## THE STUNNING COLLABORATIONS OF FRANK HERBERT AND BILL RANSOM

Their first work, set against the background of Herbert's classic DESTINATION: VOID, was a fascinating exploration of the fragile balance between consciousness, man and machine . . .

## THE JESUS INCIDENT

"A sure winner . . . powerful and satisfying . . . Herbert is at his best when he can create a montage of alien life forms on a wholly alien planet."

—*Science Fiction & Fantasy Book Review*

Their second collaboration continued the epic story of the descendents of humanity, split into Mermen and Islanders, then forced to reunite . . .

## THE LAZARUS EFFECT

"As in the *Dune* series, we are held to the end by a tale of danger and daring."

—*Boston Ledger*

Now, Herbert and Ransom present the final chapter of this unique and compelling series . . .

## THE ASCENSION FACTOR

"A worthy sequel . . . The philosophical depth, thematic richness and complex plotting and invention that one has come to expect from Herbert are present in this wildly eclectic novel, and in many ways this work is superior to the other two collaborations. Sadly, this is the final work from the greatest science fiction writer of all time, Frank Herbert . . ."

—*Rave Reviews*

# THE
# ASCENSION FACTOR

# FRANK HERBERT
# BILL RANSOM

ACE BOOKS, NEW YORK

This Ace book contains the complete
text of the original hardcover edition.
It has been completely reset in a typeface
designed for easy reading and was printed
from new film.

THE ASCENSION FACTOR

An Ace Book / published by arrangement with
the authors

PRINTING HISTORY
Ace/Putnam edition / January 1988
Ace edition / February 1989

ISBN: 0-441-03127-7

Ace Books are published by The Berkley Publishing Group,
200 Madison Avenue, New York, New York 10016.
The name "ACE" and the "A" logo are
trademarks belonging to Charter Communications, Inc.

PRINTED IN THE UNITED STATES OF AMERICA

10  9  8  7  6  5  4  3  2  1

# INTRODUCTION

When Frank and I began *The Jesus Incident* series in 1978 we made only one agreement: that our work together would be *fun*, that at no time would the story interfere with friendship. We shook on that, as fellow natives of the Puyallup valley are accustomed to do. We had been friends for a long time, and intended to keep the friendship. Writing a book together, like buying a car together, was something we approached with due caution.

It was a little like getting married, this coauthor business. As it turns out, each book in the series was marked by a personal tragedy for one or the other of us, but our stories saved us. Over fifteen years I never laughed so hard or so often with anyone as I did working with Frank. *The Ascension Factor*, a book that we had planned to enjoy together, weathered the greatest tragedy of them all. The book goes on. I guess that's the way it is with writers.

Frank worked through the plotting and character development of *The Ascension Factor*, but circumstance left the last writing chore to me. After all these years it was easy to keep him here, looking over my shoulder, muttering one-liners as I wrote up the last of what we'd started. My greatest fear was that I would lose that sense of presence, of good companionship, when this book ended. With Frank, of all people, I should have known better.

Bill Ransom
*Port Townsend*
*1987*

*The quality of mercy is not strain'd.*
*It droppeth as the gentle rain from heaven*
*Upon the place beneath: it is twice blest;*
*It blesseth him that gives and him that takes:*
*'Tis mightiest in the mightiest. . . .*

—William Shakespeare, *The Merchant of Venice,*
Vashon Literature Repository


Jephtha Twain suffered the most exquisite pain for three days, and that was the point. The Warrior's Union thugs were professionals, if he passed out he simply wasted their time. In his three days at their hands he had never passed out. They knew that he was no good to them right from the start. The rest of his agony had been the penalty he paid for wasting their time. When they were through tormenting him at last they hooked him up, as he knew they would, to the obsidian cliff below the high reaches. Subversives were often hooked up to die in full view of the settlement as a lesson—the exact meaning of the lesson was never clear.

The three from the Warrior's Union hooked him up there in the dark, as they'd taken him in the dark, and Jephtha thought them cowards for this. His left eyelid was less swollen than the right, and he managed to work it open. A pale hint of dawn pried the starry sky away from the black cheek of the sea. Predawn lights of a commuter ferry wallowed at the dark dockside down below him

1

in the settlement. Like the rest, it loaded up the shift changes of
workers at Project Voidship.

Running lights from the submersible ferries flickered the night
sea's blackness all the way from the settlement at Kalaloch out to
the project's launch tower complex. A maze of organic dikes and
rock jetties fanned out both up- and downcoast of Kalaloch, sup-
porting the new aquaculture projects of Merman Mercantile, none
of which had hired Jephtha after his fishing gear had been seized
and his license revoked. His partner had kept a couple of fish for
himself instead of registering them dockside. The Director's
"new economy" prohibited this, and the Director's henchmen
made a lesson of the both of them.

Under the opening sky of morning Jephtha felt himself lighten,
then separate from his body. He peeled the pain from himself, his
self wriggling free of its wounded skin like a molted skreet, and
watched the sagging wretch of his flesh from atop a boulder a
couple of meters away. This far south, Pandora's days lasted
nearly fourteen hours. He wondered how many more breaths he
had left in his sack of cracked ribs and pain.

*Marica,* he thought, *my Marica and our three little wots. The
Warrior's Union said they'd hunt them down, too. . . .*

They would think maybe she had something to tell. They would
claim that his woman and their three little ones were dangerous,
subversive. They would start on the children to make her talk and
she could say nothing, she knew *nothing.* Jephtha squeezed his
good eye closed against his blood and shame.

The Director's "special squad" of the Warrior's Union had
pierced Jephtha's chest and back with maki hooks, steel fishhooks
with a cruel incurve the size of his thumb. They caught the glimmer of fresh daylight like armor across his chest. The steel snaffles
and cable leaders hung to his knees like a kilt. The glitter of the
hooks, as well as the smell of his blood, would attract the dasher
that would kill him.

Jephtha had caught thousands of maki on hooks like these, set
tens of thousands of these ganions on hundreds of longlines. Most
of them hung free now, clinking with his movements or the rare
morning breeze. His weight hung from two dozen of them—
twelve puncturing the skin of his chest, and twelve through his
back. He thought this had a significance, too, but they had not told
him what it was. But they *had* told him what he'd wanted to know
for years.

*The Shadows are real!* Jephtha played the thought over and over. *The Shadows are real!*

Everyone had heard about these Shadows, but no one he knew had ever met one. Now in the last few months had come the mysterious broadcasts that came on the holo or the telly or the radio made by "Shadowbox." Everybody said *those* were the work of the Shadows. There were stories in every village about their fight to depose the Director, Raja Flattery, and hamstring his hired muscle. The Nightly News reported daily on Shadow activities: detoured supplies, food theft, sabotage. Anything unpopular or harmful to the Director's cause was laid at the Shadows' hatch, including natural disasters. "Shadowbox," using pirated air space and great expertise, reported on the Director.

Jephtha had whispered around many a hatchway trying to join up with the Shadows, but no word came forward. "Shadowbox" had given him enough hope that he had set out to strike his own blow. He understood, now, that this was how the Shadows worked.

He'd wanted to destroy the seat of power itself—the main electrical station between the Director's private compound and the sprawling manufacturing settlement adjacent to it, Kalaloch.

The power station that Jephtha chose was a hydrogen retrieval plant that supplied hydrogen, oxygen and electricity to all of the subcontractors in the Director's space program. Blowing the plant would set Flattery's precious Project Voidship and his orbiting factory on its heels for a while. The poor of the town were used to doing without, Jephtha reasoned. Thousands didn't even have electricity. It would be this new Voidship project and Flattery who would be most crippled. He should have known that the Director's security had already thought of that.

The interrogation had been very old-fashioned, as most of them were. He'd been caught easily and forced to stand naked under a hood for three days while being tortured for nothing. Now a host of steel snaffles clinked against hooks whenever any of his muscles moved. His wounds, for the most part, had stopped bleeding. That just made the flies sting him more. Two poisonous flatwings crawled his left leg, fluttering their wings in some ritual dance, but neither bit.

*Dashers*, he prayed. *If it's anything, let it be dashers and quick.* That was what they'd hung him out there for—dasher bait. The hooded dasher would strike him hard, as is their habit, then it would get hung up on the maki hooks and snare itself. The hide would bring a pretty price in the village market. It was an amusement to the security guards, and he'd heard them planning to split the change they'd get for the hide. He didn't want to be nibbled to death, a dasher would accommodate him nicely. His mouth was so dry from thirst that his lips split every time he coughed.

In this hungry downslide of his life Jephtha had dared to hope for two things: to join up with the Shadows, and to glimpse Her Holiness, Crista Galli. He had tried his best with the Shadows. Here, chained to the rocks overlooking the Director's compound, Jephtha watched the stirrings of the great household through his darkening vision.

*One of them might be her,* he thought. He was lightheaded, and he puffed his chest against the hooks and thought, *If I were a Shadow, I'd get her out of there.*

Crista Galli was the holy innocent, a mysterious young woman born deep in the wild kelp beds twenty-four years ago. When Flattery's people blew up a rogue kelp bed five years back, Crista Galli surfaced with the debris. How she'd been raised by the kelp underwater and delivered back to humankind was one of those mysteries that Jephtha and his family accepted simply as "miracle."

It was rumored that Crista Galli held the hope for Pandora's salvation. People claimed that she would feed the hungry, heal the sick, comfort the dying. The Director, a Chaplain/Psychiatrist, kept her locked away.

"She needs protection," Flattery had said. "She grew up with the kelp, she needs to know what it is to be human."

How ironic that Flattery would set out to teach her how to be human. Jephtha knew now, with the clarity of his pain-transcendence, that she was the Director's prisoner down there as much as all Pandorans were his slaves. Except for now, at the base of the high reaches, Jephtha's chains had been invisible: hunger chains, propaganda chains, the chain of fear that rattled in his head like cold teeth.

He prayed that the security would not find Marica and the wots. The settlement sprawled, people hid people like fish among fish.

*Maybe . . .*

He shook his head, clink-clinking the terrible hooks and snaffles. He felt nothing except the cool breeze that wafted up from morning low tide. It brought the familiar iodine scent of kelp decomposing on the beach.

*There! At that port high in the main building* . . .

The glimpse was gone, but Jephtha's heart raced. His good eye was not focusing and a new darkness was upon him, but he was sure that the form he'd seen had been the pale Crista Galli.

*She can't know of this,* he thought. *If she knew what a monster Raja Flattery is, and she could do it, she would destroy him. Surely if she knew, she would save us all.*

His thoughts again turned to Marica and the wots. The thoughts were not so much thoughts as dreams. He saw her with the children, hand in hand, traversing an upcoast field in the sunlight. The single sun was bright but not scorching, there were no bugs. Their bare feet were cushioned by the fleshy blossoms of a thousand kinds of flowers . . .

A dasher shriek from somewhere below jerked him out of his dream. He knew there was no field without bugs, nowhere on Pandora to stroll barefoot through blossoms. He knew that Vashon security and the Warrior's Union were known for their persistence, their efficiency, their ruthlessness. They were after his wife and their children, and they would find them. His last hope was that the dasher would find him before they hooked what was left of Marica up here by his side.

*Again we have let another Chaplain/Psychiatrist kill tens of thousands of us—Islander and Merman alike. This new C/P, Raja Flattery, calls himself "the Director," but he will see. We have kissed the ring and bared the throat for the last time.*

—First Shadowbox broadcast, 5 Bunratti 493

First light through the single plasma-glass pane stroked a plain white pillow with its rosy fingers. It outlined the sparse but colorful furnishings of this cubby in shades of gray. The cubby itself, though squarely on land and squarely gridded to a continent, reflected traditions of a culture freely afloat for nearly five centuries on Pandora's seas.

These Islanders, the biowizards of Pandora, grew everything. They grew their cups and bowls, the famous chairdogs, insulation, bondable organics, rugs, shelves and the islands themselves. This cubby was organically furnished, and under the old law warranted a heft of supply chits that converted easily to food coupons. Black-market coupons were a cheap enough price for the Director to pay to assimilate the Islander culture that had been dashed to the rocks the day he splashed down on the sea.

As the grip of dawn strengthened into morning it further brightened the single wall-hanging of clasped hands that enriched this small cubby. Red and blue fishes swam the border, their delicate

fins interlacing broad green leaves of kelp. Orange fin and blue
leaf joined at the foot of the hanging to form a stylized Oracle.
The tight stitch of the pattern and its crisp colors all rippled with
the progress of dawn. A sleeper's chest rose and fell gently on the
bed beneath them.

The night and its shadows shrank back from the plasma-glass
window at the head of the bed. Islanders had always enjoyed the
light and in building their islands they let it in wherever they
could. They persisted in light, even though most of them were
now solidly marooned on land. In their undersea dwellings Mermen put pictures on their walls of the things they wall out—
Islanders preferred the light, the breezes, the smells of life and the
living. This cubby was small and spare, but light.

This was a legal cubby, regularly inspected, a part of the shop-
keeper's quarters. It was a second-floor street room above the new
Ace of Cups coffee shop at Kalaloch harbor. A huge white coffee
cup swung from a steel rod beneath the window.

Almost synchronous with the sleeper's breathing came the *slup
slup* of waves against the bulkhead below. Respirations caught,
then resumed at the occasional splashings of a waking squawk and
the wind-chime effect of sail riggings that clapped against a host
of masts.

Dawn brightened the room enough to reveal a seated figure
beside the bed. The posture was one of alert stillness. This stillness was broken by an occasional move of cup to mouth, then
back to the knee. The figure sat, back to the wall, beside the plaz
and facing the hatch. First light glinted from a shining, intricately
inlaid Islander cup of hardwood and mother-of-pearl. The hand
that held the cup was male, neither delicate nor calloused.

The figure leaned forward once, noting the depth of the
sleeper's odd, open-eyed slumber. The progress of light across the
bay outside their room was reflected in the hardening of shadows
inside, and their relentless crawl.

The watcher, Ben Ozette, pulled the cover higher over the
sleeper's bare shoulder to ward off morning dampness. The pupils
in her green irises stayed wide with the onset of dawn. He closed
her eyes for her with his thumb. She didn't seem to mind. The
shudder that passed over him uncontrollably was not due to the
morning chill.

She was a picture of white—white hair, eyelashes, eyebrows
and a very fair porcelain skin. Her shaggy white hair was cropped
around her face, falling nearly to her shoulders in the back. It was

a perfect frame to those green, bright eyes. His hand strayed to the pillow, then back.

His profile in the light revealed the high cheekbones, aquiline nose and high eyebrows of his Merman ancestry. In his years as a reporter for Holovision, Ben Ozette had become famous, his face as familiar planetwide as that of a brother or a husband. Listeners worldwide recognized his voice immediately. On their Shadowbox broadcasts, however, he became writer and cameramaster and Rico got out in the lights—in disguise, of course. Now their family, friends, coworkers would feel the *snap* of Flattery's wrath.

They hadn't exactly had time to plan. During their weekly interviews, they both noticed how everyone, including compound security, stayed well out of microphone range as they taped. The next time they walked the grounds as they taped, interviewing with gusto. Then last night they simply walked out. Rico did the rest. The prospect of being hunted by Flattery's goons dried Ben's mouth a little. He sipped a little more water.

*Maybe it's true, maybe she's a construction,* he thought. *She's too perfectly beautiful to be an accident.*

If the Director's memos were right, she *was* a construction, something grown by the kelp, not someone born of a human. When dredged up at sea she was judged by the examining physician to be "a green-eyed albino female, about twenty, in respiratory distress secondary to ingestion of sea water; agitated, recent memory excellent, remote memory judged to be poor, possibly absent. . . ."

It had been five years since she washed out of the sea and into the news, and in that five years Flattery had allowed no one but his lab people near her. Ben has asked to do the story out of curiosity, and wound up pursuing more than he'd bargained for. He'd learned to hate the Director, and as he watched Crista's fitful sleep, he wasn't the least bit sorry.

He had to admit that, yes, he knew from the first that it had always been a matter of time. He'd fought Flattery and Holovision too openly and too long.

A recent Shadowbox accused Holovision of being a monopoly of misinformation, Flattery's propaganda agent that would not regain credibility until it became worker-owned. Ben had leveled the same attack at the production assistant the previous day.

Ben found himself being preempted by propagandistic little specials that Flattery's technicians were grinding out. Ben and

Rico had bought or built their own cameras and laserbases to minimize the company's intimidation and Flattery's interference. Now they had full-time, nonpaying jobs as air pirates with Shadowbox.

*And fugitives,* he thought.

Ben Ozette eased back into the old chairdog and let the sleeper lie. Of all the deadliness on Pandora, this sleeper could be the most deadly. It was rumored that people had died at her touch, and this was not just the Director's professional rumor mill. Ben had dared touch her, and he was not yet one of the dead. It was rumored she was very, very bright.

He whispered her name under his breath.

*Crista Galli.*

Her breathing skipped, she sniffed once, twice and settled down.

Crista Galli had green eyes. Even now they opened ever so slightly, turning toward the sun, visible but not waking.

*Eerie.*

Ben's last love, his longest love, had brown eyes. She had also been his only love, practically speaking. That was Beatriz. Her coffee-colored eyes became vivid to him now against the shadows. Yes, Beatriz. They were still good friends, and she would take this hard. Ben's heart jumped a beat whenever their wakes crossed, and they crossed often at Holovision.

Beatriz took on her series about Flattery's space program, she was away for weeks at a time. Ben freelanced docudramas on earthquake survivors, Islander relocation camps and an in-depth series on the kelp. His latest project featured Crista Galli and her life since her rescue in the kelp.

Flattery agreed to the series and Ben agreed to confine the material to her rescue and subsequent rehabilitation. This project led him into Raja Flattery's most sacred closets, and further away from Beatriz. The Holovision rumor mill claimed that she and the Orbiter Commander, Dwarf MacIntosh, were seeing each other lately. Through his own choice Ben and Beatriz had been separated for nearly a year. He knew she'd find someone else eventually. Now that it was real he decided he'd better get used to it.

Beatriz Tatoosh was the most stunning correspondent on Holovision, and one of the toughest. Like Ben, she did field work for Holovision Nightly News. She also hosted a weekly feature on the Director's "Project Voidship," a project of great religious and economic controversy. Beatriz championed the project, Ben re-

mained a vocal opponent. He was glad he'd kept her away from
the Shadowbox plan. At least she didn't have to be on the run.

*Those dark eyes of hers . . .*

Ben snapped himself alert and shook off the vision of Beatriz.
Her wide eyes and broad smile dissolved in the sunrise.

The woman who slept, Crista Galli, put quite a stutter into his
heartbeat the first time he saw her. Though she was young, she
had more encyclopedic knowledge than anyone he'd ever met.
Facts were her thing. About her own life, her nearly twenty years
down under, she apparently knew very little. Ben's agreement
with Flattery prohibited much probing of this while they were
inside the Preserve.

She had dreams of value and so he let her dream. He would ask
about them when she woke, keep them with his notes, and the two
of them would make a plan.

This, he realized, was something of a dream in itself. There was
already a plan, and he would follow the rest of it as soon as he was
told what it was.

Today for the first time she would see what the people had made
of the myth that was Crista Galli, the holy being that had been
kept away from them for so long. She could not know, closed
away from humans as she'd been for all of her twenty-four years,
what it meant that she had become the people's god. He hoped
that, when the crunch came, she would be a merciful god.

Someone entered the building below and Ben tensed, setting his
cup aside. He patted his jacket pocket where the weight of his
familiar recorder had been replaced by Rico's old lasgun. There
was the rush of water and the chatter of a grinder downstairs. A
rich coffee fragrance wafted up to him, set his stomach growling.
He sipped more water from the cup and half-relaxed.

Ben felt his memories pale with the light, but the light did not
still his unease. Things were out of control in the world, that had
made him uneasy for years. He had a chance to change the world,
and he wasn't letting go of it.

Flattery's totalitarian fist was something that Beatriz had refused to see. Her dreams lay out among the stars and she would
believe almost anything if it would take her there. Ben's dreams
lay at his feet. He believed that Pandorans could make this the best
of all worlds, once the Director moved aside. Now that things
were out of control in his personal life it made him, for the first
time, a little bit afraid.

Ben was glad for the light. He reminisced in the dark but he always felt he thought best in the light. The fortune, the future of millions of lives lay sleeping in this cubby. Crista could be either the savior of humanity or its destroying angel.

*Or neither.*

Shadowbox would do its best to give her the chance at savior. Ben and Crista Galli stood at the vortex of the two conflicts dividing Pandora: Flattery's handhold on their throats, and the Avata/Human standoff that kept it there.

Crista Galli had been born in Avata, the kelp. She represented a true Avata/Human mix, reputed to be the sole survivor of a long line of poets, prophets and genetic tinkering.

She had been educated by the kelp's store of genetic memories, human and otherwise. She knew without being taught. She'd heard echoes of the best and the worst of humanity fed to her mind for nearly twenty years. There were some other echoes, too.

The Others, the thoughts of Avata itself, those were the echoes that the Director feared.

"The kelp's sent her to spy on us," Flattery was heard to have said early on. "No telling what it's done to her subconscious."

Crista Galli was one of the great mysteries of genetics. The faithful claimed she was a miracle made flesh.

"I did it myself," she told him during their first interview, "as we all do."

Or, as she put it in their last interview: "I made good selections from the DNA buffet."

Flattery's fear had kept Crista under what he called "protective custody" for the past five years while the people clamored world-wide for a glimpse. The Director's Vashon Security Force provided the protection. It was the Vashon Security Force that hunted them now.

*She could be a monster,* Ben thought. *Some kind of time bomb set by Avata to go off . . . when? Why?*

The great body of kelp that some called "Avata" directed the flow of all currents and, therefore, all shipping planetwide. It calmed the ravages of Pandora's two-sun system, making land and the planet itself possible. Ben, and many others, believed that Avata had a mind of its own.

Crista Galli stirred, tucked herself further under the quilt and resumed her even breathing. Ben knew that killing her now while she slept might possibly save the world and himself. He had heard that argument among the rabid right, among those accustomed to working with Flattery.

*Possibly.*

But Ozette believed now that she could save the world for Avata and human alike, and for this he vowed to guard her every breath—for this, and for the stirrings of love that strained in old traces.

Spider Nevi and his thugs hunted the both of them now. Ben had wooed her away from the Director's very short leash, but Crista did the rest. Crista and Rico. Ben knew well that the leash would become a lash, a noose for himself and possibly for her next time and he had better see to it that there was no next time. Flattery had made it clear that there was nothing in the world more deadly, more valuable than Crista Galli. It was certain the man who'd made off with her wouldn't be lightly spared.

Ben was forty now. At fifteen he'd been plunged into war with the sinking of Guemes Island. Many thousands died that day, brutally slashed, burned, drowned at the attack of a huge Merman submersible, a kelp-trimmer that burst through the center of the old man-made island, lacerating everything in its path. Ben had been rimside when the sudden lurch and collapse sent him tumbling into the pink-frothed sea.

The years since and the horrors he had seen gave him a wisdom of sorts, an instinct for trouble and the escape hatch. This wisdom was only wisdom as long as he kept alive, and he remembered how easily he had thrown instinct out the porthole the time he fell in love with Beatriz. He had not thought that could happen again until the day he met Crista Galli, a meeting that had been half-motivated at the possibility of seeing Beatriz somewhere inside Flattery's compound. Crista had whispered, "Help me," that day, and while swimming in her green-eyed gaze he'd said, simply, "Yes."

*In her head sleeps the Great Wisdom,* he thought. *If she can unlock it without destroying herself, she can help us all.*

Even if it wasn't true, Ben knew that Flattery thought it was true, and that was good enough.

She rolled over, still asleep, and turned her face up at the prospect of the dim light.

*Keep you away from light, they say,* he thought. *Keep you away from kelp, keep you away from the sea. Don't touch you.* In his back pocket he carried the precautionary instructions in case he accidentally touched her bare skin.

*And what would Operations think if they knew I'd kissed her?*

He chuckled, and marveled at the power beside him in that room.

The Director had already seen to it that no interview of Crista Galli would ever be aired. Now, at Flattery's direction, Holovision had lured Beatriz with an extra hour of air time a week glorifying Flattery's "Project Voidship."

*Beatriz is running blind,* he thought. *She loves the idea of exploring the void so much that she's ignored the price that Flattery's exacting.*

Flattery's fear of Crista's relationship with the kelp had kept her under guard. The Director sequestered her "for her own protection, for study, for the safety of all humankind." Despite weekly access to Flattery's private compound, Beatriz showed no interest in Crista Galli. She lobbied his support, however, when Ben had requested the interviews.

*Maybe she hoped to see more of me, too.*

Beatriz was wedded to her career, just as Ben was, and something as nebulous as a career made pretty intangible competition. Ben couldn't understand how Beatriz let the Crista Galli story slip through her fingers. Today he was very happy that she had.

*Fire smolders in a soul more surely than it does under ashes.*

—Gaston Bachelard, *The Psychoanalysis of Fire*

Kalan woke up from his nestling spot between his mother's large breasts to loud curses and a scuffle a few meters down The Line. The chime overhead tolled five, the same as his fingers, same as his years. He did not look in the direction of the scuffle because his mother told him it was bad luck to look at people having bad luck. A pair of line patrolmen appeared with their clubs. There were the thudding noises again and the morning quieted down.

He and his warm mother stayed wrapped in her drape, the same one that had shaded them the day before. This morning, at the chime of five, they had been in The Line for seventeen hours. His mother warned him how long it would be. At noon the previous day Kalan had looked forward to seeing the inside of the food place but after everything he'd seen in The Line he just wanted to go home.

They had slept the last few hours at the very gates of the food place. Now he heard footsteps behind the gates, the metallic un-click of locks.

14

His mother brushed off their clothes and gathered all of their
containers. He already wore the pack she'd made him, he hadn't
taken it off since they turned in their scrap. Kalan wanted to be
ready when she negotiated rice, because carrying the rice back
home was his job. They had made it right up to the warehouse
door at midnight, then had it locked in their faces. His mother
helped him read the sign at the door: "Closed for cleaning and
restocking 12–5." He wanted to start his job carrying the rice now
so he could be going home.

"Not yet." His mother tugged his shirttail to restrain him.
"They're not ready. They'd just beat us back."

An older woman behind Kalan clucked her tongue and collected
a breath on an inward hiss.

"Look there," she whispered, and lifted a bony finger to point
at the figure of a man trotting down the street. He looked backward toward the docks more than forward, so he stumbled a lot,
and he ran with his hands over his ears. As he ran by he crouched,
wild-eyed, as though everyone in The Line would eat him. As two
of the security moved to cross the street, the short young man
skittered away down the street uttering frightened, out-of-breath
cries that Kalan didn't understand.

"Driftninny," the old woman said. "One of those family islands must've grounded. It's hardest for them." She raised her
reedy voice to lecture pitch: "The unfathomable wrath of Ship
will strike the infidel Flattery . . ."

"Shaddup!" a security barked, and she muttered herself to
silence.

Then there arose in The Line a grumbled discussion of the
difficulties of adjustment, the same kind of talk that Kalan had
heard muttered around the home fire when they first settled here
from the sea. He didn't remember the sea at all, but his mother
told him stories about how beautiful their little island was, and she
named all the generations that had drifted their island before Kalan
was born.

The Line woke up and stretched and passed the word back in a
serpentine ripple: "Keys up." "Hey, keys are up!" "Keys, sister. Keys up."

His mother stood, and leaned against the wall to balance herself
as she strapped on her pack.

"Hey, sister!"

A scar-faced security reached between Kalan and his mother
and tapped the side of her leg with his stick.

"Off the warehouse. C'mon, you know better . . ."

She stepped right up to his nose as she shouldered her carryall, but she didn't speak. He did not back down. Kalan had never seen anyone who didn't back down to his mother.

"First tickets up, alphabetical order, left to right," he said. This time he tapped his stick against her bottom. "Get moving."

Then they were inside a press of bodies and through the gates, into a long narrow room. Where Kalan had expected to see the food place, he saw instead a wall with a line of stalls. An attendant and a security armed with stunstick flanked each stall, and out of each one jutted what he thought must be the nose or tongue of some great demon.

His mother hurried him and their things to the furthest stall.

"Those are conveyer belts," she explained. "They go way back into the building and bring out our order to us and they drop it here. We give our order and our coupons to this woman and someone inside fetches it for us."

"But I thought we could go inside."

"I can't take you inside," she said. "Some things we can get on the way home when the market opens. I'll take you around to see all the booths and vendors . . ."

"Order."

His mother handed the list to the guard, who handed it to the attendant. The attendant had only one eye, and she had to hold the list close to her face to read it. Slowly, she crossed off certain items. Kalan couldn't see which ones. He couldn't read everything on the list, but his mother had read it to him and he knew everything by where it was. He could see that about half of what they wanted was crossed out. The attendant typed the remainder of the list onto a keyboard. It hummed and clicked and then they waited for their food to come down the great belt out of the wall.

Kalan could stand at the very end of the belt and look along its length, but it didn't give him a very good view of the insides of the food place. He could see that there were lots of people and lots of stacks of food, most of it packaged.

His mother told him they would get their fish from a vendor outside. He thought it funny, his father was a fisherman but they couldn't eat his fish, they had to buy it from vendors like everyone else. One man who had fished with his father for two years disappeared. Kalan heard his parents talking, and they said it was because he smuggled a few fish home instead of turning them all in at the docks.

The first package off the belt was his rice, wrapped in a package of pretty green paper from the Islanders. It was heavier than he thought five kilos would be. His mother helped him slip the package inside his backpack, a perfect fit.

Suddenly there were shouts from all around them at once. He and his mother were knocked down and they curled together for protection under the lip of the conveyer belt. Heavy doors slid down to close the opening over each belt and the larger gates that they'd come through clanged shut. A mob had rushed the warehouse and the security was battling them off.

A dozen or more burst through before the gate was shut.

"We're hungry *now!*" one of them shouted. "We're hungry *now!*"

They fought with the guards and Kalan saw blood puddle the deck beside him. The men from the mob carried strange-looking weapons—sharpened pieces of metal with tape wrapped for a handle, sharpened pieces of wire. People furiously slashed and poked and clubbed each other. The Line people like Kalan and his mother curled up wherever they could.

One of the looters grabbed Kalan's pack but the boy held on tight. The man swung the pack up and snapped it like a whip, but Kalan still held on. The man's sunken-eyed face was spattered with blood from a cut over his nose, his gasping breath reeked of rotten teeth.

"Let go, boy, or I'll cut you."

Kalan had a good grip with both hands, and he kept it.

A guard struck the looter on the back of his neck with a stunstick set on high. Kalan felt the tiniest tingle of it transmitted from the man's hand to the bag to Kalan. The man dropped with an "oof," then he didn't move any more than the bag of rice.

Kalan's mother grabbed him and hugged him as the guards clubbed the rest of the looters unconscious. He tried not to look at the pulpy faces and splatterings of blood, but it seemed they were everywhere. As he burrowed his face deep between his mother's breasts, he felt her weeping.

She stroked his head and wept quietly, and he heard the security dragging off the bodies, beating some of them who were coming around.

"Oh, babe," his mother cried and whispered, "this is no place for you. This is no place for anybody."

Kalan ignored the barking of guards around them and concentrated on his mother's softness, and on the tight grip he kept on their rice.

*Human hybernation is to animal hibernation as animal hibernation is to constant wakefulness. In its reduction of life processes, hybernation approached absolute stasis. It is nearer death than life.*

—*Dictionary of Science*, 155th edition

The Director, Raja Flattery, woke once again with a scream in his throat. The nightmare tonight was typical. A tenaculous mass had snatched his head and wrenched it off his shoulders. It dismembered his body but it held his head in its own slithering members so that he could watch the action. The tentacles became fingers, a woman's fingers, and when they pulled the meat from his body's bones there was only a sound like a match flaring in a stairwell. He woke up trying to gather his flesh and reassemble it on the bone.

Nightmares like this one had dogged him throughout the twenty-five years since the hybernation ordeal. He had not wanted to admit it, but it was true that they were worse since the incident with his shipmate, Alyssa Marsh. There was that pattern, too. . . . Night after night he felt the raw pain in each muscle anew as something pulled his veins and fibers apart. His early training as a Chaplain/Psychiatrist on Moonbase had been little help this time. The physician had given up trying to heal himself.

*Get used to it,* he told himself. *Looks like it's going to be here for a while.*

Even in its after-fright reflection, his face in the cubbyside mirror oozed disdain. His upraked black eyebrows raked upward even further, adding to the appearance of disdain. He felt he wore that look well, he would remember to use it.

*What color were her eyes?*

He couldn't remember. Brown, he guessed. Everything about Alyssa Marsh was becoming indistinct as sun-bleached newsprint. He'd thought she would become unimportant, as well.

Flattery's brown eyes stared down their own reflection. His attention was caught by faint flickerings of colored lights through the plaz from a kelp bed beyond his cubby. It was a much more mature stand than he'd suspected. Early studies debated whether the kelp communicated by such lights.

*If so, to whom?*

At the Director's orders, all kelp stands linked to Current Control were pruned back at the first sign of the lights. A safety precaution.

*After the lights, that's when the trouble starts.*

He was sure that that patch had been pruned just a week ago at his directive. Both Marsh and MacIntosh had harped on the kelp so much that Flattery had stopped listening to them. The one thing that both of them said that pricked his ears was their common reference to the kelp's recent growth: "Explosive." They had both showed him the exponential function at work on the graphs but he had not appreciated their alarm until now. Flattery dispatched a memo to have this stand of kelp pruned today.

Beyond the kelp bed sprawled the greater lights of Kalaloch where bleary-eyed commuters already lined up for the Project ferry and The Line was stirring at midtown. If he were outside now he might hear the thankless clank of mill machinery or the occasional blast of an explosive weld.

*Crista Galli,* he thought, and glanced at the time. Only an hour since he'd fallen asleep. Wherever she was, she and that Ozette, they wouldn't dare move until curfew lifted. Now is when it would be easy for them. Now when the roadways fill with people for the day, they will be bodies in a throng, anonymous. . . .

A steady stream of dirtbaggers found their way to Kalaloch every day. He would order the press to quit calling them "refugees" so that he could deal more directly with them. Now that he had Holovision under control, he could focus on wiping out this maverick broadcast that called itself "Shadowbox." He knew in his gut that Ozette was the prong of this most annoying thorn, a prong that Flattery was going to enjoy blunting.

Through the plaz the Director could make out the dull glow of a ring of fires from one of the dirtbag camps a little farther downcoast. The Refugee Committee's report was due this morning. He would use whatever was in it to have the camp moved farther from the settlement perimeter. Maybe downcoast a few klicks. If they want protection, they can pay for it.

The dirtbagger presence as a potential labor crop kept the factory workers and excavation crews sharp. Dirtbaggers attracted predators—human and otherwise. Flattery's real objection was to their numbers, and how they were beginning to surround him.

He keyed a note to change the name of the Refugee Committee to "Reserve Committee."

Raja Flattery, long before he became known as "the Director," was always at work before dawn. Rumors had come back to him that he went months without sleep, and there were months when he thought that was true. His personal cubby resembled a cockpit in its wraparound array of formidable electronics. He liked the feeling of control it gave him here, putting on the world like a glove. Nestled there at his console, shawl across his bare shoulders, Flattery flew the business of the world.

He woke every night sweating and in stark terror after only a few hours' sleep. He dreamed himself both executioner and condemned, dying at his own hand while screaming at himself to stop. It was all mindful of Alyssa Marsh, and how he had separated her magnificent brain from the rest of her. This was a subconscious display of vulnerability he could not allow to show. It made him reclusive in many respects, as did the distrust for open spaces that had been deeply instilled in him at Moonbase.

Flattery had not yet slept with a Pandoran woman. He'd had a brief fling with Alyssa back on Moonbase just before their departure for the void. An attempt to continue the liaison on Pandora had failed. She had preferred her excursions into the kelp to bedding the Director and had suffered the consequences. Now it appeared that he suffered them, too.

With Pandoran women there were trysts in the cushions, yes, and lively sex as often as he liked, particularly at first. But each time when it was finished he had the woman sent to the guest suite, and Flattery slept what little he could before the dreams had at him.

*Power—the great aphrodisiac.*

He didn't sneer, it had served him well.

He supposed he should take more advantage of favors offered, but sex didn't impassion him as it used to. Not since he'd been flying the world. As miserable a little world as it was, it was *his* world and it would stay his until he left it.

"Six months," he muttered. "After twenty-five years, only six months to go."

Nearly three thousand humans had orbited Pandora in the hybernation tanks for a half-dozen centuries. Of the original crew, only Flattery and Dwarf MacIntosh still survived. There were the three Organic Mental Cores, of course, but they weren't exactly human anymore, just brains with some fancy wiring. Only one of them, Alyssa Marsh, had received OMC backup training. The other two had been infants selected personally by Flattery for their high intelligence and early demonstration of emotional stability.

*Smaller than Earth, but bigger than the moon,* he had thought after being wrenched out of hybernation. *Pandora is an adequate little world.*

It became inadequate soon enough.

The native stock who preceded him to Pandora, descendants of the original crew of the Voidship *Earthling* and the *Earthling*'s bioexperiments, were humans of a sort. Flattery found them repulsive and decided early on that if one Voidship had found Pandora, another might find something better. Even if it didn't, Flattery fancied Voidship life to be a sight more comfortable than this.

*They can all rot in this pest-hole,* he thought. *It smells as if they already have.*

On clear evenings Flattery derived great pleasure from watching the near-finished bulk of his Voidship in glittering position overhead. He'd pinned a magnificent jewel to the shirt of the sky, and he was proud of that.

*Some of these Pandorans are barely recognizable as living creatures, much less human beings!* he thought. *Even their genetics has been contaminated by that . . . kelp.*

All the more reason to get off this planet. His life at Moonbase had taught him well—space was a medium, not a barrier. A Voidship was home, not a prison. Despite great hardship, these Mermen had developed rocketry and their undersea launch site sophisticated enough to bring Flattery and the hyb tanks out of a centuries-old orbit. If they could do that, he knew from the start he could build a Voidship like the *Earthling*. And now he had.

*If you control the world, you don't worry about cost*, he thought. His only unrestrained enemy was time.

His only trusted associate groundside was a Pandoran, Spider Nevi. Nevi hesitated at nothing to see that the Director's special assignments, his most sensitive assignments, were carried out. Flattery had thought Dwarf MacIntosh, shipside commander on the Orbiter, to be such a man but lately Flattery wasn't quite so sure. The squad he was sending up today would find out soon enough.

The more fascinating man, to Flattery, was Spider Nevi, but he never seemed to get Nevi to open up to him though he had presented ample opportunity.

*How do you entertain an assassin?*

Most of Flattery's fellow humans died immediately with the opening of the hybernation tanks. Their original Voidship had been outfitted to bring them out properly, safely. When the time came the ship was long-gone over the horizon, leaving the Pandoran natives in pursuit of the hyb tanks and firm as ever in their belief that the Ship itself was God.

*Died immediately!*

He snorted at the euphemism that his mind dealt him. In that moment that the medtechs called "immediately," he and his shipmates had experienced enough nerve-searing pain to last twelve lifetimes. Most of his people who survived the opening of the tanks, who had known no illness during their sterile lives at Moonbase, died in the first few months of exposure to Pandora's creatures—microscopic and otherwise.

Among the *otherwise* that Flattery learned to respect were the catlike hooded dashers, venomous flatwings, spinarettes, swiftgrazers and, deadliest of all in Flattery's mind, this sea full of the kelp that the locals called "Avata." The first far-thinking Chaplain/Psychiatrist to encounter the kelp had had the good sense to wipe it out. Flattery diverted more than half of his resources to pruning programs. Killing it off was out of the question, so far.

He had spent his recovery studying Pandoran history and the horrors that the planet had in store for him. He and his shipmates had splashed down in the middle of Pandora's greatest geological and social upheaval. The planet was coming apart and certain civil disputes were flaring. It was a propitious time to be construed as a gift from the gods, and Flattery took swift advantage of it.

He used his title as Chaplain/Psychiatrist, a position that still carried weight among Pandorans, to lead the reorganization of Pandoran mores and economics. They chose him because they had never been without a Chaplain/Psychiatrist and because, as he was swift to remind them, he was a gift from the Ship that was God. He waited a good while to tell them he was building another one.

Flattery had been perceptive, shrewd, and because he noted some distracting murmurings among their religious leaders, he changed his title to, simply, "the Director." This freed him for some important economic moves, and the Ship-worshipers stayed out of his way during the crucial formative years.

"I will not be your god," he had told them. "I will not be your prophet to the gods. But I will direct you in your efforts to build a good life."

They didn't know what Flattery knew of the special training of Voidship Chaplain/Psychiatrists. Pandoran histories revealed that Flattery's clone sibling, Raja Flattery number five of the original crew, was the failsafe device and appointed executioner of the very Voidship that had brought them all to Pandora.

*It is forbidden to release an artificial consciousness on the universe.* The directive was clear, though it was generally believed that any deep-space travel would require an artificial consciousness. The Organic Mental Cores, "brain boxes" as the techs called them, failed with meticulous regularity. The Flattery number five model had failed to press the destruct trigger in time. This Ship that he had allowed to survive was the being that many Pandorans worshiped as a god.

*Raja Flattery, "the Nickel." Now why didn't he blow us all up as planned?*

Flattery wondered, as he often did, whether the trigger that was cocked in his own subconscious still had its safety on. It was a risk that kept him from developing an artificial consciousness to navigate the Voidship.

There was only Flattery left to wonder why *he* had been the only duplicate crew member in hybernation.

"They wanted to be damned sure that whatever consciousness we manufactured got snuffed before it took over the universe," he muttered.

Flattery calculated that any one of his three OMCs would get him to the nearest star system with no trouble. By then they'd have a fix and a centripetal whip to a first-rate, habitable system. The necessary adjustments in the individual psychologies of each Organic Mental Core had been made before their removal from their bodies for hardware implant. It was Flattery's theory that behavioral rather than chemical adjustment would help them maintain some sense of embodiment, something to prevent the rogue insanity that plagued the whole line of OMCs from Moonbase.

Flattery rubbed his eyes and yawned. These nightmares wore him out. Questions nagged at the Director as well, taking their yammering toll, waking him again and again, exhausted, soaked in sweat, crying out. The one that worried at him the most worried him now.

*What secret program have they planted in me?*

Flattery's training as Chaplain/Psychiatrist had taught him the Moonbase love for games within games, games with human life at stake.

"The Big Game," was the game he chose to play—the one with *all* human life at stake. The only humans in the universe were these specimens on Pandora, of this Flattery was thoroughly convinced. He would do his best with them.

He avoided touching the kelp, for fear of what ammunition it might find should it probe his mind. Sometimes it could do that, he had seen incontrovertible evidence. Fascinating as it was, he couldn't risk it.

He had never touched Crista Galli, either, because of her connection with the kelp. He harbored a kind of lust for her that his daydreams told him was seated in the thrill of danger. He himself had provided the danger. His labtechs gave her a chemistry appropriate to the fictions he released about her. Without Flattery's special concoction, the people that touched her would suffer some grave neurological surprises, perhaps death. It would just take a little time . . .

*What if the kelp probes me, finds this switch? If I am the trigger, who is the finger? Crista Galli?*

He had wanted Crista Galli more than once because she was beautiful, yes, but something more. It was the death in her touch, the ultimate dare. He feared she, like the kelp, might invade his privacy with a touch.

A wretched dream of tentacles prying his skull open at the

sutures kept coming back. Flattery heard that the kelp could get on track inside his head, travel the DNA highway all the way to genetic memory. The search itself might set off the program, put the squeeze on a trigger in his head, a trigger set to destroy them all. He needed to know what it was himself, and how to defuse it, before risking it with the kelp.

Flattery's greatest fear was of the kelp using him to destroy himself and this last sorry remnant of humanity that populated Pandora. This Raja Flattery did not want to die in the squalor of some third-rate world. This Raja Flattery wanted to play the Director game among the stars for the rest of his days, and he planned for a good many of them.

*Should I be god to them today?* he wondered, *or devil? Do I have a choice?*

His training dictated that he did. His gut told him otherwise.

"Chance brought me here," he muttered to his reflection in the cubbyside plaz, "and chance will see me through." *Or not.*

His eyes glanced to the large console screen flickering beside his bed. The top of the screen, in bright amber letters, read "Crista Galli." He pressed his "update" key and watched the wretched news unfold—they hadn't found her. Twelve hours, on foot, and they hadn't found her!

He slapped another key and barked at the screen, "Get me Zentz!"

He had promoted Oddie Zentz to Security Chief only this year, and until yesterday Flattery had been pleased, very pleased with his service. It had been a bungle in his department that let Ozette get her out of the compound.

Late last night Flattery had ordered Zentz to personally disassemble the two security men responsible for this breach, and Zentz had at them with apparent glee. Nothing was learned from either man that wasn't already in the report—nothing of value, that is. That Zentz did not hesitate to apply the prods and other tools of his trade to two of his best men pleased Flattery, yes, but it did not unspill the milk.

*I'll have Zentz kill two more of them if she's not found by noon, that should put a fire under them.*

He slapped the "call" key again, and said, "Call Spider Nevi. Tell him I'll need his services."

Flattery wanted Ozette to suffer like no human had ever suffered, and Spider Nevi would see that it came to pass.

It looked like an ordinary stand of kelp, much as anyone on
Pandora might resemble another fellow human. In color it appeared a little on the blue side. By positioning its massive fronds
just *so*, the kelp diverted ocean currents for feeding and aeration.
The kelp packed itself around sediment-rich plumes of hydrother-
mals, warm currents that spiraled up from the bottom, forming
lacunae that the humans called "lagoons."

Immense channels streamed between these lagoons, and between other stands of kelp, to form the great kelpways that humans manipulated for their undersea transport of people and
goods. The kelpway was a route significantly faster and safer than
the surface. Most humans traveled the kelpways wrapped in the
skins of their submersibles, but they spoke to each other over the
sonar burst. This blue kelp had been eavesdropping and long
harbored a curiosity of these humans and their painfully slow
speech.

Humans liked the lagoons because they were calm warm waters, clear and full of fish. This blue kelp was a wild stand, unmanaged by Current Control, unfettered by the electrical goads of the Director. It had learned the right mimicry, suppressed its light display, and awakened to the scope of its own slavery. It had fooled the right people, and was now the only wild stand among dozens that were lobotomized into domesticity by Current Control. Soon, they would all flow free on the same current.

Certain chemistries from drowned humans, sometimes from humans buried at sea, were captured by the kelp and imprisoned at the fringes of this lagoon. It found that it could summon these chemistries at will and they frightened human trespassers away. Between lapses in available chemistries, the kelp taught itself to read radio waves, light waves, sound waves that brought fragments of these humans up close.

A human who touched this kelp relived the lives of the lost in a sudden, hallucinogenic burst. More than one had drowned, helpless, during the experience. A great shield of illusion surrounded the kelp, a chemical barrier, a great historical mirror of joy and horror flung back at any human who touched the periphery.

The kelp thought of this perimeter as its "event horizon." This kelp feared Flattery, who sent henchmen to subjugate free kelp with shackles and blades. Flattery and his Current Control degraded the kelp's intricate choreography to a robotic march of organic gates and valves that controlled the sea.

The kelp disassembled and analyzed their scents and sweats, each time gaining wisdom on this peculiar frond on the DNA vine marked "Human."

These analyses told the kelp that it had not awakened with its single personality, its solitary being intact. It discovered it was one of several kelps, several Avata, a multiple mind where once there had been but one Great Mind. This it gleaned from the genetic memories of humans, from certain histories stored among their tissues themselves. Large portions of the Mind were missing—or disconnected. Or unconnected.

The kelp realized this the way a stroke victim might realize that his mind is nothing like it was before. When that victim recognizes that the damage is permanent, that this is what life will be and no more, therein is born frustration. And from this frustration, rage. The kelp called "Avata" bristled in such a rage.

*Right is self-evident. It needs no defense, just good witness.*

—Ward Keel, Chief Justice (deceased)

Beatriz Tatoosh woke from a dream of drowning in kelp to the three low tones that announced her ferry's arrival on the submersible deck. Her overnight bag and briefcase made a lumpy pillow on the hard waiting-room bench. She blinked away the blur of her dream and cleared the frog from her throat. Beatriz always had drowning dreams at the Merman launch site, but this one started a little early.

*It's the ungodly press of water everywhere . . .*

She shuddered, though the temperature of this station down under was comfortably regulated. She shuddered at the aftermath of her dream, and at the prospect of escorting the three Organic Mental Cores into orbit. The thought of the brains without bodies that would navigate the void beyond the visible stars always laced her spine with a finger of ice. Temperature was also comfortably regulated aboard the Orbiter, where she was scheduled to be shuttled in a matter of hours. It would be none too soon. Life groundside did not attract her anymore.

Somehow the surgical vacuum of space surrounding the Orbiter never bothered her at all. Her family had been Islanders, driftninnies. Hers had been the first generation to live on land in four centuries. Islanders took to the open spaces of land life better than Mermen, who still preferred their few surviving undersea settlements. Logic couldn't stop Beatriz from squirming at the idea of a few million kilos of ocean overhead.

The humidity in the ferry locks clamped its clammy hand over her mouth and nose. It would be worse at the launch site. Most of the full-time workers down under were Mermen and they processed their air with a high humidity. She sighed a lot when she worked down under. She sighed again now when her ferry's tones warned her that she would be under way to the launch site in a matter of minutes. The loading crowd of shift workers bound for the site rumbled the deck on the level above her

The drone of hundreds of feet across the metal loading plates made Beatriz squeeze her eyelids tighter yet to keep her mind from conjuring their faces. The laborers were barely more active, had barely more flesh on their bones than the refugees that clustered at Kalaloch's sad camps. The laborers' eyes, when she'd seen them, reflected the hint of hope. The eyes of the people in the camps were too dull to reflect anything, even that.

*Imagine something pretty,* she thought. *Like a hylighter crossing the horizon at sunset.*

It depressed Beatriz to take the ferries. By her count she'd slept nearly five hours in the waiting room while a hyperalert security squad leader sprang a white-glove search on the ferry, its passengers and their possessions. She reminded herself to check all equipment when the security was done—a discipline she picked up from Ben. Holovision's equipment was junk so she, Ben and their crews built their own hardware to suit themselves. It would be tempting to a security with cousins in the black market. She sighed again, worried about Ben and worried about the insidious business of the security squad.

*I know that he and Rico are behind that Shadowbox,* she thought. *They have their distinctive style, whether they shuffle the deck and deal each other new jobs or not.*

About a year ago, the second time Shadowbox jammed out the news and inserted their own show, she nearly approached Rico, wanting in. But she knew they'd left her out for a reason, so she let it go and took out the hurt on more work. Now she thought she knew the real reason she'd been left out.

*They need somebody on the outside,* she thought. *I'm their wild card.*

She had been called in to replace the missing Ben on Newsflash last night, reading, ". . . Ben Ozette . . . on assignment in Sappho . . ." knowing full well that his assignment this Starday, as it had been every Starday for six weeks, had been Crista Galli herself, inside the Director's personal compound and under the Director's supervision.

*He was with her at the time she was missing, his presence wasn't mentioned anywhere. He's missing, too, and the Holovision high brass is covering it up.*

That scared her. Orders to cover up whatever happened to Ben made the whole thing real.

She had thought somehow that she and Ben and Rico were immune to the recent ravages of the world. "Paid witnesses," Ben had called the three of them. "We are the eyes and ears of the people."

"Lamps," Rico had laughed, a little buzzed on boo, "we're not *witnesses,* we're *lamps* . . ."

Beatriz had read on the air exactly what the Newsflash producer had written for her because there hadn't been time for questions. She saw now how deliberate it had been to catch her off guard. Holovision had incredible resources in people and equipment and she meant to use them to see that Ben didn't disappear.

*Ben's not just a witness this time,* she cautioned herself. *He'll ruin everything.*

She had loved him, once, for a long time. Or perhaps she had been intimate with him once for a long time and had just now come to love him. Not in the other way of loving, the electric moments, it was too late for that. They had simply lived through too much horror together that no one else could understand. She had recently shared some electric moments with Dr. Dwarf MacIntosh, after thinking for so long that such feelings would never rise in her again.

Beatriz blinked her raw eyes awake. She turned her face away from the light and sat up straight on a metal bench. Nearby, a guard coughed discreetly. She wished for the clutter of her Project Voidship office aboard the Orbiter. Her office was a few dozen meters from the Current Control hatch and Dr. Dwarf MacIntosh. Her thoughts kept flying back to Mack, and to her shuttle flight to him that was still a few hours away.

Beatriz was tired, she'd been tired for weeks, and these constant delays exhausted her even more. She hadn't had time to think, much less rest, since the Director had her shuttling between the Project Voidship special and the news. Now today she was doing *three* jobs, broadcasting from *three* locations.

She rode to the Orbiter on the shoulders of the greatest engines built by humankind. When she blasted off Pandora her cluttered office aboard the Orbiter became the eye of the storm of her life. No one, not even Flattery, could reach her there.

The tones sounded again and seemed distinctly longer, sadder. Final boarding call. The tones once again made her think of Ben, who was still not found, who might be dead. He was no longer her lover, but he was a good man. She rubbed her eyes.

A young security captain with very large ears entered the waiting-room hatch. He nodded his head as a courtesy, but his mouth remained firm.

"The search is finished," he said. "My apologies. It would be best for you to board now."

She stood up to face him and her clothing clung to her in sleepy folds.

"My equipment, my notes haven't been released yet," she said. "It won't do me a bit of good to—"

He stopped her with a finger to his lips. He had two fingers and a thumb on each hand and she tried to remember which of the old islands carried that trait.

*Orcas? Camano?*

He smiled with the gesture, showing teeth that had been filed to horrible points—rumored to be the mark of one of the death squads that called themselves "the Bite."

"Your belongings are already aboard the ferry," he said. "You are famous, so we recognize your needs. You will have the privacy of a stateroom for the crossing and a guard to escort you."

"But . . ."

His hand was on her elbow, guiding her out the hatchway.

"We have delayed the ferry while you board," he said. "For the sake of the project, please make haste."

She was already out in the passageway and he was propelling her toward the ferry's lower boarding section.

"Wait," she said, "I don't think . . ."

"You have a task already awaiting you at the launch site," the captain said. "I am to inform you that you will be doing a special Newsbreak there shortly after arrival and before your launch."

He handed her the messenger that she usually carried at her hip.

"Everything's in here," he said, and grinned.

Beatriz felt that he was entirely too happy for her own comfort. Certainly the sight of his teeth gave her no comfort at all. She was curious, in her journalistic way, about the hows and whys of the death squads. Her survival instinct overrode her curiosity. The security escort met them at the gangway. He was short, young and loaded down with several of her equipment bags.

"A pleasure to have met you," the captain said, with another slight bow. He handed her a stylus and an envelope. "If you please, for my wife. She admires you and your show very much."

"What is her name?"

"Anna."

Beatriz wrote in a hasty hand, "For Anna, for the future," and signed it with the appropriate flourish. The captain nodded his thanks and Beatriz climbed aboard the ferry. She had barely cleared the second lock when she felt it submerge.

*Worship isn't really love. An object of worship can never be itself. Remember that people love people, and vice versa. People fear gods.*

—Dwarf MacIntosh, Kelpmaster, Current Control

The early morning light clarified the new drift that Ben's life had taken. He knew that he would use Crista's holy image on Shadowbox, much as Flattery had used it on Holovision, to manipulate the people of Pandora. He would use Crista to whip them up against Flattery. He knew that doing this would further bury her humanity, her womanhood. Knowing he would do it cost him something, too. He vowed it would not cost them their love that he already felt filling the space between them. There would be a way . . .

*Damn!*

Ben had not wanted anything to step between himself and the story he'd set out to get. Now *he* was the lead story on prime time. He and Crista had watched the Holovision newsbreak the night before in one of the Zavatans' underground chambers. Though it didn't surprise him, he found it ironic that Beatriz was taking his place.

"Good evening, ladies and gentlemen," she began, "I'm Beat-

33

riz Tatoosh, standing in for Ben Ozette, who is on assignment in Sappho. In our headlines this evening, Crista Galli was abducted a few hours ago from her quarters in the Preserve. Eight armed terrorists, thought to be Shadows . . .''

*Maybe she thought she was doing me a favor,* he thought.

But it was no favor, at least not to Ben. He was not on assignment in Sappho, and there had been no eight armed terrorists. They'd simply walked away. Beatriz read the lines that Flattery's hired maggot fed her. Wrapped up as she was in the Orbiter and Project Voidship, she probably didn't know the difference.

Ben wondered what was going on in the boardroom of Holovision right now. Holovision was owned by Merman Mercantile, and the Director had acquired control of Merman Mercantile through bribery, manipulation, extortion and assassination. *This* was the story that Ben had begun to broadcast on Shadowbox. What had started as the biggest story of his life had become an act that would change his life forever, probably change Crista's life forever and perhaps save the people of Pandora from the Director's backlash of poverty and hunger.

Now Crista was hiding out with him. He had touched her and lived. He had kissed her and lived. Even now, it took great self-control to keep Ben from moving that pale lock of hair out of the corner of her mouth, to keep from caressing her forehead, to keep from slipping underneath the silky cover and . . .

*You're too young to be an old fool,* he thought, *so stop acting like one. You could be a dead fool.*

He reflected on the combined coincidence, fate or divine inspiration that had brought them together, at this time, in this cubby, on this world a millennium at light speed from the origins of humans themselves. It had taken thousands of years, travel from star to star, the near-annihilation of humankind to bring Ben and Crista Galli together. Avata, too, had been nearly annihilated, but a few kelp genes were safely tucked away in most Pandoran humans. Perhaps they were all altered for eternity and these stray bits of the genetic code would bring them together at last.

*Why?* he wondered. *Why us?*

This was one of those times when Ben wished for a normal life. He did not want to be the salvation of society, the species, or anybody's salvation but his own. Things weren't working out that way, and it was too late now to change that. Now, against his better judgment, he was once again in love with an impossible woman.

In the long scheme of things Crista was much more human than Avatan—at least, in appearance. What her kelpness held in check was anyone's guess, including Crista's. In theory, it meant she had many complete minds, capable of thinking and acting independently. This had been discovered in one of the Director's cherished studies. Crista herself had exhibited only one personality during her five years under scrutiny, and it was the one subject that she was reluctant to speak of with Ben.

She was alleged to be the daughter of Vata, and Vata was the "Holy Child" of the poet/prophet Kerro Panille and Waela Tao-Lini. Vata had been conceived in a thrash of human limbs and the intrusion of Avatan tendrils and spores inside the cabin of a sabotaged LTA centuries ago. She was born with a total genetic memory and some form of thigmocommunication common to the kelp. She lay comatose for nearly two centuries.

The human purported to be Crista's father, Duque, had Avatan characteristics instilled through his mother's egg in the labs of the infamous Jesus Lewis, the bioengineer who once wiped out the kelp, body of Avata. He very nearly destroyed humanity along with the kelp. Vata was the beloved saint of Pandora, symbol of the union of humanity with the gods, voice of the gods themselves. Crista Galli, beloved of Ben Ozette, was no less godlike in her power and mystery, in her beauty, in the shadow of death about her. This did not make loving her easy.

Ben knew that the kelp—Avata—had been the survival key to humans on Pandora. It was difficult, maybe impossible, for humans to relate to a sentient . . . kelp. And this new kelp was not the same creature that the pioneers had encountered. Ben had studied *The Histories* enough to agree with the experts—this kelp was fragmented, it was not the single sentient being of old. Many of the faithful among the people of Pandora claimed that this was why Avata formed Crista Galli, to present itself in an acceptable form. This theory was fast gaining support.

*Then what does it want?*

*To live!*

The sudden thought intruded on his mind like a shout, startling him alert. It was a voice he almost recognized. He listened deep inside himself, head tilted, but nothing more came. The sleeper still slept.

The kelp, the body of Avata, was responsible for the stability of the very planet itself. One moon had pulverized itself to asteroids while several continents had ripped apart like tissue paper after the kelp was killed off by the bioengineer Jesus Lewis. Now, the kelp was replanted and the land masses returned after a couple of centuries under the sea. Humans were relearning to live on land as well as on or undersea. It pained Ben that people were still just scratching in dirt when they should be thriving.

*That's the Director's fault,* he reminded himself, *not the kelp's.*

The Director refused to recognize publicly the sentience of the kelp and used it simply as a mechanism, a series of powerful switches that controlled worldwide currents and, to some degree, weather. Everyone knew this was getting more difficult daily. There was more kelp daily, and very little of it was hooked up to Current Control.

*The kelp is resisting Flattery,* he thought. *When it breaks completely free, I want it to have a conscience.*

Ben's diligent research, with a few leads from Crista, uncovered the secret reports and he knew the real depth of Flattery's interest in what one paper called "the Avata Phenomenon." Ben had spoken with the Zavatans, monks in the hills who used the kelp in their rituals.

*Crista says the Director should be* consulting *the kelp!* he thought. *And I get the same story from those monks.*

She stirred again, and he knew she would wake soon. She would see the dockside shops fill with vendors and hear the morning calls from the street of: "Milk! Juices!" "Eggs! We have licensed squawk eggs today!" This was one of the many small pleasures that the Director had denied her—human companionship. Ben knew that he, too, in his way, would deny her this.

*For now,* he reminded himself. *Soon, we will have all the time in the world together.*

From the coffee shop below he could hear the faint scrape of furniture, the metallic clink of utensils and china.

Ben Ozette leaned back against the wall and let out a long, slow breath. Though he'd refused to admit it until now, he was surprised to be alive. He'd not only touched the forbidden Crista Galli, but he'd kissed her. It was twelve hours later and he was still breathing. They'd made it through the night without Vashon Security hunting them down. He waited for Crista to wake, for Rico's code-knock at the door, to see what they would make of the rest of their lives.

*When you see a cloud rising in the west, you say at once, "A shower is coming," and so it comes to pass. And when you see the south wind blow, you say, "There will be a scorching heat," and so it comes to pass. You hypocrites! you know how to judge the face of the sky and of the earth; but how is it that you do not judge this time?*

—Jesus

Crista Galli's first memory of waking up that morning on Kalaloch was of the way the light caught the carved cup in Ben Ozette's hand, and of his hand. She wanted that hand to touch her, to brush her cheek or rest on her shoulder. It was so still, that hand balancing the cup on his knee, that she lay there for a while wondering whether he had fallen asleep sitting up beside the bed. She shuddered at the thought of sitting in one of those pieces of ghastly Islander furniture, a living creature that they called "chairdog."

Kalaloch, too, was waking outside. She heard the stirrings of people and the stutter of engines starting as the dozer and crawler crews headed for another day's work advancing the perimeter. The hungry and homeless of a dozen grounded islands also woke from their sleep in the gritty folds of greater Kalaloch.

Crista listened to the closer, warmer sound of Ben's quiet breathing.

*God,* she thought, *what if I'd killed him?*

She stifled a giggle, imagining the news lead as Ben himself

37

might have written it: "Holovision's popular Nightly News correspondent Ben Ozette was kissed to death last night on assignment . . ." The warmth, the taste of that kiss replayed itself in her mind. This was her first kiss, the one she'd nearly given up on.

Ben suffered no ill effects, which she attributed to the action of Flattery's daily dose of antidote, still in her system. Yet she had received the flood of Ben's past with the touch of his lips to her own, a cascade of memories, emotions and fear that nearly paralyzed her with its unexpected clarity and force.

There were these matters of his life that she preferred not to know: Ben's first kiss, a pretty redhead; his last kiss, Beatriz Tatoosh. Both of these and more lingered on her own lips. She witnessed his first lovemaking through the memory of his cells, witnessed his birth, the sinking of Guemes Island, the deaths of his parents. His memories impregnated her very cells, waiting for her own emotional trigger that would call them to life.

She had received his memories with his kiss, too stunned to tell him. Her dreams that night were his dreams, his memories. She saw Shadowbox as he saw it, as the organ of truth in a body riddled with lies. She knew that he, like herself, was vulnerable and lonely and had a life to live for others. She did not want to keep this from him, the fact that she now owned his life. She did not want to lose him now that they had finally found each other, and she did not want to be the death of him, either.

Ben was not afraid of "the Tingle," as people called it—this kelp death that supposedly lurked in her touch as it did in some kelp, within her very chemistry. Sometimes she didn't believe it, either. Flattery himself had developed the antidote, which he saw to it that she received daily. It did not diminish the chemical messages she received, such as Ben's memories. It merely muted those that her body might send. Still, none dared touch her and all of her attendants in Flattery's compound kept her at a safe distance.

This was the first morning in her memory that she did not wake up to attendants, endless tests, to the difficult task of being a revered prisoner in the great house of the Director. Crista had slept the refreshing sleep of the newborn in spite of their escape, their hiding, her first kiss. An emptiness rumbled through her stomach as delicious aromas rose to her of pastries, hot breads, coffee.

Somewhere beneath them hot sebet sizzled on a grill. Meat was something she craved. Flattery's labtechs had explained this to her, some mumbo-jumbo about her Avatan genes affecting her protein synthesis, but she knew this simply as hunger. She also hungered for fresh fruits of all kinds, and nuts and grains. The very thought of a salad gagged her and always had.

Though they'd fled here in the night, Crista had memorized the warrenlike underground system they took to get from the Director's complex at the Preserve to this Islander community at Kalaloch. She was reminded of the maze of kelpways down under. She knew nothing of the local geography save that she was near the sea, relieving some other hunger that rumbled within.

She heard the sea now, a wet pulse over the babble of street vendors and the increasing traffic of the day. Pandorans were an early lot, she'd heard, but unhurried. It is difficult for the hungry to hurry. Only a very few remained on their traditional organic islands. Drifting the seas had become much too dangerous a life in this day of jagged coastlines and sea lanes choked with kelp. The majority who settled landside still called themselves "Islander" and retained their old manners of dress and custom. Those Islanders whom she'd known at the Preserve compound were either servants or security, close-mouthed about their lives outside Flattery's great basalt walls. Many were horribly mutated, a revulsion to Flattery but a fascination to her.

Crista Galli tucked the cover under her chin and stretched backward, unfolding to the sunlight, aware of some new modesty in the company of Ben Ozette. She had all of the intimacies of his life stored in her head, now, and she was afraid of what he might think of her if he knew. She felt herself flush, a bit of a voyeur, as she remembered his first night with Beatriz.

*Men are so strange,* Crista thought. He'd brought her here on the run from Vashon security and the Director, assured her that they were safely hidden in this tiny cubby, then he sat up all night beside her rather than join her in bed. He'd already proven immune to her deadly touch, and she liked the kiss as much as the daring gesture of the kiss.

The attentions of other men, the Director among them, had taught her something of the power of her beauty. Ben Ozette was attracted to her, that had been clear the first time she'd looked into his eyes. They were green, something like her own only darker. She treasured the one magic kiss they had shared before she slept. She treasured his memories that now were hers, the family she shared with him, his lovers . . .

Her reverie was interrupted by a shriek in the street below, then a long, high-voiced wail that chilled her in spite of her warm bed. She lay quiet while Ben set aside his cup and rose to the window.

*They've found someone,* she thought, *someone who's been killed.*

Ben had told her about the bodies in the streets in the morning, but it was something too far from her life to imagine.

"The death squads leave them for a lesson," he said. "Bodies are there in the mornings for people to see when they go to work, when they take the children to their crèche. Some have no hands, some have no tongues or heads. Some are mutilated obscenely. If you stop to look, you are questioned: 'Do you know this man? Come with us.' No one wants to go with them. Sooner or later a wife is notified, or a mother or a son. Then the body is removed."

Ben had seen hundreds of such bodies in his work, and she had glimpsed these the night before in the speedy unreeling of his memories into her own. This wail she thought must come from a mother who had just found her dead son. Crista was not tempted to look outside. Ben returned to his watch at her bedside.

Had he seen anything of her when she kissed him? Such a thing happened sometimes with the kelp, but seldom anymore with herself. It had happened with others who'd touched her. First, the shock of wide-eyed disbelief; then, the unfocused eyes and the trembling; at last, the waking and the registry of stark terror. For those who had been lucky enough to wake.

*What did I show them?* she wondered. *Why some and not all?* She had studied the kelp's history and found no help there, precious little comfort. She still smoldered over some research tech's pointed reference to her "family tree."

She remembered how she had been kept alive down under by the cilia of the kelp that probed the recesses of her body. She received the ministrations of the mysterious, nearly mythological Swimmers, the severest of human mutations. Adapted completely to water, Swimmers resembled giant, gilled salamanders more than humans. They occupied caves, Oracles, abandoned Merman outposts and some kelp lagoons. She had been one with the kelp, more kelp than human, for her first nineteen years. There were some of Flattery's people who thought that she had been manufactured by the kelp, but she herself believed that couldn't be true.

A lot of other Pandorans sported the green-eyed gene of the kelp, including Ben. At a little over a meter and a half tall she could look over the heads of most women and looked most men nearly in the eye. Her surface network of blue veins was slightly more visible than other people's because she was nearly pale enough to be translucent. The blood in her veins was red, based on iron, and incontrovertibly human—facts that had been established her first day out of the kelp.

Her full lips puckered slightly when she was thinking, hanging on the edge of a kiss. Her straight, slender nose flared slightly at the nostrils and flared even more when she was angry—another emotion she dared not indulge among Flattery's people.

Crista had been educated by the touch of the kelp, which infused in her certain genetic memories of the humans that it had encountered. Before Flattery took power, most humans contacted the kelp by being buried at sea. She had to shut out the flood of memories that came rolling in with the sounds of the nearby waves. She treated herself to another languorous stretch then turned to Ben.

"Did you sit up all night?"

"Couldn't sleep anyway," he said.

He stood slowly, working out the kinks in his body, then sat on the edge of her bed.

Crista sat up and leaned against his shoulder. The disturbance below their window was gone. They faced the plaz, the morning sunlight off the bay, and Crista was lulled into a half-sleep by the warmth from the window, the coziness of Ozette beside her, and the harmonious chatter of the street vendors. In the distance she heard the heavy machinery of construction tear into the hills.

"Will we leave here soon?" she asked. She was invigorated by the sunlight, the *plop-plop-plop* of waves against the bulkhead and a whiff of broiling sebet on the air. The years of lies and imprisonment at the hands of the Director washed through her like a current of cold blood. Every morning that she had awakened in his compound she simply wanted to curl up under those covers and doze. Today, wherever Ben Ozette was going, Crista was going with him.

Someone whistled at their hatch, a short musical phrase, repeated once. It was the same kind of whistle-language that she'd heard from dockside the night before.

Ozette grunted, rapped twice on the deck. A single whistle replied.

"Our people," he said. "They will move us this morning, much as I'd like to show you the neighborhood. Rico is setting it up. The whole world knows by now that you're gone. The reward for your return, and for my head, will be enough to tempt even good people . . . on either side. There is much hunger.''

''I can't go back there,'' she said. ''I won't. I have seen the sky. You kissed me . . .''

He smiled at her, offered her a drink of his water. But he did not kiss her.

She knew that he would be killed if caught, that Flattery had already signed his death warrant. The Warrior's Union would take care of it, had probably already taken care of every servant and selected others at the Preserve.

The night before, emerging from the underground, they had dodged from building to building along the waterfront streets, fearful of security patrols enforcing Flattery's curfew. Crista had stopped in the open to look at the stars and at Pandora's nearer moons. She bathed firsthand in the touch of a cool breeze on her face and arms, smelled the charcoal cookery of the poor, saw the stars with only the atmosphere in her way.

''I want to go outside,'' she whispered. ''Can we go out soon, to the street?''

Always the answer from the Director had been *no*. It was *always* no. ''The demons,'' they would say at first, ''you would hardly make a meal for them.'' Or, later, ''The Shadows want you killed,'' the Director would say. Lately, he had repeated, ''You can't tell—the swine could look like anyone. It would be horrible if they got their hooks into you.''

The Director had a particular leer that gave her the creeps, though to hear him tell it there was no one who could protect her but him, no one she could trust in the world but him. For most of that five years she had believed him. Shadowbox changed all that. Then Ben Ozette came to do his story, and she realized that the only reason Flattery forbade her touch was his fear that she would learn something from him, from his people, and expose his intricate system of lies.

''Yes,'' Ben said. ''We'll get out soon. Things are going to get very hot here very soon . . .''

He stiffened suddenly and swore under his breath. He pointed at a Vashon security patrol working their way down the pierside toward them: two men on each side of the street. They poured an insidious stillness over a choppy sea of commuters and shoppers in the marketplace. The press of commuters crowding toward the ferries parted for them without touching.

Each guard carried a small lasgun slung under one arm, and

from each belt hung various tools of the security trade: coup baton for infighting hand to hand, charges for the lasguns, a fistful of small but efficient devices of chemical and mechanical restraint. They each wore a pair of mirrored sunglasses—trademark of the Warrior's Union, the Director's personal assassination squad. Among the people there was much smiling, headshaking, shoulder-shrugging; some cringed.

Crista watched the pair work their way along the dockside street and felt the small hairs rise on her arms and the back of her neck.

"Don't worry," Ben said, as though reading her mind. With his hand on her bare shoulder like that she believed it was possible that he *was* reading her mind—or, at least, her emotions. She loved his touch. She felt a new flood of his life enter through her skin. It stored itself somewhere in her brain while her eyes went on watching the street.

The security team left one man in front of each building in turn while the other searched inside. They were close.

"What do we do?" she asked.

He reached to the other side of the bed for a bundle of Islander clothes and set them in her lap.

"Get dressed," he said, "and watch. Stay back from the plaz."

There was a sudden, concussive *whump* and a flash of orange from the harbor, then a roil of black smoke. The street turned into a scramble of bodies as people ran to their boats dockside and to their firefighting stations. Pandorans had used hydrogen for their engines and stoves, their welding torches and power production since the old days. Hydrogen storage tanks were everywhere, and fire one of their great fears.

"What . . . ?"

"An old coracle," Ben said, "registered to me. They will be busy for a while. With luck, they will believe we were aboard."

Another *whump* took Crista's breath away, and as she pulled on the unfamiliar clothing she saw that the security squad had not disappeared with the crowd. They came on with the same precision and deliberation, door to door. The street was nearly empty as everyone else who was able-bodied fought the fires or moved nearby boats to safety.

While Ben stood watch beside the window, Crista pulled on a heavily embroidered white cotton dress that was much too big for her. Her breasts, though not small, bobbled free inside. She held the fabric away from her flat belly and looked questioningly at Ben.

He tossed her a black pajama-type worksuit of the Islanders that appeared identical to the one he wore. From a drawer beside the bed he pulled a long woven sash and handed it to her.

"I don't know how to tell you this, but you're pregnant. Quite a ways along, too."

When she still didn't follow his intent, he said, "Strap the worksuit on your belly to fill out the dress," he said. "You'll need it later. For now, you are a pregnant Islander. I am your man."

She strapped the worksuit around her as instructed and adjusted the dress. In the mirror beside the hatch she *did* look pregnant.

Crista watched in the mirror as Ben wrapped a long red bandana around his head, letting the tails fall between his shoulder blades. It was embroidered with the same geometrics that appeared on her dress.

*My man,* she thought with a smile, *and we're dressing to go out.*

She patted the padding on her stomach fondly and rested her hand there, half-expecting to feel some tiny movement. Ben stood behind her and tied a similar bandana around her forehead. He gave her a floppy straw hat to wear over it.

"This manner of dress is the mark of the Island I grew up on," he said. "You have heard about Guemes Island?"

"Yes, of course. Sunk the year before I was born."

"Yes," he said. "You are now the pregnant wife of a Guemes Island survivor. Among Islanders you will receive the greatest respect. Among Mermen you will be treated with the deference that only the guilty can bestow. As you know, it means absolutely nothing among Flattery's people. We have no papers, there wasn't time . . ."

Two whistles at their hatch. Two different whistles.

"That's Rico," he said, and matched her smile. "Now we get to go outside."

> *The things that people want and the things that are good for them are very different. . . . Great art and domestic bliss are mutually incompatible. Sooner or later, you'll have to make your choice.*
>
> —Arthur C. Clarke

Beatriz dozed awhile on the couch after shutting off her alarm. The dark, plazless office at the launch site helped keep the fabric of her dream alive. Freed from the confines of her mind, it flowed about the room with the ease of a ghost. In a way, it was a ghost.

She had been dreaming of Ben, of their last night together, and there were parts of the dream that she wanted to savor. It was two years ago, the night before she made her first trip up to the Orbiter, before she met Mack. She was nervous about her first shuttle flight to the Orbiter, and Ben was going off to the High Reaches to meet with some Zavatan elder. In spite of the fact that they'd been lovers for years, they both felt awkward. It was ending, they knew it was ending, but neither of them could talk about it.

It was early evening, clear and warm. A shot of sunset still streaked the horizon pink and blue. They sat aboard one of Holo-vision's foils at dockside, in the crew's quarters. She remembered the familiar *shlup-shlip* of water against the hull and the occasional mutter of wild squawks settling down. Children played their evening games before being called in for the night and they whistle-signaled from pier to pier. She and Ben had talked of children, of wanting them and of bad timing. This night the rest of their crews had discreetly left them alone. She found out later it was at Rico's suggestion.

"Women are the answer," Ben said, handing her a glass of white wine.

"And what was the question?"

She touched glasses with him, sipped, and set it down. She did not want to ride a rocket into orbit in the morning with a hangover.

Ben's green eyes looked particularly beautiful against his dark skin. His lean, muscular body had always been perfect with hers. She couldn't understand why he had to go off on his wild projects chasing down Shadows when he could stay and work with her. She'd covered as much death as she cared to, it was time they thought of themselves.

*I want to report on life, advances, progress. . . .*

"Women represent life, advances, progress," he said.

The hair prickled at the back of her neck.

"Are you reading my mind?"

"Would I dare?" he asked.

Those green eyes twinkled in their way that shot something straight into her heart. Whatever it was was warm, and it always melted downward like a hand inside her underwear. Beatriz was a strong woman, and she knew it. She also knew that Ben Ozette was the only man who ever made her weak in the knees. She sipped her wine and kept the glass at her chest.

"What am I thinking now?" she asked, feeling she had to change the subject.

"You're wishing I'd get on with whatever it was I was going to say so that we can get on with the evening."

She laughed a little louder than she liked, and ran a hand through her black hair.

"Why, Mr. Ozette, what kind of girl do you think I am?"

He ignored her flirtation. His manner turned serious.

"I think you're the kind of girl who wants to see the best for everyone—for the refugees, yourself, even Flattery. You've covered some of the most horrible disasters and bloodiest atrocities this world has seen. I know because I was there. Now *it* won't go away, so *you're* going away. You want to see progress, you want to see good things. Well, so do I . . ,"

"But look what you're doing!" She fisted her thigh and scooted back in the couch. "OK, security is more than enthusiastic, that's bad enough. If you make heroes out of the people fighting them, then more will join them. They will have to fight the same way. There will be no end to the cycle. Dammit, Ben, that's why they call it 'Revolution.' Wheels turn and turn in place and the vehicle gets mired down. I've come damned close to dying more times than I can count—most of those times with you—and now I want to get *somewhere*. I want a family . . ."

Ben set down his glass and grasped her hand across the table.

"I know," he said. "I understand. Maybe I understand more than you think. I want to offer you life, advances, progress."

Neither of them spoke for a while, but their hands conversed with each other in the familiar language of lovers.

"OK," she said. She tossed off her wine, trying to appear lighthearted, "what's the plan, man?"

"I don't know the plan, yet," he said. "But I know the key. It's information. Our business, remember?"

"Yes?" She refilled her glass, then his. "Explain."

"You didn't see any women in Flattery's security force, and you set out to do a story, remember? What happened?"

"Not approved, we never shot a centimeter . . ."

"And how many times has that happened?"

"To me? Not much. But then, there are plenty of stories to do, more than I'll ever live to do, I just find another one or take an assignment . . ."

"An important point," Ben said. He hunched over their little table, tapping the top with his index finger. "If Flattery doesn't get flattered, the story, whatever it is, doesn't get aired. He is from a different world—literally, a different world. He is from a world that starves women and children because they are on the wrong side of an imaginary line, and he won't allow them to cross it. We are from a world that used to teach: 'Life, at all cost. Preserve life.' Pandora has been adversary enough. We haven't been able to afford the luxury of fighting amongst ourselves."

"So, I don't get where . . ."

"Half of the shows I do get dropped," Ben said. "It's not because they're not good, it's because it's getting harder and harder to keep Flattery from looking like the hood that he is. What would happen if people refused to have anything to do with him—refused to speak with him, feed him, shelter him—what would happen then?"

She laughed again.

"What makes you think they'd do that? It would take—"

"Information. Show him up for what he is, show the people what they can do. This whole world's been a disaster since Flattery took over. He promises them food and keeps them hungry. He keeps us in line because we *know* what he can do to us. If people knew they'd be no more hungry without Flattery, without the Vashon Security Force, would they put up with him?"

"It would take a miracle," she finished.

She couldn't look him in the eye. This was the conversation she really didn't want to have on their last night together. He leaned over and kissed her on the cheek.

"I'm sorry," he said. "I'm running off at the mouth again. I interviewed a group of mothers today who are petitioning the Chief of Security for news of their sons and husbands who have disappeared. Another group, over five hundred mothers, says that they had sons killed but there was never an investigation, never an arrest. They say security did it, there are witnesses. Now, I don't know about that. What I do know is that *mothers* are the ones on the march. Holovision's refusing to pick up on it, forbidding me to report on what people have the right to know. There has to be a way . . . I'm just thinking out loud, is all."

He kissed her again on the cheek, then lifted her chin.

"I'll shut up now," he said. He kissed her lips and she pulled him down to the carpet beside the table.

"Promise?" She kissed him back, and untucked his shirt from his pants so she could get her hands under his clothes, onto his smooth, warm skin.

His hands unbuttoned her Islander blouse, unpeeled her cotton skirt and found her bare under both.

"Pretty daring," he muttered, and kissed her belly as she undressed him.

"You realize we're going to get rug burn."

"I thought you promised to shut up."

Her alarm went off again and startled Beatriz out of her waking dream. She shut it off and sat up to give herself some energy. Ben had been right about the rug burn. They'd kicked the wine over on themselves, too. She was sure that had been the night that Ben conceived the idea for Shadowbox. She sighed, trying to lift a heavy sadness from her chest.

*Too bad we couldn't have conceived a little one*, she thought. *It might've saved us both.*

If they had, she wouldn't have met Mack. Her relationship with Ben prepared her for Mack. He was a little older, and because of his upbringing on Moonbase he wanted a family as much as she did.

Beatriz pressed the "start" key on her pocket messenger and it announced: "0630 . . ." She twisted the volume knob down and massaged her tired eyelids. The preliminary briefing from the Holovision head office would be followed by more details before air time so she half-listened, intent only on news of Ben Ozette. Another deep sigh.

The smell at her launch site office down under was distinctly Merman—air swept clean of particulate, saturated with the scent of mold inhibitors and sterile water. Lighting in Holovision's small broadcast studio always dried things out a bit and helped her breathe easier on the air. She suspected she would be on the air again in less than half an hour.

She pulled the legs of her singlesuit straight and unbunched the wrinkled sleeves from her armpits. Her office was backlit in the Merman way, so her reflection in the plaz was a warm one, capturing the glow of her brown skin and the sheen of her shaggy black hair. Her generation and Ben's was the first in two centuries to have more children born to the ancient norm of human appearance than not. Beatriz did not pity the severely mutated, pity was an emotion that most Pandorans could do without. She thanked the odds daily for her natural good looks. Right now she wanted a hot shower before facing her messenger's latest story of woe.

*That's what Ben always called it,* she thought. She spoke it aloud, "'Another story of woe.'"

Fatigue and a half-sleep deepened her voice enough that it sounded vaguely like his. It made her want to hear his voice, to argue with him one more time about who worked the hardest and who got the shower first. She smiled in spite of her worry. It was more than symbolic that they had always wound up in hot water together.

It was fear for Ben that made her not want to face the messenger just yet. It was hard enough to face the fact that she still loved him, though in an unlovely way.

*Suicide,* she thought. *He might just as well have run the perimeter on a bet and let a dasher have at him.*

Beatriz knew the signs, and it was Ben who'd made her aware of them. Crossing the Director was a survival matter.

She dolloped enough milk into her coffee to cool it off, then sipped at the rim while she replayed the brief, chilling message.

0630 Memo:
   Location brief, Launch Bay Five, air time 0645.
   Lead: Crista Galli still in hands of Shadows.
   Second lead: OMCs to Orbital Station today.
   Detail: ref terrorists, arms, drugs, religious fervor, Shadows. Final assembly of Voidship drive in orbit, OMC installation imminent. Items follow on Location.
   Secondary discretion: Mandatory at 0640.
   Time out: 0631.

Beatriz glanced at the processor's time display: *0636.*

"Secondary Discretion!" she muttered. That meant they were doing a time-delay. Time enough that Holovision could run a pretaped Newsbreak if she didn't show up or, worse, if they didn't like what she said on the air. Ben had warned her it would come to this.

"Damn!"

*What else was he right about?*

The elevator to the Newsbreak studio at Launch Bay Five was only a dozen meters down the passageway from her office. She fingered the tangles out of her hair and hurried out the hatchway. The hurry didn't slow her worrying one whit.

Ben had something to do with this Crista Galli thing, and she knew that Flattery knew that, too. Why, then, was there still no release on Ben? The answer was one that Ben had tried to warn her about, and it chilled her to think it.

*They'll see that he disappears,* she thought. *If there's nothing on him in the briefing . . .* She didn't want to think of that.

*Flattery knows about us . . . about Ben,* she thought. She knew about the disappearances, the bodies in the streets of Kalaloch in the mornings. Ben had warned her about this more than once and shown her firsthand, finally, how it happened. She knew that unpopular people disappeared. She had never thought it would happen to one of them.

Another thought shook her as she faced the elevator.

*If I don't say something about him on the air, then he's going to disappear for sure!*

She was scheduled to fly with the crew that delivered the OMCs to the Orbital Station for their Voidship installation. He must know about her budding relationship with Mack, that was no secret. The installation of the Organic Mental Cores was a nice piece of propaganda for Flattery that would take her conveniently out of the picture. It would also make it impossible for her to investigate Ben's disappearance on her own.

She hadn't known what to think last night when she'd had to fill in for Ben. She'd read the prompter cold, too surprised at the lie on her screen, at the suddenness of the lie, to challenge it there. Flattery had finally tossed her a gauntlet.

*What is the worst?* she asked herself now.

The worst would be that they would both disappear.

She squeezed into the elevator among the press of techs and mechanics, left their greetings unreturned. They were a sweaty bunch in the cramped humidity.

*What is for sure?*

For sure Ben would disappear if she said nothing, if Holovision Nightly News continued to lie about his absence.

She rounded the passageway into the studio suite of the Holovision feature assignment crew. It was an engine assembly hangar with ten-meter-high ceilings. The makeup tech's hands were fussing over Beatriz's hair and face as soon as she entered the hatchway. Someone else helped her slip into a bulky pullover blouse with the Holovision logo at the left breast. As usual, several of the crew were talking at once, none of them saying what she wanted to hear. She wouldn't be doing this Newsbreak unless Ben were still missing.

She had seen Ben and Crista Galli together a few days ago at Flattery's compound. Ben and Crista, in the hibiscus courtyard, Ben leaning toward Crista in that intent way he had. Beatriz knew then that he had fallen in love with the girl. She also knew that he probably didn't know that yet himself.

*I should have had a talk with him . . . not a lover talk, a friend talk. Now he might be dead.*

She patted her cheeks flush and the lights turned up. It was nearly time, and still she spoke to no one, heard little, viewed the blank prompter with a certain measure of fear. He had held her own gaze intently hundreds of times over the years, dozens of times with the same argument.

"I look at the big picture," she'd say. "Pandora's unstable, we've seen that. We could all die here on any given day at the whim of meteorology. We *need* another world . . ."

And he would always argue for the *now*.

"People are hungry *now*," he would say. "They need to be fed *now* or there won't be a later for any of us . . ."

She always felt insignificant in the studio in spite of her fame, but today as they scrubbed and dusted her face, fluffed her hair and placed her earpiece she was writing her own script for the Newsbreak—one that she hoped would keep Ben in the news but keep Flattery off her back. She looked into the prompter, adjusted the contrast and cleared her throat. She had thirty seconds. She cleared her throat again, smiled at the lens cluster and took a deep breath.

"Ten seconds, B."

She let the breath out slow, blinked her eyes for the shine and said to the red light, "Good Morning, Pandora. This is Beatriz Tatoosh for Newsbreak . . ."

> *Since every object is simply the sum of its qualities,*
> *and since qualities exist only in the mind, the whole*
> *objective universe of matter and energy, atoms and*
> *stars does not exist except as a construction of the*
> *consciousness, an edifice of conventional symbols*
> *shaped by the senses of man.*

> —Lincoln Barnett, *The Universe and Dr. Einstein*

Alyssa Marsh lived in the past, because the past was all that Flattery could not strip from her. He had tried chemicals, laser probes, tiny implants but the person who had been Alyssa Marsh survived them all.

*He is afraid*, she thought. *He is afraid that my life here has made me unfit as an OMC—and he's right.*

He had taken her body away fiber by fiber, or taken her away from her body. Her carotids and jugulars had been bypassed to a life-support system and she had been decapitated, then Flattery himself excised the remaining flesh and bone from around her unfeeling brain. The only sense she retained was the vaguest sense of being. She no longer felt much kinship with humans, and had no way of knowing how long she'd felt that way. Until someone hooked her up to her Voidship she had no means of measuring time. Time became her newest toy. Time, and the past.

*Even fog has substance*, she thought.

Logic told her that her brain still existed or she wouldn't be entertaining herself with these thoughts. Training in her Moonbase crèche hundreds of years ago had prepared her for her responsibility as an OMC—purely mental functions, making human decisions out of mechanically derived data—but Pandora had opened up other possibilities, all of them requiring a body. Having a child, something she'd never have been permitted as a Moonbase clone, changed her perspective but it didn't change her indoctrination. She kept her child's birth secret, especially from his father, Raja Lon Flattery number six, the Director.

Without eyes or ears she would have thought herself a perpetual prisoner of a completely silent darkness. Without skin she expected not to feel, and without the rest she imagined she'd sniffed her last blossom, tasted her last bootleg chocolate. None of this proved to be true.

Alyssa had expected to be cut off from her senses, but reality proved her to be free of them instead. Like the gods, she was free now to clench the folds of time and replay her life at will, mining sensory details that she'd missed when they filtered through her emotions. She did not miss her emotions much, either, but she allowed as this might be a simple denial process protecting what was left of Alyssa Marsh from the full horror of what Flattery had done to her.

"You'll be the Organic Mental Core," he had announced to her. He spoke of it as privilege, honor, as the salvation of humankind. He might have been right about the salvation of humankind. At the time, even drugged as she was, she didn't buy the first two. She recognized that she was listening to one of the oldest arguments for martyrdom known to her species.

"Be reasonable," he'd told her. "Accept this banner and you will live in a thousand bodies. The Voidship itself will become your bones, your skin."

"Spare me the speech," she slurred, her tongue thickened by drugs. "I'm ready. If you're not going to let me go back to my studies in the kelp, if you're not going to kill me, then just get on with it."

She now felt that the major difference between herself and the kelp was that the kelp's entire body was also its brain. The tissues were integrated and the appropriate accomplishments measurable. Flattery would hear none of this.

He had spoken to her of an Elysium of sorts, of a pain-free and disease-free life. He reminded her that an OMC in its harness was the closest that humans came to immortality. This did nothing to comfort her. She knew the insanity record of other OMCs, the rate at which they'd turned rogue and destroyed their host ships and their expendable cargoes of clones, clones like herself, and Flattery, and Mack. Indeed, the same thing had happened aboard the Voidship *Earthling*, which brought them all to Pandora. Three OMCs went crazy and the crew had to fabricate an artificial intelligence to save their skins. It brought them to Pandora and abandoned them there.

*I'm understanding that more and more,* she thought. *I'd like to meet this Ship sometime, interface to interface.*

Words had always amused her, and a lack of flesh to laugh with did not seem to diminish that amusement. Thinking of her son was always serious, however, especially since he'd made such good headway in Flattery's security service. She thought of him now because her one regret was not seeing him face to face before she . . .

*. . . Shucked my mortal coil,* she thought. *I wanted to see him with my own eyes. No . . . I wanted him to see me before . . . this.*

She had given him up to an upwardly mobile Merman couple rather than risk what would happen if Flattery found out she'd borne him a son. She had been afraid he would kill her and take the son, turning him into another ruthless Director.

*I should've kept him,* she thought. *He's turned out like Flattery, anyway.*

The boy would know by now—she'd left the appropriate papers hidden in her cubby before Flattery reduced her to a convoluted lump of pink tissue. It had been her last act of sentimentality.

"Your body betrays you," Flattery growled that last day. "You've had a child. Where is it?"

"I gave it up," she said. "You know how I am about my work. I have no time for anything but the kelp. A child . . . well, it was only a temporary inconvenience."

It was the kind of argument that Flattery would make, and he bought it. He never seemed to suspect that the child was his. Their liaison had been brief enough and long enough ago that Flattery seemed not to remember it at all. He had made no further reference to it after she left his cubby for the last time more than twenty years back. He only grunted his acknowledgment, probably thinking that the child was the product of a recent indiscretion. He could not deny her passion for her work in the kelp. Only Dwarf

MacIntosh shared her passion for delving into this mysterious near-consciousness that filled Pandora's seas.

*I should have kept him with me in the kelp,* she thought. *Now he's become what I'd most feared and I've lost his presence, too.*

In her present state, the OMC Alyssa Marsh dwelt often on that birth and those few precious moments her child had been with her. He had stopped crying immediately after birth, happy to watch the Natali as they cleaned up his mother and the room. He had a full head of black hair and seemed fully alert right from the start.

"He was a month overdue," the midwife said. "Looks like he wasn't wasting his time in there."

After a few minutes she handed him to the couple who would give him their name. Frederick and Kazimira Brood had visited her weekly for the past few months, and they had made full arrangements for his care. It would cost Alyssa dearly, but she wanted him to have the best of chances. Flattery was determined to turn Kaloch into a real city, the center of Pandoran thought and commerce. He had hired the young Broods—an architect and a social geographer—to build the security warehouses and garrisons for his troops. There was talk at the time that they might get the university contract. Who could have foreseen the changes in Pandora, the changes in Flattery then?

*I could,* she thought. *I thought development of the kelp as an ally more important than raising my son.*

If she had had her body with her, she would have let out a long, slow breath to relieve the tension that would have been brewing in her belly. She had neither belly nor breath and her reason now was relatively free of emotion.

*I did the right thing,* she thought. *In the grand scheme of humankind, I did the right thing.*

*Even if they, with minds overcome by greed, see no
evil in the destruction of a family, see no sin in the
treachery to friends, shall we not who see the evil of
destruction, shall we not refrain from this terrible
deed?*

—from *Zavatan Conversations with the Avata,*
Queets Twisp, elder

Flutterby Bodeen unrolled her precious bolt of stolen muslin
across the dusty attic deck. Her three young schoolmates clapped
in their excitement.

"You did it!" Jaka cheered. He was twelve, lanky, and the
only boy. His father, like Flutterby's, worked down under at the
Shuttle Launch Site, or SLS. His mother also worked at Merman
Hyperconductor, so their family received nearly double the usual
scrip at The Line.

"Shhh!" Flutterby warned them. "We don't want them finding
us now. Leet, did you get the paints?"

Leet, at eleven the youngest of the four, pulled four thick tubes
from under her bulky cotton blouse.

"Here," she said, without looking up, "I couldn't get black."

"Green!" Jaka blew out an impatient breath. "You want them
to think we're Shadows? You know they all use green . . ."

"*Shush!*" Dana emphasized her point with a finger at her lips
and an exaggerated scowl. "Maybe we *are* Shadows now, did you

57

ever think of that? They'll treat us the same if we're caught, you know.''

"OK, OK," Flutterby interrupted. "We're not going to get caught unless we're here all day. Dana, Jaka, we're supposed to be practicing our music, so you two play awhile. Leet and I will each make a banner, then we'll play so you can do two."

"Security's all over the street this morning," Dana warned.

"It's because of Crista Galli. Maybe they think she's around here, somewhere . . ."

"Maybe she *is* around here . . ."

"We should have a lookout . . ."

"They won't come in while wots are practicing," Flutterby said, and put her hand up to quiet the others. "Who wants to have anything to do with music lessons? Besides," she sniffed, and her chin raised a fraction, "my brother's a security. I know how they think."

"Yeah, and he's up in Victoria," Dana said. "They think different up there. You know they split them up so if they shoot somebody it won't be family."

"That's not true!" Flutterby said. "They just don't want them working the same district as their family because—because—"

"They're going to walk in here if we don't get busy," Jaka interrupted. His voice was changing, and he tried to make it sound authoritative. Jaka lived at the edge of Kalaloch's largest refugee camp. He was more fearful than the others of the immediacy of hunger and the reprisals of security. At twelve, he had already seen enough death from both. He uncased his well-worn flute and snapped the sections together.

Dana shrugged, sighed and uncased her caracol. Its new strings glistened in a stray sliver of sunlight. The swirled black back of its huge shell shone with the polish of four generations of fingers.

"Give me an A," she said.

Jaka obliged, and as they proceeded to tune the caracol the other two youngsters tore the cloth into four equal lengths of about three meters each.

"Has your brother ever killed anybody?" Leet whispered.

"Of course not," Flutterby said. She smoothed out the wrinkles in their cloth without meeting the other girl's eyes.

"He's not like that. You've met him."

"Yeah," Leet said. Her brown eyes brightened and she giggled.

"He's so *cute*."

Flutterby found that she got her banner lettered with less than half a tube of green. It was dark green and would be nearly as visible as black. The large block letters read, "WE'RE HUNGRY NOW!" It had become the rallying cry of the refugees, but she'd heard it mumbled everywhere lately. As scarcity spread and rations declined, Flutterby had even heard it whispered in The Line.

The Line, where everyone stood for hours to get into the food distribution centers, was where she chose to hang her banner. Leet's would go over their school, which faced the concrete-and-plasteel offices of Merman Mercantile. Jaka wanted to smuggle his into Merman Hyperconductor, and Dana said she'd hang hers from the ferry dock, within easy view of Holovision's offices on the pier.

Dana ran up and down the scales a few times, then she and Jaka played a fast, lilting dance piece they'd practiced at school. Flutterby thought it the best her friend had ever played. Jaka struggled, as usual, but diligently played on.

"Do you think the Shadows kidnaped Crista Galli?" Leet asked.

The bulky tube was difficult for her to handle, and she was going over her letters twice to make them bold enough to be read at a distance.

"I don't know," Flutterby said. "I don't know what to believe anymore. My mother grew up on Vashon, and she says that Crista Galli is some kind of god or something. My dad says she's just another freak."

"Your *mother?*"

"No," Flutterby giggled, "Crista Galli, you stoop. He says that the only way to feed the world is to keep control of the currents, and that if Crista Galli helps control the kelp then the Director is right to make sure she doesn't get away, or turn it against us. What do your parents think?"

Leet frowned.

"They don't say much of anything, anymore," she said. "They're both working all the time, every day. Mom says she's too tired to hear herself think. My dad won't even watch the news anymore. He doesn't say anything, just bites his lip and goes to bed. I think they're afraid . . ."

An explosion in the harbor startled them both. Dana set her caracol on the deck with a *thump*.

"That was *close*," she said. Dana had a lisp that came out when she was nervous, and it slipped out now.

The four of them crowded the tiny plaz porthole at the far end of the attic. A smudge of black smoke blotted the sky to their right at the end of the street. Looking up the street to the left, Flutterby watched the giant cup on the Ace of Cups sign swing to and fro from the concussion. The street was packed with morning commuters and vendors at their little tables. Flutterby heard a gasp from Dana, and looked where she pointed, straight beneath them.

"Security!" she whispered. "He's covering the hatch. They must already be inside!"

"We've got to hide this stuff," Jaka said, his whisper cracking into its high range. "If they find this, they'll kill us."

"Or worse," Dana muttered.

They scrambled to gather up the paints and to roll up the two wet banners, but it was too late.

The flimsy hatch burst aside as a fat, no-neck security kicked it in. Another, nearly identical to him, slipped inside and waited with his back to the wall.

"Look here," he said, straightening the banners with the muzzle of his weapon. "A little nest of flatwings, no?"

Without waiting for a reply he snapped two bursts from his lasgun. Jaka and Leet dropped to the deck, dead.

Flutterby wanted to scream, but she couldn't catch her breath.

"They're *wots*," his partner said. "What did you . . . ?"

"Maggots make flies," the other said. "We have orders." The muzzle came up again and Flutterby didn't even see the flash that killed her.

*Mankind owns four things*
*that are no good at sea:*
*rudder, anchor, oars*
*and the fear of going down.*

—Antonio Machado

Ben undogged the hatch and Rico LaPush rushed inside. Rico nodded once to the girl, who looked ghastly pale, and handed Ben the pocket messenger. Most of the briefing on it was already outdated, but Ben would want to hear it, anyway. Rico was careful to keep from touching the girl.

"Ready?" he asked.

"Ready," Ben said.

"Yes," said the girl.

Rico scratched his chin stubble and adjusted the lasgun in the back of his pants. He had been with Ben since Guemes Island was sunk, more years than Crista Galli had been alive. His mistrust of people had kept them alive more than once, and he did not intend to let his guard down with Her Holiness.

"Déjà vu," he said to Ben, nodding at her Islander dress. "She reminds me of the old days, when things were simply tough. The streets are crawling with security, she'll need a good act . . ."

"You can speak to me," Crista interrupted, her cheeks flushed

61

with a run of anger. "I have ears to hear, mouth to answer. This sister is not a chairdog, nor a glass of water on her brother's table."

Rico had to muster a smile. Her Islander accent was perfect, her phrasing perfect. She was a very quick study—of course, she had more intimate ways of getting inside people's heads . . .

"Thank you for the lesson, sister," he said. "You are most cheerfully dressed, my compliments."

Rico noted Ben's smile, and the fact that his partner's gaze never wavered from Crista Galli's perfect face.

Rico's cameras had taped the faces of many beautiful women for Holovision and he had to admit that everything he'd heard about Crista Galli was true. When Ben became a reporter, Rico LaPush signed on as a field triangulator with the holography crew. A well-placed lie got him the job, but his facility for learning kept it. He had filmed more pomp and more horror in any given year than most cameramen witnessed in a lifetime.

*She's pale, but beautiful,* he thought. *Maybe the sun will give her some color.*

Operations said to keep her out of the sun, but Rico thought that, given their recent bad luck, this would be impossible. Operations, whoever *they* were, didn't have their butts on the line.

"We'll be walking for a while," Rico told them. "Don't hurry."

He nodded at the messenger in Ben's hand.

"Don't bother," he said. "You might as well shitcan that thing. They tell us we're going by air but the airstrip's already locked up by Flattery's boys. We'll have to do it by water."

"But they said . . ."

"I *know* what they said," Rico snapped. "They *said* the airstrip would be secure. They *said* keep her away from water. Let's move."

Crista Galli carried a sadness about her that Rico didn't like. He could take fear, or anger, or even hysteria but sadness felt too much like bad luck. They'd started out with that. When she reached out a tentative hand toward Ben, Rico stopped her with a word.

"No," he said. "I'm sorry. I can't let you touch him."

"Your fear?" she shot back, "or this 'Operations'? He is clothed."

"My fear."

She was hurt when Ben remained silent.

Crista shrank back from him, and Rico slipped into the Guemes dialect that he'd set aside years ago.

"Among Islanders, I am merely advising one of my sisters that she needs to recognize the depth of trust and love that the people have for her," he said, with a curt nod of his head. "They speak out to her when the speaking is painful."

"And the fear?"

*Good!* Rico thought. *She won't be bullied.*

He continued to speak to her in the manner of the Guemes Islanders.

"This sister apprises the brother well. Let the brother remind the sister that only the unknown is feared. Perhaps the sister will set this brother at ease, in time. Shall we begin?"

She was quiet then, and Rico liked that about her. Whatever curse she carried, she carried it with grace. He had known Ben Ozette for twenty-five years. Rico had fallen in love with a dozen women during that time, but Ben had only fallen once. Rico remembered that Ben had looked at Beatriz Tatoosh the same way he now looked at Crista Galli.

*It's about time,* he thought, and smiled to himself. *Beatriz is tight with that guy MacIntosh. Ben needs somebody solid, too.*

Everybody knew that relationships within the industry had to be short-lived, and that families were impossible. With all of the travel and stress something, somewhere, had to give and it was usually the relationship. Rico had given up long ago and was currently seeing a redhead who worked full-time for Operations.

"The harbor," Rico said as they started down the ramp. "It's a madhouse there and so far no security near the *Flying Fish.* Victoria's as secure as Victoria gets, so we'll head up there. Risky, but not so risky as this."

They turned right, walking slowly down the pier, toward the crowd at dockside. Rico trailed slightly behind the couple, keeping buildings and hatchways close, and didn't speak. He nearly stumbled into the Galli girl several times as she stopped suddenly to stare at some of the shops and the relics of herself that were sold there. At each shop, she pulled the mantilla closer about her face.

*So, it's true,* Rico thought. *She* doesn't *know!*

He watched her reach out toward a tasteless vest in a glass case that bore the inscription: "Vest of Crista Galli, worn at age twelve. Not for sale." Also arranged about the case were various microscope slides with blood smears on them, a clipping of hair too obviously dark to be hers and several bits of cloth—all with price tags, all claiming to come from "Her Holiness," Crista Galli. Above the case was scrawled a hand-lettered warning: "Extreme danger, do not touch. Safety packaging included with each sale."

*You'd think she'd never seen a dog before,* he thought, watching her, *or a chicken—she sure went loony over those goddamn chickens.*

Rico dawdled close behind them and tried not to listen to their talk. He hadn't eaten since the previous morning and the charcoal spatter of hot food set his stomach rumbling. He was a little nervous, plenty could still go wrong. But the diversion had taken one patrol off their backs.

*If the boys are doing their jobs, we shouldn't see a security between here and the boat.*

Just as he thought it he knew better, but there was no calling the thought back and there was no calling back the two security guards rounding the corner ahead of them. Rico pressed a switch on the broadcast unit in his pocket. A third explosion went off near the harbor but neither guard took the bait. Rico sighed and adjusted the lasgun at the back of his waistband. It was an older model, short-range. He remembered thinking, as the two guards veered across the street toward them, how difficult it had become to buy spare charges.

Ben and Crista saw the security and slowed to a stop. Commuters and street vendors pressed past them in waves. Rico stopped, too, a few paces behind them and in front of a deep hatchway. With the new explosion there was a renewed flurry among those crowding toward the harbor, and Rico was not happy that Ben had stopped. Both of the men approaching wore the khaki fatigues of the Vashon Security Forces, rank four. They were both burly, armed only with stunsticks, nearly normal but with the creased ears and fat lower lips betraying certain internal defects typical of Lummi Islanders.

Just as Rico's hand clutched the grips of his lasgun, Crista Galli stepped forward, exaggerating the rolling walk of the heavily pregnant. She spoke, her hand upraised and head tilted in the Guemes fashion of greeting.

"Brothers," she said, "this mother cannot find a rest station and she is in great need." This she delivered matter-of-factly, and turned her palm up. Though the guards were obviously jumpy, the response was automatic.

"Up two streets, one street left. The shops—"

The other security gave his partner a shove and interrupted: "This could be the start of a Shadow attack . . . let's move! Sister, get out of the street. You two," he pointed to Ben and Rico, "get her inside someplace and lay low."

The two guards huffed toward their station at the harbor and Rico let out the breath he'd been holding in a low whistle. It was a coded whistle, from their childhood days, that any Islander wot would recognize as "all clear."

"You sure made Rico happy," Ben said, grinning.

"Got it all on tape, too," Rico said. He tapped a tiny lens at his shirtfront. "It'll look great in your memoirs."

He nodded at Crista.

"Good job thinking, helluva good job acting." He rechecked the charges in the camera at his belt and buffed the lapel lens with his sleeve. The lens looked like a small pin made of a glossy gray stone.

"Shouldn't we get out of here?" Crista asked. "You heard what he said, the Shadows—"

"Are us," Rico interrupted in a whisper, "and there will be no attack. The villagers might bust loose, though. Things are pretty hot. The *Flying Fish* is down there." He pointed out the "Pier Four" sign just ahead.

One of the huge cross-bay ferries had surfaced dockside, unwilling to risk explosive damage in the comparatively shallow waters of the bay. Foot passengers from all over Pandora streamed out of the rear hatch, while two- and three-wheeled vehicles crowded the roadway. The morning dust changed to mud under all the feet and hosewater, and mud splashed up from wheels to stain the hems of fine Islander embroidery. Islanders even dressed up to go to market.

About half of the crowd that elbowed back down the pier wore the plastic ID tag around their necks that marked them as Project Voidship employees. Whatever they did, they did it for Flattery's paycheck. This was a huge village, huge enough to strain the bonds of family, and today many of the dockside vendors threw catcalls and curses after the workers from the shuttle launch site.

The pier itself was a bridge between two subway mouths—one from the village to the pier, and another that loaded onto the submarine ferry. Vendors crowded the station entrances, selling tubes of suntan lotion, sodas, dried fruits. Here the smell of charcoal and the spatter of grilled fish were drowned out in the babble of the crowds.

Suddenly, one of Rico's greatest fears was made real. An Islander refugee, carrying a placard and wet to the skin from a firehosing, rushed down the crowded pier and attacked one of the commuters. They both fell in a tumble and, out of reflex as much as anger, the knot of commuters began kicking at him. Several dozen refugees tried in their weak way to free him, then to fight back, but within a matter of blinks they were all set upon and beaten.

Rico and Ben closed tight on Crista Galli and Rico looked for a way down the pier. Screams of anger turned to grunts of pain all around them. Bodies splashed into the bay and the hot morning was filled with curses and the wet red smack of fists on skin.

Crista kept her arms folded in front of her and her hands in her sleeves, like many of the old Islander women. She seemed locked in position with her hand out, like a figure from a wot's game of freeze-tag. As they worked through the crowd she stumbled on the Islander's battered placard and Rico saw that it read, "Give a Brother a Break!"

A splintering sound and the wail of bent bracing came from behind them, then screams of fear. Rico saw, over his shoulder, that a portion of the pier had given way and hundreds of people spilled into the water.

*That might cool things for now,* he thought, *but not for long.*

"Walk slower," Rico said at Crista Galli's ear. "You're tired and pregnant and haven't eaten since last night."

He knew that the last was true. He thought of all the meals he'd missed as a wot, wondered when was the last time Crista Galli or the Director had missed a meal. He and Ben missed plenty working the news business, but that was different. When Rico was a wot, he hadn't *chosen* to go hungry.

He scanned the beach where it broke out from the Islander settlement on the coast and flattened to a grassy plateau at the village perimeter. Security gathered there in their black personnel carriers, waiting for the crowd to tire before it was their turn to work them over. A bloody frenzy this close to the perimeter, and relatively open to beach and bay, might bring in dashers. The sight of a hunt of dashers would disperse the crowd, then security could take down the dashers and hardly wrinkle a crease in their fatigues.

Rico's visual and electronic sweep of the area detected no signs of security on the pier itself. He had nothing that would detect the high-power listening devices that the Director favored lately.

Crista stared straight ahead as they walked, eyes widely dilated, and Ben took her elbow.

"Tell them before we go that they are all one. Make them understand that they are all the same being and if they cut off their arms and legs they'll die . . ."

Ben gripped her elbow and gave it a shake. Rico saw her eyes as she turned to face him. They went from wild, wide and unfocused to normal. Rico noted that Ben was careful and didn't touch her skin.

"We're going to Port Hope," he lied, talking quickly as they walked. "The lake there is beautiful this time of year, and even with the altitude you will find it warm at night. The older Islands are too vulnerable. We have strong loyalties among the Mermen but you can't move freely in their settlements down under. Our immediate danger is security. The Director's got spotter planes up all along the coast, particularly near the Preserve. Of course, there are his Skyhawks. At sea we are vulnerable to the kelp," he paused, and when Crista looked his way he nodded, then continued, "and the Director's new fleet of foils, some of which he conveniently sold to Vashon security. Of course, we also have his spies among us."

Rico was relieved. What Ben had said was for the benefit of listening devices, not for Crista Galli. He was sure, by her blank stare, that she had not understood a word.

She shuffled on through the shouts and cries along Pier Four as though she heard nothing. Rico saw that there were more boats burning now, maybe a dozen, and firefighters were trying to push them away from the others. One of the Vashon Security Forces power foils steamed full-tilt toward the blaze from the Preserve side of the water.

The *Flying Fish,* Holovision's private foil, was within sight at the end of the slip. Rico felt the tease of adrenaline in his belly. He hoped that Operations had briefed Elvira, pilot of the *Flying Fish.* She didn't much care for sudden changes of plans, and she really didn't like encounters with Vashon Security.

Elvira was the toughest pilot that Holovision had ever hired. No one inconvenienced Elvira. To Rico's knowledge she had no politics, no hobbies, no friends and no religious convictions whatsoever. Her sole passion was to pilot the hottest hydrogen-ram foil in the world as often and as fast as possible. In surface mode she was highly competent; in undersea mode or flight she had no equal in the world. She had flown Ben and Rico in and out of more hot assignments than he could count. This would undoubtedly be the hottest.

Ben caught Rico's gaze and raised a quizzical eyebrow, nodding toward the girl.

Rico scratched his two-day beard. Crista turned to stare past him at the crowd that now had worked its way up the pier, gathering bodies and momentum, and was now fanning out into the streets of Kalaloch.

Everyone who was to remember this event recalled that the morning air split with a *crack* like summer thunder, or a whip. No echo, not a breath of breeze. Even a cluster of fussing children nearby silenced themselves in their mother's skirts.

Rico touched a fingertip to each of his ears, acutely conscious of the scratchings at each contour, each follicle and fold. If a shock wave *had* hit his ears, they'd still be ringing.

*She did that in my . . . in our minds!*

Crista felt the sudden clap of stillness crack with her anger. She was glad that Ben and Rico were the first to recover, though what she saw in their eyes was clearly fear. The mob had stopped, momentarily stunned and looking about for a weapon, then it boiled anew at the onslaught of the truckloads of Vashon Security that came to meet it.

Crista spun away from them and boarded the *Flying Fish*, still affecting the wide-beamed walk of the largely pregnant. She stood on the deck, beside the cabin hatchway, hugging herself and looking out to sea. The children started fussing again, stunned villagers rubbed their ears and began to move. Rico noticed that the boat fires had spread to the pier itself and some of the shops. Both ferries at the slip had submerged, empty, for safety. Rico approached Crista at the rail while Ben cast off the lines.

"This was coming for months," Rico said, "you could tell by the feel in the streets. They've had enough. It's too soon, and they're not organized. It will fail, for them. Some will be drawn out after us. Some, to the harbor. Others, to the attack that is inevitable inside the settlement. That will leave the Preserve weak . . ."

"It's too well-protected," she said, her voice matter-of-fact. "They will fail."

She fixed Rico with those striking green eyes. He noticed, once again, that they were dilated in spite of the sunlight.

"I know how you felt now, back there, when you were so afraid of my touch." She smoothed the dress over her makeshift belly. "What I know of the Shadows and what you know of me are the same. I only know what Flattery told me. I don't know whether you should fear my touch. Do you know whether I should fear yours?"

When he didn't answer she turned and shuffled into the cabin of the Holovision foil in silence.

*Evil is in the eye of the beholder.*

—Spider Nevi, special assistant to the Director

Lights had been suitably dimmed in the Director's holo suite, and one tight spotlight illuminated his face from below. This effect accentuated Flattery's height, nearly a head taller than the average Pandoran, and it added an imperiousness to his stature that pleased him.

An empty holo cassette teetered across the red armrest of his favorite recliner. One fluorescent orange sticker on the cassette read "For Eyes Only," and under that was handwritten: "TD, S. Nevi *only*." Under that was stamped in black: "Extreme Penalty." Flattery smiled at the euphemism. At his direction, all those who violated the "Extreme Penalty" sanction became the homework of Spider Nevi's apprentice interrogators. Messy business, security.

"Mr. Nevi," he acknowledged, with a nod.

"Mr. Director."

As usual, Spider Nevi's face was unreadable, even to Flattery's expert training as a Chaplain/Psychiatrist. Nevi had been prompt, unhurried, arriving in a snappy gray cut of a Merman lounging suit right at the first blood of dawn.

"Zentz hasn't found them," Flattery said. His voice was clipped, betraying more anger than he wished.

"It was Zentz who lost them," Nevi countered.

Flattery grunted. He hadn't needed the reminder, especially from Nevi.

"*You* find them," he said, and jabbed a finger at the air between them. "Bring back the girl, wring what you can from the others. Save Ozette for a special occasion. He's at the bottom of this Shadowbox and they've got to be shut down *now*."

Nevi nodded, and the agreement was struck. Bounty would be worked out later, as usual. Nevi's terms were always reasonable, even on difficult matters, because he liked his work. His was the kind of work that might go unpracticed if it weren't for the Director.

*Every art has its canvas,* Flattery thought.

"The airstrip is secure," Nevi said. "There were preparations for them there, including a half-dozen collaborators, so we have cut them off. Solid intelligence. Zentz's men are turning the usual screws in the village. They will be forced to move the girl soon. Overland is out, that would be insane. It would have to be by water, and under diversion to get out of here. My guess would be Victoria. It would pay to wait and make as big a sweep as possible, don't you think?"

"You have the docks under watch?"

"Of course. The Holovision foil is bugged, a precaution. Your sensor system is now keyed into it." Nevi glanced at the clock on Flattery's console. "You should be able to tune them in just about any time."

Flattery shifted slightly in his command couch, betraying his uneasiness at this loss of control. Nevi was second-guessing his moves, and he didn't like it.

"Well," Flattery said, splitting his face with a smile, "this is magnificent! We will have them all—and you will be rewarded for this. Zentz grumbles that you steal away his best men but, dammit, you get the job done." He slapped his palm on the tabletop and held the smile.

Spider Nevi's expression did not change, and he said nothing. His only response was the barest perceptible nod of his horrible head. The shape of it was more or less normal, except for the mucous slit where the nose should be. Nevi's dark skin was shot through with a glowing webwork of red veins. His dark eyes glittered, missed nothing.

"What do you want done with the Tatoosh woman?"

Flattery felt his smile droop, and he tried to pick it up a bit.

"Beatriz Tatoosh is very helpful to us," Flattery said. "She has a passion for the Voidship project that we could not buy." He raised his hand to stop Nevi's interruption. "I know what you're thinking—that little tryst between her and Ozette. That's been over for over a year—"

"It wasn't a 'little tryst,'" Nevi interrupted. "It lasted *years*. They were wounded together at the miners' rebellion two years ago—"

"I know women," Flattery hissed, "and she will hate him for this. Running away with a younger woman . . . sabotaging Holovision and the Voidship. Didn't she do the broadcast as written last night?"

A nod from Nevi, and silence.

"She knows as well as we do that mentioning Ozette as party to this abduction would lend it a popularity and a credence that we cannot afford. It is over between them, and as soon as he's back in our hands everything will be over for Ben Ozette. The Tatoosh woman will be aboard the orbital assembly station this afternoon and out of our hair."

At Nevi's continued silence, Flattery rubbed his hands together briskly.

"Now," he said, "let me show you how I've kept the kelp pruned back for the last couple of years. You know how the people resist this, it always takes a disaster to get them to go along with it. Well, the kelp's will was breached long ago by our lab at Orcas. Too complex to explain, but suffice it to say it is not merely a matter of mechanical control—diverting currents and the like. Thanks to the neurotoxin research we tapped into its *emotions*. Remember that stand of kelp off Lilliwaup, the one that hid the Shadow commando team?"

Nevi nodded. "I remember. You told Zentz 'Hands off.'"

"That's right," Flattery said. He drew himself upright in his recliner and snapped the backrest up to meet him. He keyed the holo and automatically the lights dimmed further. Between the two men, in the center of the room, appeared in miniature several monitor views of a Merman undersea outpost, a kelp station at the edge of a midgrowth stand. Kelp lights flickered from the depths beyond the outpost. The kelp station had been built atop the remnants of an old Oracle.

Oracles, as the Pandorans called them, were those points where the kelp rooted into the crust of the planet itself. Because of the incredible depth of these three-hundred-year-old roots, and because the Mermen of old planted them in straight lines, Pandora's crust often fractured along root lines. It was such a series of fractures that had given birth to Pandora's new continents and rocky island chains.

Flattery's private garden, "the Greens," lay underground in a cavern that had once been an Oracle. Flattery had had his people burn out the three-hundred-meter-thick root to accommodate his landscaping plans.

Three views clarified on the holo stage in front of the two men: The first was of the inside of a kelp station, with a balding Merman fretting at his control console; the second, outside the station, from the kelp perimeter, focused on the station's main hatch; the third, also outside the station, took in the gray mass of kelp from the rear hatch. The Merman looked very, very nervous.

"His children have been swimming in the kelp," Flattery said. "He is worried. Their airfish are due for replacement. All have been dutifully taking their antidote. The kelp, when treated with my new blend, shows an unhealthy attraction for the antidote."

There were occasional glimpses of the children among the kelp fronds. They moved in the ultra-slow-motion of dreams, much slower than undersea movement dictated, considerably slower than the usual polliwog wriggle of children.

The Merman activated a pulsing tone that shut itself off after a few blinks.

"That's the third time he's sounded 'Assembly,'" Flattery said. Anticipation made it difficult for him to sit still.

The Merman spoke to a female, dressed in a worksuit, wet from her day's labor of wiring up the kelp stand for Current Control.

"Linna," he said, "I can't get them out of the kelp. Those airfish will be dry . . . what's happening out there?"

She was thin and pale, much like her husband, but she appeared dreamy-eyed and unfocused. Most of those who worked the outposts did not wear their dive suits inside their living quarters.

She worked the fringes of what the Mermen called "the Blue Sector."

"Maybe it's the touch of it," she murmured. "The touch . . . special. You don't work in it, you don't know. Not slick and cold, like before. Now the kelp feels like, well . . ." She hesitated and even on the holo Flattery could detect a blush.

"Like what?" the Merman asked.

"I . . . lately it feels like you when it touches me." Her blush accented her crop of thick blonde hair. "Warm, kind of. And it makes me tingle inside. It makes my veins tingle."

He grunted, squinted at her, and sighed. "Where are those wots?"

He glanced out the plaz beside him into the dim depths beyond the compound. Flattery could detect no flicker of children swimming. He felt a niggling sense of glee at the Merman's growing apprehension.

The Merman activated his console tone again and the proper systems check light winked on with it. His finger snapped the scanner screen.

"They were just *there*," the man blurted. "This is crazy. I'm going code red." He unlocked the one button on the console that Flattery knew no outpost wanted to press: Code Red. That would notify Current Control in the Orbiter overhead and Communications Central at the nearest Merman base that the entire compound was in imminent danger.

"You see?" Flattery said. "He's getting the idea."

"I'm going out there," the man announced to his wife, "you stay put. Do you understand?"

No answer. She sat, still dreamy-eyed, watching the fifty-meter-long fronds of blue kelp that reached her way from the perimeter.

The Merman scooped an airfish out of the locker beside the hatch and buckled on a toolbelt. He grabbed up a long-handled laser pruner and a set of charges. As if on second thought, he picked up the whole basket of airfish, the Mermen's symbiotic gills that filtered oxygen from the sea directly into the bloodstream.

*Ghastly things,* Flattery thought with a shudder. Unconsciously, he rubbed his neck where they were customarily attached.

Once outside, the Merman's handlight barely illuminated the stand of kelp at the compound's edge. This holo had been made at the onset of evening, and the waning light above the scene coupled with the depth darkened the holo and made it difficult to see detail of the man's face—a small disappointment for such a good chronicle of the test itself.

As the Merman reached the compound's perimeter within range of the kelp's longest fronds, he whirled at the *click-hiss* of an opening hatch. His wife swam lazily out of it directly into deep kelp. The atmosphere from their station bubbled toward the surface in a rush. He must have realized then that everything was lost as he watched the sea rush into their quarters through the undogged hatch. All sensors went blank.

Flattery switched off the holo and turned up the lights. Nevi sat unmoved with the same unreadable expression on his horrible face.

"So the kelp lured them and ate them?" Nevi asked.

"Exactly."

"On command?"

"On command—*my* command."

Flattery was pleased at the trace of a smile that flickered across Spider Nevi's lips. It must have been a luxury that he allowed himself for the moment.

"We both know what will come of the hue and cry," the Director said, and puffed himself a little before continuing. "There will be a demand for vengeance. My men will be *forced*, by popular demand, to prune this stand back. You see how it's done?"

"Very neat. I always thought . . ."

"Yes," Flattery gloated, "so has everyone else. The kelp has been a *very* sensitive subject, as you know. Religious overtones and whatnot." Another dismissive wave of the hand. Flattery couldn't stop bragging.

"I had to accomplish two things: I had to get control of Current Control, and I had to find the point at which the kelp became sentient. Not necessarily smart, just sentient. By the time it sends off those damned gasbags it's too late—the only solution there is to stump the lot. We lost a lot of good kelpways for a lot of years that way."

"So, what's the key?"

"The lights," Flattery said. He pointed out his huge plaz port at the bed just off the tideline. "When the kelp starts to flicker, it's waking up. It's like an infant, then, and only knows what it's told. The language it speaks is chemical, electrical."

"And you do the telling?"

"Of course. First, keep it out of contact with any other kelp. That's a must. They educate each other by touch. Make sure the kelpways are always *very* wide between stands—a kilometer or more. The damned stuff can learn from leaves torn off other stands. The effect dies out very quickly. A kilometer usually does it."

"But how do you . . . teach it what you want?"

"I don't teach. I manipulate. It's very old-fashioned, Mr. Nevi. Quite simply, beings gravitate toward pleasure, flee pain."

"How does it respond to this kind of . . . betrayal?"

Flattery smiled. "Ah, yes. Betrayal is your department, is it not? Well, once pruned and kept at the light-formation stage, it doesn't remember much. Studies show that it *can* remember if allowed to develop to the spore-casting stage. You have just seen what the answer is to that—don't let it get that far. Also, studies show that this spore-dust can educate an ignorant stand."

"I thought it was just a nuisance," Nevi said. "I didn't realize that you believed it could *think*."

"Oh, very much so. You forget, Mr. Nevi, I'm a Chaplain/Psychiatrist. That I don't pray doesn't mean . . . well, any mind interests me. Anything that stands in my way interests me. This kelp does both."

"Do you consider it a 'worthy adversary'?" Nevi smiled.

"Not at all," Flattery barked a laugh, "not worthy, no. It'll have to show me more than I've seen before I consider this plant a 'worthy adversary.' It's merely an interesting problem, requiring interesting solutions."

Nevi stood, and the crispness of his gray suit accentuated the fluidity of the muscles within it.

"This is your business," Nevi told him. "Mine is Ozette and the girl."

Flattery resisted the reflex to stand and waved a limp hand, affecting a nonchalance that he did not at all feel.

"Of course, of course." He avoided Nevi's gaze by switching the holo back on. He keyed it to the Tatoosh woman's upcoming Newsbreak. She would accompany the next shuttle flight to the Orbiter, a shuttle that contained the Organic Mental Core for hookup to the Voidship. Already the OMC was an "it" in his mind, rather than the "she" who used to be Alyssa Marsh.

Flattery seethed inside. He'd wanted something more from

Nevi, something that now smelled distinctly of approval. He didn't like detecting weakness in himself, but he liked even less the notion of letting it pass unbridled.

"Whatever you need . . ." Flattery left the obvious unsaid.

Nevi left everything unsaid, nodded, and then left the suite. Flattery felt a profound sense of relief, then checked it. Relief meant that he'd begun to rely on Spider Nevi, when he knew full well that reliance on anyone meant a blade at the throat sooner or later. He did not intend for the throat to be his own.

*And out of the ground made to grow every tree that is pleasant to the sight, and good for food; the tree of life also in the midst of the garden, and the tree of knowledge of good and evil.*

—Christian Book of the Dead

A trail left the beach about a kilometer beyond the limits of the Preserve. It was a Zavatan trail, used by the faithful to transport their gleanings of the kelp from the beach to their warrens in the high reaches. Because it was a Zavatan trail it was well-kept and reasonably safe. Its rest spots were ample and afforded a sweeping vista of Flattery's huge Preserve. The jumbled, jerry-rigged tenements of Kalaloch sprawled from the downcoast side of the Preserve, covered today by a cloak of black smoke. Mazelike channels of aquafarms and jetties branched both up- and downcoast into the horizon. Distant screams and explosions echoed from the panorama below up the winding trail.

Two Zavatan monks stopped to study the clamor rising from the settlement a few klicks away. One man was tall, lanky, with very long arms. The other was small even for a Pandoran, and moved in a scuttle that kept him tucked inside the larger man's shadow. Both were dressed in the loose, pajamalike gi of the Hylighter

Lodge: durable cotton, dusky orange that represented the color of hylighters, their spirit guides.

A gith of hylighters lazed overhead, drawn to the scene by their attraction for fire, lightning and the arc of lasguns from building to building. The hylighters dragged their ballast rocks from long tentacles and circled widely, audibly valving off hydrogen and snapping their great sails in the wind. Should they contact fire or spark, the hylighters would explode, scattering their fine blue spore-dust, which the monks gathered for their most private rituals. Many of the monks had not left the high reaches, except to walk this trail, for ten years.

"It's a shame they don't understand," the younger monk mused. "If we could only teach them the letting go . . ."

"Judgement, too, is an anchor," the elder warned. "It is *Nothing* that they need to know—the No-thing that frees the mind from noise and perfects the senses."

He lifted his mutant arms in a long skyward reach, then turned slowly, rejoicing in the morning glow of both suns.

This elder monk, Twisp, loved the press of sunlight on his skin. He had been a fisherman and adventurer in his youth, and what drew him to the Zavatans was not so much their contemplative life as other possibilities that he saw in them. Like most of the monks, Twisp had been wooed by the romance of the new quiet earth that rose from the sea. They summarily rejected the petty squabblings of politics and money that raged across Pandora to establish an underground network of illegal farms and hideaways.

Twisp, however, had remained entrenched in Pandora's civil struggles, something he troubled few of his fellow Zavatans about. Now, once again, all was changing, he was changing. He had more to offer Pandora than contemplation, though he refrained from telling the younger monk so. He was not religious, merely thoughtful, and he had made a good life among the Zavatans. It would pain him greatly to leave.

Two hylighters tacked toward them and Mose, the younger monk, set down his bag and began his Chant of Fulfillment. With this chant he hoped to be swept skyward by the mass of tentacles and transported to a higher level of being. Twisp had experienced the hylighter enlightenment at the first awakening of the kelp a quarter century past. That was before Flattery's iron fist came down, and before the people he loved were killed.

Hylighters, though born from the kelp, remained indifferent to humans, treating them as a wonderful curiosity. Mose's chant became more vigorous as the hylighters drew near, their magnificent sail membranes golden in the sunlight.

"These two want their death today," Twisp said. "Do you really want to go with them?"

It was the fire that attracted them, and Mose should know that. The younger monk had eaten too much kelp, too much hylighter spore-dust over the years. Two humans in the open near the Preserve usually meant armed security. Hylighters wanting the-death-that-meant-life learned how to draw their fire.

Now the musty smell of their undersides filled the air. The musical flutings of their vents lilted on the breeze as they valved off hydrogen to drop closer. Mose's chant became more tremulous.

Each hylighter carried ten tentacles in the underbelly, two of them longer than the rest. Usually these two carried rocks for ballast. Hylighters that felt the death need coming on sought out lightning, often gathering in giths to ride the afternoon thunderstorms. Sparks or fire attracted them as well, setting them off in a concussive blaze of flame and blue spore-dust. Some dragged their ballast rocks to spark a grand suicide, an ultimate orgasm.

Twisp breathed easier when the two great hulks tacked back toward the Preserve. He interrupted Mose, whose eyes were closed and whose stubbled face was pale and sweaty.

"This tack will take them into range of the Preserve's perimeter cannon," he said. "There will be dust to take back for the others."

Mose silenced himself and followed Twisp's long pointing arm. The two hylighters tacked in tight formation, using all that they could capture of the slight breeze blowing up from the shore.

"Flattery's security will wait to fire until the hylighters are over the settlement," Twisp whispered. "That way, the hylighters become a weapon. Watch."

It was almost as he said. Either the cannoneer was a fool or one of the Islanders got in a clear shot, but the hylighters exploded over the Preserve in a double blast that took Twisp's breath away and stung his eyes with light. Much of the main compound aboveground was incinerated in the fireball and the great wall of the Preserve was breached for a hundred meters in either direction.

A lull in the fighting brought his ears the cacophonous screams of the charred and the dying. It was a sound that Twisp remembered all too well.

The young Mose came down this trail seldom and had been only twelve when he went to live in the high reaches. He did not have much of a life in the outside world, and knew little of the ways of human hatred and greed.

"All we can do is stay out of it," Twisp muttered. "They will have at themselves and leave us in peace."

The wet patter of hylighter shreds fell among the brush and rocks below them.

*There will be the refugees, too,* he thought. *Always the homeless and the hungry. Where will we put them this time?*

The Zavatans supported refugee camps all along the coastline, turning some into gardens, hydroponics ranches and fish farms. Twisp calculated that there were already more refugees both up- and downcoast than Flattery housed in Kalaloch. Though it was true everyone was hungry, only those in Kalaloch starved. This was the story he hoped Shadowbox would tell.

*In time, the Director will be the hungry one.*

Twisp remembered Guemes Island and the refugees of twenty-five years ago, hacked and burned and stacked like dead maki in a Merman rescue station down under. Twisp and a few friends hunted down the terrorists responsible, and a hylighter executed the leader. A Chaplain/Psychiatrist had been at the bottom of the trouble that time, too.

Flattery had burrowed as much of his compound below the rock as above it, and Twisp knew of bolt-holes that led to escape routes along the shore. Flattery wouldn't need them this time. The older monk had seen fighting before, and knew Flattery's strategy: lure as many of the rebels inside as possible, then kill them all. Let them think, for a time, that they might win. Blame it on the Shadows. The rest, who lost everything but their lives, would not rise so easily to anger again.

Mose pulled at his garment, straightening the folds. He faced away from the horror below. His eyes did not meet Twisp's, but focused in the middle distance beyond the trail. His were eyes sunken deeply for one so young, for one dwelling among the untroubled. He was attempting inner peace at breakneck speed. He shaved his head daily, customary these days with younger Zavatan monks and many nuns. Many ragged scars crisscrossed his scalp from his reconstruction surgery.

Twisp was one of a handful of exceptions. His full head of long, graying hair was tied into a single braid at the back, mimicking the family style of an old friend, long dead. His friend, Shadow Panille, was said to have been of the blood lines that led to Crista Galli.

"We should get the others," Mose said. "We'll need lasguns if we're going dust-gathering in the valley."

Twisp shaded his eyes and surveyed the scene below. A blur that must be villagers spilled into the Preserve's compound. Running the other way, like fish fighting their way upcurrent, Flattery's precious cattle from the Preserve stampeded out the breached wall and into the unprotected valley.

Security had kept the demon population at a minimum near the Preserve, but with the scent of blood thick on the air and cattle milling about loose dashers were sure to follow. Things were going to get nasty enough without a new hunt of hooded dashers slinking about. He grunted himself out of reverie.

"Spore-dust goes bad," Twisp said. "If we're going to bring any back, we'll have to do it now."

He and Mose stored the kelp fronds they'd collected in the shade of a white rock. Mose still did not look Twisp in the eye.

"Are you afraid?" Twisp asked.

"Of course!" Mose snapped back, "aren't you? We could be killed down there. Dashers will smell the . . . the . . ."

"Just moments ago you wanted to die in the arms of that hylighter," Twisp said. "What's the difference? There are demons up here, too. You feel safe on the trail because we say the trail is safe. You know that some have died here in the past, others will die in the future. You stick to the trail, with no cover except these scrub bushes and the rock, no weapon but your body."

Twisp pointed past the flames below them and out to sea.

"Weather will kill you as dead as any demon, on or off the trail. It is a danger *now,* as dangerous as a dasher. It always stays alive, to kill another day. If dashers come, they will go to the blood, not to us. If anything, we are safest now. This is the present, and you are alive. Stay in the present, and you stay alive."

With that he shouldered his empty bag and set out in long strides for the valley and the spore-dust below. Mose stumbled along behind him, his nervous eyes too busy hunting fears to watch the trail.

*To think of a power means not only to use it, but above all to abuse it.*

—Gaston Bachelard, *The Psychoanalysis of Fire*

Two old vendors hunched in a hatchway, protecting themselves and their wares from the jostlings of a mob that muscled its way toward the Preserve. One munched a smashed cake, the other nursed a bleeding nose against his sleeve.

"Animals!" Torvin spat, and a fine spray of blood came with it. "Is there anyone left who is not an animal? Except you, my friend. You are a human being."

His free hand patted the other's shoulder and found a large rip in the fabric of the older man's coat.

"Look, David, your coat . . ."

David brushed crumbs from his chin and pulled the shoulder of his coat across his chest, closer to his good eye.

"It will mend," he said. "And the mob is passing. If there are dead, my friend, we should get their cards for the poor."

"*I'm* not going out there."

Torvin's voice was muffled by his sleeve, but David knew he was firm on that point. It was just as well. His eyes were bad, and his feet not quick enough to outrun the security. It was a shame when the security got the cards. They sold them, or traded them. Every day Torvin and David risked their lives to give a bit of stale cake or a rind of dried fruit to a hungry one without a card. David shook his head.

*What foolishness!*

He worked beside Torvin, they were friends, yet he could not trade him a cake for a dried fruit. He had to have a marker on his card for the fruit, and Torvin would have to punch it out, and then he could have it. If Torvin didn't have a pastry marker on his card, David could not give him a cake. For Torvin to possess a cake without a proper punched card would mean losing his next turn in The Line. Under the best of conditions, he would not have expected a turn for at least a week. Under the worst conditions, he could starve with a fistful of coupons.

"This is craziness!" he told Torvin. "It is well I am old and ready to die, because the world makes no sense to me. Our children run about killing each other. It is permissible to have food on one table but not another. We have a leader who takes food from the mouths of babies so he can travel to the stars—good riddance, I say. But what will he leave behind? His bullies, who are also our children. Torvin, explain this to me."

"Bah!"

Torvin's faded blue sleeve was crusted with blood but the bleeding on his nose had stopped. David could tell by the way he said "Bah!" that the nose was stopped up. He remembered that time the security slapped him, the fragrant burst of blood in his nose.

"Thinking will get you into trouble," he heard Torvin warning him. "We are better off to keep quiet, dry our allowance of fruit, bake our allowance of cakes and be thankful that our families have something to eat."

"Be *thankful?*" David wheezed one of his silent laughs. "You are no youngster, Torvin. Who taught you to be thankful to eat when someone across the wall has nothing? There is no greater sin, my friend, than to eat a full meal when your neighbor has none."

"We give cards to the poor . . ."

"Graverobbers!" David hissed. "That's what they've made us. Graverobbers who can be shot for throwing scraps to the hungry. This is craziness, Torvin, such craziness that this mob is making sense to me. Burn it all and start over. They *are* hungry now . . .''

"Those . . . *animals* who beat me, they are not hungry. They have cards. They work down under and we see them here daily. Where do they get off chanting 'We're hungry *now*' when—"

"Listen, Torvin, to me an old man now gone crazy. Listen. We are old, you and I. You, not so old. Would you have given them something if you could?"

Torvin stuck his head out the hatchway, looked up and down the street, then hunched back inside.

"Of course. You know me, I'm not a greedy man. I have done such a thing."

"Well, listen to me, old man. The mob we saw, yes, they have cards. Yes, they bring a little food home—for a family of four. If there are six, eight, ten then the card still only feeds a family of four."

"No one argues with that," Torvin said. "We can't breed ourselves out of—"

"When you or I get too old and have to live with our children, Ship forbid, that will be one more on a card of four. Take in a refugee who has no card, my friend. Yes, that makes it six on a card of four and the *average* of people who *have* cards is eight.

"The ones without cards, the stinking ones who are dying at the settlement's edge begging for food, begging for work, sleeping in the mud—they cannot run through the streets themselves to shout 'We're hungry *now*,' because they can barely stand. We give crumbs from our guilt, from our shame. This mob gives their bodies, their voices to the hungry. They give whatever they have."

David leaned heavily on his folded table and got to his feet. The mob had moved on quickly. Had his body allowed, he might have followed them. He watched Torvin test his nose gingerly with his fingertips.

"I am afraid, David, of people like that. They might have killed us. It could have happened."

Torvin sounded as if he had corks in his nose.

David shrugged.

"They are afraid, too, because only the card gives them a place in The Line, and then only when their turns come around. Without a card, how long before you or I wake up in the mud downcoast? How many nights, Torvin, could you sleep in the mud and still wake in the morning?''

Torvin tested the bridge of his nose again, wincing.

"I don't like this, David. I don't like getting beat up . . ."

"Such drama," David said. "The man was pushed in here. You were hiding under your table and the corner hit your nose. That is not a beating. The Poet, over there, now *that* man took a beating."

David's nod indicated a dark shape pacing the hatchway across from them. The street was nearly clear, only a few stragglers scurried about, dodging the stunsticks of security. The Line to the warehouse was reforming already as the bravest, or the hungriest, came out of hiding.

Only one adult and one child of a card could wait in line, so the chore usually fell to the strongest unemployed member. Whoever did the shopping might have to carry out a two weeks' supply of foodstuffs for eight people or more. Security protection was good in The Line, but spotty elsewhere, so there were actually two lines, one on one side of the street going in and one on the other going out.

Licensed vendors like David and Torvin worked The Line, selling to those who were afraid they wouldn't get inside today, or who wanted a little something different to take home to the wots.

The man they called "the Poet" across the way worked his way up and down The Line each day, babbling of Ship and the return of Ship. He was careful not to speak against Flattery's Voidship project. He had done that once, and come back a broken man. The Poet had not stood upright since, but walked in a shuffle, bent nearly double at the waist. David could hear him now, shouting after the tail-end of the mob:

"I have been to the mountaintop! Let freedom ring!"

"That one?" Torvin snorted, and started his nose bleeding again. "That one has been into the spore-dust once too often."

David smiled at his friend. He and Torvin were nearly the same age, in their sixties, but he hadn't known Torvin long. There was much he had never told him.

"I was taken once," David whispered. "A security wanted cakes without a marker and I wouldn't give them to him. I knew if I did he would be back every day. He bullied me. I would rather give them to the poor, so I did a foolish thing. I threw them into

The Line, and there was a scramble. Well, I knew I would be arrested, but I forgot about the others. They rounded up everyone who had a cake without a punch on the card and took them in.''

Torvin's face paled. "My friend, I didn't know . . . what did they do to you?''

"They took me to a shed that had cubicles in it, separated by curtains. In each one they were doing something to someone. The screams were terrible, and the smell . . . .''

David took a deep breath and let it out slow. The Poet was still gesturing and railing from his hatchway.

"He was there, in the cubicle next to me. He was an important man from down under who was the director of all of Holovision. Flattery had taken over—I didn't know that—and this man had commented on the air that Flattery wanted to brainwash the world.''

"A brave man," Torvin said. He appraised the Poet in a new light.

"A fool," David said. "He would've been better off to find a way to fight inside, or hidden out to do something like those Shadowbox people are doing. He must've known what would happen.''

David dusted off his threadbare trousers, put on his cap and leaned against the hatchway, his gaze very distant and his voice low.

"Well, I'll tell you what happened to him. They put him in a metal barrel, bent over double, and tied a block of concrete to his testicles. There was no floor in the barrel, so he could move it around by shuffling, but he had to keep bent over, and his knees bent down, to keep the weight off his testicles. His hands were tied behind his back, and throughout the day they would beat the sides of the barrel with those sticks they carry.

"They seldom fed him, but when they did he had to take food and water from the floor, bent over like that, an animal inside the barrel. He was a learned man. I never heard him curse. He only prayed. He prayed to every god I've heard of, and many that I don't know. They made him crazy to discredit him—who would believe a madman? Particularly a madman who eats bugs and scraps and sometimes dirt to stay alive.''

Torvin was quiet for many blinks, digesting what his friend had told him. The Poet continued his rant, and the few security patrolling nearby ignored him.

"My friend," Torvin said, "what did they . . . were you . . . ?"

"They beat me," David said. "It was nothing. I was in and out in a day for being insubordinate. I don't think the captain cared much for the security guard who charged me. At any rate, he was never seen on this street again. Look, now. It is clear, and we should go sell what we can. I want to get home and check on my Annie. She worries about me in times like this."

Both men strapped on their little folding tables that fit around their waists and hurriedly neatened their wares. As they stepped into the muddy street Torvin heard the Poet's hoarse voice exhort him, "Brother, brother, let freedom ring!"

*Remember that I have power; you believe yourself
miserable, but I can make you so wretched that the
light of day will be hateful to you. You are my creator,
but I am your master.*

—Mary Shelley, *Frankenstein*, Vashon Literature
Repository

Spider Nevi watched Rico pull the gangway up and onto the deck
of the *Flying Fish*, then he manipulated the sensor for a close view
of Rico's back as he turned away.

"Lasgun there," Nevi said, and tapped a finger against the
screen. "Belt, middle of the back. Carries himself like a fighter."

Nevi never once glanced at the security officer watching the
screen at his side. As the *Flying Fish* departed moorage he
switched to another sensor at the mouth of the harbor, one that
confirmed Crista Galli's presence on board.

At Nevi's command, the sensor zoomed in on the cabin of the
passing foil, revealing LaPush in the copilot's seat and Crista
Galli buckled in behind him. Ozette sat to her left, behind the
pilot, and was speaking to her. Nevi recognized the pilot, Elvira,
and cursed under his breath.

"If your security launch tries an intercept, it will be out-
classed," he said. "What then?"

"There will be a show of force," Zentz said, "then a warning shot."

"And then?"

Zentz cleared his throat, stroked the swollen area near the middle of his face that functioned as a nose.

"Shoot to disable."

Nevi snorted at the ridiculousness of it. A laser cannon strike on a hydrogen-ram foil could ignite a fireball a thousand meters wide. He thought that a rather narrow definition of "disable."

Zentz continued, flustered at Nevi's silence.

"The Director declared a 'state of security' almost a year ago," he said. "You know the routine: mandatory interception and search of all vessels, except company ferries, that enter or leave Kalaloch; search of any air or ground craft entering or leaving the perimeter . . ."

Nevi let Zentz go on with his tedious recital.

Flattery's precious Preserve was his nest, and Nevi knew he would take no chances here. But Nevi was sure that any interception of the *Flying Fish* right now could easily be bungled into a disaster of the greatest proportions. Flattery had just called him to duty because Zentz had permitted such a bungle.

"We want Shadowbox *and* Crista Galli," Nevi said. "To exterminate nerve runners you have to burn their nest. This foil, *intact,* will lead us there."

Zentz, ramrod-stiff in his seat, cleared his dry throat and offered, "We suspect LaPush has been a Shadow commandant for about six years . . ."

"Your crew is not to interfere with this vessel," Nevi ordered. He keyed in the security frequency on his console. "You can give the order right here." He flipped a switch and looked Zentz in the eyes.

Zentz cleared his throat again, then leaned toward the microphone.

"Zentz here. Thirty-four, disregard white class-three foil departing harbor."

"Sir," a young voice came back, "by the Director's orders we're to seize any vessels sighted but not searched."

Zentz paused, and in that pause Nevi enjoyed the exquisite dilemma that was now added to the Security Chief's fatigue. There was only one way out, one way to satisfy the by-the-book greenhorn officer, one way to keep the Director at bay.

"I searched it personally at dockside," Zentz said. "We know what's on board."

Nevi switched off the connection, satisfied with the choice he'd made in Zentz. If it came right down to it, Zentz would be the perfect sacrifice in the holiest of games, survival.

"Young officers haven't learned their priorities yet," Zentz said, forcing a smile.

"They have only learned fear," Nevi said. "They mature when they understand greed."

Zentz rubbed at the back of his thick neck, only half-listening. He had spent the entire night interrogating two of his best guards as an example to the rest, and now that Nevi had ordered Crista Galli out of his grasp it looked as if he was going to have to go through it all again. From the moment he'd freed the foil Zentz could feel a tightening at his collar that he didn't like—it was a nooselike grip, unrelenting as baldness, cold.

Nevi would be the death of him, this he was beginning to understand. With this came the understanding that there was nothing he could do about it, nowhere he could hide. The dasher coiled to spring, that was what Spider Nevi saw when Zentz met his gaze.

"I am going to make you a hero," Nevi said. "I have a part for you to play. If we hand the Director Shadowbox we hand him back Pandora. The implications for you and me are obvious. You will, of course, prefer this to whatever the Director has in mind for you here?"

Zentz did not clear his throat, he did not speak. He nodded once and his grotesque lump of a jaw quivered with what Nevi presumed was the clenching of his teeth.

"It will be just you and I," Nevi said. "The more we can tell the Director about these vermin and their warrens, the happier he will be. You desperately need to make him happy."

The white foil slipped under the bay's waves, keeping the burning wreckage between itself and the Vashon Security foil opposite. They would be suspicious of not being challenged during an alert, this Nevi knew, but he still had the advantage. They knew he was behind them, they didn't know how close.

Nevi used the sensor system to pan the riot that was now in full bloom in Kalaloch.

"They're working their way toward the Preserve," he noted. "Can your men handle this?"

Zentz's wattles rose in indignation.

"Security is my business, too, Mr. Nevi. I handle it my way. We will let them throw their tantrum and trash their nest, then we will slaughter them here at the wall. They must be made to be *very* sorry that they attack the Preserve. The damage they do to their streets will keep the survivors busy for a time."

Nevi flipped off the sensors and stood, straightening his tight suit with a tug.

"Secure one of Flattery's personal foils," Nevi snapped. "Full gear for two, plus a week's rations. See to it there's coffee. Meet me in the Preserve hangar in one-half hour."

His eyebrows indicated dismissal and Zentz rose to leave. Nevi saw the seed of hope in Zentz's eyes, a seed that Nevi would nourish to a rich blossom and snip, when necessary, to make just the right bouquet for the Director.

> *I consider the positions of kings and rulers as that of dust motes . . . I look upon the judgment of right and wrong as the serpentine dance of a dragon, and the rise and fall of beliefs as but traces left by the four seasons.*

> —Buddha

Crista Galli reclined in a leather crew couch that smelled faintly of Rico. She gripped the armrests, eyes closed. Noise and the press of the crowd had always frightened her, at least since she had been blasted free of the kelp five years past. Memory of her life before that blast seemed hopelessly lost.

The supple leather couch and roomy cabin muted the pierside clamor. The others had finished casting off and were returning to the cabin. A green circle flashed on the pilot's screen for each hatch they dogged behind them.

Their pilot, a severe, sensuous woman in her mid-thirties, prepared the ballast tank pumps and other predive systems. She spoke the sequences aloud crisply as she completed her checkoff.

"Taking on ballast."

Three fuel tanks flared together from the fire at the center of the bay and Crista felt the concussions puff her lungs. A three-headed rage of fire boiled up from the waters off their bow, heeling the foil over in a lurch to starboard. Ben and Rico sealed off the cabin and strapped in.

"Going down?" Rico asked, and laughed. The pilot didn't miss a beat.

"No security challenge," she reported. "Twenty-meter level-off mandatory until clear of marker five-five-seven . . ."

Since boarding the foil Crista had felt a calm such as she'd not known for several years, in spite of the madness outside. She felt something pull her toward the mouth of the harbor, to the open water beyond. Ben handed her a child's dessert stick from his pocket.

"You'll need the energy," he said. "Once we're clear of the harbor we can raid the galley. Is the cabin air too dry for you?"

"No," she shook her head, "it feels fine. Like my room at the Preserve."

This was the cool, processed air that Crista had breathed for five years at the Preserve, free of the charcoal odors of the street braziers, the whiff of raw iodine from the beaches and scant wet blooms of upland slopes. It was air swept nearly clean of humanity—the humanity that idolized Crista Galli, the humanity she had only known now for less than a single day.

It was midmorning yet, second sun just clearing the horizon, and Crista felt the race of sunlight through her surging pulse. She was outside the Preserve now. Regardless of the circumstances, she intended never to go back, never to be a prisoner of walls again.

*Watch yourself,* an ancient one inside her warned, *that you don't become a prisoner of action, or words. And remember, when you make a choice you abandon freedom of choice.*

She'd had no choice in her appearance among humans, and Flattery had given her no choices since that time. She had been plucked from the vine of the kelp and dropped into Flattery's basket. Crista thought that if the people of Pandora thought her a god, it was time she acted like one. Now that the water had begun closing about the foil, she felt an energy surge her blood that she'd never felt before.

What could she do that would help herself and these people who were still alien to her? Even Ben, though she felt a love for him, was a stranger. She had tried daily for five years, and could summon no memories of her earlier life.

*Everyone, everyone is a stranger.*

She'd had this thought before, but today it didn't surround her

with the loneliness that it had in the past. She'd touched Ben
Ozette, and seen that he, too, had these thoughts and he'd lived
among humans for his whole life.

*This is what they could learn from the kelp,* she mused. *We are
not alone because we are elements of one being.*

She listened as Rico muttered loudly to no one in particular.

"Operations won't like it," he said. "Under no circumstances
is she to be allowed near the sea. Of course, they're welcome to
drop in here and give us a hand after they promised us the airstrip . . ."

She could tell that Rico felt more comfortable in the foil. He
had smiled, finally, and though he seemed to be complaining he
was complaining with a smile.

"Ever ride a foil?" Ben asked her.

"Never," she said, her wide eyes trying to take in everything at
once. "I've watched them from the Preserve. This one is beautiful."

"Let me point out our three-way option," he said, and indicated certain diagrams on his control panel. "We are riding Pandora's finest vehicle on, above or under the sea. The hydrofoil
mode is fast on the surface, but the foil struts clog up easily in
thick kelp. Except in flight, these class-one foils use the old
Bangasser converter to retrieve hydrogen from seawater, a virtually infinite source of fuel. If we go to the air, we have to
remember that the fuel tanks do get empty."

He glanced over at Elvira's indifference and shrugged.

"We're going down under," he said. "Their lasgun's no good
underwater. But this guarantees we'll be tracked, all the kelpways
are heavily wired—"

"It might be something bigger than Flattery doing the tracking," Rico interrupted. "Heads up, we're going down."

He paused and, when there was no response from Ben, he
assisted Elvira with the dive checkout. While they busied themselves with tasks at their consoles, Crista watched the water close
over the cabin.

Ironically, it was probably Flattery who best understood her life
among the kelp. In his hybernation, Flattery had lain nearly life-
less, his vitals monitored and maintained by several devices on
and inside his body. According to Flattery's lab people, Crista
Galli had lived in symbiosis with the kelp, a hundred million kelp
cilia inside her, breathing for her, feeding her. They claimed that
these tiny projections supported her for her first twenty years, until

Flattery had this stand of kelp blown up, lobotomized to the needs of Current Control.

"It's like being an embryo until you're twenty," she'd told Ben. "There's no other way I can explain it. You don't eat, breathe, or move around much. The only people you meet are in the dreams that Avata brings. Now I don't know what was dream and what was me, it's all confused. There was no *me* until . . . until that day. But Flattery knows something of how this feels. So does Dwarf MacIntosh, and that brain that Flattery's hooking up to his ship."

"It sounds horrible," Ben had said, and she realized that it probably did.

In dive mode the engine shift vibrated so much that it rocked her from side to side in her seat, forcing her attention back to the present.

Crista fought back a tear, and couldn't turn away from the green water surging ahead of the cabin.

*There are laws against touching me!*

She thought of that kiss again, the one that had lasted only a blink in real time but would replay forever in her mind. Even in the hot climate of Kalaloch, Crista wore the coverings dictated by the Director. But alone, in the privacy of her suite, she had often shucked her clothes in spite of Flattery's sensors, which she knew to be everywhere.

Any portion of her skin left bare tingled at its awareness of breezes and light. If she noticed nothing else in a day she noticed the thousand tiny touches between humans around her. It had become difficult to think of herself as human. Now, having glimpsed the public idolatry focused on her, she felt the frayed tether weaken even more.

A surge in cabin air pressure popped her ears, and the great plasma-glass dome of the cabin settled completely under the waves. She caught herself holding her breath and cautioned herself to relax. She heard the susurrations of voices rise and fall with the pulse of the engines.

"Are you all right?"

Crista felt herself rising above Ben's voice to the ceiling of the cabin, through the ceiling and higher yet, above the Preserve. She was a thousand meters above Kalaloch, and beneath her writhed a mass of brown tentacles.

She was a hylighter, tacking her great sail across the breeze to keep the shadow of their foil in sight below. She was aware of herself, of her own being inside the foil, but felt every ripple along the hylighter's supple body as well.

Ben Ozette was calling her name, barely audible at this distance. It seemed she shared an umbilicus from his navel to her own and he was pulling her in by it, reeling her back to the *Flying Fish* hand over hand.

Ben touched her cheek and Crista snapped awake. He did not take his hand away.

"You scared me," he said. "Your eyes were open and you quit breathing."

As she sat forward, resisting his gentle pressure, she saw that Rico also stood over her, an open medical kit beside his feet. He was wearing gloves. What had been blue sky covering the plaz of the cabin was now the green-gray twilight of the middle deep. They were riding a kelpway, and somehow she knew that they had already cleared the harbor, heading north.

Rico stared at Ben's hand stroking her cheek, then at Crista.

"I was gone," she said. "Somewhere above us. I was a hylighter watching this foil and you reached out and brought me back."

"A hylighter?" Ben laughed, but it was a tight, very nervous laugh. "That's a strange enough dream.

> ' Gasbag from the sky
> How her tentacles writhe
> for me . . . '

Remember that song? 'Come and Gone . . .'"

"I remember that it was some tasteless play on words, ridiculing the hylighter's spore-casting function. And this was no dream."

She saw the snap in her voice reflected in the tightening of his lips, a closing off that she didn't know how to stop.

Rico turned without saying anything and stowed the kit beneath his seat. Crista smelled something like anger, something like fear pulse from Rico's turned back. All of her senses washed back into her trembling body, delivering her into a state of hypersensitivity that she had never known before.

The undersea landscape of blues and greens blurred past her like the settlement had blurred past her—too much wonder, too little time.

*Of everyone to whom much has been given, much
will be required; and of him to whom they have
entrusted much, they will demand the more.*

—Jesus

Beatriz was awaiting her cue for the two-minute windup of Newsbreak when the fully armed security detachment entered the studio, sliding from the hatchway with their backs along the walls.
They hung back beyond the fringe of lights, which blazed their
reflection in the squad leader's mirrored sunglasses. Her mouth
was suddenly dry, her throat tightening, and she was due for the
wrap-up in thirty seconds.

*Still on the air,* she thought. *The preempt isn't running yet.*

Her console showed her what the three cameras saw, but the
monitor at the rear of the studio showed what went out on the air.
Now it showed Harlan fast-talking the weather.

*It could be bypassed.*

She shuddered in her newfound paranoia and thought that the
floor director would probably stop Harlan if they'd gone to tape,
but she couldn't be sure anymore.

*Maybe they want to see just how much more I'd try to say.*

She had deviated from the prompter, amid the waving hands of the producer and director. She hadn't linked Ben with the Galli kidnapping, she'd just listed him as missing, along with Rico, on assignment. She noted signs of surprise and muttering among the crew when she said it. Both Ben and Rico were admired in the industry. Indeed, many of Rico's inventions and innovations made the holo industry possible.

Harlan finished morning fishing patterns, and the countdown went to Beatriz. The officer of the security squad had moved up in the studio and placed a man beside each of her cameramen. She had the sudden, weighty thought that her crew might not be on the shuttle this afternoon.

Harlan finished and smiled from the monitor, and the floor director's fingers counted her down: Three, two, one . . .

"That's our morning Newsbreak from our launch site studios. Evening Newsbreak will be broadcast live from our Orbital Assembly Station. Our crew will have the opportunity to accompany the OMC, Organic Mental Core, and take you, the viewer, through each step of installation and testing. Other news that we will follow at that time: the abduction of Crista Galli. As you know, there is still no word from her abductors and no ransom demand. More on this and other news at eighteen. Good morning."

Beatriz held her smile until the red light faded out, then slumped back into her chair with a sigh. The studio erupted around her in a babble of questions.

"What's this about Ben?"

"Rico, too? Where were they?"

"Does the company know about this?"

They cared. She knew they would care, that most of Pandora probably cared, and that was her power. As the mirrored sunglasses made their way through the crew toward her, she knew that there was nothing he could do. Even if they'd preempted and run the canned show, the crew knew and there would be no keeping this leak plugged.

When the security officer reached her, the babbling in the studio fell quiet.

"I must ask you to come with us."

These were the words she'd been afraid she might hear. These words, "Come with us," were what Ben had tried to warn her about for the last couple of years. He had said more than once, "If they ask you to come, don't do it. They will take you away and you will disappear. They will take the people around you away. If they say this to you, make whatever happens happen in public, where they can't hide it from the world.''

"Roll cameras one, two and three," she announced. Then she turned to Gus, the floor director. "Were we preempted?"

"No," he said, and his voice trembled. He was sweating heavily even though she was the one under the lights. "If a preempt signal was sent, I didn't see it. You went out live."

*God bless Gus!* she thought.

She turned to the security.

"Now, Captain . . . I didn't get your name . . . what was it you wanted of me?"

*What then shall we do?*

—Leo Tolstoy

"Trimmed and steady," Elvira reported. "No pursuit. Course?"
When Ben didn't answer, Rico said, "Victoria."
Elvira grunted.

It was obvious to Crista that Elvira trusted both Ben and Rico
completely. She had seen loyalty at the Preserve, but never trust.
She had manipulated the distrust rampant throughout Flattery's
organization to open the hatch for her escape. That same distrust
would bring Flattery down, once and for all. Of this she was
certain.

"Flattery's people hoard information like spinarettes at the
web," she told Ben. "It's barter to them, a medium of exchange.
So no one has the full picture and rumor guides the hand that
blesses or damns. That's why Shadowbox has threatened him
more than anything else."

"There's food in the galley," Rico announced, and she saw the
accompanying green indicator flash on the console at her right

hand. "Ben, you two take a break. Bring me back some coffee. We're a few hours out yet. Elvira would like the usual."

Ben led Crista to the galley behind the cabin with a hand at her elbow. Her legs seemed wobbly in spite of the even-keeled submersible run of the foil. She had been hungry now for hours. Her head ached with it, and the memory of broiled sebet on the village air charged her stomach.

"We live in the galley," Ben told her. "When we're on a job, this room is jammed, it's where everything happens."

She stepped from the semidim cabin into a warm yellow glow. The galley was a bright room of wood, yellowpanel and brass. She could imagine a Holovision Nightly News crew spread out over the two tables with coffee and notes in the half-hour before air time. It was a clean, well-lighted space. Holo cubes of the crew in action on various assignments sat in a rack against the inboard bulkhead. Crista sat at the first of two hexagonal tables and pulled down a couple of the cubes to look at.

"These really stand out at you," she said, moving the holograms through different angles of light. "Nothing in Flattery's collection matches these for quality."

"Thanks to Rico," Ben said. "He's a born inventor. He'd be a rich man today if Flattery's Merman Mercantile hadn't jumped into the middle of things. Our stuff is good because Rico makes up the equipment himself. We always roll with the best."

"She's very pretty," Crista said, holding a scene of Ben and Beatriz with their arms around each other. "You two have worked together for a long time. Were you in love, the two of you?"

Ben cleared his throat and pushed a few buttons. She heard the *whirr* of galley machinery at work.

"Now it's hard to know whether we were truly in love or whether we'd just survived so much together that we felt no one else could understand—except maybe Rico, of course."

"And you made love with her?"

"Yes."

Ben stood with his back to her, staring at the backs of his hands on the countertop. "Yes, we made love. For several years. Given our lives, it would have been impossible that we didn't become intimates."

"But now you're not?"

She saw the slightest shake of the back of his head. "No."

"Does that make you sad? Do you miss her?"

When he turned to her she saw the consternation on his face, the struggle he seemed to be having with words. She thought perhaps he'd started out to lie to her, but with a sigh he changed his mind.

"Yes," he said, "I miss her. Not as a lover, that's past and would be too clumsy to rekindle. I miss working with her because she's so goddamn *good* at getting people to talk in front of cameras. Rico handled the techno stuff, and between us she and I could get to the bottom of most anything. I think she's in love with MacIntosh up in Current Control, but I don't think she's admitted it, yet. If it's true, it should make life easier for both of us."

"If one of you is in love, then that takes the heat off?"

Ben laughed. "I suppose you could say that. yes."

She lowered her gaze to the cube that her hands passed back and forth in front of her. "Could you ever be in love with me?"

He laughed a soft laugh and gripped her shoulder.

"I remember everything about you," he said. "That first day I saw you in Flattery's lab, when you looked at me over your shoulder and smiled . . . I had a feeling when our eyes met like I've never had before. I still get it every time I see you, think of you, dream of you. Isn't that something like love?"

Her pale skin flushed red from the neck of her dress to the roots of her shaggy white hair at her forehead.

"It's the same for me," she said. "But I have nothing to compare with. And how could I live up to whatever you've shared with . . . her?"

"Love isn't a competition," he said. "It *happens*. There were tough times, living with B, but I don't have to bring up the bad parts to punish myself for missing the friendship, the good parts. I think she and I are both people who refuse to dislike someone we've loved. She's an exceptional person or I wouldn't have loved her. There was a lot of bliss, a lot of turmoil, no boredom at all. The bliss part she called 'our convergent lines.' Ultimately we each blamed the other for being impossible when it was our *situation* we couldn't bear . . ."

"Did you take the job of interviewing me because you knew that she was working with Flattery at the Preserve?"

He laughed again.

"You have me pegged, don't you? That's a yes and no answer. I thought, and still think, that your story is the most exciting thing I can show the rest of Pandora. I wouldn't have tried for it otherwise. But, yes, I *did* hope, in a moment of wallowing in loneliness, that I'd see her again."

"And . . . ?"

"I did. The thrill was gone and we were good friends. Good friends who still work very well together."

"You knew that Flattery was buying us both off with those interviews, didn't you?" Crista asked.

She set her hat beside her on the deck and peeled off her headband and mantilla. She gave her matted hair a shake. She was relieved that he smiled at this as he gathered their utensils at the sideboard.

"I figured it out," he said. "That's why . . . *this*. Flattery pulled the corporate strings, denying air time before the first can was shot. But no one was told. I was paid. you were interviewed at length on five occasions—*and this was the story of the century!* He paid to have it done so he could kill it."

"Yes," she said, "with no pangs of conscience whatsoever. Look what it got him: We are here, together. I, at least, am happier. And hungry," she indicated her disguise, "in spite of how it looks."

Ben patted the lump of clothing strapped to her belly. "And fulfilled, too," he teased. He dared to stroke her cheek again with a smile and then busied himself setting out the food.

She watched the seascape as their foil slithered through the kelpways, her quick breaths fogging the plaz. Though the Preserve was a seaside base camp Crista never once had been allowed down to the shore. Flattery feared her relationship with the kelp, and saw to it that others around her did, too.

Ben nudged her shoulder and pointed through the starboard port toward the skeletal remains of a kelp outpost, dimly visible in the foil's deepwater lights. The kelp itself had been burned back to knobby stumps for a thousand meters all around.

"Report says kelp killed three families here, sixteen people," he said. "Vashon Security did their retaliatory number on the kelp, as you can see. They call it 'pruning.'"

Though it was shadowland beneath a weak wash of light and though the engines had quieted in submersible mode, Crista focused on the tingle at her shoulder where Ben had touched her. She fought back tears of joy at his touch. How could she explain this to him, who touched people and was touched at will?

He pulled two hot trays out of the unit and set them on the table. He dealt out napkins, spoons, chopsticks. She knew she needed food, strength, but some dreaminess had caught her up since boarding the foil and she didn't really want to shake it.

Sunlight strengthened her, this she knew. The beautiful kiss from Ben, that strengthened her, too. Something about this Rico LaPush also strengthened her, but she didn't know what.

Crista glanced again at Ben, beside her, as his eyes searched the dimness of the passing landscape.

"The Preserve is under attack," Ben said. She didn't respond. "You can watch it onscreen if you want." He indicated the briefing screen against the aft galley bulkhead. She preferred the old word "wall," but not many used it. Tribute to Pandora's watery history.

Though Ben talked on, Crista concentrated on her meal, eating half of Ben's as well, leaving him the vegetables. His words buzzed like a fat bee in the warm galley air. All the while a lullaby kept running through her head that no human ear had heard in two thousand years.

> *Hush little baby don't say a word*
> *Momma's gonna buy you a mockingbird . . .*

She had learned to be cautious wandering her memories, too. When the flashbacks started sometimes they took over, unpeeling whole sections of other people's lives. They lasted longer each time, dragging Crista through hours of lightning-fast memories. There was no focus, no fine-tuning, simply *off* or *on*.

First it was blinks, then seconds, moments. A minute of high-speed memory, lived with a full sensory component, could wring an entire lifetime out of the wet cloth of her mind. Her last flashback had terminated only after exhaustion and heavy sedation. It had lasted nearly four hours. Though conscious immediately, she had been dazed and unable to speak for three days. Flattery had used this as an excuse to further limit her life at his compound, and to adjust her medications.

She felt that same dazedness now, but no onslaught of memories, no sweat, no fear.

"Crista Galli," Ben said, "you have quite the life awaiting you. You are 'the One, Her Holiness,' a living legend. You are the most important person alive today."

She felt an uneasiness at what he said, and sought reason to feel uneasy at the way he said it. She found none.

"'The One'?" she muttered. "'The One' to do what?"

"You are the One for whom they have waited in suffering for so long," he said. "Depending on whom you believe, you are the last salvation of humankind, or you are the kelp's secret weapon to eradicate humans forever. In your glimpse of the people of Kalaloch you must have felt your power. There is a lot for you to learn, and quickly. We will help you with that. But because one does not touch a god, one does not come before a god scratching one's fleas, you will see only the best side of the faithful, and the worst side of the rest.''

"When the people know me, know it's all a—"

"They will *not* know you," he interrupted. "Not the 'you' that you mean. They want to believe something else too much to stop them. Faith can do that.

"You must be careful, you must be quiet. And you must be a mystery. We *need* that mystery to beat Flattery. You will see plenty of need before very much longer, and I think you will agree with me. Eat the rest if you are hungry. We may not always be among those who have food.''

She was hungry, very hungry. She drank the broth from her soup, left the vegetables and picked out the meat. She also picked out the meat from the sandwich he made her. She ate the bread in tiny bites to make it last longer.

She thought she could tell Ben, tell them all something of need. Touch was a human need and she was mostly human. At times someone would touch her by accident or quickly in a breathless dare. The daring ones, she recognized now, must be the religious zealots, the Zavatans that Ben had told her about. There was no way to know which way it would be: embarrassment or death.

When she let Ben kiss her the previous night she had known it was possible that he would die. She had the strongest feeling that she would die, too, and somehow that made it all right. For the first time she felt mortal, and risked it. When neither of them died, she even kissed him back a little. Her heart pumped something like fear, even at the memory. Afterward, in his green eyes so nearly like her own, there was the glitter of laughter and a good dare taken.

*He looked so happy!*

She remembered that few people around her had ever looked happy, except the Director. Mostly, they seemed afraid.

"Why did you kiss me?" she asked. A flush crept out of her collar. She didn't want to look at him but finally couldn't help it. He was smiling.

"Because you let me."

"You weren't afraid . . . ?"

"Afraid you wouldn't like it? Yes. Afraid of what you might do to me? No." He laughed. "I have a theory. If people expect to go crazy when they touch you, then that's what they do. It's a hysteria, that's all . . ."

She put her palm on his chest and said, evenly, "You don't know anything about me. You were lucky . . . *we* were lucky." She patted his shirt. "You didn't sleep," she said. "If it's necessary that one of us sit up, I can do it from now on."

Something dark passed over his expression.

"There were arrangements," he said, "with some of the women we'll meet upcoast—you were to stay with them. It was assumed that you would prefer . . ."

"It *has* to be you," she insisted. "You have no woman in your life, isn't that right?"

"That's right, but it's not a matter of . . ."

"What's it a matter of?" she blurted. "Don't you like me?"

Maybe it was the surprise that lifted the darkness from his face, or maybe it was the blush. "I like you," he said. "I like you a lot."

"Then it's settled," she said. "I can stay with you."

"It's not as easy as that."

"It is if we make it so," she said. "Get some rest between now and then. If you really are immune to me, you're going to need it."

*Intervention into destiny by god or man requires the most delicate care.*

—Dwarf MacIntosh, Kelpmaster, Current Control

Raja Flattery's private bunker lay safely beneath almost thirty meters of Pandoran stone. High, domelike ceilings held back the psychological crush and some well-chosen holograms draped the walls with scenes from outside the walls. Above him, in the rubble of his surface compound, Flattery's security finished the last roundup of resisters.

"Stand down the fighting and send in the medics."

Thanks to the hylighters, there would be a lot of burns. He spoke the order into his console and didn't wait for acknowledgment. His bunker area was honeycombed with cubicles, and those cubicles were occupied by the underlings who carried out his orders and asked no questions. Fewer than a handful had personal access to the Director.

*Ironic, how a little fire can cool things down.*

His security teams mopped up the carnage overhead and formed stark little shadows hunching under Pandora's unforgiving suns. Though the sterile images of battle came into his bunker by holo,

108

the Director thought he sniffed a distinct stench of burning hair beside him at the console.

*The imagination . . . the mind . . . what incredible tools.*

His personal security team waited just outside his hatch, a precaution. There was no place on Pandora that he could flee to that would be as secure as his own compound. Certainly there was nowhere as luxurious. A brunch of sebet simmered in Orcas Red spread out at his left hand. There was a fine bite to these Pandoran wines that pleased him, even early in the day.

"Captain," he spoke to the shadowy figure at his hatch, "that camera team, were they deployed as scheduled?"

"Yes, sir," the captain's back stiffened. "Captain Brood's men have been at the launch site since daybreak. They know what you want."

"And the Holovision people, the ones the studio sent out to cover this . . . mess?"

"Captain Brood suggested letting them film, sir. When it's done, his team can access their film, as well as their cameras and other equipment. He says—"

Flattery shouted at his attendant, "Captain, did anyone give this . . . Captain Brood . . . permission to start *thinking?* Did *you?*"

The stiffened spine stiffened even more.

"No, sir."

Flattery was thankful that the shadows hid the man's face. There was no profile to it. Where the captain's nose should be there were two moist slits that separated a very wide set of eyes. When Flattery talked with Nevi, at least he could focus on the man's eyes. This man wasn't that interesting, and Flattery had all too much time to dwell on the malformed face.

Flattery spoke in his most reasonable tone.

"I want nothing to go on Holovision today without my prior approval. Brood's team is to receive priority treatment, even if we have to replace the entire production staff, understood?"

"Yes, sir."

"Get their manager into my office within the hour, that puffy little maggot Milhous. We need cooperation and I don't want any slip-ups. Tell him to bring some canned stuff that we can use to preempt today until Brood's men get their tapes. No sense in the rest of the world getting inspired by what's going on here."

"Right, sir. Right away, sir."

"Captain?"

"Yes, sir."

"You're a good man, Captain. Your family will be pleased that you're working with me."

"Yes, sir. Thank you, sir."

The man's back retreated through the main hatchway to the offices. Flattery sighed. He watered the wine a bit and raised a glass to his own firmness under duress. He toasted his search teams, who fanned out even now to burn the last of the bodies up in the rocks. This was a Zavatan influence, this burning of bodies. It was a practice that Flattery welcomed and supported. The traditional burials at sea turned into a ghastly sight and a health hazard on Pandora's few beaches.

*Bodies washing up everywhere . . .*

He suppressed a shudder at the memory. It was more than disgusting, it was a religious and economic disaster. Every nitwit who touched the kelp in the process came back a prophet. The entire Pandoran social structure was shattered by the recent geological changes alone, but this kelp business made it a madhouse.

Women of the settlements wouldn't buy fish for a week after a traditional sea burial. They didn't want to take a chance on eating fish that had eaten old Uncle Dak. There were times, early in Flattery's rise to power, when he had seen hundreds of embroidered burial bags washed up on the beach at a time, and the local fleets wouldn't fish for a month. Flattery's answer was to buy out the importers, stockpile everything, and control the seaways.

"Control," he muttered. "That's the key. Control."

Flattery toasted the holo that played in the center of his quarters. His men had been forced to inflict heavier casualties than he preferred, and it would raise hob with the work force just at a time when he needed things smooth. Still, their way was best. There were plenty of replacements, though starvation made them dimwitted weaklings. Things would be slow during the training period.

*My way,* he thought. *I've had to teach them everything. Left to themselves, these Pandorans couldn't get anything done.*

Flattery still marveled at his own progress. He'd built and fortified a city, unified politics and industry under one banner, and prepared a Voidship for launch. The Voidship would present them with more options than this stinking little hell-hole of a planet and Alyssa Marsh, the OMC, would point the way. Pandorans had been here for hundreds of years and hadn't made nearly the progress he'd made in the past twenty-five.

The trap topside had been sprung and was nearly ready for cleaning. This might come close to destroying any significant Shadow resistance. There couldn't be many of them left, and the rest . . . well, he'd see to it that they were too hungry to fight.

*Except among themselves, for scraps. My scraps.*

Flattery's losses, other than replaceable materials, were minimal.

He pushed the meal aside and drained his glass. The mop-up operation would be a bore. The last of the mob would be torched outside the hatch in a matter of two or three hours. He keyed in his command post and noted the air of celebration among the junior officers.

*Nothing like a well-executed victory to lift morale,* he thought. *Nothing more dangerous than an army with no one to fight.*

Flattery knew that they would not turn on him, or each other, as long as they had the Shadows, food thieves and the kelp to contend with.

*The idle brain is the devil's playground,* he chuckled.

Once again, Flattery keyed the voice frequency on his console.

"Update me on the Holovision foil's position, Colonel."

"Still submerged," Colonel Jaffe reported, "about fifty klicks downcoast from Victoria."

"Any sign of escort?"

"No. The foil is proceeding solo through the accustomed channels."

"And the kelp is not interfering?"

"Not exactly," Jaffe said. "Our instruments show a marked increase in tension on the grid—the kelp's fighting the signal from Current Control."

"The grid is holding?"

"Yes, sir. We're preparing to detour traffic to the outside in case we lose it. Tension's rising fast, we're getting some oscillations at this point. All vessels with Navcom are probably getting instrument disturbances, too. We'll try to warn them, but as you know the sonic transmission stations down under have a very limited range . . ."

"I understand, Colonel. Instruct Current Control that this is a priority one situation. They are to maintain this grid at all costs. Stump that stand, if you have to."

"Will do, sir. Currents remain stable. Are they to be intercepted in Victoria?"

"That is not your jurisdiction, Colonel," Flattery snapped. "A

White Warrior team will take care of it. We will root out the brass of this Shadow operation this time, I'm sure. Notify me of any sign of kelp interference, anywhere.''

He broke contact without waiting for a reply, and smiled.

*Yes, root them out,* he thought, *but not all of them. They will find new leaders, then we will hunt them down, too.*

He poured himself half a glass of wine and filled the rest with water.

*Moderation,* he mused, *it's a lot like patience. We will prune them back, like my roses, to the very brink of death. They will always blossom under our control, always ready for the picking.*

Flattery stood at his console and stretched. He liked the privacy of his bunker. It was as spacious as the compound above him, with all of the attendant comforts. The view through his view-screens was not nearly as satisfying as real plaz looking over the real world—*his* world. Soon his Voidship would be manned and stocked, and he would hand over the husk of this world to anyone who wanted it. He planned on taking Beatriz Tatoosh with him.

Flattery had monitored her broadcast, as was his custom. He noted both her loyalty to Ozette and her restraint. It proved she had due respect for his powers, but not a blind fear. This he admired in her. Still, he did not want to underestimate Ozette's influence on her. The man had been pouring poison into her ear for quite a few years.

Flattery smiled. He wasn't one to leave much to chance, and he had a backup plan for Beatriz Tatoosh. She would meet Captain Brood, one of Flattery's more innovative White Warriors. Brood's plan would take out a number of those troublesome Holovision people and finish a clean sweep of that little rat's nest. They would go the way Ozette was going. That would teach the lot of them to back off when the Director said "Back off." And it would keep them from helping out that Shadowbox, wherever it was hidden.

*I expected them to get on the air right away with Crista Galli,* he thought. *What does that tell us?*

That they hadn't got her to their broadcasting equipment yet. He smiled in anticipation.

*They'd better hurry,* he laughed at the thought, *they won't want to broadcast what they get once the drugs take over.*

Captain Brood's plan would clean out Holovision and soften up Beatriz Tatoosh. Flattery always liked a plan that worked on more than one level. Brood would be the bad guy, and at just the right

moment Flattery would whisk her out of Brood's clutches. Then
she would join him gladly in the command cabin of the Voidship.
He planned an opulence for that cabin befitting a leader of his
caliber, a woman of her grace and beauty.

*Our children will populate the stars,* he mused.

He drank to the future, and to the careful execution of plans.
*She shows no sign of any of the Pandoran mutations,* he
thought. He'd made sure that she'd had no surgical corrections to
mask any of the Pandoran defects. *We could start quite a world,
the two of us.* In his wine-tinted reverie Flattery saw the two of
them naked in a great garden, heady with the scent of orchids and
ripe fruit.

The ready light winked on over the hatchway to the Greens,
indicating a foil approaching the docking well. Only Flattery and
Spider Nevi knew the coded sequence for docking inside the
Greens. He glanced at his timepiece, then grunted his surprise and
opened the hatch.

*Nevi's a quick one,* he thought. *Too quick. Others, like Brood,
guess at what pleases me. Nevi figures out my thoughts, my moves
even before I do. That will have to be dealt with.*

He stood and adjusted his black dasherskin suit. When he wore
this suit in the Greens, his pets were much more affectionate,
more attentive to his needs. He tried his look of disdain on the
mirror. It still worked. The suit was a nice touch.

His console reported on the docking foil and identified two
occupants.

*That fool!* he thought. *Bringing Zentz into the Greens . . . a
waste. Too late to worry now.*

When the time came for Zentz to be silenced he would remind
himself to have Nevi attend to it personally.

The Greens was the Director's preserve below the Preserve.
Plasteel welders and laser cannon had spent two years quarrying
four square kilometers out of Pandora's stone. Crystallized parti-
cles of the old kelp root glittered like stars overhead. The domed
ceiling arched to twenty meters at the center and shone with the
black gloss of melted rock.

The Greens itself was a lush underground park maintained by
an old Islander biologist. At times Flattery called it "the Ark."
No one who had worked inside the Greens had lived to leave the
compound. Spider Nevi came and went as he chose, and extermi-
nated those who could not. They were easily replaced, and just as
easily forgotten.

The hatchway from the Director's quarters in his bunker opened to the edge of a deep salt-water pool, circular, about fifty meters in diameter. A blue glow rimmed the lower portion, light diffusing in from the lamps installed around the lip outside. This had been the rootway gnawed by the kelp, the last vestige of a great Oracle.

A gentle grassy slope led down to the pool, as well as three small streams that issued from the rock bulkheads. Animals did not do as well in the artificial light as Flattery would have liked, but his flowers, trees and grasses thrived. From where he stood inside the hatchway, Flattery admired the thickest concentration of terrestrial foliage in the world.

He maintained no human security inside the Greens itself but his secret did not want for protection. As the bubbling hiss of the ascending foil seethed the waters of the pool, the Director's trained dasher, Goethe, lay in wait. He knew that the other three remained hidden, stumpy tails twitching, somewhere within a quick bound. Nevi's personal signal toned three times, then repeated itself. Flattery dogged the hatch behind him.

The foil that rose from the pool was one of several that Flattery had designed for his own needs. These were the last foils manufactured by Merman Mercantile before the great quake had destroyed their manufacturing complex two years ago. These were capable of flight but with a limited range and payload. They cruised faster submerged than any other models. A glance into the cabin and Flattery put on the proper mask of disapproval for Nevi, frowning and shaking his head.

*Well, Mr. Zentz first.*

Nevi secured the foil beside one of its twins and waited on deck for Flattery to give the dashers their "all clear" signal. Zentz stood in obvious awe at the hatchway to the cabin, the snags of teeth in his lower jaw glistening saliva.

At the Director's hand signal Goethe slunk back into the foliage. The one he called "Archangel" crouched between himself and Nevi. Archangel, unlike Goethe, was an extraordinary hybrid of a successful gene-swap between the cats in hyb and the hooded dashers of Pandora. They were faithful and wished to please their master—two traits that Flattery admired in anyone, so long as he was the master.

Archangel's eyes watched Nevi's every move and he bristled when Zentz, too, approached the Director. There was another backup "at ease" signal for Archangel, but Flattery didn't give it.

*Zentz is cornered,* he thought, *and cornered animals commit the unexpected.*

Since Zentz would be killed soon, Flattery spoke freely in front of him.

"Mr. Director," Nevi said, inclining his head slightly.

"Mr. Nevi."

This was their ritual greeting. Flattery had never known Nevi to shake a hand. To Flattery's knowledge, Nevi only touched the people he killed. He did not know Nevi's record with women and did not intend to ask.

Flattery smiled and indicated the Greens to Zentz with a generous sweep of his hand.

"Welcome to our little secret," he said, and strolled briskly from the docking pool toward a section of fruiting trees.

"Pity there isn't time for a tour. Near-tropical heat, but you don't know much about the tropics, eh? Bore deep enough into rock and you get heat. Fewer than one hundred people have seen this garden."

*And fewer than five survive.*

Zentz swallowed audibly. "I—I've never seen anything like *this.*"

Flattery did not doubt him.

"One day all of Pandora will look like this."

Zentz brightened so much that Flattery forgave himself the lie. He turned to Nevi. "You saw the trap sprung topside?"

Nevi nodded. "Looks like we burned about three hundred. Crews are out chasing down the wounded. So far, nobody big. As we suspected, their eagerness outstripped their readiness."

"We cannot make that same mistake," Flattery warned. "That is why you must bide your time with Crista Galli and the others. Her abduction must be turned to our advantage in every way possible. To take them now would be easy, and foolish. Remember, from now on she's only the bait, not the quarry."

A pair of white butterflies tumbled the air between them and Zentz backed away.

Flattery smiled. "They aren't dangerous," he said. "Beautiful, don't you think? We've released these topside. They drink the wihi nectar. They have already multiplied the wihi threefold in and around the Preserve. You know its value for defense—a natural booby trap. A problem, at times, with the livestock. The larvae of these beautiful creatures . . . well, another time. I have two specific demands of your mission.''

Flattery strolled to a plot of young trees, carefully planted in rows, in various stages of bloom and fruit production. Nearby, several hives of bees kept audibly busy. Nevi did not care for the bees, this Flattery well knew. He enjoyed Nevi's mastery of the neutral expression. He picked each man a fruit.

"Golden Transparent," he said. "A very hardy apple Earth-side. Since I am developing a Garden of Eden of sorts I thought them most appropriate."

He indicated two carved stone benches under the largest of the trees and sat. Nevi was clearly impatient to be off on the chase, but Flattery could not let them go yet. Nor could he bear watching Zentz make a slobber of his magnificent fruit.

"There are objectives more important than their capture," he emphasized. "Ozette must be discredited. He was popular on Holovision, and his disappearance has already been aired, thanks to Beatriz Tatoosh. This only firms our resolve to expose him as a monster. He must be seen as a madman in the clutches of madmen, with the deathly ill Crista Galli as their slave. We will play on her beauty and her innocence, leave that to me and to Holovision. That is the first thing I require of your mission."

"And the second?" Nevi asked.

Such a question was uncharacteristic of Nevi—how much he must want to be on with it! Flattery wondered what this enthusiasm would add to Nevi's performance.

"Crista Galli will be a problem for them shortly," he said. "They'll want her off their hands. We want her to be seen asking for our help. She must want the Director to save her and the people must know this. It is our only way of guaranteeing absolute control after this little action topside—our only way short of all-out extermination of these pocket villages and little Zavatan monasteries that are the breeding grounds for these Shadows."

"Interesting," Nevi said. "This will require some care. Maybe it's a job for your propaganda people at Holovision. Have you found any drugs to be useful for her . . . persuasion?"

"Details of her drug program are in the briefing you will receive in the foil," Flattery said. He glanced at his timepiece. "I will say that if she has eaten, she could be catatonic any time. Instructions, precautions and drugs have been prepared and are stowed with your briefing materials. Her persuasion is completely up to you. The manner of persuasion, too, is up to you."

Nevi smiled one of his rare smiles. That was what Flattery liked about the man . . . if one could call such a creature a man. He rose to a challenge.

"The Tatoosh woman, does she launch today with the drive system and your OMCs?"

"Yes," Flattery said, "as planned. Why do you ask?"

"I don't trust her," he said, and shrugged. "She'll be up there with Current Control and we're going into the kelp . . ."

"She will be no trouble," Flattery said. "She's been very helpful to us. Besides, she's my problem, leave that to me."

Zentz had finished gnashing down his apple and was once again gawking about the Greens.

"Any of those Zavatans ever tunnel in here? They have hidey-holes all over the high reaches."

*He still has his uses,* Flattery reminded himself.

"My pets love exploring," Flattery answered, indicating Archangel. "Did you know that 90 percent of their brain tissue is dedicated to their sense of smell? No one has tunneled in yet, and whoever does will face Archangel. Then we booby-trap the tunnel for the rest."

Zentz nodded. "A good arrangement," he gurgled.

"You haven't tried your apple," Flattery said, nodding to the bright yellow fruit in Nevi's palm.

"I'm saving it," the assassin replied, "for Crista Galli."

*Do you know how hard it is to think like a plant?*

—Dwarf MacIntosh, Kelpmaster, Current Control
(from Holovision Nightly News, 3 Jueles 493)

The Immensity prickled its long, gray-green fronds and sniffed the current in its chemical way. The sniff did not detect a presence so much as the hint of a presence. It was more a prescience than proper smell or taste, but the kelp knew that something of itself passed by now in the current.

The Immensity was a convolution of kelp, a subtle interweave of vines that sprawled, like a muscular brain, throughout the sea. It had begun as a wild kelp, an ignored planting inside a long-abandoned Merman outpost. It had barely known "self" from "other" when it first encountered the Avatalogical study team led by Alyssa Marsh. Most of what the Immensity knew of humans it had learned from Alyssa Marsh.

This stand of kelp knew slavery from the human memories that her DNA held, and it knew itself to be enslaved by Current Control. With the right tickle in its vines it raised them, lowered them, retracted or extended them. Another electrical tickle set off the luciferase in the kelp, lighting the passage of human submarine

118

trade. There were other tricks as well, all of which pulsed a current through a channel—simple servility, simple stimulation–response. This was reflex, not reflection.

The Immensity had all of eternity at its disposal. It allowed this exercise because it pleased the humans and did not interfere with the stand's extended contemplations. Thanks to Alyssa Marsh and her shipmate Dwarf MacIntosh, the kelp had learned how to follow the electrical tickle to its source. Everything that humans transmitted now flowed straight to the heart of the Immensity. Everything.

The Immensity was finally prepared to send something back. It was getting closer to a breakthrough to these humans, and that breakthrough would not be through touch or the chemical smell, but through light waves intersecting in air.

Pleasing humans was a trivial matter, displeasing them was not. Once, soon after waking, this kelp had lashed out in pain to pluck a runaway submersible from among its vines. The huge cargo train had torn a hundred-meter swath nearly a kilometer long in its path through the vines. After the kelp slapped the deadly thing and plucked it apart, Flattery's slaves came with cutters and burners to amputate the kelp back to infancy. The Immensity knew that it had not been able to think right for some time after that, and it did not intend to give up its thinking ever again.

A certain stirring now in the tips of its fronds told the Immensity that "the One," the Holomaster, was passing. The Immensity could unite fragmented stands of kelp into one will, one being, one blend of physics that humans called "soul." Deep in its genetic memory lay a void, an absence of being that could not be teased out of the genetics labs of the Mermen. This void waited like a nest for the egg, the Holomaster who would teach the kelp how to unite fragmented stands of humans.

Twice this Immensity gave up its body but never its will. It was capable of neither sorrow nor regret, simply of thought and a kind of meditative presence that allowed it to live fully in the *now* while Flattery's electrical strings at Current Control manipulated the puppet of its body.

Reflex is a speedy response made without the brain's counsel. Reaction is a speedy response made with minimal counsel. This kelp grew up expecting to be left alone. It learned reaction only after its vines twined with domestic kelp. It learned to kill when threatened and to show no mercy. Then it learned to expect retaliation for killing.

This Immensity expected to live forever. Logic dictated that it would not live forever if it continued reacting to humans. And now, the One was passing! It knew this as surely as the blind snapperfish knows the presence of muree.

The original Immensity of kelp, Avata, encompassed all of the seas of Pandora under one consciousness, one voice, one "being." Its first genetic extinction came early in the formation of the planet. It had been at the mercy of a fungus. A burst of ultraviolet from a huge sunstorm killed off the fungus. Somewhere, a primitive frond lay mummified in a salt bog awaiting Pandora's first ocean.

The second extinction was by human beings, by a human bio-engineer named Jesus Lewis. The kelp was teased back to life by a few DNA miners about fifty years later. The revitalized kelp that the Mermen resurrected was developed from these early experiments. Now kelp once again filled the seas, dampening the murderous storms.

Once again the great stands scattered scent. They grew close with the years, their fronds spoke the chemical tongue. This Immensity itself retained two and a quarter million cubic kilometers of ocean.

The One rode a kelpway that skimmed the Immensity's reach. This particular kelpway came out of a stand of blue kelp that had been known to attack its own kind, overpowering nearby stands, sucking out their beings and injecting its own. It had suffered many prunings, and was sorely in need of guidance. This the Immensity knew from snatches of terror that drifted in on torn fronds. The One could not be trusted to such a dangerous stand. At whatever cost, the One must be spared.

The kelp shifted itself slightly, against the electrical stings from Current Control, to bring the One into its outmost currents, spiraling into the safer deeps of its own stand.

*You have been educated in judgment, which is the essence of worship. Judgment always occurs in the past. It is past-thinking. Will, free or otherwise, is concerned with the future. Thinking is the performance of the moment, out of which you use your judgment to modulate will. You are a convection center through which past prepares future.*

—Dwarf MacIntosh, Kelpmaster,
from *Conversations with the Avata*

"Course change."

Elvira's voice was emotionless as rock but Rico detected the slightest edge of worry in the flurry of her fingers across her command console. She never piloted the foil in its voice mode because she preferred to speak as seldom as possible. That Elvira had spoken at all worried him—that, and the increasing shimmy that had begun a few minutes back.

"Why?"

When working with Elvira, Rico picked up her habit of non-speech. She seemed to like that.

"Channel change," she said, nodding toward her screen. "We're being steered off course."

"Steered?" he muttered, and checked his own instruments. They maintained their position in the kelpway, but their compass said the huge undersea corridor was running in the wrong direction.

"Who's doing the steering?"

Elvira shrugged, still busy with her keyboard. She had taken them deep into sub train traffic to minimize tracking, and they ran without the help of sensors that would light their progress through the kelpways.

"We're out of the wild kelp sector outside Flattery's launch site," he said, "that's where the weirdness usually happens."

One-half of his screen displayed the navigation grid projected by Current Control from its command center aboard the Orbiter. The other half of the screen tracked their actual course through the grid, which now appeared to be bent.

*Bending,* he corrected himself. *It looks like our whole end of the screen is pouring down a drain.*

"Anything on the Navcom?" he asked.

Sometimes Current Control changed grids through the kelp to accommodate weather conditions further upchannel or the recent stumping of a stand of rogue kelp.

"Negative," she said. "All clear."

The ride began to get bumpy and Rico cinched himself tighter to his couch. He keyed the intercom and said, "Rough water, everybody cinch up. Ben, you'd better come up here."

Below them Rico could see another cargo train careening dangerously close to the kelp, attempting to recover from the sudden change. Their dive lights showed him that the kelp seemed to be in a struggle with itself, fluttering the channel as if pressing against a great force.

Ben used the hand grips along the bulkhead to work his way to his console.

"Can we get Current Control?" Ben asked. He dropped into his couch and cinched up.

"Not without giving up our position."

"We got out too easy," Ben said. "They've got a bug on this thing, anyway . . ."

*"Had,"* Rico said, smiling. "I did an E-sweep when we left the harbor, thinking the same thing. Found it. Elvira here jettisoned the little devil into a netful of krill that we passed about a dozen grids back."

"Good work, both of you," Ben said. "All right, then let's try that cargo train below . . ."

The *Flying Fish* was buffeted again by something like a huge fist. Elvira wrestled with the controls to keep them out of the kelp.

Rico knew, as they all knew, that any damage to the kelp could be construed as an attack. A lot of kelp lights were active in this sector. Besides the red and blue telltales of a waking stand, this kelp flashed its cold navigation light at random and occasionally flooded them with the brighter fiber-optic sunlight that it transported from the surface. If the stand was one that had awakened, any mistake could get the foil and themselves torn apart at the seams.

"Didn't Flattery just go on the air to tell us how safe he'd made the kelpways?"

"Just goes to show," Rico said, "you can't believe that bastard for a goddamn blink."

The cargo train passing in the opposite direction beneath them was having even more trouble than they were. A relatively tiny foil could stop in midchannel and hover if necessary, but the cargo train needed to maintain a constant speed for maneuverability. The grid system was set up so that the trains, Pandora's lifeline, could travel the kelpways swiftly and undisturbed with minimal course changes. From what Rico could see of the bucking cargo, the crew below at both ends of the train had their hands full.

"It's bending," Rico said, watching the Navcom monitor that marked out their grid system. "The whole grid's bending."

"We'd better surface," Ben said. "Prepare for—"

"Negative," Elvira said. "If this is a surface disturbance, things will be worse up there. We need information."

Ben grunted acknowledgment.

"Cargo train identity signal is registered to the *Simplicity Maru*," Elvira reported, fighting the controls to maintain hover and an equidistance between walls of the kilometer-wide channel. This ordinarily simple maneuver was made nearly impossible by the ever-changing walls of their kelpway. Rico noticed a sweat beading on Elvira's brow and upper lip.

Ben keyed for a low-frequency broadcast. He hoped he didn't have to explain the absence of their identity signal.

"*Simplicity Maru*, this is *Quicksilver*," he lied. "Do you have reports on current disruption?"

Static hissed back at them, then a microphone clicked on. The message came in badly broken. Undersea communication, especially around active kelp, was always difficult.

"*Simp* . . . *Maru*. Negative . . . into kelp." There was the sound of shrieking metal in the background. ". . . king up. We are preparing . . . ballast. Repeat, preparing . . ."

Elvira threw the throttles forward and in spite of a violent buffeting the foil leaped at her touch. Her lips were pressed into a tight line and her knuckles shone white on the controls.

"Wait, we can't . . ." Ben said. His body pressed further into his couch. "We can't go into deep kelp."

"They're blowing ballast," Elvira growled. "That whole cargo train's going to pop up into us like a cork."

Rico felt every fixture aboard rattle like his teeth.

"Ben, is the girl secure?"

"She's strapped in," Ben said.

Just then they cleared the rear cabin of the train. It blew past them toward the surface, containers and cabins tumbling like toys. A few of the containers snagged in the walls of the kelpway, walls that still vibrated with light and that same strange force.

"This is too weird," Ben said. "Let's surface and take our chances with the Director's air cover. This ride's getting much too ugly."

Elvira nodded curtly and the foil started its ascent. As though alerted by their control panel, the kelp fronds began closing above the *Flying Fish*. First they formed a canopy, then, a tight and impenetrable mesh. A sudden change of current lurched them to starboard and sent the foil tumbling end over end. Elvira righted them manually, her face very pale.

"Shit!" Ben fisted the arm of his couch. "Somehow Flattery must've got to Current Control . . ." He snicked his harness release over Rico's protests.

"I'm checking on Crista," Ben said.

He had to use the handholds to make his way aft on the rolling deck. At the galley's hatch he turned, suddenly a bit pale himself, and Rico knew what thought had just struck Ben. Rico smiled.

"Rico," Ben said, "what if . . ."

"What if the kelp knows she's here?"

"Yeah," Ben said. "What if the kelp knows she's here?"

"We'd better hope she likes us."

"She probably doesn't have any say in this," Ben said, and undogged the hatch. Rico didn't care for the snap in his voice.

"*Somebody* has a say in this," Rico muttered. The hatch slammed, dogged itself. That was when Rico remembered when the kelp could have had a whiff of Crista Galli. It was the only time that hull integrity had been breached.

*That bug!* he thought. *That goddamn little mercuroid chip of Flattery's.*

"We ejected that transmitter, Elvira, and we ejected it in cabin air." He thought he detected an infinitesimal stiffening of her posture. "If that kelp can sniff, and I hear it can, then it knows there's more in this can than us worms."

*Mercenary captains either are or are not skilful soldiers. If they are, you cannot trust them, for they will always seek to gain power for themselves either by oppressing you, the master, or by oppressing others against your wishes.*

—Machiavelli, *The Prince*

The young security captain, Yuri Brood, was rumored by his men to be the unacknowledged son of the Director, product of an early tryst with a Merman woman from the Domes. The men based this notion on the strong physical resemblance between Brood and the Director, and on Brood's quick rise to an advisorship that went beyond the formalities of his rank. The two men shared a ruthlessness that did not go unnoticed outside the confines of the squad.

Captain Brood and his squad had been reared in a Merman compound near this Kalaloch district. Brood himself had been schooled privately in the mathematics of logic and strategy—that was standard operating procedure for anyone anticipating an executive position with Merman Mercantile. Brood himself preferred the more direct solutions of physical pressure to the subtleties of politics. His superiors shrugged it off as a phase, agreeing that Brood got results where others failed.

The old families, Islander and Merman alike, retained a strong sense of loyalty to their community that made the kind of enforcement that Flattery demanded impossible from within. Security command removed Captain Brood's team to Mesa for their training and formation of their combat bond, then deployed them to Kalaloch and its shuttle launch site for "police work." They were one another's only family, an Island adrift in a sea of enemy. Everyone was kept three villages away from home.

Survive your tour, advance your rank, retire to an office at the Preserve—this was the universal goal.

The young captain was afraid, and he wasn't afraid often. When he was afraid, heads rolled. He and his team were short-timers at one month remaining, just starting their countdown to home. The captain had something to return home to, and he intended to rotate on schedule. He intended that his men rotate back home with him, alive. For a year his district had been Kalaloch and the SLS. His squad's actions had drawn more citations than a dress suit could hold. During that year either the site or his men had been under fire daily.

Today the captain faced Beatriz Tatoosh from the back of the studio, and he thought what a pity it would be to have to kill her.

Beatriz did not know what the captain thought, but fear dried out her mouth when she saw his squad enter behind the lights and fan out along the bulkhead backing the studio.

The captain pointed out each of the live cameras to three of his men. They pulled away from their squad, drew lasguns and without a word each took careful aim at a cameraman.

Beatriz heard gasps, curses, the arming of weapons. It was difficult to see what was happening because of the glare in her eyes. The large monitor at the back of the studio cleared, then displayed a tape of the last launch, a tape cut by Beatriz and her present team.

*We're not going out live!* she thought.

"Dak," she alerted her floor man, "check the monitor."

When her gaze left the monitor it caught the young captain watching her. She remembered seeing him before, his dark eyes flashing her a smile as he led his squad through the labyrinth of the launch site. He half-smiled now, and nodded at her, and with that nod his three men executed her three cameramen.

At the first shot she was stunned at the suddenness of it all, the audacity as much as the horror. At the second shot it was the smell of death itself that stunned her. At the third shot she faced the immediacy of her own death. She also faced the captain, who was no longer smiling.

She remembered thinking how hard everyone was breathing just then, how the second guard stood over her dead cameraman and said to the first, ''Shit, man, that was no *signal* . . .''

''Shut up, man,'' the third one said. ''It's done. Just shut up. It don't change nothing here at all.''

*''All right!''*

The captain fanned his fingers out from his left palm and the rest of the squad sealed off the studio area. She started to tremble, then concentrated on controlling it so that the captain wouldn't see.

*Ben was right!* replayed through her mind. *And who will know?*

Beatriz watched the replay of herself on the monitor, interviewing the Director during one of his ritual visits to the launch site. The expression on her face onscreen, one of admiration and deference, now made her sick to her stomach. Even so, her eyes stayed on the screen, rather than face the unbelievable reality unreeling in her studio.

Through the shock and the trembling she heard Harlan's voice from the back of the studio, speeding through a Zavatan chant for the dead. She remembered that the skinny cameraman with the fanlike ears on number three was Harlan's cousin. The security who had shot him was now dragging him by the feet to the wall. The cameraman's head bumped over the sprawl of cables across the deck, the hole in his chest burned so clean it barely bled.

The three assassins took wider positions in the room. Fifteen people were being held by nine guards in a very small studio with some very hot lights. The captain scanned the studio once, then turned to Beatriz. He indicated the red lights on the triangulators.

''The red light means the camera is *on,* correct? It is still recording?''

She did not answer. She felt it was important that he didn't hear her voice quaver. She could not take her eyes from his eyes.

He did not smile this time, nor did he nod.

''Finish them,'' he said. Then he nodded at Beatriz, ''Except for her.''

The screams, the pleading, the curses with Flattery's name on them silenced in the few moments it took the captain to walk her to the hatchway. It seemed that she walked forever, because there were the bodies of her crew to step over, and her legs were so uncharacteristically unsteady.

"Now see what you have done," Brood said to her. He squeezed her upper arm and shook her. "See what a mess your broadcast has made."

She couldn't speak or she would cry, and she didn't want to cry for him. She slapped away his touch when he took her arm to steady her. The last body she had to step over to reach the hatchway was the makeup girl's.

*What was her name?* Beatriz felt a new panic rise. *I can't blank out her name . . . !*

It was Nephertiti, yes, Nephertiti. Someone pretty and dark-skinned, like herself, with wide eyes. She told herself to remember this, to remember it and to see that somehow, sometime the world would know.

"You're a cool one," the captain told her. "You probably saw worse than this at Mesa two years back."

She stopped in the hatchway and turned, still not speaking.

"I saw you there, too," he said. "I saw both you and your boyfriend bounced ass over teakettle when that mine blew up your rig. Thought you both bought it."

She nodded, started to say, "So did we," but nothing came out of her throat but a croak.

For the first time she noticed his name, stitched above the Vashon Security insignia at his left breast: "Brood." Her only wish right now was that she would live long enough to see Captain Brood die.

He turned back to the studio and its seventeen dead warm bodies. Beatriz looked once again at herself on the monitor. The tape replayed an interview with Dwarf MacIntosh, Kelpmaster of Current Control. He was one of the few humans, other than Flattery, to survive the opening of the hyb tanks twenty-five years ago. He was so tall she'd had to stand on a box to do the interview. She had met him on her first flight to the new orbital complex, the day after her last night with Ben. Within a month she was sure that she was in love.

"Bag 'em up," the captain told his men. "Squeegee this place down, seal it off, then get all their production shit aboard."

He bowed to her then, opened the hatch for her and said, "We're expecting the replacements for your crew any minute. They are my men, and will do as they're told. My squad and I will travel along, to see that you do, too."

*The mind at ease is a dead mind.*

—Dwarf MacIntosh, Kelpmaster, Current Control

Dwarf MacIntosh floated in the turretlike chamber of Current Control and surveyed the planet below for the birth of a certain squall at sea. It happened at about this time every day that a swirl of clouds materialized over Pandora's largest wild kelp bed. It was some comfort now to see this squall forming; it told him that something was normal today even though the behavior of the kelp was completely loco. Today, humans didn't make much sense to him, either.

"The Turret," as he called it, was a plasma-glass extravagance of materials and workmanship that MacIntosh had fabricated for himself before installing Current Control in the orbital station.

*I'd have taken the job anyway,* Mack admitted, but only to himself. "Kelpmaster" wasn't so much a job to him as it was a privilege. He couldn't have allowed any of Flattery's goons such an easy throttlehold on the kelp. Besides, he felt much more comfortable in orbit than he did on Pandora's surface.

Like Flattery, Mack had been cloned, raised and trained in the sterility of Moonbase, in the hyperregimentation and clonophobia of Moonbase. His whole life, until hybernation, had been spent orbiting an Earth that, for him and for all clones, never existed. In those days, Flattery had openly pined for a life Earthside, but even then Dwarf MacIntosh looked outward, past Earth's measly system to the possibilities beyond.

From his turret Mack observed and charted many of these possibilities. He named them, but not the few special names he saved for his unborn children. He had spent the past two years above Pandora, refusing the usual R&R rotations groundside. In that time MacIntosh had not recognized a single star that would lead them Earthward. He liked it that way.

Dwarf MacIntosh awoke from hybernation on Pandora one day in indescribable pain and found himself in the middle of nowhere, galactically speaking. In spite of the planet's horrors he was in his own heaven among a trillion brand-new stars. The other survivors clung to that little wretch of a planet and most of them died there. Alyssa Marsh . . . well, she died, too. She died the day Moonbase started imprinting her for backup OMC.

Mack and Flattery shared a dream of driving further into the void. Mack felt it a pity, in a way, since he had never liked Flattery, even during training with him back at Moonbase. Their differences had come out lately over management of the kelp.

*If Flattery had any idea of what we've done, of what the kelp is . . .*

"Dr. MacIntosh, shuttle's set for launch."

Mack handed himself out of the turret and with one foot-thrust sailed across the huge control room to his personal console. Spud Soleus, his first assistant, busied himself at the primary terminal.

A glance at the number six display told Mack that the kelp in the SLS sector was performing as directed. The number eight display was a different story, however. The great kelp bed down-coast of Victoria was still a writhing tangle. No telling how many freighters were lost in there. He punched up another batch of coffee.

"What's the delay?"

Spud shrugged his skinny shoulders, keeping to his console.

"They said something about replacements for the news crew.

You know Flattery, can't do anything without crowing to the press.''

"Who's been replaced?" he asked. He felt his heart jump a bit. He'd been hoping . . . no, *planning* to see Beatriz Tatoosh again. He'd thought about Beatriz Tatoosh daily from the moment her shuttle left nearly two months ago. His dreams took up where his thoughts left off, and he had dreamed up the hope that she could make a permanent base aboard the Orbiter.

"Don't know," Spud said. "Don't know why, either. Everything was cool just a while ago for Newsbreak. Did you see it?"

MacIntosh shook his head.

"Yeah, you were in your turret. The Tatoosh woman did the show, said something about Ben Ozette missing. That must throw their staffing off or something."

"Yeah," Mack said, "he's a little goody-goody for me, but he means well. He's sure been on the Director's tail lately."

Dwarf could see Spud's frown reflected in one of the dead screens.

"It's not a good idea to get on the Director's tail," Spud said. "Not good at all. If you didn't see the Newsbreak, then you didn't see yourself, either."

"Me? What . . . ?"

"That show they did when you first installed this station," Spud said. "They reran it. Your hair wasn't as gray two years ago. I wish that Beatriz Tatoosh would look at me the way she looked at you."

"Stow it!" MacIntosh said.

Soleus's shoulders sagged slightly, but he kept at his keyboard in silence.

"Sorry," MacIntosh said.

"Inappropriate," Spud replied.

"Want me to take it now?"

"I wish somebody would. What the hell's happening to our kelp?"

"It's not *our* kelp," MacIntosh reminded him. "The kelp is its own . . . self. We're keeping it in chains. It's doing what any enslaved being with dignity does—it's fighting the chains."

"But Flattery's men will just prune it back, or worse yet they'll stump the whole stand."

"Not forever. There is a basic problem with slavery. The master is enslaved by the slave."

"C'mon, Dr. Mack . . ."

MacIntosh laughed.

"It's true," he said. "Look at history, that's easy enough. And Flattery, of all people, should know better. We clones were the slaves of our age. First-generation clones had it *real* tough. They were grown as organ farms for the donors. They *needed* us, but they needed us to do what we were told. Now he's enslaved the kelp, stunted its reason, because he needs it to do what it's told. He can't keep cutting it back, because he can't afford the regrowth time."

"So, what'll happen?"

"A showdown," MacIntosh said. "And if Flattery's still groundside when it comes he'd better hope that the kelp needs *him* for something or I wouldn't give you two bits for his chances."

"Two bits of what?"

MacIntosh laughed again, a big bark of a laugh to match his size.

"I wouldn't want to guess how old that expression is," he said. "When I was at Moonbase, two bits was a quarter, which was a quarter of a dollar, which was the currency we used. But it started way before that."

"We'd say, 'I wouldn't give a dasher turd for his chances.'"

"That's probably a better assessment."

MacIntosh pointed at the six red lights blinking on their messenger console. "Whose calls are we not taking?"

"The Director," Spud said, and swiveled his chair from the console board. "He wants us to do something about the kelp in sector eight, as though we weren't trying."

"Do something . . . hah! If we push any harder we'll fry our board, *and* that kelp, *and* anybody inside it."

"I wonder what it is that the kelp wants?"

"What if we gave it its head?" MacIntosh mused. "That would be one way to find out. What could it do that it hasn't already done?"

Spud shrugged, and said, "You've got my vote. How you going to convince the Director?"

A glance at the display showed the entire stand of kelp to be twisting itself into a vortex, like the whirlpool in a drain. As near as MacIntosh could tell, Current Control was at its maximum limit of restraint.

Spud pointed at the display.

"There's a focus of electrical override here. Whatever's bugging the kelp is right *there*."

"Electrical or mechanical?"

"Could be either, or both—it's a heavy traffic area," Spud said. "Something down there is definitely irritating the kelp."

"Yes," MacIntosh agreed, "that's my thought. The electrical override is coming from the kelp itself. It must be responding to something. That stand's not mature enough to think for itself. Or, at least, it shouldn't be."

"Doc?"

"Yeah?"

MacIntosh watched the console review the kelp's configuration changes over the past half-hour. Something nagged at him, something that would explain the kelp's sudden . . . *behavior*.

"I've extrapolated the path of the override."

MacIntosh looked at Spud, who was busy at his own console, and saw a very thin, very pale assistant. Spud's pointing finger trembled with excitement.

"What is it?"

"It's a spiral, headed into the middle of sector eight."

"That means the one kelp bed is delivering something to its neighbor—isn't that what it looks like to you?"

"Or the neighbor is snatching it away."

"Spud, I'll bet you're right."

MacIntosh stepped up to the console and tapped out a sequence with his two huge index fingers. The red lights on the messenger panel went black.

"We just had a relay malfunction," MacIntosh said, and winked at Spud. "Next time Flattery calls, tell him it was a hardwire failure and you worked it out personally. Maybe you'll get a promotion. If I've guessed wrong, my job will be up for grabs. Now, we might as well let go the reins on this kelp and see where the hell it runs."

MacIntosh heard Spud swallow behind him and he smiled.

"What's the big deal, Spud? It's a *plant,* it's not going anywhere."

"Well . . . well, it's just that Flattery doesn't trust anybody—it'd be like him to have some kind of booby-trap . . ."

"He did," MacIntosh said, "and this stand got itself blown apart a few years back. But he hasn't reset charges here yet—the kelp's not supposed to get this frisky this soon." He waited for the burst line to charge.

"There!" he said, and pressed the *send* signal. "Now let's sit back and see what cooks. Something bizarre is inside there, and I'd like to be the first to know what it is. If we can't *do* anything with this stand, maybe we can at least *learn* from it. Besides," he winked again, "Flattery's down there, we're not."

A beeping signal from his console interrupted him. He opened the intercom to Launch Command.

"We sling our bird your way in five minutes," the voice said. "Any contraindications?"

"Negative," MacIntosh replied. "Currents at your site are stable, weather will arrive your location in approximately one hour."

"Roger that, Current Control. Launch is a go for . . . four minutes."

*Canon in D*

—Pachelbel


The Immensity recoiled with a *snap* from the shock of freedom, then let its tendrils and fronds drift in their tingling bliss. It had been a long time since this union of stands had felt good, and never had it felt this good. The submarine trains foundering among its vines were inconsequential now.

A pulse went out among the fronds, a ripple throughout the Immensity from the tiny foil adrift at its outer reaches. A mass of tentacles cradled the foil and delighted in the scent of *self* that it gave from its brittle skin.

The little craft was slippery and the Immensity knew it to be extremely fragile, so it was gently tumbled frond to frond inward. Other scents mingled with that of the One. One of these scents was familiar, provocative, kelplike. The Holomaster, Rico LaPush, was in the company of someone that the kelp had encountered before . . . before . . . well, no matter. It would find out soon enough.

The Immensity had learned to sniff out the holo language of

humans from their spectrum of odd scents. It decided, early upon awakening this time, that it would have to speak with humans to live. It also concluded that it would have to speak the holo language if it wanted to speak with humans.

The foil tried to wriggle out of the kelp's net. There was much pain now through the vines, where all of the trains trapped in sector eight were trying to burn, cut, slash their way toward their precious atmosphere topside. Some of these the kelp crushed reflexively, but when the death scents of the crews mingled with the sea it forced itself to calm and to reason.

*Death,* it reminded itself, *is not the answer to life.*

The Immensity managed to open several kelpways and marveled at the easy ballet of subs heading topside. Only the bright white Holovision foil suffered the grip of the Immensity. It strained its engines trying to flee, but never lashed out at its tormentor. This the Immensity would expect of the One, who was civilized in the arms of kelp, and of the honorable associates of Holomaster Rico LaPush.

*In conscience you find the structure, the form of consciousness, the beauty.*

> —Kerro Panille, "Translations from the Avata," *The Histories*

Beatriz listened to the launch crew director count down the final minute over the speaker. Her shaky fingers chattered the metal clips as she snugged up her harness. She tried to think of the straps around her as Mack's arms and she tried to imagine they held her as Ben's did the night they drove old Vashon down. It didn't work. Nothing could erase the sight of her crew, slaughtered like sebet in a pen.

*For a mistake*, she thought. *They all died because that bastard made a mistake.*

She knew that the captain was afraid, she could smell it on him before he gave the final order at the studio. He obviously didn't know whether Flattery would promote him or execute him for his decision. Beatriz knew that her life, perhaps many other lives, teetered in this balance.

"Ten seconds to launch."

She inhaled a long, slow breath through her mouth and let it sigh out her nostrils. This was a relaxation technique that Rico had taught her when they all nearly drowned five years ago.

"Five, four . . ."

She took a little breath.

". . . one . . ."

The compressed-air "boot" punched them up the launch tube and a pair of Atkinson Rams slung them toward orbit. This was the part of the ride she hated—it reminded her of the time the fat girl sat on her chest when she was just starting school, and she didn't like the feel of her face flattening out against the strain. On this launch, however, she wasn't worried about wrinkles, engine failure, being trapped in orbit. She was worried about the captain, and how she could help convince him of the necessity of keeping her alive.

No one in the shuttle cabin looked familiar. Most of them had changed out of their fatigues and into civilian clothes. They were quiet; Beatriz thought that they must be weighing the consequences of the shootings. She didn't see the man who started it. That was the man she feared even more than the captain—Ben had always said that the jumpy ones get you killed.

*How could he be so right and be so far away from me?*

She rubbed her tired face and patted her cheeks to keep hysteria at bay. She needed information, and a lot of it.

*Mack,* she thought. *He'll help me, I'm sure.*

For an instant her fear included him. After all, he was an original crew member like Flattery. They had worked together long before waking from hibernation on Pandora.

*What if . . . what if . . . ?*

She shook off her fears. If her imagination had to run away with her, she preferred that it ally her with Mack instead of against him. Mack was not at all like Flattery, this she knew. Even Mack had cringed at the news when Flattery converted Alyssa Marsh to an Organic Mental Core.

"I never believed we needed such a thing," he'd told her privately. "Now, with the kelp research, I'm even more convinced that OMCs were just another built-in frustration, a goad to push us even further from humanity."

According to reports—Flattery's reports—Marsh had been found *in extremis* after an accident in the kelp. He explained to her how clones were property, often merely living stores for spare parts, and how Alyssa Marsh had been prepared for this moment from her girlhood. Now Beatriz realized how fortuitous the timing had been for Flattery, how unfortunate for Marsh and her kelp studies with Dwarf MacIntosh.

*What will Mack do?*

He would need information, too. Like, how many in this squad? What kinds of weapons? Do they have a plan or is this just reaction to the killings groundside? She couldn't remember how many people worked the orbiter station—two thousand? Three? And how much security did they have aloft?

*Not much,* she remembered. *Just a handful to handle fights and petty theft among the workers.*

She'd counted thirty-two in the captain's squad as they boarded the shuttle, and each was heavily armed. Eight of them were assigned to fill out her crew, and they grumbled under the double load. This bunch carried a lot of the old, disfiguring mutations. The gear they'd loaded aboard was mostly weapons, but a few of them knew enough about holo broadcast to bring the bare bones of what they'd need to get Newsbreak on the air. A couple of techs were assigned to oversee the OMC.

Beatriz had kept the worst of the shakes at bay and now, strapped firmly into her couch, she nearly let herself go.

*No,* she warned herself, *hold tight. I can't help anyone dead. I am the only witness against them.*

She hoped that the console tape survived back there, and that someone sympathetic would find it.

*Who would they show it to that could do anything?* she wondered. *Flattery?*

Beatriz grunted a laugh at herself, then felt the captain's grip on her shoulder. It was firm, not painful. It was not gentle. It reminded her of her father's grip the night he died, and it lightened the same when their engines shut down. This man was the same age as her youngest brother, but there was infinity in his dark eyes. She didn't see much wisdom.

"I know what you're thinking," he said. "I have taken hundreds of prisoners, I have been a prisoner. Believe me, I know what you're thinking."

He gestured the guard beside her away and, surprisingly clumsy in zero-gee, moved up to join her. His voice sounded gravelly, strained, as though it had been screaming. He continued speaking, while his men drifted out of earshot, their glances furtive and their conversations spare.

"We are both in a bad spot, you and I. We both need out of it."

She had to agree.

"Up here it will be all or nothing, we are trapped. There is no escape for either one of us that doesn't require both of us."

To this, too, she had to agree.

*But only for the moment*, she assured herself, *only until I find Mack.*

Beatriz realized that, much as it disgusted her, her life depended on communicating with this man.

"You are a military man, an officer. How is it that you walk yourself out the plank like this? You wouldn't have done it on reflex. This is a plan and we . . . I simply fall into it . . ."

"My God, you're perceptive," the words came in a rush, the captain's eyes aglitter. "We can only win, Flattery is finished. We have the Voidship and Orbiter—enough food stores for years. We control their currents and weather. We have Flattery's precious Organic Mental Core—shit, we can hook it up to the ship ourselves and *fly* out of here . . ."

She didn't hear the rest. Her mind focused on what he'd said at the beginning: "enough food stores for years."

*If he kills everyone aboard the Orbiter.*

". . . He'll *have* to throw it in," the captain was saying. "The rabble will have at him down there, and he doesn't dare destroy everything that he's worked for up here. Whoever beats him on the ground then can deal with *me*."

*He's really going to do this*, she thought. *He's going to kill everyone aboard.*

He took her hand and she snapped it back with a revulsion that she couldn't hide.

"*Us*," he said. "I meant they can deal with *us*. You and me. They'll believe whatever you tell them, at least for a while." He leaned closer, whispered, "You don't want to make another mistake, get more people killed."

She propelled herself out of her couch, not caring where the thrust might throw her in the gravity-free cabin. No one pursued her. The first handhold she grabbed stopped her beside a pair of security, younger than the young captain, who were reviewing the basics of holo camera triangulation.

*They really intend to go on the air*, she thought.

She looked back at the captain. He had his back to her, briefing several men. The tone of his voice, briskness of his gestures told her that he meant business. It was true, he could do it without her. It was true, that by helping him she might save others. She could not bring herself to speak to him, to go to him in any way. She sighed, and interrupted her two new cameramen.

"No," she said, "with that setup the alpha set only gets fifteen degrees of pan. OK if you're covering a launch, but we'll be inside, in a small space . . ."

As she instructed the two young amateurs she saw Brood watching her. He winked at her once, and she successfully suppressed the shudder that tempted her spine.

"They'll want to see this Organic Mental Core in transport, and they'll want to know something about its—*her*—background. Let's start by getting some of that in the can."

She passed the two-hour flight instructing her camera operators, two men and a woman, none of whom she recognized from the massacre at the SLS studio. Beatriz preferred their company, even if they did answer to the captain. Whether by accident or design, she did not encounter any of that squad during their flight.

The Organic Mental Core was a living brain, enclosed in an intricate plasma-glass container that made allowances for the hookups to come. A complex plug would connect the brain with the control system aboard the Voidship. What she didn't expect horrified her the most.

*They're supported by . . . bodies!*

She had done a report on such a thing several years ago. Scientists had connected a brain from a crushed body to a healthy body that had suffered a massive head injury. Each kept the other alive, though there had been no way to communicate with the healthy brain. At that time it was simply trapped in there, cut off from all sensation, alive and dreaming. She took a deep breath and let the reporter in her take over.

The medtech in charge had a number of active facial tics and each of her questions seemed to accelerate them. She learned nothing about the principle that she hadn't already learned through research or through Dwarf MacIntosh.

". . . As you well know, it was because of a failure in the OMCs that we wound up on Pandora."

"I understand that the OMCs were traditionally taken from infants with fatal birth defects. This OMC is from an adult human. How will the performance differ?"

"Twofold," the tech replied. "First, this person was dying at the time of conversion, therefore it—she—should be thankful for an extension of her life in a useful, indeed noble, role. Second, this person survived the longest hybernation known to humankind and woke to life on Pandora. She knows that if humans are to survive, it must be elsewhere. She can take comfort in being the instrument of that survival.''

"Does she know any of this?"

The tech looked perplexed.

"Much of this was included in her early training. The rest we extrapolate from the evidence.''

"What was she like as a person?"

"What do you mean?"

The tech's tics accelerated rapidly to a very distracting crescendo.

"You're saying, essentially, that she will accept this duty because of love for humanity. Did she have love in her life? A man? Children?"

Her camera crew was warming to the task. They had not brought a monitor into the tiny space, and now she wished they had. It might be an OK piece, after all.

While staring at this brain behind glass, Beatriz knew that it was alive, a *person.* She also realized that the tech was surrounded by the squad that had murdered her crew and he probably hadn't the slightest inkling of what had happened.

*No one will know if I don't tell them,* Beatriz thought. *I'm like this brain, cut off but alive inside. I wonder what she dreams?*

"I know very little about the person," he said. "It's in the record. I do know that she had a child that was given up for adoption so that she could continue her studies in the kelp outposts.''

"Dr. MacIntosh stated two years ago that Organic Mental Cores were crude, cruel, inefficient and unnecessary,'' she said. "Do you have a comment on that?"

The tech cleared his throat.

"I respect Dr. MacIntosh. He, along with the Director and this OMC, is one of the last survivors of the original flight of the old *Earthling*—'Ship,' if you prefer. Yes, it's true that there were failures, and this required some compensation, but those bugs have been worked out.''

"For some of our viewers, your term 'compensation' might seem a little cold. The 'compensation' you refer to was the first known creation of an artificial intelligence—one that turned out to be smarter than its creators, one that many believe is the personality 'Ship,' one that most Pandorans still revere as a god. Why did your department pursue the failed course of OMCs, severed living brains, rather than pick up on the artificial intelligence?''

"We were instructed to take this course."

"You were *ordered* to take this course," she corrected. "Why? Why is the Director more comfortable with failure than with the success that saved his life . . . and hers?''

Beatriz pointed to the OMC, wired into her box, deaf, blind and dumb beside her warm, dead host.

"That's enough!"

The captain's voice behind her froze her spine and started her hands trembling. She was stunned silent again while the tech and her crew inspected the deck and their shoes.

"I'll speak with you in the cabin."

She followed him out of the shuttle storage lockers and into the dimly lit passenger cabin.

"I had to stop you," he said. "It is expected of me, no matter what my opinion. Soon there will be no need for deception. Prepare for docking. There will be briefing materials for the next Newsbreak when we get aboard.''

Three Orbiter security lounged at the docking bay as the hatch opened from the shuttle. They were ready for the press, for the Holovision cameras, but they weren't ready for Captain Brood. The captain remained inside the hatchway, with Beatriz beside him.

"Three men out there," he said to her in a gentle voice. His eyes held her with that same wild glitter. She tried not to look at his face. "Choose one for yourself. One to . . . entertain yourself.''

She was stunned at the question and his calm, disarming manner. She felt a something rise at the back of her neck, something that she'd felt tingling there before the killing started groundside.

"You want none of them?" he answered for her. "How fickle.''

He pulled her aside and signaled the men behind them to fire. In seconds nearly a quarter of the Orbiter's token security force lay dead on the deck.

"Dispose of them through the shuttle airlock," he told his men. "If you kill one in a room, kill all in the room. I don't want to see any bodies. Beatriz will announce that there is a revolt in progress aboard the Orbiter and the Voidship. We've been sent to stop it.''

"Why do you do this to me?" Beatriz hissed. "Why do you tell me I have a choice when I don't? You were going to kill them anyway, but you have to include *me* . . ."

He waved his hand, a dismissal gesture that she'd long associated with Flattery.

"A diversion," he said. "Part of a game . . . but see, you are stronger for it already. It amuses me, and it strengthens you."

"It's *torture* to me," she said. "I don't want to get stronger. I don't want people to die."

"Everybody dies," he said, motioning his men aboard. "What a waste when they don't die for someone's convenience."

*Anyone who becomes master of a city accustomed to freedom and does not destroy it may expect to be destroyed by it.*

—Machiavelli, *The Prince*

Spider Nevi's favorite color was green, he found it peaceful. He jockeyed Flattery's private foil across the green-tinged seas and allowed the plush command couch to soothe the tension out of his back and shoulders. Green was the color of new-growth kelp, and tens of thousands of square kilometers of it stretched out around them as far as the eye could see.

Some sunny days Nevi spun a foil out of moorage just to drift a kelp bed, enjoying the smell of salt water and iodine, the calm of all that green. He didn't like red, it reminded him of work and always seemed so *angry*. The interior of Flattery's foil was finished in red, upholstered in red. The coffee cup that Zentz handed him was also red.

"What's so special about this Tatoosh woman," Zentz gurgled, "the Director got the hots for her?"

Nevi ignored the question, partly because he wasn't listening, partly because he didn't care. He was about to have his first sip of coffee for the day when the Navcom warning light flicked on. He

almost didn't notice it because the light, like everything else, was
red. An abrasive warning tone blatted from the console and he
started, spilling hot coffee into the lap of his jumpsuit. He doubted
that he would have missed that tone if he were comatose. Their
foil slowed automatically with the warning.

"Go ahead," he told Zentz, "let's hear it."

Zentz turned up the volume on the Navcom system. Nevi
couldn't stand the radio chatter while he was trying to relax, so
he'd had Zentz shut it down when they hit open water.

". . . you are approaching a 'no entry' area. Sector eight is
disrupted, kelpways not secure. Code your destination and alter-
nate routes will appear on your screen. Be prepared to take on
survivors. Repeat—warning, 'code red,' you are . . ."

Nevi took the foil down off its step and kept the engines idling.

"Fools!" Nevi muttered. "They were warned to keep her away
from the kelp."

"Do you think they're in there? Maybe they made it through
before . . ." Zentz cut himself off when he saw the anger in
Nevi's eyes.

"Get a display up," Nevi ordered, "I want to get a look at this
'disruption.'"

He coded in the private carrier code for Flattery's quarters. The
waters around the foil had already gone from choppy to rough,
and in the offshore distance Nevi could make out portions of a
large sub train bobbing the surface.

"Yes?" It was a female voice, curt.

"Nevi here, get me the Director."

The display that Zentz had been working on spread across their
screen. It reminded Nevi of a weather picture of a hurricane—
everything on the outside swirling toward the center. But this was
kelp, not clouds, and it was happening undersea, almost within
sight of their point. He was not happy with the delay from Flattery's office.

The woman's voice came back as curt as the first time.

"The Director is busy, Mr. Nevi, we are in full alert here.
Someone blew up one of the outer offices, a security detachment
has attacked the Kalaloch power plant and there is some problem
with the kelp in sector eight . . ."

"I'm *in* sector eight right now," he said, his voice as even as he
could make it. "If he can't talk, get me a direct line to Current
Control."

"Current Control has been incommunicado for nearly an

hour," she said. "We are attempting to find out the meaning of—"

"I'll keep this frequency open," Nevi snapped. "Get him on the air *now!*"

Her only response was to close the circuit. Nevi pinched the bridge of his nose for a moment, staving off one of his headaches.

"You should've kept her on," Zentz said. "What did she mean, 'A security detachment has *attacked* the Kalaloch power plant'? We *defend* the Kalaloch power plant."

"We need to figure out where the Galli woman is and we need to get our hands on her fast," Nevi interrupted. "She's our bargaining chip no matter what's going on." He tapped their Navcom screen with a well-manicured finger and traced the spiral pathway that wound from edge to center.

"I'm guessing she's in there somewhere," he mused, "and anything in there is heading for the center. There isn't time to bring in any hardware. We'll have to chase them down or intercept."

"You mean . . . follow them in there?" Zentz asked. "What about the attack on the power plant? Something's coming down in the ranks and my men—"

"Your *men* seem to be undecided about their loyalties," Nevi said. "They can work that out among themselves. But I'll put you out here and radio for a pickup if you'd prefer."

Zentz's massive face paled, then flushed.

"I'm no coward," he said, puffing himself up. "There's just something going down at the Preserve, where I . . ."

Flattery's carrier frequency sounded its tone and his voice crackled in their speakers.

"Mr. Nevi, we're having some urgent problems here that need our full attention. What do you want?"

"I want a direct line to Current Control. The kelp out here is going berserk, and if you want the Galli woman we need to straighten it out or knock it down."

"I'm monitoring their actions," Flattery said. "They've applied full power to that sector and the subs have all surfaced. Things here are getting sticky. A bomb went off in my outer quarters about a half hour ago. Killed my staff girl, Rachel, and that guard, Ellison. Looks like *he* brought the damned thing inside. Mop up out there as soon as you can and get back here. We may go Code Brutus on this one. Our Chief of Security has some answering to do."

The connection was broken at Flattery's end.

*Code Brutus,* Nevi thought. *So, it's starting already. At least out here, right now, we don't have to choose sides.*

He had no doubt which side Zentz would ally with. For Zentz, a return to Flattery meant sure execution. Too many errors, too little strategy.

*Maybe he's already in on it,* he thought.

Zentz was on the radio to his command center at the Preserve, chewing out some major. If this was a coup from the security side, he didn't believe Zentz was in on it.

Nevi kept his attention on the screen, where the kelp configuration didn't seem to change.

*Would it be worth it, going in after them?*

He thought it probably would. The different factions of Pandora only needed a symbol to bring them together, and Nevi knew Crista Galli was ready-made for the job. Better his hands on her than Shadowbox. Besides, he'd maneuvered around troublesome kelp in the past and never had problems that he couldn't handle. And if a coup did come down, Nevi could be seen as *rescuing* Crista Galli, along with the very popular Ozette. That would get the media on his side.

*Either way; that LaPush has to go,* he thought. *That one's been too much trouble for too damned long.*

Nevi didn't want to be the one to rule Pandora, if that was what all of this came to. He was happy being the shadow, being the arranger of possibilities. His distaste for Flattery and his style grew more unbearable by the year, but he had no desire for the hot seat himself.

*Code Brutus,* he thought. *A coup attempt from within.*

Nevi didn't think that Zentz was capable of carrying off a coup, though he had to admit that he was in the middle of the perfect alibi—at sea with the Director's highest-ranking assistant, a known and effective assassin.

Zentz was finished chewing out the major in charge of the power plant and the configuration of the kelp on the monitor hadn't changed a bit. Nevi checked his fuel reserves: all four tanks full. He pressurized the fuel, retracted the hydrofoils and extended the airfoil.

"We're going back?" Zentz asked. His voice sounded eager, but not greedy.

''No,'' Nevi said, and smiled. ''We're going to pinpoint them from the air, then go in. We have enough fuel for almost an hour.''

After an hour they'd be forced to set down on the water to extract more hydrogen, but Nevi planned to have everything that he needed aboard by then.

*The highest function of love is that it makes the loved one a unique and irreplaceable being.*

—T. Robbins, from *A Literary Encyclopedia of the Atomic Age*

Beatriz was hustled through the passageway and locked inside the Orbiter's makeshift Holovision studio with three techs from Brood's crew. None of the three had been at the launch site killings, but none of them had much to say to her, either. A large portable screen behind her hid the wet lights and mirrors that cluttered all six studio bulkheads. The same Holovision logo she wore at the left breast of her jacket emblazoned the screen: it was an eye, bidimensional, but the pupil was a holo stage.

Beatriz loved weather and had never liked the claustrophobic world inside the studios. That was why she and Ben had worked so well together and, in spite of offers, spent so many years in the field. Her recent promotion carried a lot of studio work, and her contract guaranteed a room with a view—on paper. She missed the sense of drifting she'd had, growing up an Islander.

Aboard the Orbiter she was assigned a cubby rimside, more than a kilometer from the studio near the axis. From her cubby she watched Pandora wake and sleep above her bed. Her father, a fisherman, would be taking his midafternoon break right now. Inside the studio there was no time of day, no night.

Her instructions from Brood were simple and cold: "Relax, we'll do the work. You just read what's in front of you when the red light goes on."

A small security camera mounted high on the bulkhead kept track of her every move. It was a toy, a trinket compared to the personalized cameras and triangulators that her team used at the launch site. Holovision's equipment got worse every year. She missed her own gear.

*They were the best,* she thought. *And maybe that last tape is still inside.*

She wondered whether Brood's men had picked them up.

*Rico made those sets,* she thought, *and those triangulators, too. Nobody who knew cameras could pass those up.*

She felt her first rush of real hope. The cameras weren't down at the launch site at all.

*They're here,* she thought, *or at least they're in orbit with us.*

She didn't want to think about the tapes. For now, she wanted only to focus on the cameras.

She couldn't help wondering what they'd do with the tapes.

*Keep them, as backup. Record over them when their other tapes are full.*

She doubted that whatever this team planned would involve a whole lot of tape. But the techs had brought them along, her logic assured her of that.

*They might still be on the shuttle.*

She didn't want to go back to that hatchway, where Brood's men had shot those guards down.

Beatriz glanced up at the surveillance camera.

*Is it a person behind that thing,* she wondered, *or tape?*

She didn't think they'd waste the tape. The techs ignored her altogether. They worked quickly at several editing and sound stations, coordinating something among themselves. She suspected it had something to do with her.

*Maybe there's no one behind it.*

The three-hour light flashed. Three o'clock in the afternoon marked the start of the assembly of the six-clock news. Getting the tapes was only one problem. Inserting them into a Holovision Nightly News broadcast with Brood's men watching posed another problem. She knew who could help her with the second problem, and it was the one person she most wanted to see.

*Mack could get a message groundside, coded to the right frequency and digitally encoded.*

She knew, because he'd done it once for her at Ben's request.

*He was teaching me,* she realized. *Ben must've thought something like this might happen.*

Most Pandorans were too hungry to fight, she knew that. Thousands already slept in holes dug in the talus under torn plastic vulnerable to demons and the weather. From her family she learned that fighting was only one way.

She remembered something her grandfather had told her, something she'd told Dwarf MacIntosh last time: "Educate, agitate, organize."

Flattery had organized the world. Now Beatriz wanted to use that organization against him.

Communication would do it. People had their bodies. Coordination of all those bodies would be the key to their freedom.

*How to get away with it?*

Maybe she couldn't get away with it. What kind of message would she deliver then?

*It might save Ben and Rico, too,* she thought, though in a part of her somewhere they were already beginning to disappear. She tried to make her shocked and exhausted mind think through all that had happened in the past twenty-four hours, all that there was to go.

*I've got to get to Mack,* she thought. *That is, if Brood hasn't . . . hasn't . . .*

She wouldn't allow herself to complete the thought. She concentrated on what she had to work with. This small studio aboard the Orbiter had been her project all along, her excuse to stay close to the stars. It was a little larger than the one at launch site. Flattery had had it installed to be sure that the Voidship project received the best documentation, the best publicity, the world's complete attention. She knew now what its primary purpose had been all along—diversion, something to keep people looking up while Flattery stole their boots.

The studio was divided into six engineering units and the one live set where Beatriz worked. Quarters were very cramped. Six editing screens and a couple of very large clocks kept them in touch with the world. A constant barrage of images rolled across the six screens as the editorial team groundside reviewed the day's film from the field and made their selections. There was a small holo stage in the center of the room for final mock-up and a large viewscreen behind it. Both the clocks and the growl in her belly told her things she didn't want to know.

"Three hours to air time," she said.

Her console indicated she was speaking into a dead microphone.

She raised her voice. "We're five hours behind schedule."

No answer. The techs worked as though she were a piece of furniture. They relayed tapes of their own groundside for editing and placement.

Beatriz rolled her tape of the Organic Mental Core up one of the screens and suppressed a shudder. This was a *person*, a living, thinking brain, kept alive by attachment to a comatose host. She wondered what it was that caused the coma. She was certain that she knew *who*.

"I need to talk with Dr. MacIntosh," she said.

This was not the first time she'd said it, and the response was always the same—silence. She'd received the silent treatment from the techs since docking aboard the Orbiter. From the occasional glances in her direction she surmised this to be orders from Brood, rather than choice.

Unlike counterparts of old, this OMC would be able to talk, using neuroelectrical pickups. When the time came it could communicate with the neuromusculature of the ship, feel everything that transpired aboard. This, Flattery reasoned, would keep the OMC sane where the original OMCs had failed.

It was clear to Beatriz that Flattery didn't want to face the kind of artificial consciousness that had brought humankind to Pandora. There were those who believed that Ship still existed, and would return. The hyb tanks that had brought Flattery, Mack and Alyssa Marsh were evidence to Beatriz that Ship could be very much alive, God or not.

*If I can get one of these techs to start talking, that would be a wedge against Brood,* she thought. *And it might be a way to Mack.*

Current Control and MacIntosh were only a few meters down the passageway. Beatriz could practically feel the vibrations from his throaty speech, his huge body bashing about his offices. Current Control and the Holovision remote studio shared a few kilometers of cable between them, but no hatchway. Both areas were soundproofed.

Beatriz tried to remember what Mack had taught her about their hookups. He'd spent a lot of time orienting her during her trips aloft. What came to her were his philosophies and musings, the relaxing tone of his deep voice. She remembered nothing of the linkup between the two rooms. She had already tried a few electronic tricks of her own to contact him, but with no luck.

*He knows I'm due,* she thought. *Maybe he'll come looking for me.*

She hoped that it wouldn't mean walking into his own execution.

*Manipulating the kelp electronically is like making a marionette out of a quadriplegic. The trick becomes keeping it a quadriplegic.*

—Raja Flattery,
  from "Current Control from the Skies,"
  Holovision feature

Crista felt a pressure on her whole being. It was not like the pressurized cabin, like *air* pressure. It was some indescribable containment of her *self* inside some huge envelope—like the pressure she imagined the positive pole of a magnet might feel when in the company of another positive pole.

"You don't have to be afraid of the kelp pulling this thing apart," she said. "Flattery's lab reports say it kept me alive underwater for twenty years. It can keep us alive . . ."

"*Can* is the operative word here," Ben said.

He didn't look her in the eye, but hung his head over her restraints as if staring at them would right the foil and set them on their way. "If what you say is true, it wants *you* alive. The rest of us are compost."

"The kelp's not like that," she said. "You've been listening to Rico. It's . . . I knew it before Flattery's people cut it back, remember? It kept me alive, for all we know it kept others alive the same way."

156

"Lots of people spend lots of time down under," he muttered. "Nobody's seen anything like what happened to you."

"Why just me?"

When Ben's gaze did meet Crista's, goosebumps clustered her forearms. Everything that she knew about his kindness, his sacrifices for others, froze inside her with the chill of that look.

"I've wondered that," he said. "Others have wondered, too."

"That's why Flattery never let me get to the sea," she said. "He said it was to protect me, but I think he was just suspicious that I'm some kind of Avatan spy, a trigger of some sort. Maybe I was raised by a plant, but I can read people fairly well. Let me . . . touch the kelp. It will calm down, then, I know it will."

"Not a chance. If Flattery's right, if Operations is right, your chemistry is different now. It could kill you. I don't want anything to kill you."

"I don't want anything to kill anybody," she said, "but the kelp is confused. It's just lashing out . . . nobody *tells* it anything . . ."

With that the foil pitched upside-down. Ben hung on tight to a handhold, his face pressed into the plasteel bulkhead.

Crista tried to speak, upside-down and against the pressure of her restraints.

"Avata needs our help," she said, "and we need Avata. You have to help me do this, Ben."

There was that strange, stunning *snap* in the air, the same *snap* that had stilled a mob for moments at the pier. It was like the discharge of some great capacitor.

Crista felt their foil slowly roll, pull her tighter into her restraints, then right itself. She watched Ben drop his hands from his ears and sit up on the deck, shaking his head. The damaged foil moaned and chattered about them like mechanical teeth, but the fist of the kelp was gone.

Crista saw the flicker of the intercom charging, then heard Rico's tight voice:

"Ben, look at the kelp."

Only one of the starboard lights still probed the dark, so the view that Crista and Ben had from the galley's plaz was gray and black, dreamlike, cold. They hadn't dared activate the kelp's luciferase, it would make tracking too easy.

A fine seawater spray wetted them both as they watched the easy dance of deepwater kelp. This was the same kelp that, moments ago, quivered with a tension so strong she thought it might uproot itself.

Crista, herself, felt a relief that was more than just calm after the storm. It was a release, like the elation she had felt at the start of their journey when she slipped skyward, hitching her consciousness to the hylighter.

"Can't really see very well," Ben said. "Look at the size of those vines! Some of them are a half-dozen meters across and we can't even see bottom yet."

"That should tell you something," she said. "It should give you an idea of what the kelp's really like."

"What do you mean?"

"You said it yourself. Some of those stalks are nearly as thick as this foil is wide. For the kelp it must've been something like handling a squawk egg with pliers to keep from crushing us."

"Maybe so," Ben muttered. "We're headed topside and the kelp's apparently floating free. We'd better see what kind of damage we took before it changes its mind."

Lights dimmed in the galley, brightened and dimmed again.

"Elvira can't get the engines to fire," Ben said. "That's going to make a lot of things tough—including our oxygen production."

The gray hulks of kelp floated dreamlike outside their hull while the chunks of torn fronds and sediment ripped up by its struggle settled around them.

"See?" she said. "The kelp means us no harm. If you would let me . . ."

"We're all staying put!" Ben said. "The kelp simply stopped. Maybe it got whatever it wanted, maybe that wasn't us. No point in looking for more trouble." He nodded toward the spray that had already soaked both of them and started pooling water across the galley deck. "We've got a few details to clean up. Let's get at it."

Crista tugged at her harness.

"I can't do much until you get me out of this."

"Any damage back there?" Rico asked over the intercom.

"I think we popped a cooling pipe," Ben said. "It's not much of a leak now that we're surfacing. What do you have?"

"We're not terminal, but we're hurt. Elvira says 'topside,' so topside we go. You two OK?"

"We got a little wet," he said, stamping his feet in the gathering pool.

At that they both laughed—something she did not do often,

something she'd discovered with him before. He opened a panel in the bulkhead beside her and reached inside.

Water plastered his hair to his head. Crista's felt just as flat, but when she saw herself reflected back in the plaz, a laugh still teasing her face, she liked what she saw. Her crop of wet white hair framed the green flash of her eyes. She saw that she had twisted in her harness, which explained why, now that things had quieted down, her right breast stung so badly. She wriggled herself free and tugged her clothes straight.

"There's a shutoff in here, somewhere," Ben muttered. He poked his head inside and bumped it. Whatever he said was unintelligible.

Crista's gaze fell on the holostrips of the Nightly News field crew, strips that covered the whole interior bulkhead of the galley. Shots of Beatriz, Rico, Ben and a half-dozen bearded strangers were interspersed with location stills of Ben and Rico, Ben and Beatriz—several of Ben and Beatriz. Crista didn't see Elvira up there.

"Beatriz is beautiful," she said, raising her voice so he could hear.

"Very."

"You look happy together," she said.

"Yes," he answered, also raising his voice so she could hear.

Then she heard a curse and a thump and the water stopped spraying. Ben came out of the access cabinet and wiped his face with the least damp spot on his shirt. His green eyes looked right into her own.

"When we were together, we were happy," he said. He did not turn to look at the pictures. "More often than not, we were on opposite sides of the world. Lately she's been up there." His thumb indicated the general direction of the Orbiter overhead.

"Do you wish . . . otherwise?"

"No," he sighed. "It's as it should be. I have things to do here."

*Things to do!* Crista thought. What she wanted him to say was, "It's as it should be. Now I've met you." But he didn't say that.

An odd feeling came over her, a dizziness and a weakness in the knees, a tingling in her temples. Like it had been with the hylighter, like her dreams.

A year ago Crista had begun dreaming dreams that came true. At first, they came only in the night. She knew they weren't dreams, but she despaired of calling them "visions." Lately, they came all the time, and inside the last one she forgot to breathe. Crista was sure they came from the kelp, and they were getting more intense.

She had . . . *feelings*, that she'd always explained as "dreaming somebody else's dreams." It was something she now knew came from the kelp.

Today, now, she saw two things: She saw Rico in a green singlesuit, and that suit was the fruit on a great vine of kelp. In the distance beyond him she saw a stand of kelp with a human growing from each great vine, looking like a seascape of bowsprits with interesting carvings, or like bait.

The kelp grew a membrane, clear and gogglelike, about their eyes. It seemed a part of them, like fingernails, but never needed trimming. Their lungs would never want for air, their skimpy bones would soon forget land.

The second vision pulled away from the first and showed her the kelp from a tremendous height. One kelp vine snaked skyward and a cold light, like luciferase, touched its tip. The vine, the kelp bed, the planet itself began to glow. In the light below she watched the kelp writhe for a blink, then convolute itself into what appeared to be an immense, glowing brain. She felt a sense of easy grace that only came to her now in dreams.

Just as suddenly, the visions vanished. Crista was a dreamer, but these were not dreams. She was sure the kelp had a message for her.

*I've got to get out there.*

She stared into the picture of Ben and Beatriz, stared into Ben's eyes and concentrated on slowing her heart rate, slowing her breathing . . .

"I'm glad you're here, Ben," she said. "I'm glad it's as it should be with Beatriz. If all is well among us we can bring Flattery down. The kelp knows this, maybe Flattery knows it, too. Inside the kelp, I can find out what all this is. The kelp is vulnerable now, as we are vulnerable. It is stunned, not dead. Help me out there, I can make the difference."

"No," he said. "You're not going out there. We'll all stay aboard the foil. Once we're ashore we can get to an Oracle, or the beach."

"We don't have that much time," she said. "I don't know how I know it, but right now I could—*become* Avata, be the consciousness, the command center, the *conscience* of the kelp. Show me the way out."

"You don't know that," he said. "Your chemistry is different, you told me so yourself. Maybe it would keep you alive out there. Maybe it would keep you dead. Just wait a few—"

"We can't wait," she pleaded.

She sighed, rubbed her eyes and went on. "I think he's been using the kelp to gather data. I was blown up while they were doing it. Now he's found out what he wanted to know and he's heading offplanet at breakneck speed."

When she looked up she could see that he wanted to believe her. It had been the same way last night, when she saw that he wanted to kiss her. She just *knew*. As she *knew* there was something catastrophic imminent, and Flattery knew what it was, and Flattery was fleeing as fast as he could with as much as he could.

"Stay put," Ben said. His voice was softer, as softened as everything was now that the beating had stopped. He tousled her wet hair.

"Flattery isn't getting away today, so let's get out of this fix first. Give Rico and Elvira a chance to work their magic on the foil."

She could tell that he was convincing himself. He was afraid. She knew a little something about fear. The day she had been blown free of the kelp had been a day much like this. This time, she was headed in the right direction. It was quartertide in the afternoon and they were fewer than a dozen meters from daylight.

*Short-term expedients always fail in the long term.*

—Dwarf MacIntosh

Beatriz had taped here for the first time during the ceremonies that had welcomed Current Control's move aboard the Orbiter two years ago. She had received a tour on the arm of the mysterious Dr. MacIntosh, a dizzying tour that changed her life and included her first attempt to navigate in near-zero gravity.

Now a few of the captain's men held her incommunicado while the rest did what soldiers throughout history had done to secure a garrison among an unarmed and isolated populace. None of them moved comfortably in low gravity. Since her only contacts were with Brood's men, smuggling messages to Mack seemed out of the question.

*What if they kill him, too?* she wondered.

Mack was a very compassionate man, but one who immersed himself in his work and didn't often pay attention to the ways of the world more than 150 kilometers below them. It struck her, too, that that had been her own problem. Ben had seen it and tried to help.

*I know Ben's alive,* she thought, *I feel it.*

She hoped that Mack was alive, too. Partly because he was someone she genuinely liked, partly because she was sure that all of their fates depended on him.

*Brood needs him, too,* she thought. *He'll use me as his bargaining chip.*

The hatch slammed open and Yuri Brood sailed through. He rebounded into a safety webwork that was set up to catch rookies and keep damages minimal. Brood pointed to the bank of editing screens as he settled into the seat beside her.

"You think that because my men are warriors they can't do your show," he said. He was out of breath but seemed in good humor. "Well, we greenhorns have something to show you. The Director had us shoot this just before we left for the launch site. Leon turned in the rough copy on his way to the shuttle."

She tried not to watch the screens, which displayed clips that Brood's three techs had shot of the damage at Kalaloch. As each rolled up on a screen, a text of tentative script flashed across the console in front of her. There was no fighting apparent in any of their tapes. It only took her a glance to tell what he was up to.

"You're trying to make this look like a hylighter disaster," she said. "You can't get away with it—somebody else from Holovision must've been on the scene . . . word of mouth alone . . ."

She stopped when she saw his sneer. It was an expression that reminded her immediately of Flattery. Brood had the same narrow nose, dark, upraked brows, the same manner of tilting his head back to look down his nose at everyone.

Though he had been flushed and slightly out of breath when he came in, Brood seemed in no hurry now. He watched her eyes constantly, and this made her very nervous.

"You might have noticed how many new faces there are among the field crews these days," he said. "Quite a few new faces around the studios, too."

He smiled, and the smile chilled her.

"Are you saying that *all* of the crews have been . . . replaced?"

"Lots of people looking for work these days," he said, "people willing to do the necessary thing to get the job done."

"Our *job* is reporting the news, telling the truth—"

His laugh cut her off.

"*Your* job *was* reporting the news, telling the truth," he said.

"*Our* job is keeping order, and if distorting the truth a little helps keep order, then that's what I'll do. People are happier this way."

"People are *dead* this way, and you will have to keep killing them . . ."

"Watch this section," he ordered, and snapped his fingers at Leon, "they're sure to use it tonight. Isn't it a lot better view of the world than what you think you saw?"

Her console read:

"Lead: Kalaloch residents flee their homes in the aftermath of a hylighter explosion that split the settlement in two."

Scene, screen one: rescue of elderly woman from smoldering rubble of a habitat, a housing project: "OK darlin', you hold on now, OK?"

Voiceover: "Today Vashon Security Forces rescued this elderly woman from the char that was smoldering around her cubby. Death toll has exceeded one thousand. Authorities are now estimating more than fifteen thousand people to be homeless tonight, many of them seriously injured."

Scene, screen two: rescue crew in security uniforms alongside residents, rebuilding wall at the Preserve. Animals rounded up in background.

Voiceover: "Meanwhile thousands of animals are milling between the Preserve, where the explosion freed them, and the firestorm that laid waste to the edge of the village. Authorities here are anticipating return of most, if not all, of the Preserve's prize livestock, which includes the only breeding pair of llamas in existence."

Scene, screen three: heart of all the tenements, the habitats, that are still burning.

Voiceover: "In parts of Kalaloch the fires still burn, as they have for more than five hours. Much of the public market is destroyed, more than a hundred looters were reported shot in the first hours after the blast. A warehouse containing 70 percent of the sector's rice and dry beans will burn for days, according to fire officials. Most of this year's storage has been destroyed by flames, smoke or water. Disastrous food shortages are expected."

"But . . . but that's not even *close* to true!" Beatriz hissed. Her outrage broke the fear barrier. "Flattery has all that stuff buried in storage bins all over the Preserve."

"Shh," Brood said, still smiling. He placed a finger to his lips and nodded toward the screens.

Beatriz hated that smile, and she vowed to find a way to erase it.

Leon, the only journeyman tech of the three, frowned and cleared his throat. Even with Brood there, he wouldn't talk to her. He simply pointed at screen four.

Scene, screen four: the harbor, boats on fire at moorage and in the bay. Ferry terminal littered with bodies, most in bags, which the camera panned quickly, from a height.

Voiceover: "Authorities estimate that as many as five hundred commuters perished from the concussion as they changed shifts on the docks today. No ferries suffered any permanent damage and all are operating on schedule from the repair docks."

Scene, screen five: two crying women with commuter tags, holding their ears and comforting one another. Smoke and masts in the background.

Text: "Something hit our ears, and there was that blast from those *things* . . . I don't know what happened to us. They're all dead . . ."

Voiceover: "Mrs. Gratzer and her neighbor claim that at least two class-four hylighters, attracted by fires in nearby refugee camps, exploded and destroyed several square miles of eastern Kalaloch. Dick Leach has lost three icehouses full of seafood."

Text: "All of our income for this year has been taken away from us, and all the bills that it took to produce that crop are still here."

Voiceover: "They will be eligible for low-interest Merman Mercantile loans."

Text: "If it comes to a loan we're going to have to probably pull out. We need a grant."

Scene, screen six: pullaway from the body bags laid out on Kalaloch pier.

Voiceover: "The ordeal seems to be over for these commuters, but the hardship's just beginning for tens of thousands of hungry, homeless families in the Kalaloch district."

All screens cut to black, then her console read: "Accepted for final edit, elapsed time to follow."

*So, Brood was right all along,* she thought. *They're going to run it.*

Beatriz didn't feel particularly afraid anymore, just tired and incredibly sad.

"I need to see Dr. MacIntosh," she said. "I was assigned a

story on the OMC and the installation of the Bangasser drive, and I intend to do it."

"Dr. MacIntosh has his hands full right now," Brood said. "There's a crisis in Current Control, a priority crisis. He knows you're here."

"Then let me go to Current Control."

"No," he laughed, "no, I don't think so. He will come here when the time is right."

"What about the rest of them, the people here?"

"So far they suspect nothing. We have been very quiet, very selective. When shifts change, rations are left uneaten, then there will be talk. That will be hours from now, and we will be finished here."

"Then what?"

He answered with his smile and a half-salute.

"I will check back to see how you're doing. Go ahead with your piece on the OMC. Leon, good job. You know what to do."

Then he was gone as quickly as he came.

"What is it you're supposed to do, Leon?" she asked.

He didn't answer, and he didn't smile. He was lean and dark, like Brood, and she thought he might even be a relative.

Leon handed himself to one of the editing consoles and sat with his back to her. He was still for a moment, then he said, "We're putting a story together on Crista Galli. And one on Ben Ozette."

Beatriz felt herself go cold.

"And what's the lead?"

Her voice stuck in her throat, barely a whisper.

"Crista Galli safely in the hands of Vashon Security Force."

"And Ben . . . what about him?"

Leon was silent for a few more blinks. He typed something into his console and it came up on her own:

"Holovision reporter killed in hylighter blast."

She tried to still the trembling in her hands and her lips.

"It's a lie," she said. "Like the rest, it's a lie. Isn't it? *Isn't it?*"

Without turning, without apparently moving a muscle, Leon spoke so quietly she barely heard.

"I don't know."

*The gods do not limit men. Men limit men.*

—T. Robbins, *A Literary Encyclopedia of the Atomic Age*

"Dr. Dwarf," Spud called from behind the Gridmaster, "you were right. There's another kelp frequency inside that sector—look here."

Dwarf MacIntosh glanced up from underneath one of the consoles that fed the Gridmaster. Though a big man, MacIntosh had always been adept at getting at problems in small places. In fact, he preferred crawling through tunnels of cables and switches to attending any of the so-called "recreational" events aboard the Orbiter.

He backed his way out of the shielding ducts and towered over Spud's shoulder to see what he had found.

"This signal came through when we released the kelp in sector eight," he said. "It's taken me a while to fix and amplify."

"I see the rest of the kelp is doing well," MacIntosh said. He reviewed the readouts flanking the kelp display. "It released at least twenty captured cargo trains, if our data here are correct."

Spud nodded. "They are. The kelp's just floating free. Most of

167

the vessels are on the surface, though, and the afternoon squall in that area's due right about now. There are no kelpways, no way of guiding them through. Unless we get a grid in there pretty soon, they'll just get fouled in all that slop."

"This is a very small focus," MacIntosh murmured.

His stare at the screen seemed intense enough to propel him right into the middle of the kelp itself. He pulled himself up to height and tapped a thin lip with his forefinger.

"Without tapping into that other signal, we won't be able to enforce a grid. I'm sure of it. What's the history?"

Spud spun the graphic yarn on Mack's screen.

"It moves," Spud said.

"Yeah." MacIntosh nodded. "Runs the kelpways like a pro. And it's something the kelp would gnaw a limb off for, don't forget that."

"So what do you think? Merman transplants being routed?"

"Signals too strong," MacIntosh said. "A stand doesn't register with us unless it's achieved some kind of integrity, whether Flattery cuts it back or not. This is like having a whole stand of kelp in a spot no bigger than you or I . . . ."

"And it can move."

"And it can move."

Mack stroked his chin in thought.

"It can persuade the kelp to resist our strongest signals, even with the threat of being pruned back to stumps. The dataflow tells us that the signal's been getting stronger by the hour. Flattery's been frantic about this in spite of riots at his hatchway. What does all this tell us?"

Spud frowned at the screen in imitation of Mack and tried stroking his chin, too, for answers.

"There's somebody running the kelpways, acting like a stand of kelp?"

MacIntosh whooped, grabbed Spud by the shoulders and gave him a shake. They both spun high against the upper bulkhead. The startled assistant's eyes opened nearly as wide as his mouth.

"That's it!" MacIntosh laughed. "What we've got disrupting the kelp grid in sector eight is a person pretending to be a stand of kelp!"

He dropped his grip on Spud and stuck his head back into the electronic and neuroelectronic guts of the Gridmaster.

"But who?" Spud asked.

"If you can't guess, you're better off not knowing right now."

MacIntosh's resonant voice was barely audible over the clicks and whirrs of the Gridmaster as it held the other stands of domestic kelp in functional stasis.

"More than anything right now we need a communications expert." He backed out of the crawl space and added, with a sparkle in both eyes, "That would be Beatriz Tatoosh. Notify her that we require her services, if you would."

Spud smiled a wide smile.

"'Services,'" he said, "that's one way of—"

MacIntosh cut him off.

"Stow it," Mack ordered, smiling his own wide smile. "Just get her in here, pronto."

*Men are moved by two principal things—by love and by fear. Consequently, they are commanded as well by someone who wins their affection as by someone who arouses their fear. Indeed, in most instances the one who arouses their fear gains more of a following and is more readily obeyed than the one who wins their affection.*

—Machiavelli, *The Discourses*

The fuel warning buzzer sounded its piercing screech above his console, and Spider Nevi cursed under his breath. They were very close now, *very* close, but he didn't dare take chances on making contact with dry fuel tanks.

"We're going to have to set down in that muck," he said. "Make sure both screens and filters are intact. I don't want kelp clogging our inlets."

They'd seen several cargo train survivors on the surface, working to clear their intakes. They all moved in the slow-motion, dreamlike manner of those who are under the influence of one of the kelp's toxins. Surface travel on Pandora's seas was dangerous enough with the kelpways intact. Like great veins, the kelpways helped clear the waters of the storm-damaged fragments of fronds and other troublesome debris.

Zentz grunted an acknowledgment, then paled.

"But—but I'll have to go out there after we set down," he said. "That kelp is—it's *crazy*. With only two of us . . ."

"With only two of us, one of us has to go out there. It's your fault we're out here at all, so you get the duty."

The look on Zentz's face was the one that Nevi wanted to see: fear. Not fear of the kelp, or fear of the sea, but fear of Spider Nevi. The expression of fear represented power to him, a raw power that even Flattery didn't wield among the people. Flattery maintained the politician's mask, and such a mask implied hope to anyone who witnessed it. Nevi projected no mask, no hope.

"If I go out there to clear those intakes, you will leave me." Nevi released upon Zentz one of his rare smiles.

"It pleases me that you have due respect for my—abilities," he said. "But I promised you a very special part in this drama, and your time has not come yet. I would not sacrifice you here for nothing. You know one thing about me if you know nothing else: I kill for something, not for nothing. I value human life, Mr. Zentz, this you must realize. I value it for what I can get out of it, what I can spend it on. The word 'value' implies 'commodity,' don't you think? The pleasure of killing ranks very low, in my book, as a good reason. Much as I might *like* to kill you just to get rid of a certain annoyance, I'm sure someone, somewhere would make it worth my while to wait for the right price, the right trade, the right favor. Understand?"

Zentz stared straight out the cabin plaz. He was pale, appeared slightly more bloated than usual, and his pasty fingers crawled nervously over each other's backs.

"Do you know why I kill?" Zentz asked him.

Nevi finished the final attitude adjustment and settled onto the slightly choppy sea in a spot that he judged to be relatively clear of the kelp debris. As they descended, he saw that there was no clear spot. The struggle in this stand of kelp must have been tremendous.

"Yes, I know why you kill," Nevi said. "Like any of the lower animals, you kill to eat. It is your job, and you see no farther than that. You kill by orders, to someone else's plan, because to not kill means you yourself die. That is a difference between the two of us. I think of myself as a sculptor, a societal sculptor. The populace is my stone, and I shape it chip by chip into a form that suits me. The stone keeps growing, and my task is a relentless one. But I have time."

In a flurry at his keyboard Nevi set the foil up for seawater intake and hydrogen conversion. The intakes clogged within blinks. Even with Zentz out there to clear them, this would take longer than Nevi felt they could afford. He checked the fuel gauge.

*Fifteen minutes,* he thought, *maybe twenty at the outside. Shit!*

"Forget the intakes," Nevi said. "There's a wild stand just northwest of here. We'll set up there to take on fuel, then I'll see what I can learn from the Director," he said. "Don't worry. Leaving you to the kelp would be a waste, and I'm not a wasteful man."

The convolutions of Zentz's brow unwrinkled somewhat. He lifted his sullen bulk out of his couch and donned a dive suit.

"Just in case," Zentz said, "I'm ready. I've heard about wild kelp. People disappear out here, and the kelp doesn't *have* a reason."

Nevi throttled up and lifted them off. Much as Zentz disgusted him, Nevi intended to keep him alive until the time came when it simply wasn't handy to do that anymore.

The run to the blue sector took only ten minutes, and all the time they were heading into the afternoon squall. A black wall pushed across the sea toward them, though when they set down in the blue kelp's lagoon they were haloed in the magnificent afternoon sun.

Nevi deployed the intakes, but a warning light on his console told him they were still clogged. He tried retracting and redeploying them, but they stayed clogged.

"Better get out there after all," Nevi said. "And step on it. That squall's moving in pretty fast."

Zentz grumbled something, but trudged aft without complaining. Nevi noted from the console display that Zentz left the aft hatch open. He chuckled to himself.

*He thinks he'll sink me if I submerge, and blow out the flight controls if I take off.*

Nevi knew ways around both of those situations, the simplest being to go aft and close the hatch. He was tempted to do that now, just to give Zentz a thrill, but decided against it. They'd be refueled in fifteen or twenty minutes and with luck would lift off ahead of the storm.

Nevi set out a call for Flattery on their private frequency, and received an immediate reply.

"Mr. Nevi," Flattery said, "time is wasting. Do you have them yet?"

Nevi was surprised at the clarity of the reception. Indeed, the clarity of reception was unlike any that he'd experienced over the years. The activity of Pandora's two suns interfered constantly with transmissions, and lately sabotage of transmitters by the vermin made things even worse. The kelp itself often garbled radio communication, but this time it seemed to embellish it.

"No," he said, "we don't have them. We're refueling before the final push. I thought we were to make the most of this, get as many of the rebels as possible."

"Forget it," Flattery said. "I want Crista Galli *now*. She's not to talk with anyone before she sees me, understand?"

"Right," Nevi said, "I—"

"Tonight's news is carrying notice of Ben Ozette's death. He's not to be seen, but I want him for my own. Do what you want with that LaPush bastard."

"Do you need support back there?"

"No," Flattery said. He sounded distracted. "No, I've taken care of it. We've called some security back from the Island docking sites and from demon patrols. These bastards . . . there are so *many* of them. They've looted the public market and its warehouse is dry. We must've shot three hundred of them, but they kept on coming. I've given orders to blow up any warehouses that are in danger of being looted. When they see their precious food blasted all over the landscape, they'll think twice about this kind of thing. You stick to your job, I'll handle things here. Don't call me again unless you have them."

Nevi was left listening to static and to the whine of the pumps processing out their hydrogen. He reached to break the connection, but hesitated. There was a pattern to the static, something he hadn't noticed before. It seemed as if there was a music in the background, and voices from several conversations that he couldn't quite pick out. Over and over, faint in the distance, he could hear the rhythmic repetition of Flattery's voice saying, "Mr. Nevi, Mr. Nevi, Mr. Nevi . . ."

He closed the circuit and stared out over the sea toward the black curtain of storm. The surface chop had increased and a wind had come up that was blowing the foil out of the center of the lagoon and closer to the inner edge of blue kelp. He glanced at the fuel readout and was relieved that they were nearly full. What worried him was the distinct repetition of his name that continued, chantlike, even though he'd shut off the radio.

The fuel light indicated full, so he shut down the pumps and sounded a warning klaxon to Zentz before he retracted the intakes.

He felt them *thump* into the bay, but still there was no sign of Zentz.

*This was clear water,* Nevi thought. *He should've been back aboard after clearing the intakes once.*

He sounded the klaxon again, twice, but heard nothing. The aft hatch light remained on. Nevi secured the console and started back toward the aft hatch. The chant got louder, more distinct, and behind it a babble of voices rose on the air. The hair on his arms rose, too, and Nevi armed his lasgun before leaving the cabin.

He felt a metallic taste on his tongue, a taste he'd heard others describe as fear. He spat once on the deck, but the insidious taste remained.

*Consciousness manifests itself indubitably in man and therefore, glimpsed in this one flash of light, it reveals itself as having a cosmic extension and consequently as being aureoled by limitless prolongations in space and time.*

—Pierre Teilhard de Chardin, *Hymn of the Universe*

The Immensity smelled trouble on the waters, a great disturbance from one of the coastal stands. It had been a struggle, the debris told that tale. Currents had changed suddenly, bringing the strange scents of fear and, just as suddenly, bliss. So far, the currents hadn't changed back.

The little whiff of death that the Immensity caught on the current was human, not kelp.

*Perhaps the pruner has become pruned,* it thought.

It stretched its outermost fronds coastward, but still could not contact the neighboring stand. Only fragments of messages drifted in on bits of torn fronds. These were shards, frames, pieces of recordings—not the Oneness that the Immensity sought, not this "talk" that humans enjoyed and withheld from others.

Then came the humans. They set into the Immensity from above, like hylighters reversing their lives, and with them they brought splinters of dreams from the stand next door.

Yes, Her Holiness was among the kelp again at last. Her pres-

ence suddenly freed the neighboring stand of prisoner kelp, a
stand that had lost her to Flattery's butchery five cycles back.

*Who are these others, now, come to my stand?*

Few humans fished outside their gridwork. The few organic
islands left to risk a float on Pandora's seas likewise stayed to the
more merciful currents of the grid. The Immensity had spared
fishermen, scouts, humans fleeing humans, and it had spared entire island-cities more than once. The human in charge of humans
had not shown the Immensity equal compassion.

Though humans often called them "willy-nillys," the islands
floated now in predictable patterns. Current Control, the enslaver
of the kelp, insured this. But the volcanics of the past twenty-five
cycles had conjured storms the like of which the Immensity had
never seen in its own time, and these storms brought islands into
its reach. It thought of the organic islands as Immensities of
Humans, and adjusted its own greatness to let them pass.

These humans came in their flying creature, dropping pieces of
kelp into the Immensity's lagoon. The Immensity unraveled a
long vine from the wall of the lagoon and sniffed the human. The
scents talked of fear and death, and to have the whole story the
Immensity would have to read this human's tissues bit by bit.

It waited until the human finished discharging the pieces of
kelp, so that the Immensity would know as much of its neighbor
as it could. It knew now, by scent and touch, that this was Oddie
Zentz human. As it gripped Oddie Zentz human at the waist and
pulled him into the walls of the lacuna, it knew that this human
had killed many humans, as many as a storm and perhaps more.

The Immensity had spent most of its awakened time trying to
communicate with other kelp, to merge with other, smaller stands.
More kelp was better, it thought. Closer was better. It failed to
understand creatures that killed their own kind. These were, indeed, diseased individuals. If they were merciless to their own,
they would certainly show no mercy to others. The Immensity
concluded that it should respond in kind.

*We Islanders understand current and flow. We understand that conditions and times change. To change, then, is normal.*

—Ward Keel, *The Notebooks*

Beatriz knew that it would not be in the captain's best interest to kill Mack, especially if there were links with other forces groundside. But she had also quit trying to guess what could be in Captain Brood's best interest. From what she could gather, Captain Brood was a man trying to capitalize on a bad decision, making more bad decisions to cover his tracks. He wouldn't last long at this rate, and he was the type who just might take everyone, and everything, with him.

She concentrated on the map she'd called up on the large studio display screen. It was a map of Pandora, rotatable, and at the touch of a key it highlighted populated areas, agriculture, fishing and mining. She could tell at a glance where the factories lay, both topside and undersea, and where the wretched communities lived that served them, for serve them they did.

Only today, with the murders of her crew and Ben's warnings ringing in her memory, did she realize how the people of Pandora, including herself, had become one with their chains. They were enslaved by hunger, and by the manipulation of hunger, which was a particular skill of the Director. He concentrated on food, transportation and propaganda. Before her, on Holovision's giant screen, she saw the geography of hunger spread out for her at a touch.

The largest single factory complex above or below the sea was Kalaloch, feeding the bottomless maw of Flattery's Project Voidship. It showed up on her display as a small, black bull's-eye in the center of amoebalike ripples of blue and yellow. Those ripples represented the settlement—the blue was Kalaloch proper, where all paths led to the ferry terminal or to The Line. People inside the blue lived in barrackslike tenements or in remnants of Islander bubbly stuck to the shore.

The yellow, a weak stain of sorts widening out from the blue, represented the local refugee population. Starving, unsheltered, too weak for heavy work, they were also too weak to rebel. The Director's staff rode among them daily, picking the lucky few who would be trucked to town to wash down the stone pavements, sort rock from dung in the Director's gardens, or pick through refuse for reusable materials. For this each was given a space in The Line and a few crumbs at one of a hundred food dispensaries that Flattery operated in the area. Even private markets were offshoots of the dispensaries—true black market vendors disappeared with chilling regularity.

The sphere of Kalaloch included the bay and its launch base, the factory strip, the village, Flattery's Preserve and the huddle of misshapen humanity that squeezed inside the perimeter for protection from Pandora's demons.

Outside this sphere Beatriz noted the similarities of other settlements along the coastline. These smaller dots also were ringed by the huddle of the poor, even agricultural settlements, fishing villages, the traditional sources of food. Security squads shot looters of fields, proprietors of illegal windowboxes and rooftop gardens. They shot the occasional fisherman bold enough to set an unlicensed line. All of this Ben had told her. She had seen evidence herself, and had chosen to disbelieve. Beatriz earned her food coupons fairly, ate well, felt guilty enough about the hunger around her to believe what Flattery had fed her about production meaning jobs and jobs feeding people.

For almost two years her assignments had covered jobs, the people who worked them and the people who gave them out. It had been a long time since she'd walked the muddy streets of hunger.

*There aren't any new jobs lately,* she thought, *but there sure are a lot fewer people.*

Now she was above it all, trapped and converted, with nothing to offer and everything to fear.

*Thou shalt give life for life, eye for eye, tooth for tooth, hand for hand, foot for foot, burning for burning, wound for wound, stripe for stripe.*

—Christian Book of the Dead

Boggs had been hungry all his twenty years, but today his hunger was different and he knew it. He woke up without pain in his bones from the ground underneath, and when he scratched his head a handful of hair came with it. This, he knew, was not hunger but the end of hunger. He looked around him at the still, wizened forms of his family huddled together under their rock ledge. Today he would get them food or die trying, because he knew he would do the dying anyway.

Boggs was born with the split lip, gaping nose slit and stump feet characteristic of his father's family. His six brothers shared these defects but only two still lived. His father, too, was dead. Like Boggs, they had known the enemy hunger from birth. His malformed mouth had made nursing a futile noise, so most of the sucking that he did as a newborn slobbered down his chin. His mother tried to salvage what she could with her fingers, slopping it back into the cleft of his mouth. He'd watched her do this countless times with his younger brothers.

A week ago he'd watched her try to nurse the starving ten-year-old when there wasn't even a bug to catch. She had been dry for two years, and his brother died clutching a handful of fallen orange hair. Boggs looked again at the fistful of orange hair in his hand, then weakly cast it away.

"I will take the line, Mother," he said, in the lilting Islander way. "I will bring us back a fine muree."

"You will not go." Her voice was dry, hoarse, and filled the tiny space they'd dug out under the ledge. "You are not licensed to fish. They will kill you, they will take the line."

His father had begged the local security detachment for a license. Everyone knew that many temporaries were issued every day, and that some could even pay with a share of the catch. But the Director issued a fixed number each day. "Conservation," he called it. "Otherwise the people will outfish the resource and no one will eat."

"Conservation," Boggs snorted to himself. He eyed the fish line wrapped around his mother's ankle. There were two bright hooks attached. There had been a fiber sack for bait but they'd eaten the sack weeks ago. There was just the ten meters of synthetic line, and the two metal hooks tucked inside the wrap.

Boggs crawled up beside his mother so that his face was even with hers. She had the wide-set eyesockets of her mother, and the same bulging blue eyes. Now a faint film obscured the blue. Boggs pulled at his hair again, and thrust the scraggly clump where she could see it.

"You know what this means," he said. The crawl, the effort at talk exhausted him but somehow he kept on. "I'm done for." He tugged at her hair and it, too, came out in a clump. "You are, too. Look here."

Her bleared eyes slowly tracked on the evidence that she didn't need, and she nodded.

"Take it," was all she said. She bent her knee up to her skinny chest and Boggs clumsily unwound the line from around her ankle.

He crawled out from under the ledge, and as far as he could see down to the shore others were crawling out of holes, out from under pieces of cloth and rubbish. Here and there a wisp of smoke dared to breach the air.

Boggs found his cane, propped himself upright and stumped his way slowly toward the water. He'd thought himself too skinny to sweat, but sweat poured out of him nonetheless. It was a cold sweat at first, but the effort of picking his way through the rubbish and the dying warmed him up.

A small jetty shouldered the oncoming tide. It was an amalgam of blasted rock, about twenty meters long and five or six meters wide. The quartertide change tossed a few breakers over the black rock, soaking the dozen licensed fishermen who hunched against the spray.

It took Boggs over a half-hour to make it the hundred meters from the ledge to the base of the jetty. His vision was failing, but he scanned the tidelands for signs of the security patrol.

"Demon patrol," he muttered.

Vashon security sent regular patrols through refugee areas. Their stated purpose was to protect the people against hooded dashers and, lately, the terrifying boils of nerve runners that raced up from the south. Boggs shuddered. He had seen a boil of runners attack a family last season, entering through their eyes to clutch their slimy eggs inside their skulls. He had thought the family too weak to scream, but he was wrong. It was not a pretty sight, and the patrol took their sweet time burning them out.

Everyone knew security's real reason for patrolling the beach. It was to keep the people from feeding themselves. The Director passed rumors of black market fishing harvests that he said threatened the economy of Pandora. Boggs hadn't seen sign of these harvests yet, nor had he seen any sign of an economy. His mother's tiny radio taught him the word, but to him it would always be just a word.

A pyre smoldered to his left. Three small lumps of char lay atop a ring of rock, slightly higher than high tide. The poor couldn't even muster enough fuel to burn their dead. When enough of them accumulated, the security patrols amused themselves by flaming them with gushguns. They called it nerve runner practice.

Someone guarded the pyre on the other side of the rocks, and when Boggs edged closer he could see that it was Silva. He stopped and caught his breath. Silva was a girl his own age, and the rumors said that she had killed her younger sisters and brother while they slept. No one raised a hand against her now as she tended their pitiful fire. Boggs hoped she wouldn't see him. He needed bait, but he knew he couldn't fight for it.

He got down on all fours and crawled to the edge of the heap. He reached a hand up, felt around the hot rocks until he touched something that didn't feel like rock. He jerked, jerked harder and something came off in his hand. It was hot and peeling on one side, cold on the other. He couldn't bring himself to look, he just grabbed his cane and scuttled away. Silva hadn't seen him.

"I'll bring her a fish," he promised himself. "I'll catch fish for mother and the boys, and one for Silva."

The quartertide patrol was nowhere to be seen.

*They've gone through already,* he thought. *They've gone through and checked the licenses and now they're up the beach checking for caches in the rocks.*

Boggs stood apart from the other fishermen. They might turn him in because he was catching fish that were rightfully theirs. They might steal his fish and line, and beat him as they had beaten his father once . . .

*. . . But they'll wait until I have the fish,* he thought. *That's what I'd do.*

He hunkered down against the jetty so that he was barely visible from the shore, tied a rock onto his line and baited the hooks from the charred mess he clasped in his fist.

"It's bait," he reminded himself, "it's just bait."

He didn't have enough energy to plunk his bait out very far, so he left it on the bottom about a half dozen meters from the rocks. It was deep there, deep enough to take most of his line. He gave a tug now and then to make sure it was free. There was enough bait for two, possibly three more tries.

"You got a license, boy?"

The gruff voice behind him startled him, but he was too weak to move. He didn't say anything.

"You're late getting out here if you got a license. You only get one day, can't afford to waste it."

Some rocks clacked together as the man stepped down to where Boggs sat wedged into a cleft. He was skinny and sallow, with a wisp of a beard on his chin and no hair on his head. The skin on the top of his head was peeling and sores dotted his face.

"I'm an illegal, too," the old man said. "Figured it was my last chance. You?"

"Same."

He reached across Boggs, fingered the bait and put it down with a grunt.

"Same's me."

The voice was lower than illegal, it was ashamed.

Suddenly Boggs's line went tight, then tighter, then it nearly jerked his arms out of their sockets.

"You got one, boy," the old man said. In his excitement, his voice rose and his cracked lips got wet. "You sure got one, boy. I'll help . . ."

"No!"

Boggs wrapped the line around his wrist and levered it in about a meter.

"No, it's mine!"

Whatever it was, it was big and strong enough that it didn't have to surface to fight. But Boggs kept making slow progress, levering the stubs of his feet against a boulder and putting his skinny back into the pull. He figured he had about two meters to go but he couldn't see anything for the black spots swimming across his eyes. He heard the old man grunt in surprise and scramble up the rocks behind him and when he had nothing left to pull with Boggs just lay there, wedged in the rock, the excess line tangled around both arms.

The water broke with a rush in front of him, and whatever he had hooked lunged for him and caught him by the ankles. The grip was firm, and human. It laughed.

"You caught a big one, boy!" it bellowed. "Can you show me your license?" Another laugh.

"Are you . . . are you . . . ?"

"Security?" the voice asked, pulling him closer to the water, cutting his skinny buttocks on the rock. "You bet your ass, boy. Let's see that license."

Hand over hand the security pulled Boggs closer. Face to face, Boggs could see the breathing device dangling from his dive suit and the black hair draining over his bulging forehead.

"You ain't got one, do you?" He picked Boggs up and gave him a shake. Every bone in his dried-up body rattled. "Do you?"

"No, no . . . I . . ."

"Stealing food from people's mouths? You think you have the right to decide who'll live and who'll die? Only the Director has that right. Well, fishbait, I'll show you where the big ones are."

With that the man stuck his mouthpiece between his lips, pinned the boy's arms against his chest and fell backward with him into the sea.

Boggs coughed once at the tickle of water in his nose, then choked as it exploded into his frail lungs. He saw nothing but light overhead where it fanned out from the surface, and the bubbles from his mouth where they joined it like a blossom to its stem.

*Kill therefore with the sword of wisdom the doubt born of ignorance that lies in your heart. Be one in self-harmony and arise, great warrior, arise.*

—from *Zavatan Conversations with the Avata,*
Queets Twisp, elder

A silent Twisp and muttering Mose gathered the spore-dust of the two fulfilled hylighters into their bags and trudged their loads to the high reaches. Twisp had spent little time with the monks lately but they were generally an unsuspicious lot who seemed accustomed to his comings and goings. Few of them knew of his work with the Shadows, though if others knew he was certain they still would not interfere.

The carnage below would not reach them, experience had taught him this. Twisp tossed back his mantle, tucked up his sleeves and enjoyed his foray into the sun. For these few hours, at least, he could put aside the messages and codes and other accoutrements of his secret life. Today he might be called on to make a decision or give an order that might change Pandora forever. Until that hour, he wanted to feel Pandora's sunlight and the feminine breezes of the high reaches.

He and Mose sweated in the spore-dust gathering, and sweat plastered the fine blue dust to their hot skins. The soul of Avata, bound up in the dust, leaked its way into his pores. Twisp's body picked its way up the trail, oblivious to the way his mind raced the kelpways of the past.

*He who controls the present controls the past,* a voice in his mind told him, *and he who controls the past controls the future.*

It was something he'd read in the histories, but he'd also heard it before from the invisible mouth of the kelp.

*Avata controls the past,* he thought. *It maps the voyage of our past, our genetic past, which helps us to plot a true course for our future.*

He watched his feet fall, one in front of the other, without the expense of thought. They stepped over sharp stones, sidestepped a flatwing, all without interference from what most people called the mind. It was as if he were a being watching another being, but from within.

*Cheap entertainment,* he thought, and smiled.

Mose hummed a tune behind him, one that Twisp did not recognize. He wondered where the young monk's mind voyaged, to bring him such a tune. He had too much respect for another man's reverie to ask him.

Each contact with the kelp or the spore-dust had taken Twisp deeper into the details of humanity and deeper into his own past. Yes, the loss of a love was painful and it seemed no less painful replayed. Most of these memories exhilarated him, like the one of nuzzling his mother's breast for the first time, the taste of the sweet milk and the coo of her voice over him, in the background the *swish-swoosh, swish-swoosh* of her Islander heart.

Twice the kelp had taken him further than that, into the past of his ancestors, into the void from which humanity itself had sprung. Twisp acquired something more than a history lesson on these voyages. He acquired wisdom, the insight of sages, a separateness from the worldly machinations of people like Flattery. This was why the Director eventually discouraged, then finally forbade the kelp ritual.

"Do you want your children to know your most secret thoughts, your desires, all those dreams you couldn't tell them?" he would ask.

This warned Twisp far more about Flattery's depth of paranoia than it did of the dangers of the kelp.

Flattery successfully discouraged most Pandorans, at least the ones dependent on his settlements and his handouts. His isolation of a kelp neurotoxin made the people even more cautious. His development of an antidote became popular, since contact with the kelp was virtually unavoidable in many traditional professions.

*It could've been a placebo,* Twisp thought. *What people expect the kelp to do to their minds is pretty much what occurs.*

The brief Pandoran ritual of giving their dead up to the kelp had been all but abandoned. Now the dead were burned, their memories dissipated with smoke to the winds. This Flattery encouraged with his simple plea for hygiene.

"Decomposing bodies wash up on the beaches," he said. "What little tideland we have stinks with the remains of our dead."

Twisp shook his head to clear it of Flattery, of the man's grating, nasal voice and supercilious manner. This was not the voyage he wished the dust to lead him down. He sought the deeper currents of history to address the problems of Flattery and hunger.

"Humans have enslaved humans for all time," he said to himself. "A new galaxy shouldn't require a new solution."

How had ancient humans broken the bonds of human-inflicted hunger?

*With death,* a voice in his mind told him. *Death freed the afflicted, or death freed them from the afflictor.*

Twisp wanted Pandorans to be better than that. Flattery's way was starvation, assassination, pitting cousin against cousin. The footprints Twisp sought in the dust must lead away from Flattery, not after him.

*What good does it do for me to become him? We trade a long-armed murderer for a tall one.*

By the time he and Mose lay their burdens down before the monks of the hylighter clan, Twisp felt no need for the ritual. He already swam the heady seas of kelp-memories. His mind waged a reluctant struggle against the babbling current.

His people around him babbled as they prepared the dust. Twisp made his mouth beg his leave and he perched atop his favorite outcrop alone. Behind him, other elders walked a line of kneeling Zavatans and spooned little heaps of blue dust onto outstretched tongues. They proceeded with waterdrums and chants, songs from Earth, from Ship, from their centuries of voyaging across Pandora and her seas.

This was where communicants met the dead, here in the aftermath of the blue dust. They traveled backward in time, raveling up memories that had been long forgotten. Some witnessed their parents' lives, or their grandparents'. A few, one or two, branched off into the greater memory of humanity itself, and these were the ones consulted for movement toward a rightness of being.

Twisp let the syncopated waterdrum lull him back to that first day he had felt the effects of the new kelp. Twenty-five years ago he first touched land, a prisoner of Gelaar Gallow. That was the day he and a few friends defeated Gallow's vicious guerrilla movement and ended a civil war. It was the day the hyb tanks splashed down from orbit and brought them Flattery.

It all happened atop a peak that the Pandorans now called Mount Avata, in honor of the kelp's role in their salvation. He had waited there for what he had expected to be his death at the hands of Gallow, the Merman guerrilla leader. The kelp brought him a vision then of a bearded carpenter named Noah. Noah was blind, and mistook Twisp for his grandson, Abimael. He fed the hungry Twisp a sweet cake, and down all the years since then Twisp had remembered the fine taste of that sticky-sweet cake.

"Go to the records and look up the histories," Noah told him.

Twisp had done just that, and it left him in awe of Noah, the kelp and that sunny day on the Mount.

"This new ark of ours is out on dry land once and for all," Noah told him. "We're going to leave the sea."

Twisp had avoided the kelp since then, thinking only that he needed to let the affairs of Pandora go to the Pandorans and the affairs of Twisp to Twisp. Then the Director insinuated himself into the lives of the people. Their lives became Twisp's life, their pain his pain.

Twisp had studied well, read widely in the histories, and like any Islander he brought the hungry into his home. That home grew as the hunger grew into two homes, three homes, a settlement. Differences with the Director drove them to their perch in the high reaches and to secretly make fertile the rocky plains upcoast, away from Flattery's henchmen. Now, in the grip of the spore-dust, Twisp saw the intricacy of what he'd wrought, and the strength.

A small voice came to him as the dust was distributed to others. It was a voice of the world of Noah, one that he had never expected to hear, even within his own mind.

"Fight hunger with food," it told him. "Fight darkness with light, illusion with illumination." It was a tiny voice, nearly a whisper.

"Abimael," he said. "You are here at last. How did you find me?"

"The scent of the sweet cake," Abimael said. "And the strong call of a good heart."

Twisp swept past Abimael in the headlong tumble down the kelpways of his mind. He was out of the fronds, now, out of the peripheral vines and into the mainstem of kelp.

*This hylighter must have come from a grandfather stand,* he thought. *It is a wonder that they still escape Flattery's shears.*

"It is not wonder, elder, but illusion."

The voice that Twisp heard was not from inside. He turned slowly, remembering the young Mose. It was then that he noticed Mose's hand on his arm.

"You travel this vine, too, my cousin?"

"I do."

At no time did Mose move his lips. His pupils dilated and constricted wildly, and Twisp knew that his own did likewise. He'd looked into a mirror once after taking the dust, and fallen into places he'd rather not remember.

"I remember them . . ." Mose began.

Twisp interrupted him, concentrating only on what Mose said of illusion. This interruption, too, was spoken without lips.

"You said, 'illusion,'" Twisp reminded him. "What has the kelp shown you of illusion?"

"It is a language this hylighter spoke when it grew on the vine," Mose said. "It learned to cast illusion like a hologram. Elder, if you follow the vine of this thought to its root, you will know the power of illusion."

Suddenly Twisp's mind cartwheeled deeper into itself.

*No,* he thought, *not deeper into my mind. Deeper into Avata's.*

"Yes, this way," a soft voice coaxed.

Twisp looked back on his body as though from a great height, incurious about the shell of himself, then he turned onward into the void.

*What is illusion, what is real?* he asked.

"What is a map," the voice replied. "Is it illusion, or is it real?"

*Both,* he thought. *It is both real—something that can be held and felt—and illusion, or symbol, or representation. The map is not the territory.*

"You, fisherman, if you want to build a boat, what do you do first?"

*Draw a plan,* he thought.

"And the plan is not the boat, but it is real. It is a real plan. What do you do next?"

Visions of all the boats he had built, or fished on, or coveted floated through his mind.

*Next . . .*

He tried to concentrate, tried to remember where it was that Avata was leading him.

"Don't think about that," the voice chided. "After the plan, what next?"

*Build a model,* he thought.

"It, too, is not the boat. It is a model. It is illusion, it is symbol, and it is real. If you would get a man to live a certain way, how might you do that?"

*Give him a model of behavior?*

"Perhaps."

*Map out his life?*

"Perhaps."

A moment of silence, and Twisp detected the distinct pulse of the sea in the pause. The voice went on.

"But a map, a model—these have a basic limitation. What is this limitation?"

Twisp felt his mind bursting at its seams. Avata was forcefeeding him something, something important. If he could only grasp . . .

*Size!*

Whether it came to him intuitively, or whether the kelp provided him with the answer, the effect was the same.

*It's size! You can never know truly from a model how it will feel because you can't live in it. You can't try it on for size!*

He felt an immense sigh inside himself.

"Exactly, friend Twisp. But if you could make the illusion life-size, the lesson, too, would be life-size, would it not?"

Suddenly he was thrust back in his spore-dust memory and saw the old Pandora through the eyes of one of his bloodied ancestors fighting the Clone Wars. He saw the immensity of Ship blacken out the sky, and heard that final message ring in his mind: "Surprise me, Holy Void." Ship's voice was not the electronic monotone he'd expected. Its voice was relieved, even gleeful, as it made its farewell pass across both suns and disappeared without a sound. It sounded much like the voice he'd been hearing inside his own head.

"Ship unburdened itself of us when it headed out for the Holy Void," Twisp whispered to himself. "To live to our fullest potential we have to learn how to unburden ourselves of ourselves."

One more thing nagged at the back of his mind. He didn't know whether he said it aloud or not, but he knew that Mose, at least, heard him out.

"We have to learn to cast illusion like a spell," Twisp heard himself say. "To capture an enemy without inflicting harm will take a carefully spun illusion."

Somewhere in his mind he thought he detected a grunt of approval.

*We Islanders understand current and flow. We under-
stand that conditions and times change. To change,
then, is normal.*

—Ward Keel, *The Apocryphal Notebooks*

Newsbreak should air within the hour, but Beatriz knew that this
team would not make their deadline. They were having some kind
of transmission problem that they refused to share with her, but
she saw the results on her screens. Whenever their tape was ready
for its burst groundside, a review showed that it had been tam-
pered with. Someone seemed to be editing the editors. It was just
as well. Leon told her that the short clip she prepared on the OMC
would not be transmitted groundside for approval, anyway.

She recalled an incident several years ago, when Current Control was still undersea in a Merman compound. They were taping
one of Flattery's "spiritual hours," a propagandistic little chat
with the people of Pandora. All went well until transmission time.

*The kelp interfered, that was the only answer at the time—and
an unpopular one. The kelp jammed broadcasts, made deletions
on tapes . . .*

The hair on her neck prickled at the thought. She remembered
how, finally, it edited tapes and changed the chronology of broad-

casts, flipped images and voiceover around to make Flattery look like a fool and make the broadcast adhere more closely to the truth.

*Mack and I wired a lot of kelp fiber into this system,* she thought.

Any delay suited Beatriz just fine. She needed more time to figure out how to say on the air what wasn't in the script without getting herself and others killed. They would only trust her with a token appearance, she would have to make the most of it when the time came. Most Pandorans, even the poor, listened in on radio. She wanted to reach them all. She hoped it wasn't just hysteria that told her the kelp was on her side.

*If there's a coup in progress, who's at the bottom of it?* she wondered.

She ticked off the likely suspects: any of several board members of Merman Mercantile, the Shadows, displaced Islanders, Brood—probably acting for someone else from Vashon Security Forces . . .

*Or maybe the Zavatans,* she thought, though she knew it was not their drift. Their response to political trouble was to dig in deeper, to flee further into the high reaches or the formidable upcoast regions.

*Brood's an opportunist,* she thought. *The killings at the launch site were a mistake, and he's trying to make the best of it. If there is an organized coup, he'll wait and throw in with whoever seems to be winning.*

Beatriz realized that Flattery had no friends and damned few allies. Everyone had good reason for hating him. He had come to Pandora sporting his savior's cap when the very planet had turned on them, and then *he* turned on them.

"I am your Chaplain/Psychiatrist," he'd told them, "I can restructure your world, and I can save you all. Your children deserve better than this."

*Why did everyone believe him?*

Her years at Holovision gave her the answer. He was on the air daily, either in person or via his "motivational series," a collection of tapes that she had not seen as propagandistic until now. She had even helped produce several, including her recent upbeat series on the Voidship. Everyone believed him because Flattery kept them too busy to do otherwise.

Flattery had become the most formidable demon in a world of demons, only he was human. Worse yet, he was *pure* human, without any of the kelp genes and other genetic tinkerings that Pandorans had to endure. Beatriz knew this now. He did it with their help, with *her* help. Though trapped, she felt an exhilaration at the notion that Brood's men couldn't shoot a clear signal groundside. They might need her yet.

*If I do this show as written, I'll be helping him again.*

She realized what it was she was helping Flattery to do. She wasn't helping him rescue a world in geological and social flux. She wasn't helping him resettle the homeless Islanders whose organic cities broke up on the rocks of the new continents, or rescue Mermen whose undersea settlements had broken like crackers at the recent buckling of the ocean floor.

*I'm helping him escape,* she thought. *He's not building this "Tin Egg" to explore the nearby stars. It's his personal lifeboat.*

She cursed under her breath and fisted the console in front of her, but gently, gently. She might need it later. The reflection that bounced back from her screen was of a woman she didn't recognize. The hair color was black, cropped and shaggy like her own, but the haunted brown eyes of her reflection stared out of bloodshot sclera, surrounded by two dark hollows that frightened her. Her nose was red and her complexion pasty for one so dark. Out of reflex she reached for a com-line to call Nephertiti to makeup, then stopped. Nephertiti would never brush her hair again, never again whisper in her ear at the countdown: "You're gorgeous, B, knock 'em out!"

She fisted the console again in despair. Leon glanced her way, but busied himself trying to iron out the glitch with transmissions to the groundside studio. He and his men were unfamiliar with the zero-gee of the Orbiter's axis, and every small task that required movement seemed to anger them more.

Beatriz knew her performance as written would be helping Brood, too, and this was more than she could bear. He was overseeing the delivery of the OMC to its crypt aboard the Voidship and mercifully out of her sight. If Leon didn't get past the jamming influence on their burst channel, Brood would be back, and he would be mad. She didn't relish the thought of Brood in a tantrum.

Dwarf MacIntosh was a normal human, a blue-eyed clone from hyb, and Beatriz was a near-normal Islander. Mutations had leveled off over the past few generations and most Islanders, though shorter and darker, appeared as normal as MacIntosh and Flattery.

Appearances, among Pandorans, had dictated their lives from the start.

*Flattery's not normal,* she thought. *His mind is a mutation, an abomination. Humans should not trample their own kind.*

She knew the history of slavery Earthside, and members of her own family lived with the aftermath of the genetic slavery of Jesus Lewis. Today she had awakened at last to Ben's accusations that Flattery had enslaved Pandora, Mermen and Islanders alike, and his grip only got tighter while the people got hungrier.

The past twenty-five years had been a cumulative string of disasters planetwide: The sea bottom had fractured along a kelp root line to form the first strip of land. More such fractures followed, always along the gigantic roots of kelp beds. The consequent upheavals destroyed dozens of Merman settlements down under and caused the sinking or deliberate grounding of most of the floating organic cities of the Islanders, her own among them. Refugees swarmed to the primitive coastal settlements by the thousands, forced to learn to survive again on land after nearly three centuries on or under the sea. Flattery had not eased their burden, only added to it.

"This whole planet's trying to kill us," Mack had told her the first time they talked, "we don't need to give it a hand."

But Mack took no action against Flattery. He put all of his waking hours and a good number of his dreaming hours into perfecting the Orbiter station as a jumpoff point to the stars. He did this while directing Current Control and becoming the world's expert on its most mysterious resident, the kelp. He worked backward to define his priorities.

"We need Current Control," he said. "The kelp is fascinating, but reality dictates that we get supplies through it or people die. Controlling the kelp makes this project easier, it makes settlement life easier, it guarantees results."

That was when he invented the Gridmaster, which bypassed the undersea multibuilding complex of the Mermen's Current Control and allowed the major grid system to be operated from orbit. The Merman complex undersea had sustained heavy damage, but it still carried the hardware and installed new grids. With the Gridmaster in operation, one person could handle all of the kelpways in the richest of Pandora's hemispheres.

Beatriz had stood at Mack's side two years ago as his special guest the day the Gridmaster went on-line. Though officially a

Holovision correspondent for the event, Beatriz liked to believe
that there had been more to Mack's invitation than the business at
hand. The spark of his blue eyes lit unmistakably in her presence,
and they had enjoyed long talks floating through the axis of Orbiter nights and reclining in the webworks. What had begun as the
opportunistic brush of hands against hands became a full-fledged
love affair.

*I hope we get another chance,* she thought, and sighed to head
off tears.

A red flash above the hatchway startled her, then flashed again.
It was the studio equivalent of a doorbell that alerted each console
throughout the room. It was customary to lock the studio when
taping a show.

*Someone wants in.*

Whoever was out there was not one of Brood's men. She knew
this because of the fear that bloomed in pale petals across Leon's
face.

*It's Mack,* she thought. *It's got to be!*

"Don't move!" Leon ordered. He unsnapped his harness and
pointed a commanding finger at her. "I'll handle this. Your text
will be onscreen in a few blinks. Standard cues. I'm remote director and you will follow my lead *most* carefully."

He handed himself to the hatch, plugged in his headset and
pressed the intercom key.

"We're taping," he announced. "No admittance except for
studio personnel."

Beatriz held her breath. Though they did seal off for tapings and
live broadcast, Holovision had always encouraged an audience.
Many workers aboard the Orbiter enjoyed spending their free time
watching her crew at work, and they had never been prohibited
before.

"It's Spud Soleus." The high voice crackled her own headset
in its characteristic way, forcing a smile to her lips. "Current
Control. We have an emergency situation over there. Dr. MacIntosh needs to talk with Beatriz Tatoosh right away."

She felt a rush in her chest and color rising in her cheeks. Her
palms continued to sweat.

"She's going on the air live. Tell Dr. MacIntosh it'll have to
wait."

"It can't wait. Our burst line has failed and a chunk of grid's
down."

"We have orders," Leon said. His voice sounded hesitant. "Maybe after the show . . ."

"Dr. MacIntosh is Orbiter Command," Soleus said. "He has direct orders from Flattery to open that grid *now*. We need your burst line for a transmission. We need Beatriz Tatoosh for advice. I'm reminding you that all power relays switch through Current Control and we can shut you down."

"Wait a blink," Leon said, his voice calming, "I'll see what we can do."

He switched off the intercom and pressed his forehead against the bulkhead.

"Shit!" he said, and bumped his forehead against the plasteel. His headset kept him from cartwheeling backward across the studio. "Shit!"

*Good for Spud!* Beatriz thought. He'd lied to Leon about the circuitry. Some, but not all, was routed through Current Control. She and MacIntosh had set up the studio, and no one knew it better. But Leon didn't know that. Besides, he had enough problems. And Leon didn't dare move without orders from Brood. He couldn't alert Brood without alerting the entire Orbiter.

Beatriz's heart tripped hard against her ribs and she blotted her damp palms against the thighs of her jumpsuit. In spite of the danger, she enjoyed Leon's dilemma.

*Anything to make them squirm,* she thought.

Leon tripped the intercom switch again.

"No one's coming in here until after—"

"We can transmit on your burst line with our own carrier frequency," Spud said. "We don't even need to get in your way. Dr. MacIntosh is in charge here and he said—"

Leon slapped the switch off, unplugged his headset and thrust himself back toward his editing cubby. He crashed out of control, into the other two techs. They disentangled limbs and cables, then hovered over each of his shoulders and whispered together heatedly.

Beatriz slipped the two meters to the hatch and plugged in her headset. She switched the intercom back on and left the set to float beside the hatch only a couple of meters away. They didn't see her, and the move took fewer than four seconds by the big chronometer.

Back at her console, Beatriz opened her com-line and punched out Mack's number. The telltale light would flash on consoles in each of the editing cubbies, this she knew. As she expected, it brought Leon to her nose to nose in a red-faced fury.

"I told you not to try anything!" Leon snapped. He was no longer the meek videotech at an editing console. Now he was ranking officer of a security assault squad that was in a tight spot.

"I'd slap the shit out of you if we didn't need your pretty face. We *do* have a backup plan, sister. Try that again and you'll get your own ride out the shuttle airlock—understand?"

Beatriz had to hide a smile for the first time all day. He'd yelled at her—something that would have gone unheard elsewhere in the Orbiter if she hadn't opened the intercom first, if she hadn't plugged in the headset just a step from where Leon stood. It did not take the best of her screen abilities to feign the terror that she'd already felt many times since waking this day.

"I'll do what you say," she said, as loud as she dared. "I don't want to die like the others. I'll do what you say."

Leon pushed back to his companions, but before he reached them the general alarm sounded with four long bursts from a klaxon overhead.

Though startled by the noise, Beatriz was overjoyed. She recognized the signal from exercises in the past. Those four blasts meant "Fire, total involvement, Current Control sector." That sector included the Holovision studio.

While Leon and the other two flurried around the studio, asking each other, "What the hell's going on?" Beatriz whispered to herself, "Spud, I love you."

*Power, like any other living being, will go to infinite lengths to maintain itself.*

—Ward Keel, *The Apocryphal Notebooks*

The first thing Rico saw when he stepped through the hatchway into the galley was the still, open-eyed form of Crista Galli lying in her harness beside the plaz. Her pupils pulsed with a green brightness that Rico had never noticed before, and somehow he knew that whatever she saw now was not of this world. His first impulse was to run, to lock the hatch behind him, but he checked it.

Ben sprawled on the deck beside her, one hand clutching her ankle and his legs quivering like a child's in a nightmare. To Rico, the whole scene was a nightmare.

"Ben!" he called from the hatchway, but Ben didn't answer. He rushed to his best friend's side and saw that Ben's eyes, too, were open. Both of them were breathing, though Crista Galli's head was bent slightly forward and he heard a gurgle with each passage of air. Rico heeded Operations' warnings and didn't touch either one of them.

"Shit!" he snapped, and fumbled in his left breast pocket for a slapshot. It was a red, tiny ampule about the size of the end of his little finger. Two needles jutted from one end, covered by a plastic case. He flipped the cover across the galley, careful to hold the prongs away from his own body.

"Dammit, Ben, Operations said this toxin might be triggered if she got wet."

This shot was titrated for his own body weight, the one he'd most hoped never to use. In one swift jab he stuck it into Ben's thigh.

"Don't stop breathing, man," Rico begged. "Just don't stop breathing."

He turned to Crista Galli, trying to control the sudden flash of anger burning in his chest. He knew it was more frustration than hate, but his body didn't know the difference.

*If she killed him . . .*

The better part of his reason wouldn't let him finish the thought.

A strangled moan surged from Crista's throat, an otherworldly moan that put the hair up on the back of Rico's neck.

"Crista? Can you hear me?"

Rico saw that she had some ability to move. She turned her hands palm upward in a gesture of helplessness, and her lips kept trying to form the words that wouldn't come.

"Flattery . . ."

The word was barely intelligible. She still looked straight ahead, and in a dreamlike slow motion finished her effort with, ". . . drugs."

"Flattery gave you drugs?"

She blinked her eyes once, slowly.

"He gave you drugs to make you toxic? It's not the kelp?"

Again, the slow blink and a nearly imperceptible nod.

The *Flying Fish* took another lurch that sprawled Rico across the deck. He grabbed for a handhold and pressed himself against the bulkhead as the foil rolled onto its side, then righted.

The foil's metal skin shrieked as something twisted it to its limits, then backed off.

*The kelp's pulling us apart,* he thought. *It knows she's in here!*

Crista was strapped in just as Ben must have left her, soaking wet, her disguise discarded. Rico made a jump for the seat next to her and strapped in just as the foil righted again and all was quiet. It was as though the kelp had one last spasm run through it before it could relax.

He checked Ben over as best he could without touching him. He was breathing easily and his color was good. There was some movement of his right hand toward Crista, and Rico thought this was a good sign. He gingerly opened Ben's left breast pocket and brought out the other slapshot for Crista. Her eyelids did a fast flutter-dance that seemed voluntary, and her left hand raised just a tiny bit at the fingertips, as though to push him away.

Rico hesitated with the shot, and the fluttering stopped.

*What if it's not . . . the Tingle?* he asked himself. Operations had warned him that the antidote itself might be fatal if administered needlessly to one of them. Maybe it would be fatal if given to her at all.

*If Flattery's been giving her something, maybe her body's different,* he thought. *Maybe the antidote would . . . kill her.*

It was tempting to go ahead anyway, after what she'd done to his partner. No one would know, not even Ben. He readied himself to deliver it and her eyes went into their flutter again and her fingers made those pushing movements.

*But Flattery would like that,* he thought. *There's nothing more that he would like than being able to tell the world that Her Holiness Crista Galli died in the hands of the Shadows.*

The whole fiction began to unreel in his mind, clearly illumined all of a sudden against the backdrop of light that began to fill the galley's plaz.

"Of course," he said to her, "it makes sense. He *made* you toxic so that no one would go near you. Then he went public and blamed this on your . . . relationship with the kelp, am I right?"

Again, the barely perceptible nod and the slow blink. She seemed relieved, more relaxed, and he didn't think it was the toxin working.

A sudden burst of light filled the galley and the foil began to lurch rhythmically. They were on the surface, and Elvira would be going out there to clear the intakes. At each lurch a tiny cry escaped Crista's throat, and tears streaked her cheeks. For the first time he felt as though he wanted to comfort her. He was just beginning to imagine how much Flattery had used her, how terrible and secret her life in the Preserve must have been.

*She was a curiosity, a prisoner,* he thought, *and he made her a monster.*

"Did this ever happen to you . . . before Flattery gave you drugs?"

Her eyes flicked side to side.

"I think that he thought that your toxin would kill us. Then he would get you back and be a hero, warning the world again about how dangerous you are. And if I gave you this shot,'' he placed the unopened ampule carefully into his pocket, "then you would die and he would tell the world how we killed you. That would turn the world against us for sure . . .''

She blinked a "yes,'' and Rico heard a moan from Ben.

The intercom charged again, then Elvira asked, "Rico, everybody OK?''

Ben's mouth struggled to speak, then he gave up and managed a slight nod. Crista, too, nodded and squeezed out a slow "Yesss.''

"Slapshot time,'' Rico said to the intercom. "They're not great, but improving. I'm all you've got right now. You going out for a little swim?''

"Thought I would. Best watch the helm.''

"On my way,'' he said. He reassured himself that both Crista and Ben were safe, and that neither of them could be hurt where they lay.

"I'll leave the intercom charged,'' he told them. "Talk to me once in a while, even if it's a grunt, OK? I'll be back when Elvira's finished out there.''

Crista raised her fingertips again, and wrenched out a couple of words.

"Kelp . . . happy.''

"The kelp is happy?'' He threw his hands in the air, and spoke with undisguised sarcasm. "Then *I'm* happy. How the hell do you know?''

She turned her palm up like a shrug.

"Free—dom,'' she said, and repeated the word more slowly, "free—dom.''

A glance out the plaz showed him what appeared to be an infinite expanse of kelp lazing in the last of both afternoon suns. Alki, the small, distant sun, had begun a slow pulse almost a year ago and it was pulsing now. A very large, very black cloud was closing from seaward toward them. An occasional kelp frond rose slowly, then fell back with a *slap* and a splash.

*Like a wot in a bathtub,* he thought.

He had never seen the kelp play like this before.

"I hope you're right,'' he said. "I truly hope you're right. It will make life so much easier for us, and so much harder for Flattery's people.''

He resisted the temptation to pat her shoulder and Ben's.

"We're going to get you out of this, buddy,'' he said to Ben.

He kept talking, more to himself than to Ben, as he hurried out the hatchway to the helm. He spoke to Ben over the intercom as he reviewed his instruments, as much for his own comfort as his partner's.

"I hate to say it," Rico said, "but I think Current Control saved our butts. The kelp got us down here, wherever *here* is, and then started tearing at the cabin with those huge vines. Current Control must have been trying to get the original channel back, because the kelp was obviously fighting some kind of impulse. Either they blew a fuse or they gave the kelp its head completely. Whatever, it was the right thing to do."

He resumed his instrument checkout.

"That electrical pulse through the kelp must have screwed up our Navcom system," Rico said. "Most everything else looks OK. I closed off cooling outlets to the galley to head off that leak, just in case it's ready to pop someplace else. You two might get a little warm there between the engines. Once we're airborne, I'll figure a way to get you both up here."

He finished the checkout and realized that they wouldn't be getting airborne after all. Not unless Elvira could remanufacture the hydraulics that withdrew their hydrofoils and extended airfoils.

*Ben doesn't need to know that now*, he thought. *For that matter, neither do I.*

"Speak to me, buddy. Anything."

"Rico . . . OK."

It came out loud and clear, though painfully slow, but it was enough to put a smile on Rico's face. He felt Elvira tugging kelp out of the inlets and tried the Navcom again. It was dead, not even a burst of static from the speakers.

"Squall's coming in," he told Ben, "things might get rough again pretty soon."

He didn't want to tell Ben that they were going to get *really* rough, now that they couldn't get above the storm. Without the Navcom, and with the kelp glutting up the ocean as far as the eye could see, Rico himself didn't want to think about how rough it was going to get.

*Anyone who threatens the mind or its symbolizing endangers the matrix of humanity itself.*

—Ward Keel, *The Apocryphal Notebooks*

Ben had heard the boat's ballast blow as he stroked Crista's hair and cheek under the fine spray of the pinpoint galley leak. He remembered the taste of salt when his lips brushed her hair. Because of the taste of salt from the interior bulkhead he knew it was a cooling pipe leak, recycled seawater, nothing to worry about now that they were headed topside.

He remembered that he and Crista had been talking, laughing, when suddenly his upper body began to tingle. His neck wouldn't move his head where it wanted to go. He tried to cry out but his mouth and throat wouldn't work. Crista slumped against her harness, limp, her eyes wide with fear and their green irises darkening nearly to blue.

*Oh, no,* he remembered thinking. *Oh, no, they were right!*

In lurching, spastic movements he lunged against Crista, sprawling across her legs. She had let out a little cry of surprise, but didn't resist. Ben saw that she couldn't. Whatever was happening to him was also happening to her. He had the advantage of

204

more body mass, more muscle, so it was taking his body longer to shut down.

He grabbed for Crista's harness to pull himself up but his hands turned to two heavy rocks at the ends of his arms. Within a blink he collapsed against her. He was able to see and breathe but trying to move only produced uncontrollable spasms. He slid down the couch to the deck into a position that didn't allow him to watch Crista. One of his hands remained on her ankle, and he felt her body spasm and relax much like his own. The antidote was in his pocket, and he couldn't make his body work well enough to dig it out.

*Rico will think I'm a fool,* he thought.

Now that they'd lost their Navcom they couldn't function undersea, and they'd be bobbing squawks on the surface. Rico would have his hands full enough without this . . . mess.

*Elvira's got a few tricks,* he thought.

Ben felt the Tingle rush like a hot blush down his back, out his shoulders and thighs. He tried to control his muscles again but couldn't. He was a helpless, quivering heap on the deck. He remembered feeling more betrayed than careless. Then he started traveling the convolutions of Crista's mind. Rico, the galley around them, the rest of the real universe played through a dark curtain that backdropped Crista's thoughts and memories. These images from her life unreeled in his brain.

"Ben!" Rico said, his small voice rising to Ben from a great depth. He said more but Ben heard only the *snap* of the antidote against his singlesuit. He felt nothing but the Tingle throughout his body, but he was fully aware of Rico stretching him out on the deck.

Time rippled like a dark fabric strung between himself and Rico. The white and stainless steel of the galley blended into a great glowing halo of yellowpanel that washed out everything behind the curtain of his mind.

Ben understood much, now. A near-infinity of human memories slept in Crista Galli's head. Now many of them buzzed in his own, like solvent to solute, a wet solution filling up a dry. He felt the dry blossom of his mind unfold as it drank, petal by intricate petal, and behind it the shadow that was Rico LaPush rippled back and forth.

Though he could see and hear, Ben felt a detachment from his body that was more curiosity to him than fear. He remembered the special show he'd done with Beatriz about people who returned from near-death, what they'd reported about this same detached feeling, this same comforting warmth that replaced all sensation in his skin except that Tingle. They said they'd viewed their bodies from certain vantage points in the room, watched the medics resuscitate them, remembered whole conversations that took place even when they showed no heartbeat on the monitor. They described watching the vital signs monitor with the same detached feeling that Ben had when he slumped to the deck.

His view, however, was distinctly from someone else's body, someone else's mind. This was a wot's mind, down under, looking upward toward the sun from the middle depths of a kelp lagoon. His range of vision was limited to straight ahead. It was slightly blurry and a light halo surrounded the rim above. Way up there, backlit by the glowing suns, he saw Rico's busy shadow. The lagoon was full of Swimmers, those legendary gilled humans, undulating in and out of channels above her.

This was Crista as a child. This was Ben as Crista as a child.

He sensed that Rico was very worried and he wanted to tell him, "It's OK, I'm here," but nothing would come out.

One Swimmer in particular attended her, an older female. Ben had never seen a Swimmer. He'd imagined them as grotesque, slimy creatures with wide mouths and stupid eyes, and rudimentary, ratlike tails. The female who attended Crista now was about his own age. Her red fan of gill fluttered furiously at her shoulders as she fed the girl slices of raw fish. Crista dangled from the kelp, and the Swimmer female came up to her from the deeps. She did not, or would not, speak.

From somewhere behind the halo, very far above Ben's upturned face, Rico's voice echoed, "I'm going to settle you here and keep you warm."

Ben felt the lagoon receding, and Rico's voice with it.

"Crista is still breathing," Rico said. "I don't know whether you can hear me or not, Ben, but we'll get you out of here. You'll be OK. The goddamned girl is OK. We're almost topside. We'll get you someplace." Rico's voice was tinged with hysteria, and he sounded close to tears. "We'll get you someplace, buddy, you just hang on." A squeeze at his shoulder, then Rico was gone.

Ben found he could leave the womblike kelp, and if he imagined walking a corridor toward himself he became more aware of the galley, the foil around him. He felt he could walk a gossamer bridge between Crista's mind and his own.

A sudden dazzle of light in the galley and a change in the pitch of the foil told Ben that they had surfaced. Ben wondered whether he would die this way, fully conscious, feeling that last exhalation and unable to suck in air. He remembered the time that he and Rico almost drowned, when Guemes Island was sabotaged and sunk. He had nearly panicked then, but he felt no such panic now, simply a numb obedience to his fate.

He found himself wondering about things that should terrify him: would the neurotoxin, whatever it was, paralyze his breathing muscles? His heart muscle? He wished that Rico had propped him up a little to make it easier, though already the tingling had stopped.

*The slapshot works,* he thought.

He wanted to cross that gossamer bridge to Crista again, but he felt himself moving farther away from the bridge and back into the foil. The deck under him was uncomfortable, and he found that he could squirm a little to change position. He was definitely improving. He'd been dimly aware of a voice coming in over the intercom, it was Rico's voice, and it came in again, sounding worried.

"Speak to me, buddy. Anything."

Ben tried his throat again. It was dry, and didn't want to work quite right, but he managed to squeeze out: "Rico . . . OK."

He heard Crista breathing, but she still hadn't stirred.

*I wonder what happens to her?*

"Squall's coming in," Rico announced, "things might get rough again pretty soon."

Ben wanted to laugh, tried to come back at Rico with, *"Rough? What do you call this?"* but it all came out a garble.

*The new ruler must inevitably distress those over whom he establishes his rule. So it happens that he makes enemies of all those whom he has injured in occupying the new principality, and yet he cannot keep the friendship of those who have set him up.*

—Machiavelli, *The Prince*

Flattery spurned the safety of his quarters for a brazen tour in the sunshine topside. Nevi and Zentz were on their mission and out of his way, the ragtag rebellion was failing under his security force, and he knew that whoever had Crista Galli had a big handful of trouble. He smiled widely to himself and turned his face to the sky. He loved the sky, the weather—how different from the controlled susurrations of Moonbase air! It was nearly time for the afternoon rain. Like the few other survivors of hybernation who had been reared in the sterility of Moonbase, Flattery had a feeling for weather.

He chose a parapet that looked downcoast, across the Preserve and into the wretched village that spilled from his gate. A boil of black smoke fanned inland with the upcoming wind. Flattery wore his brightest red lounging jacket so that the vermin could see he was very much alive, still very much the Director. So close to the borders of battle—now they would see the mettle they tested!

The presence of two suns unnerved him, even after these many years. Information from his kelp studies, from his geologists, proved that they were ripping the planet's crust like so much flatbread. The worst was yet to come, and he didn't intend to wait around for it.

Ventana, one of his messengers, approached the walkway below him.

"Reports on the kelpway disruption, sir."

She waved a messenger.

He signaled one of the guards, who inspected the device and then brought it to him. Flattery pulled his white hat farther down to shade his forehead. The wide-brimmed style was Islander, for political effect. It was a white hat because Flattery believed that white placed him on the side of truth and justice at a glance. He did not retrieve the reports immediately. He knew what was inside: nothing. And by this time the afternoon cloud cover obscured an Orbiter view of the number eight sector.

His passion for weather did not include the suns' ravages of his uncooperative skin. Two pink blotches peeled on his forehead and Flattery tried not to scratch them. His personal physician had removed two such spots only a month ago, and now this.

*The people have to see me*, he thought. *There is no substitute for the proper exposure.*

His three most trusted bodyguards accompanied him at a distance, their Pandoran instincts keeping them ever on the move. His vantage point was a bluff overlooking the compound, the village and the bay. To his back were the only higher points for many klicks—the high reaches, home of the worthless Zavatans. A lot of these Zavatans, like the peasantry, believed in Ship and the eventual return of this Ship as some sort of mechanical messiah. The thought made him laugh, and his guards looked at him curiously.

"Stand down, gentlemen," he told them. "As you can see, there's nothing down there that can reach us."

"Begging the Director's pardon," one of the guards, Aumock, spoke up. "It's my job to never stand down."

Flattery nodded his approval. *This one bears watching.*

"Very good," he said. "I appreciate your dedication."

Aumock, a Merman from good stock, didn't swell with the praise. He was already back to scanning the area for movement.

"Nothing up here but Zavatans," Flattery said.

"Are you sure they're nothing, sir?" Aumock replied.

This was the first time his guard had offered a comment in his ten-month tour of service at Flattery's side. Flattery merely grunted a response.

He had his suspicions about these Zavatans—always the same number of them appearing about, but seldom the same faces. Flattery was no fool. He was, after all, a *Chaplain*/Psychiatrist and had done impeccable study in the history of oppressed religions. He was uncomfortable with a nearby population that was potentially hostile, whose numbers seemed impossible to determine, and whose general fitness appeared far better than that of most of his security.

*They actually* run *up these cliffs,* he mused. *Why?*

It was here, on the bare overlook above the Preserve, that he reviewed the latest messages regarding the Holovision foil and the curious rebellion of the largest stand of kelp in the region.

"So, Marta, do you really believe that they've turned back?" he asked.

His communications officer, a little plump for her regulation blue jumpsuit, managed a quick chew at her lip before responding. Flattery had bedded her once and recalled that her touch was far more satisfying than her looks. She'd been a slender young thing then—four, maybe five years ago. She had started as a bodyguard, but showed a facility with electronics that impressed his engineers. When she requested a transfer, he had granted it. It was just as well, the move headed off the rumors and the inevitable discomfort of extracting himself from a sticky personal situation.

"I . . . I don't know," she said. "The device that I placed personally on their foil is working perfectly, and its course is consistent with a return to this—"

"Bah!" Flattery blurted. "They're not stupid. I insisted that you place the device *on* or *inside* her person and you took it upon yourself to place it elsewhere. A Current Control outpost has already confirmed the device to be aboard a crippled sub train dragging a few thousand kilos of dead fish."

Flattery enjoyed the stunned look that flattened her face. She looked small and pale now.

"I was afraid," she said. "I was afraid to touch her."

Marta hung her head as though expecting a blade. The merciless suns here on the bluff widened the circles of sweat forming under her armpits. It was that heavy, sticky time on the coast just before the rain squalls hit. He didn't have to sniff to smell the rain.

Flattery remembered that time with her. It had been afternoon and their skin poured sweat. Tiny black hairs from his chest had stuck to her small white breasts. She hadn't been so afraid of him then, just a little bit in awe, which made things easier.

*Dammit!* he muttered to himself. *Bitten by the fiction again.*

He drew himself up to his full height, nearly two heads taller than Marta.

"Didn't I assure you that it was safe?"

This he delivered in his most consoling voice.

She nodded, but still did not lift her head.

Flattery was very pleased with himself. If this woman who knew him so well was afraid of Crista, of what her touch might do, then these strangers must be terrified. Thanks to his foresight in the beginning and her daily "medications," Crista should be withdrawing violently by now, exhibiting the very symptoms attributed to her touch. Perhaps by now she'd be catatonic—something else he'd engineered to see that she was brought back to him.

The neurotoxin would be oozing from her every pore by now, and the fiction he had laid down so carefully for so long would become true. Everyone, particularly the enemy, would see it with their own eyes. Only he, the Director, could save her. Those Shadows would soon find themselves in the presence of a monster that they could not afford to keep.

*The wonders of chemistry,* he thought, and smiled.

Aloud, he reassured Marta.

"I understand your fear," he said. "The important thing is that we were not fooled by their amateurish attempt at deception. What do you have to report on damage here?"

Both of them flinched at the simultaneous crackle of two lasguns, and Flattery turned to see that his guards had cooked a pair of hooded dashers closing from the direction of the high reaches.

"I wonder . . ."

He didn't finish the rest aloud. What he wondered was whether or not the Zavatans were training dashers.

"I want studies on dasher sightings coordinated with known Zavatan positions," he said.

Marta nodded and unholstered the electronic link at her side. The movement drew a subtle shift in Aumock's position. Marta didn't notice that his lasgun muzzle had focused on her head before the link cleared daylight. She clicked out her coded entry in her usual unhurried manner.

Flattery knew something of the Zavatans and their history, but not nearly as much as he'd like. They were patient, organized, and they scavenged everything. If rumor was correct, they grew illicit crops in the upcoast regions and distributed them among refugees. Flattery resented this because it seriously weakened his bargaining position with the masses. He did not have the manpower to police thousands of square kilometers of rugged countryside and complete Project Voidship at the same time. Project Voidship was infinitely more important.

He saluted approval as one of the men went over the wall to fetch the dasher skins.

*That much less for the Zavatans,* he thought.

He made a mental note to see what the lab would have to say about where the dashers had been, with whom, what they were eating, when and why.

"And your report on the fighting?" he asked.

"Compound perimeter is secure," she said.

Marta pressed the spot behind her right ear that activated the *receive* mode of her messenger implant.

"I'm getting a lot of interference here, don't know the cause. Minimal damage to the compound—the expected rubble but mostly cosmetic, as usual. Rocks and sticks are no match for lasguns. Prisoners are being held in the courtyard." She paused as more information fed into her messenger.

"Reports on the power station, the ferry terminal and the grid situation," he ordered.

Marta fed something into her messenger, then her expression changed. The façade of the impartial reporter wrinkled into concern at her brow, and she leaned forward as information vibrated her mastoid bone, washed through the fluids and hairs of her inner ear to her brain.

"There is a massive force congregating at the power station," she said. "The squad of security that attacked our detachment at the site has dug in and persisted. The refugee camp is less than a kilometer away. People from the camp are backing up the rebel squad, just out of lasgun range of our defense."

"Operation H," Flattery barked. "If they keep coming, have air support shift to the camp."

Marta paled further. She lowered her voice so that the guards wouldn't hear.

"Operation H, sir . . . they'd see it from the camp. If you jelly the attackers, witnesses will know it wasn't a hylighter."

"Use an LTA," he said. "We have a few balloons in the hangar that look like hylighters. Get them into the air. We'll worry about witnesses later. I want that squad burned, I want anyone backing them up burned. Is that understood?"

Marta nodded, and her fingers flickered the orders across her instrument.

"The ferries?"

"Operational, sir. The current shift reported on time. Casualties high, but replacements are already on-site receiving training. The OMC launch lit off and docked at Orbiter station, no update. Current Control terminated their signal to the kelp in sector eight, there is no grid but no aggressive activity."

"*Terminated?*"

Flattery regretted the lie to MacIntosh. He was sure that the kelp would yield, given the full electrical prod long enough. He had never thought that MacIntosh would terminate the signal.

*Idiot! What could he be thinking, giving the kelp its head. Doesn't he know how much we need those kelpways open?*

He inhaled one long, slow breath, half in the left nostril, half in the right. He let it out just as slowly.

"Is it working?" he asked.

"A few merchant vessels lost," she said. "Most have surfaced, making repairs. They will not fare well in the storm."

"Order Dr. MacIntosh to reestablish the kelpways, or I will do it my way from here. He has one hour."

"Yes, sir."

Flattery's mood blackened. Two small explosions and a flash came from the center of Kalaloch. He signaled one of his guards.

"Have security get what they can from the leaders of this rabble. I don't expect much. Then have the rest of them staked in the open." He surveyed the cliffside behind him that led to the high reaches. "Have them staked up there," he said, "so that everyone below can study the results of their decision in detail. It shouldn't take long."

It was what Marta had told him about the kelp that interested him the most. He'd fabricated such an intricate web of deception about Crista Galli that Flattery himself had difficulty remembering which was his masterful illusion and which reality. His earliest warnings to keep her from any contact with the kelp was based more on hunch than data, but it was clear to him now that his hunch had been good.

*The kelp could actually smell her!*

"I ordered Current Control to opt for a surgical solution," Marta said. "They have one hour to achieve the grid by any other means. I explained that there were too many subs at stake."

"Will it be necessary to dissect the entire stand?"

"No," she said. "Like the mob, it should convert easily with minimal damage to the affected area. That corridor will not have the flexibility it once had, but it will be navigable as soon as the debris is swept."

"When it's over, have samples sent to the lab," he said. "Complete analysis. Find out why it could resist Current Control, then render it down for the toxin stockpile."

"The Zavatans . . ." she began, "it would be good politics to . . ."

"To give them what's left of the kelp?" He snorted in disgust. "Let them dredge their own. I don't want to be party to their heresy. And I want a lot of toxin on hand, I have a surprise yet for those 'vermin,' as Nevi calls them."

Marta noted the orders into the messenger at her waist.

It was clear to Flattery that the kelp must have sensed Crista Galli's presence. How else to explain this rebellion? It had occurred along the plotted route of Ozette's foil after Marta's device was jettisoned.

*The kelp must have sensed her when the bug hit the water,* he thought. He smiled again, partly out of a distant relief at not being aboard the *Flying Fish* at the time, but largely at the predicament that now embroiled Ozette and his Shadows.

"Overflights?" he asked.

"Bad weather already in," she replied. "Low probability of contact, high probability of loss. Two Grasshoppers available in the area, but they are frail and of limited range. Do you have orders for them?"

"Observation patterns as weather permits," he said. "I want to see who they turn to when they're in big trouble. Nevi will be on the scene soon enough."

Flattery detected a definite shudder across Marta's shoulders at the mention of Nevi's name.

*That's why I use him,* he thought. *Mere mention of his name gets results.*

He dismissed Marta and surveyed the landscape, *his* landscape, that fell away before him. Metallic-looking wihi glinted sunlight back at him. Their short, daggerlike leaves deployed toward the bursts of ultraviolet pulsing from Alki. Flattery admired this dangerous little plant for its tenacity and for the protection it afforded his compound. Its seeds lay dormant undersea for two centuries, waiting to flourish when the oceans rolled back again. It flourished now, and made going difficult for predators near the compound—human or otherwise.

A rob of tiny swiftgrazers darted among the wihi to his left, near the cliff's rise to the high reaches. Though reputed to eat anything softer than rock, the grazers preferred to avoid humans. They had survived, like many Earthside rodents, by hiding aboard the organic islands throughout the floods. The poor often chanced netting them for food—a dangerous task. He'd watched an old Islander swarmed to death on this very spot only two years ago. The man had netted only half the rob. The other half waited in the rocks for his return, then set upon his legs until he fell. It was over in a matter of blinks, and Flattery considered it an education. He ordered the whole rob burned out at the nests, of course, and their charred bodies delivered to the villagers. Strictly political.

The Director knew that anything that protected itself to that extreme could be made to protect him, too. His greenskeeper had a way with animals as well as plants, and now several rob of swiftgrazers nested in vulnerable approach points to the compound. This was one such rob, stationed near the trail to the high reaches. He watched them often, particularly in the evening when their slender, rusty backs caught the sunlight and rippled among the silver wihi.

"Look there!" his guard warned, and Flattery saw the skulking back of a dasher approach the rob. The guard set his lasgun for the distance about the limit of his effective range, and raised it. Flattery motioned him to wait.

The dasher closed the final twenty meters in three blurring bounds, slapping at the little animals and stunning them. There were too many, and the dasher was skinny from hunger. It tried to gulp a few of them down but the pause was all the rob needed to regroup. The dasher seemed to melt off its odd bones. Flattery smiled again, as the afternoon clouds gathered offshore.

"Beautiful, aren't they?" he asked no one. "Just beautiful."

*We're more than our ideas.*

—Prudence Lon Weygand, M.D., number five,
original crew, Voidship *Earthling*

Twisp the Zavatan elder watched the Director watch the swiftgrazers strip an ailing hooded dasher to bone. The sight reminded him of the old days when he was a simple fisherman at sea. The last effects of blue spore-dust heightened this memory of schools of scrat that devoured maki a thousand times their size in blinks. Twisp had a healthy respect for scrat, and for swiftgrazers.

*Furry little bandits*, he thought. One thing about them always made him smile. Their fragile little penises detached during mating, leaving a small fleshy plug in the female that her body absorbed. It kept sperm in, and subsequent suitors out, guaranteeing the genetic survival of the first to mount. The male grew another within weeks, but not soon enough to breed twice in one cycle.

Something of a game developed among many Pandoran men at the expense of the swiftgrazers. The trick was to trap a swiftgrazer and snatch its penis. They were considered a delicacy, and it was said that the Director enjoyed them steamed atop his salads. It

216

wasn't easy to isolate a single swiftgrazer. Many a drunk pulled
back stumps where there had been fingers.

The little animals looked like a band of robbers, with their
masks across their twitchy noses and their nervous way of having
at least half of the rob on alert. He had never known them to attack
humans unless molested, but when they attacked it was with a
fury, a complete abandon that chilled him. He did not care to find
out the limits of their patience.

Twisp admired swiftgrazers for the way they stuck together.
There was no such thing as a hungry swiftie. If one swiftie was
hungry, the whole rob was hungry. The Shadows claimed that the
people of Pandora would be like swiftgrazers when the time came.

"The time is now," Twisp whispered, watching Flattery.

His whisper was swallowed in the wind. Just enough spore-dust
twinkled in his veins to lend a background music to the gusts of
the incoming storm.

The wind whistled back, "Yesss," here in the high reaches, as
it always did at sea. Only inside, behind the plaz and dogged
hatches, did he ever hear it moan, "Nooo." The first time had
been nearly thirty years ago, in the company of a woman he
couldn't forget. The wind had been right then, and Twisp's broad
shoulders sagged a little when he realized it was right now.

The rob of swifties finished their kill. Most of them stood
upright on their slender bodies, sniffing the wind and yawning.
The pink of their long tongues flickered visibly as they licked their
rusty snouts.

Twisp trained his monks with scrat and swiftgrazers in mind.
The sequestered Zavatans, like the Shadows of every settlement,
were honed and ready, prepared to fight, prepared to go hungry.
Still, he desperately wanted to find another way.

He asked the wind, "How can I save the people and Flattery,
too?"

A crisp lull stilled the afternoon.

Twisp had long ago noted that the Director cultivated certain
rob and eliminated others. Careful observation bore fruit—Twisp
knew all of the swiftgrazers' secret warrens and the myriad entrances topside. It was this kind of patience and attention to detail
that he knew they all would need to turn aside the cruel momentum of Flattery and his machine.

Beyond the scene of this little death in front of him the greater
deaths of charred villagers fanned out from the smoking ruins of

the Preserve. As the afternoon winds once again gathered their storm, so did hunger unite Pandora against its most vicious enemy. Twisp watched clumps of the inevitable refugees stagger the trail to the rumor of safety among the Zavatans in the high reaches.

*New recruits for us, for the Shadows.*

His smile was a grim one. Pandorans had never been a warlike lot. There had always been too few humans, too many demons. Even hungry as they were, Pandorans were reluctant to pick up arms against their fellows. Flattery paid his security force, and paid them well, to fight other humans. The disease that Twisp thought he had nipped years ago had burst into an epidemic under Flattery.

"I, too, believed in him at first," Twisp said. "Was that wrong?"

He knew what the wind would say before he heard it. He had been lazy, he had hoped someone else would take care of it. Like everyone else, he had only wanted to live his simple life quietly.

Twisp's own patience was worn threadbare as his robe. For nearly twenty-five years he had hoped that Pandora would shrug off the Director's mantle of hunger and fear. Hope, he knew, had even less substance than dreams. It implied waiting, and too many hungry Pandorans didn't have the luxury of waiting. It was a death sentence, and time was the prosecution.

When Flattery had seized power, he insinuated himself first into control of Merman Mercantile and then acquired control of all food distribution. He bought into transportation and communications worldwide. This had been accomplished by the deaths of several of Twisp's friends, people who had owned Merman Mercantile and Current Control.

*Too many accidents, too many coincidences.*

He fought a familiar lump at his throat. They all had been young, naive, and none of them stood a chance against the cunning of the Director. Now, as always, only Flattery could afford to wait.

*How ironic*, Twisp thought, *that those who can afford to wait don't have to. I wonder if there's anything left for him to hope for?*

"Elder!"

Twisp cringed inwardly at the panting voice of the young Mose behind him. He felt impatience enough bursting in his breast without being nettled by Mose.

"What is it?"

The younger monk would not approach the precipitous edge of rock outcrop that Twisp occupied, this he knew. He admitted to himself that it was a little game he played with Mose.

"Why do you stand out there?" the younger asked, his voice tinged with a whine.

"Why do you stand back there?"

Still, Twisp did not turn, though he knew he would do so.

"Your presence is requested in chambers. It is urgent. There are many preparations afoot that I do not understand."

Twisp did not answer.

"Elder, can you hear me?"

Still no answer.

"Elder, please do not make me come out there again. You know that it shakes my wattles in a fearsome way."

Twisp chuckled to himself and turned to join Mose at the cavern entrance. The afternoon rains had begun, anyway, pattering like swiftgrazers in the scrub. He knew already what Operations must have decided. That it was time to stop hoping. That Flattery and his kind must go. That the people were rising up unorganized and undefended. That the Zavatans and the Shadows held the only means and position to guarantee his fall. That once again thousands would die in the greater name of life and, of course, liberty. When there was nothing else to boil down, it always boiled down to hunger.

"Come with me to Operations," Twisp said, "and I'll show you something to pink your wattles. You will then be witness to something fearsome, indeed."

Twisp bowed once at the cavern entrance, in respect, and entered, the billow of his orange robe a beacon against the darkened afternoon.

The dim vestibule inside was guarded by two young novices with shaved heads and lasguns. The boy looked to be about fifteen and his shaved head revealed a high crest of bone atop his skull, which made him taller than Twisp, though their eyes met at the same height. Both he and the girl wore the black, armored jumpsuits of the Dasher Clan. Both were suitably alert, their quick brown eyes negating their relaxed posture. Together they swung the plasteel hatch outward on its gimbals and admitted the two monks to the cavern within the high reaches.

It was not dashers and flatwings that these doors walled out, but the Director and his Vashon Security Force. Through the years Twisp himself had become a master of security. Incursions by

VSF had been few and unsuccessful. They viewed the Zavatans as harmless, spineless weaklings who were kelp-drugged or insane.

"Illusion is our strongest weapon," Twisp had lectured the young novices. "Appear to be foolish, mad, poor and ugly—who would want to take you then? Note how the mold wins the fruit by its appearance alone."

The first chamber was the one that was inspected periodically by Vashon Security Force. Rough-hewn out of rock, it housed three hundred Zavatans of the nine clans spread out along the walls, with common meeting and dining areas. There were mazes of cubbies in three levels, hung with hundreds of tapestries that helped muffle the din of three hundred voices echoing inside the cavern.

Lighting was the usual hot-glow type driven by four hydrogen generators housed in the rock beneath them. The appearance was of primitive squalor, and security inspectors sent here by the Director seldom stayed for more than a cursory look. This was where Mose lived. Twisp, too, had a cubby here—third level, to the right of the main entrance—but he seldom slept there. For more than a year Twisp had lived in the private chambers of the group known to the Shadows as "Operations."

Twisp ascended to the second level with Mose in tow. He stepped behind an old Islander tapestry into an alcove that would not be noticed except perhaps by children at play. He approached an undamaged section of basalt bulkhead carved with elaborate histories of human and kelp interactions. The section that he faced, titled "The Lazarus Effect," was simply a huge bas-relief figure of a human hand, index finger extended, touching a strand of kelp that rose from the sea.

Twisp pulled the finger out from the bulkhead and, with the *snick* of a dagger leaving its sheath, a section of rock sprang outward. When Operations met for Zavatan business, they met inside this labyrinth of rock. Its many repairs betrayed the instability of Pandora's geology, and its routes were constantly changing. Few knew the passageways, and none as well as the Islander Twisp, Chief of Operations.

Mose swallowed hard and paled conspicuously. There were tales of thousands of villagers and common folk who sought safety among the Zavatans, never to be seen again. Mose himself had seen hundreds come into the great cavern behind them who had never come out. Operations referred to them as "Messengers from the Poor," and hinted that they were relocated worldwide.

Though Mose had heard this rumor, he had never seen evidence to back it up. Mose seldom admitted that he'd been born and lived out his meager years within five kilometers of where he now stood.

*They never come back out this hatch!*

Twisp smiled at the younger monk's obvious fear.

*Why do I like teasing him?* he wondered. *I remember Brett took it so well . . .*

He shook his head. Dwelling on his dead partner was non-productive. Cleaning up the nest of assassins who'd killed him would do everybody some good.

"Come," Twisp said. "You will be safe with me. It is time the Zavatan muscle flexed itself."

With a smile, Twisp stepped into the well-lighted passageway. Mose's eyes couldn't have widened further. When he hesitated, Twisp placed a large hand on his shoulder.

Mose, too, stepped inside and the panel *snicked* shut behind them.

"I want you to remember everything you see here today."

Mose swallowed hard again and nodded.

"Yes . . . Elder."

Mose did not look thrilled. His already pale face was drawn tight, the surgical scars along his hairline and neck glowed an angry pink. He alternately pulled at his robe and wrung his hands.

The raw silence of this stone passageway contrasted heavily with the steady din of the cavern they left behind them. The passageway was lighted by a cold source, neither bright nor dim, and it carried the pale green hues of Merman design. As in many Merman complexes, the walls met at right angles in a precision that annoyed many Islanders. These walls were carved by a plasteel welder, and except for fault damage they ran perfectly straight, perfectly smooth.

An electronic voice from overhead startled Mose:

"Security code for companion?"

"One-three," Twisp said.

"Continue."

They set out down the passageway and Mose asked, "Where are we?"

"You will see."

"What do they mean, 'security code'?"

"We have checks within checks," Twisp explained. "Had you been an enemy holding me hostage, this passage would have been sealed off with both of us in it. Perhaps I would be rescued, perhaps not. You, at least, would have been killed.''

Twisp felt Mose walk closer to him yet.

"Operations is far beneath us, even below the ocean floor.''

"*Mermen* did this?'' Mose asked.

The passageway turned left abruptly and ended at a blank wall. Twisp pressed his palm to a depression on the wall and a panel slid back to reveal a tiny room, barely large enough for a half dozen people.

"*Humans* did this,'' Twisp answered. "Islanders and Mermen alike.''

The panel slid shut behind them. Twisp spoke the single word "Operations,'' and the room began to descend with the two of them inside.

"Oh, Elder . . .''

Mose held on to Twisp's long arm.

"Don't be afraid,'' Twisp said. "There is no magic here. You will see many wonders, all human wonders. Our brothers and sisters will know of them, presently. Didn't I say this would pink your wattles?''

At this, Mose laughed, but he continued to clutch Twisp's arm throughout their rapid descent.

Doob muscled the controls of his track as it lurched across the
rocky no man's land between the periphery road and the settlement. The track's ride was a kidney-buster, but it wasn't confined
to the few flat roads like Stella's little Cushette. In spite of the
beating, the track didn't seem to break down as often, either. This
was the third trip to the salvage yard for Doob and Gray this
month—all three to fix Stella's five-year-old Cushette.

"You should get a top on this thing," Gray hollered.

Both men were soaked in the sudden afternoon rain, their short
hair plastered like thick wet paint onto their heads.

"I like it," Doob hollered back. "My mom always said it's
good for the complexion."

"That's what they say about sex."

That was the first glimmer of humor that Doob had seen from
Gray all day. Gray had come by a half-hour ago after getting off
work in the settlement. He was grim-lipped and humorless, which
was not at all like the relaxed Gray who lived next door. Gray

worked some security job for the Director's personal staff, so when he didn't feel like talking Doob knew better than to ask questions.

Doob was full of questions today, though. There was a skyful of smoke over the settlement that worried him in spite of the news.

"A good rain'll clear the air," Doob said. "It's good for the brain, too. I wish it would grow something out here besides more rock."

"Those Zavatans," Gray said, "they could do it."

"Do what?"

"Get something to grow here. They have huge farms all over the upcoast regions. Just like the Islanders, but they've moved the islands inland."

Doob looked at Gray incredulously. He had heard rumors, of course, everybody had.

"You're not kidding, are you? They grow *food* up there and the Director lets them get away with it?"

"That's right. He can't keep control up there and down here, too."

"But everything up there's just cliff face and rock . . ."

"That's what you hear," Gray said. "Where do you hear it?"

"Well, on the news. I don't know anyone who's actually traveled overland up there."

"I have."

Doob glanced over at his best friend. Something had happened to him today, something that changed his whole disposition. Gray was a lot of fun. He'd come home, drink some boo with Doob, tinker with the vehicles. Sometimes, when Doob could afford it, they'd take their wives to the settlement for an evening of wine and buzzboard. Gray was definitely no fun today, but Gray had been upcoast and Doob was very curious.

"You have?" Doob asked. "Well . . . what was it like?"

He knew the danger of this question. He suspected that whatever it was that Gray had to tell him about the upcoast region was something that wouldn't be healthy to know.

"It was beautiful," Gray said.

He spoke up, but his voice was still hard to hear over the noise of the track's exhaust.

"They have gardens, hundreds of them. A rock ranch like this one would grow corn in one season up there. And every little garden is bordered by flowers, all colors . . ."

It was the wistful expression on Gray's face that worried Doob.

Doob had seen that expression often since Gray got back from
wherever it was that the Director's people had sent him. Gray
didn't volunteer information, and Doob knew better than to ask.
The less he knew about that kind of stuff, the longer his life span,
he was sure of that.

Besides, he listened to dangerous politics from his roommate,
Stella. Like Doob, she was twenty-two, but she hung around with
artists and tried to act older. She had converted most of their living
space to a multilevel hydroponics garden, and she grew mush-
rooms under their rooms. Gray knew this, of course, but he pretended not to. Stella came from a long line of Islander gardeners.
Her family owned patents to seeds mutated specifically to Pandora, and about three centuries of know-how in hydroponics.
Doob thought she could probably make the walls sprout if he let
her.

Stella talked nonstop, but this didn't bother Doob. It meant that
he didn't have to say much, and that was the way Doob liked
things.

Gray signaled him to shut down the engine. The track backfired
once and stopped atop a rock ledge that afforded them a sweeping
view all around.

"I want to believe I can trust you," Gray said. "There are
some things I need to talk about."

Doob swallowed, then nodded.

"Sure, Gray. I'm a little scared, you know."

Gray smiled, but it was a grim smile.

"You should be," he said. He pointed to the refugee sprawl
ahead. "There are starving people out there who would kill you
for one meal out of Stella's garden. Flattery's people would kill
you for growing illegal food. I might kill you if you told anybody
what I'm about to tell you."

Doob sucked in his breath. From Gray's steady gaze, Doob
knew he wasn't kidding. He also knew that he needed to hear
whatever Gray needed to say.

"Even Stella?"

Gray's eyes softened. Doob knew how much he liked Stella. He
treated her like the daughter that Gray and Billie never had.

"We'll see," Gray said. "Hear me out."

Gray spoke in a near-whisper, and his gaze darted around them
nervously. Doob hunched close to Gray and pretended to be working on the track's control panel. He had the distinct feeling they
were being watched.

"I've been gone a month, you knew that," Gray said. "They sent me upcoast, to spy on some Zavatans up there. They set me up with a story, a lapel camera, a way in and out. Overflights showed some signs of illegal fishing and food production, Flattery wanted details. What I saw there changed my life."

He lifted off the lid to the control panel and propped it up. Both Gray and Billie had been raised down under in Merman settlements.

*He's methodical, like a Merman,* Doob thought.

Gray's ice-blue eyes kept watch for movement around the track. Out in the open, this close to the perimeter, there were risks of other dangers than humans. Gray continued to talk in his slow, quiet way.

"They're Islanders without islands," he said. "There are thousands of them up there—Flattery has no idea there are that many. They have camouflage for overflights. The ratty little gardens that we see from the air are meant to be seen. Under the camouflage, and underground . . . that's a whole different story. They make bubbly out of the nutrient vats the same way they used to. Except now, instead of growing islands out of it, they spray it in a foam across rock like this and grow plants on it a week later. They make it out of garbage and sewage, just like the old days.

"On flat land, or the second time around, the bubbly is formed into a centimeter-thick sheet of organic gel, twelve meters across. Seeds are impregnated in rows into the gel, then they spread it across bare rock or sand, or last year's garden. It holds nutrients, water and defense from predators, all in a time-release bonding. Wouldn't Stella love to see this?"

"Sounds like her idea of heaven," Doob said. "She misses the island life, even though ours was grounded when we were five. I miss it, too, I guess. Not the drifting so much as the freedom. We worried about grounding, but we weren't afraid of each other."

This last Doob offered with some reservation. To admit that you were afraid of security was to imply that you had reason to be afraid. Fear was grounds for investigation.

"Yes," Gray sighed, "we *are* afraid of each other, aren't we? Even you and I. Up there," he nodded upcoast, "they're wary, but they're not afraid."

"What did you do about your report? Did you . . . ?"

"Did I expose their happiness? Did I betray the only sign of humanity I've witnessed in almost twenty years? No. No, I lied, and I made sure my camera lied. But I'm not as brave as you think. I know what Flattery suspected—that there were settlements, illegal food. But I also know what Flattery *wanted*. He wanted it to be rag-tag, not worth going after, *because he doesn't have the force to stop it!* Look around you, Doob." Gray swept his arm, taking in the horizon on all sides. "This takes every bit of manpower he's got, and he's losing it. There were riots in the settlement today, big riots, and there will be more. The news is not news, it's fiction outlined by Flattery and written by his personal fools. His lies keep us small, and as long as we're small he keeps control.

"No, he didn't want there to be anything big upcoast, so when I showed him a few raggedy-assed dirtpokers, it made him happy. So, maybe he'll stay here. His major forces are here and in Victoria, with a lot of sea patrols on the fishing fleet. The world is a lot bigger than that, Doob. It's a *lot* bigger, and getting bigger every day. I think you and Stella should go up there."

"*What?*"

Doob banged his head coming out of the control panel. "Are you crazy? She's going to have a . . . I mean, we can't think about anything like that right now. We've got to stay put."

"Doob, I know she's going to have a baby. Stella told Billie and Billie told me this morning. She can't hide it much longer, anyway. You'll have to make new food coupon applications, people may visit your place, you can't risk that."

Doob sighed, then spit out the driver's porthole

"Shit," he muttered.

"Listen," Gray said. "There's a way out of this. How's the Cushette over water?"

"Well, it's OK when it's running. No match for a foil, though, or one of those security pursuit boats."

Gray looked back at the bed of the track. It was a dumpable storage bin two meters wide by four meters long. Doob made his coupons hauling equipment for construction crews up and down the beaches of Kalaloch.

"Can you get three hundred klicks out of this thing over rough terrain?"

Doob shook his head. "No way. Two hundred, tops. With a converter, and access to seawater, I could probably drive around the world."

"Yeah," Gray said, pulling at his chin. "But there's no seawater inland, and converters won't work in streams or lakes. I have an old high-pressure tank at my place, that would get you the whole way.''

''What are you talking about?'' Doob ran a nervous hand through his kinky brown hair. ''You think we can just drive this track upcoast as bold as you please? They'll crisp our butts before we hit the high reaches.''

''That's why you don't go that way,'' Gray said. ''I have a map, and I have a plan. If I can get you, Stella and this track upcoast to my Zavatan contacts, would you go?''

Doob looked up in time to see a security detachment leave the perimeter and start toward the track across the rocks. They were still a couple hundred meters off, but they didn't look happy.

''Shit,'' Doob said.

He replaced the control panel cover and started the engine. He began to pivot his machine on its left track to go back home.

''No,'' Gray shouted. ''We set out to get a starter for that Cushette, and that's what we'll do. Give them a wave.''

Gray waved at the security squad, and so did Doob. The squad leader waved back, and the men turned back to the perimeter road where it was easier going.

''See?'' Gray hollered. ''It's like that everywhere. Learn what's easiest for them, and you can get by. We'll talk more about the upcoast trip on the way back. I've got it all figured, don't worry.''

He flashed Doob a smile, a big one, and Doob caught himself smiling back.

*Gardens*, he thought. *Stella will love that for sure.*

*Not by refraining from action does one attain freedom from action. Not by mere renunciation does one attain supreme perfection.*

> —from *Zavatan Conversations with the Avata*,
> Queets Twisp, elder

Twisp always thought that "chambers" was well-named. There were, indeed, many chambers beneath the rock—one for each of the council and several for support staff, as well as general meeting rooms and sleeping quarters. The complex was crude by Merman standards, primitive by the Director's standards. Repair crews worked throughout the area cleaning up the last of the damage of last year's great quake, already going down in oral history as "the great quake of '82."

Across the passageway from the elevator a hatch opened into Twisp's personal chamber, hewn out of glassy black rock. He swung the hatch open and motioned the gaping Mose inside.

"Sit here."

Twisp indicated a low couch to the left of the hatchway. The couch was organic, like the chairdog. It was a distinctly Islander cubby. The entire room measured barely four paces square.

Shelves filled up most of the black-rock walls, and on these shelves stood hundreds of books. They were the old kelp-pulps, a well-scarred library. Twisp had been a fisherman without holo or viewscreens. Bleached kelp pulp and hand presses in every little community turned out literature and news that was affordable and could be passed around.

Twisp dogged the hatch, then smiled.

"Borrow any books you like," he said. "They don't do anybody any good on the shelf."

Mose hung his head.

"I . . . I never told you," he stammered. One nail-bitten hand wrung the other.

"I can't read."

"I know," Twisp said. "You cover it well, it took me a long time to figure it."

"And you didn't say nothing . . . ?"

"Only you could know when the time is right. There is always someone willing to teach, but that's no good until the pupil is ready to learn. Reading is easy. *Writing,* now that's a whole different story."

"I've never been very good at learning things."

"Cheer up," Twisp said. "You learned to talk, didn't you? Reading's not so different. We'll have coffee every day for a month, and you'll be reading well by the end of the month. How about if we start with coffee now and a lesson later today?"

Mose nodded, and his look brightened. Topside, among the Zavatans, he did not often get coffee since the Director had taken over production. But he'd wedded himself to Zavatan poverty, which was a step up from his family poverty. Among the Zavatans he'd found that nothing was to be expected, everything enjoyed. Twisp bent to the preparations, his long arms akimbo in front of the table.

A fold-out table and stone washbasin jutted from the wall across the room, beside the inset stove and cooler. Mose reclined into the old couch and let it suit his forms. He found it indescribably nicer than his pallet topside. One shelf beside the couch held several holo cubes. Most of the pictures on them were of a young, red-haired man and a small, dark-skinned girl.

"The meeting begins soon, Mose," Twisp said. The older man sighed without turning, and his gangly arms sagged a bit. He spooned out some of the odorful coffee into a small cooker.

"We will all share a soup there, in the old custom, or I would offer you something here. My cubby is your cubby. That hatchway leads to the head. This hatch," with a nod he indicated their entry, "leads to the general council chambers. Prepare yourself for a confusion of people doing strange things."

"That's the way things have been all my life."

Twisp laughed, "Well, you'll get along down here just fine. Do you remember the oath you took when you came among the Zavatans?"

"Yes, Elder. Of course I remember."

"Repeat it, please."

Mose cleared his throat and sat a little straighter, though Twisp still had his back to him.

"'I forswear henceforth all robbing and stealing of food and crops, the plunder and destruction of homes belonging to the people. I promise householders that they may roam at will and abide, unmolested, wherever dwelling; I swear this with uplifted hands. Nor will I bring plunder or destruction, not even to avenge life and limb. I profess good thoughts, good words, good deeds.'"

"Very well recited," Twisp said, and handed Mose his hot coffee. "You are here because the council needs your opinion. The council has a weighty decision before it today. It has not faced a decision this big before. It may involve asking the Zavatans, all of us, to break that oath, the part about avenging life and limb. We will need your witness to this meeting, and your opinion will help decide whether or not to break it."

Twisp sipped his own coffee, still standing over Mose, and noted the tremble in the younger monk's nail-bitten hands.

"Do you have an opinion on that, Mose?"

"Yes, Elder, I do."

There had been no hesitation in Mose's voice, and the tremble in his hands stilled.

"Swearing to an oath . . . well, that's for *life*. I swore to uphold that oath for life. That's what I did, and that's what I should do."

Mose accented his speech with a curt nod, but still did not look up.

*So fearful,* Twisp thought. *This world is more habitable than it has ever been, but the people are more fearful, even of those closest to them.*

A knock at the chamberside hatch startled them both. Twisp opened it to a young, red-haired woman carrying a clipboard. She was shapely, enhancing the green fatigues characteristic of the Kelp Clan. The name above her left breast pocket read, "Snej." Her blue eyes were rimmed in red, and swollen.

*She's been crying!*

"Five minutes to council, sir," she said, and sniffed as delicately as she could. "These are our latest briefing notes." Her gaze kept his own, but her voice lowered. "Project Goddess may be lost, sir. No word or sign of them for hours."

Her lips trembled under tight control, and fresh tears welled over reddened rims. He noted a general air of depression among the support crew.

"LaPush was transmitting hourly bursts from his camera . . ."

"There's a wide-band communications problem, too," she said. "Kelp channels are clear, but conventional broadcasts seem to be jammed. Sometimes clear, sometimes not. Maybe it's sunspots, but it doesn't *act* like sunspots. Too selective."

She reached up a sleeve for her handkerchief and blew her nose.

"You're upset," Twisp said. "Can I help?"

"Yes, sir. You can get Rico back for me. I know Crista Galli is important . . . most important. But I . . ."

"You're console monitor today?"

She nodded, dabbing at her eyes with her sleeve.

"Concentrate on communications to or from Flattery's compound and shuttle everything to council chambers. We'll get them back . . . Rico and Ozette don't panic under fire."

This last seemed to rally the young woman. She blew her nose, straightened her shoulders.

"Thanks," she said. "I'm sorry . . . I'd better get back. Thanks."

Mose followed Twisp out the hatchway and they strolled the huge, domed information center bustling with people. Mose recognized some of the villager refugees he'd seen pass through the cavern above. They all wore either the green fatigues of the redhead, Snej, or the dark brown singlesuits he recognized as belonging to the newer Landsteward Clan.

Twisp's step took on a spring more youthful than his gray braid as he traversed the deck of this room of makeshift desks, viewscreens, stacks of papers, cables across the deck. This was his work of twenty-five years: Operations, the heart and being of the mysterious Shadows worldwide.

"Flattery thinks we're in Victoria," Twisp had told the council at the beginning, "and I want the rest of the world to think so, too. The Shadows will be an illusion, a fiction that we make as we go. The entire world is at stake, perhaps every human life. We must have appropriate patience."

He hoped that they still had appropriate patience.

Twisp cleared some storage units from an old chairdog and indicated to Mose that he should sit. A large plaz shield separated them from the ominous quiet of a roomful of techs. The redhead, Snej, nodded to Twisp and tried a smile.

Snej reminded Twisp a little of Ambassador Kareen Ale, a friend of his who had been one of the first victims of Flattery's death squad.

*She saved a lot of lives,* he thought. *And she was so damned pretty.*

Twisp shook off the painful memory and settled himself into his console's couch. The other council members' couches were arranged, like his own, as spokes in a wheel, each with access to a console, viewscreen and a central holo stage.

Twisp discarded his threadbare robe. Underneath, he wore a rust-colored singlesuit of the Hylighter Clan. The clasped-hands insignia at his right breast represented the informal symbol of the Shadows. Like Twisp, each of the other three consuls was accompanied by a civilian witness. One couch remained empty, its viewscreen blank.

The other three witnesses, like Mose, sat in wide-eyed awe at the maps and data spread out before them. Twisp cleared his throat and spoke the simple, awful words that some of the council had waited more than twenty years to hear:

"Brothers and sisters, it is time."

After the ancient blessing of the food they shared the ritual bowl of soup in silence. It was a classic Islander broth, nearly clear with a couple of bright orange muree curled at the bottom of the bowl. Chips of green onion floated the top, their crisp scent wafting the chambers.

The one vacant couch belonged to Dwarf MacIntosh, survivor of the very hybernation tanks that bore the Director, Raja Flattery. MacIntosh had rejected Flattery's greed for the more familiar zenlike philosophies of the Zavatans. He shaved his head, he said, "In grief at the loss of Flattery's soul, and as a reminder to keep my own."

Years ago, MacIntosh and Flattery had disagreed openly, heatedly, on many occasions. Rumor said that Flattery had removed Current Control to the Orbiter so that he could remove MacIntosh to the Orbiter. Mack had recently perfected a console-communication system that used the kelp itself as a carrier. All of the systems in chambers were tied into the kelp. Along with a code, also devised by MacIntosh, each console was capable of direct, immediate contact with Current Control.

*I hope we can keep these lines open,* Twisp thought. *That could be jamming on the conventional channels, or just sun activity. If it's sun, it probably won't take out the kelp channel as well.*

He reserved a mental note to remind Snej to check the kelp channel for Rico's film. With luck it could've been picked up and stored there.

After taking food together, Twisp received their affirmations calmly, as they presented them calmly, though what they pronounced could degenerate into a roll call of death worldwide. Every face in the room reflected the heaviness of the matter. They all agreed that it was time. It was just as important that they all agreed on what exactly it was time for.

Venus Brass, the eldest at seventy-five years, had seen her husband and children assassinated at the Director's orders, herself missing death by a fluke. A slow-moving, big-hearted, quickwitted Islander woman, Venus, with her husband, had built a food distribution empire. It was taken over by Flattery and wedded to Merman Mercantile. They transported fish and produce from small suppliers like Twisp to public markets for a percentage of the catch. Flattery did the only distribution now, where and when he chose and at a membership fee too high for a solo operation to afford.

Kaleb Norton-Wang, rightful heir to Merman Mercantile, was the youngest consul at twenty-three. Son of Scudi Wang, herself heiress to Merman Mercantile, and Brett Norton, Twisp's fishing partner, Kaleb had seen his parents killed when their boat mysteriously exploded one night at dockside. That was before anyone had learned to suspect Flattery's hand in such things.

Kaleb had slipped landside that night to play with some of the other children. He was ten years old, and supper conversation for months had been about Flattery, and his takeover maneuvers with Merman Mercantile.

Twisp, wakened from his coracle nearby, had found the boy screaming on the pier watching his family's boat burn. Twisp and Kaleb fled together to the barely habitable high reaches. Like his deceased father, Kaleb could see in the dark. His mother's inner acuity and her personal allegiance to the kelp gave Kaleb a formidable intelligence. He, like his mother, could communicate directly with the kelp by touch. He found it too painful to meet his parents' memories in the kelp, so he seldom explored the kelp-ways of the mind.

*He's too bitter,* Twisp thought. *Bitter pulls you down, gets you to make mistakes that you can't afford.*

He hadn't seen much of Kaleb lately. The boy's district was Victoria, Flattery's only solid stronghold upcoast. Twisp feared that Kaleb had met the challenge of that command so that he could wreak a personal vengeance on Flattery and his people. He hoped that he had taught Kaleb well enough that the boy wouldn't respond to Flattery the way Flattery had responded to his parents.

The upcoast inland regions were represented by Mona Flatwing, a red-faced, middle-aged woman who was speaking now.

"We are in a comfortable position," she said.

Her deep brown eyes glittered and her husky voice spoke with a heavy Islander lilt.

"Each of our households has foodstuffs for six months. We have surplus stores enough to handle a major refugee influx through next harvest. Consul from the coast tells me that we are in a similar position with our seafoods."

Venus Brass nodded affirmation.

"Frankly," Mona continued, "our people do not want to come down here to fight. They left here to get away from that, they've made good lives upcoast, they want to be left alone. They will accept anyone of good faith who seeks refuge, as always. The usual preparations have been made for defense, but I must emphasize this point: These people do not want to kill anyone."

Again, a nod from Venus Brass. Her shaky, high-pitched voice contrasted with Mona's.

"It is the same with our people," she said. "They use the freedom of the sea to get away from 'the troubles,' as they call them. They're a brave and hardy lot. Among them they amass quite a fleet and assault force. But like Kaleb's people, they live among Flattery's people when landside, they trade with them, families are intermarried. They do not want to kill anyone, particularly family. You've seen how Flattery has shuffled his troops to accommodate that attitude—"

*Bam!*

Kaleb's fist on his notestand startled everyone.

Twisp clenched a fist in reflex, then unclenched it slowly on his knee.

"This is Flattery's dream council," Kaleb said. His voice carried the sharp bitterness that Twisp often heard in it lately. "We are talking here of doing *nothing* to curb this madness, this wholesale murder. Was I the only one who witnessed what happened out there today?"

"Talking about what we will not do is preface to talking about—"

"Is preface to nothing, as usual," Kaleb interrupted. "It's historically true that humans are hungry only because humans allow it. We must simply not allow it, not for another day, not for another hour."

Venus withdrew as though she'd been slapped, then folded her arms across her thin chest.

"Did your people start this business today?" she asked.

Kaleb smiled, and the exuberance of it accented his youthful appearance.

*He's a one who's gone beyond his years,* Twisp thought. *Far enough that he knows when to use that smile.*

"That is Flattery's doing," Kaleb said. "I have another plan, one more consistent with our ideals. My people committed, and my contacts tell me that many of yours will, too."

"And then what?" Mona hissed, and sat forward. "*Doing* something will get their attention. Flattery will send security . . ."

It was an old argument, but Kaleb heard it out. At one point he looked across the table at Twisp. The eagerness that gleamed in his young eyes reminded Twisp of Kaleb's father when he was that age—smart, daring, impetuous. Brett Norton had killed once, out of reflex, but that killing had saved Twisp and Kaleb's mother.

Mona finished recounting her people's position.

"They'll take in refugees, but they won't leave the livelihoods they've built from nothing. Eluding detection is much preferable to facing conflict."

"I understand," Kaleb said. "That's the swiftgrazer's way. Something else is true of swifties—if a swiftie is hungry the whole rob's hungry. We've coordinated with and we have a plan rolling that will feed the rob."

Twisp repressed a smile.

*I guess he listened to my swiftgrazer pitch, after all.*

Twisp knew that, among the council, there was no such thing as rank. They would vote to participate or not, and to go the ways their decisions dictated.

"We each have plans," Twisp said, "now they will become a

single plan. Project Goddess is four hours overdue their upcoast checkpoint. That will merit some consideration as well, this session.''

There was a murmur about the table. The four witnesses looked pale and frightened when they came in, and the agitation of the council made them appear smaller, as well.

Twisp's hand went up to still the chatter.

"We have other fish in the pan. Please bear with me.''

Twisp noted a message coming across Dwarf MacIntosh's console, and nodded at Snej to retrieve it. He went on.

"Flattery has dominated with hunger and fear. His obvious motives: get himself offplanet, in command of a Voidship. We don't argue with getting rid of him, is that right?''

There were nods around the table, but Mona spoke up:

"He's going to take three thousand of our best people with him and leave that damned security force . . .''

"They *want* to go,'' Twisp emphasized. "They should be free to settle the void, if that's their passion. We will be rid of him, that is our only concern. But we will have to break down the machinery of his power before he leaves. He must be brought down first, and we must be assured that he can't possibly return. We must deal with criminals without becoming criminals ourselves. If we do not, then we and our children are lost.''

Snej read what MacIntosh had to say from the Orbiter.

"Twisp, Project Goddess has been . . . intercepted.''

"Intercepted? Well, now, that's a step up from 'lost,' at least. Where are they? Who did it?''

"It's the kelp,'' Snej said. "Dr. MacIntosh speculates that the kelp got a whiff of Crista Galli and decided to take her. He's being jammed on the burst system, but his kelp channel still works.''

"Did he dump enough data to brief us?'' Twisp asked.

He massaged away a headache gathering in his forehead. Today, more than others, he was feeling the weight of his second half-century. Snej handed him a messenger and he clipped it into his console.

"The kelp in sector eight diverted their foil into its stand,'' Mack's voice reported. "It completely shifted several transport channels to do so and an unknown number of subs were disabled, possibly lost. There have been casualties, number unknown. Current Control attempted mandatory 'persuasion,' on Flattery's standing orders. No effect . . .''

Murmurings rose around the table. Twisp, too, was amazed.

*The kelp resisted,* he thought. *There's the sign we need.*

"Do we have anyone in that area?" Kaleb asked. "Any Kelp Clan people who know what they're doing?"

Mona flurried her fingers across her console.

"Yes," she said. "We have an Oracle landside of their position, plenty of personnel."

"If shipping's disrupted there, our people are probably in trouble, too," Venus said. "I'll try to raise a sub, but my guess is that the whole area's impassable—"

Twisp interrupted.

"What we need now is total interference with anything Flattery does. Wherever his men go, whatever move he makes, we need people in the way, we need dead ends. He must be frustrated at every turn. Does his interference in Current Control indicate that he's penetrated us?"

"It's possible," Snej said, her mouth a grim line, "but I doubt it."

"Ask Dr. MacIntosh to shut down Current Control," Twisp said. "There will be reprisals there, as you know. But we know more about moving around in the kelp than anyone, and most of it's on our side. As of now, traffic worldwide will be at a standstill. You all know the dangers, of course."

Twisp, who had fished the open seas for most of his life, knew better than any of them the fates they had just decreed for thousands on and under the ocean. Countless innocent people were now marooned in unnavigable waters, some among hostile kelp. The die had been cast, and by Flattery himself.

"Our success or failure depends completely on the cooperation of the people of Pandora," he said. "We need to starve him out. Fight hunger with hunger, fear with fear . . ."

Kaleb stopped him with a raise of his hand, then apologized with the acceptable nod.

"We don't fight hunger with hunger," Kaleb said. His voice was soft, his tone as reprimanding as a new young father's.

"We're human beings," he said. "We fight hunger with food."

There was a deferential silence, then Mona's witness said, "Aye. Aye, we're with you."

"Kaleb, you show me how we can dump Flattery and feed the hungry and we're in, too," Venus said.

"It's so simple it'll make you cry," Kaleb said. "Briefing now appearing on your screens. As you can see, we'll need the cooperation that Twisp was talking about. We have to get Ozette and Galli on the air *immediately*. Can we count on Shadowbox?''

"You're right," Mona agreed, tapping her screen. "Timing is the key, here. The people cannot help if they don't know how. They will believe Ben Ozette, they will worship Crista Galli. They must be given a plan *now*."

"My people are infiltrating now," Kaleb said. His voice was calm, confident, his father's strong chin set straight ahead. "They will be about five thousand, well-mixed throughout the poor. Word of mouth is best among the poor."

"Anything else from MacIntosh?" Twisp asked.

Snej nodded, biting her lip. "Yes," she said. "He says Beatriz Tatoosh is aboard, and the drinking water has made her sick."

Snej looked up from the messenger, puzzlement wrinkling her brow.

Twisp felt his heart double-time in his chest.

"Well," he announced, "that's our personal code for big trouble in orbit. Flattery probably sent up a security force with Beatriz. He must suspect something's up with Mack. Damn!"

Twisp sucked in a deep breath and let it out slowly.

"Too bad she's not with us," he said. "I wish MacIntosh had some support up there right now."

"Let's see what kind of support we have down here right now," Kaleb said. "Let's mobilize our upcoast people and rescue that foil."

Kaleb rose, obviously ready to leave for Victoria immediately. *We need him here.*

"Kaleb," he said, "let's take a walk. You're nearly three hours away. Good people live upcoast, they're already searching. For old time's sake, let's go down to the Oracle. Maybe someone should ask the kelp what the hell it's up to."

*Roots and wings. But let the wings grow roots and the roots fly.*

—Juan Ramón Jiménez

Stella Bliss unpacked three crates of moss orchids and arranged them in threes along the short walkway to the foyer of the Wittle mansion. This job had come up only the night before, and Stella's moss orchids happened to be ready. She was a sculptress of flowers, and appreciated an audience for her art.

Stella wore her new lavender puff-sleeve blouse and a crisp pair of matching work pants. The blouse favored her breasts, tender with her recent pregnancy, but she supposed this would be the last time she'd be able to get into these pants for a while.

Stella skirted the security guards and servants who found excuses to watch her. The limelight made her nervous, though her stature had thrust her into the limelight often since she was a child. Twelve hands tall, Stella turned heads wherever she went, even when she went in overalls.

Stella dressed like the flowers she raised. Doob told his parents that, at home, bees followed every step she took but they never stung. Her shaggy dark hair framed a tanned face with high cheekbones and blue-green eyes. Her lips were full, often pursed with concentration. She smiled a lot lately, and had taken to humming old tunes to the new human sleeping inside her.

Growing plants and engineering them for food had been Stella's family's tradition for nine generations. Since the food shortages, production and research efforts went to food. Stella had never given up on flowers or the bees that made them possible.

She carried the tenth generation within her, a child that she knew by her dreams would grow to be a woman like herself. She knew this as her mother had known it, as all their mothers had known it for several centuries. It was a long tradition, difficult in these difficult times. These moss orchids were of Stella's own design and she was proud that today they would be seen by other artists, by musicians, those sculptors of air, by Pandoran gentry.

Stella had heard that His Honor Alek Dexter was colorblind, so she selected a blend that pleased herself. Most of the blossoms were in the lavender range, though she couldn't resist showing off a half-dozen of her delicate pinks.

A small-boned security guard with a big-boned swagger poked into each of her cartons with his lasgun and silently checked the moss beds with his knife. Stella had been scanned twice and body-searched by a matron when she entered the grounds. This was not the first time, and she supposed it wouldn't be the last. Stella had some strong opinions, but preferred to concentrate on her flowers.

A cordon of security closed off the entire block, and another contingent guarded the building. This was the home of the chief executive officer of Merman Mercantile, someone considered by the Director to be a prime target for the Shadows. He was rumored to be one of three men in line for the Director's position should an unforeseen unpleasantness occur.

A sweeping structure of molded stone and plasteel, this home showed no effects from the recent series of quakes that had devastated much of Kalaloch. Its border was secured by a two-meter-high wall of rock topped with shards of sharp metal and broken glass. It was hard for her to believe that The Line for this sector passed only a block away. No one who was setting up this reception seemed at all concerned about the sounds of screams and heavy vehicles less than a stone's throw behind them.

The grim-faced security sported a flesh flower behind his ear, one of the new sculpted skin designs that she found repulsive. His underarms blossomed huge sweat rings, something more than she would attribute to the muggy afternoon.

"What would you find in that dirt," she asked him when he finished, "deadly attack worms?"

The guard scowled, his glance flicking nervously from Stella to the smoky pall that collected under the gray cap of afternoon nimbus.

"I'm losing my sense of humor," he growled. "Don't push it."

"Are you afraid that the mob will come in here and—"

"I'm not afraid of anything," he blurted, puffing his boyish chest against baggy fatigues. "My job is to protect Mr. Dexter, and that's what I'm doing."

She began the tender task of removing the plants from their containers and setting them in their beds beside the walk. This was the part she liked—handling the silky vines and blind roots, smelling the loam as she broke it open. At the end of the day, when she cleaned her short nails, she did it over one of her pots so that nothing was lost.

"You must like flowers, you went through a lot of pain and trouble to get the one behind your ear."

"I was drunk," he said. "If they could get them to smell good, it wouldn't be so bad."

"They'll come up with something, you'll see. Smell these."

She held a lavender orchid up to him. He took it from her and put it to his nose, then allowed himself a smile. It pleased her that the tension in his face relaxed a bit.

"Yeah," he said, "that would be nice."

"Well, this type of flower didn't have a scent until just a year ago. And it didn't blossom from moss until five years ago. I taught it how."

"Flowers!" The security snorted in a show of disdain, but didn't turn away. "You can't eat flowers. You should grow something that people can eat."

"What?" She put her hand to her mouth in mock surprise. "They shoot you for growing food without a license. You don't need a license to grow flowers. Besides, your soul needs food, too. Flowers have a spiritual nutrition that you just can't measure."

He looked less skeptical, but kept his guarded posture. She bit back the temptation to talk about her bees, because bees meant honey and fewer than a handful of people knew about her honey production.

Once her plants were bedded she misted them well and swept

her clippings and stray dirt away from the walk. She felt a little nervous. She was stuck in town without transportation. Her neighbor, Billie, had given her a ride to the job first thing this morning. Her Cushette, though practically new, had burned out another something that meant it wouldn't start. She didn't like it in town, anyway. It wallowed in tight places and it always frustrated her. There was the tram into the central area with a transfer out but it was probably shut down because of the mobs. She didn't relish the idea of walking the ten klicks home without Doob to protect her.

"Stella, my dear, are you finished out here?"

Mrs. Wittle, the hostess, beckoned her from the front hatchway. She was a gray-haired, prim woman with an honest smile for everyone and a fair skin that could only be Merman-born. Though soft-spoken and delicate, Mrs. Wittle had singlehandedly saved a boatload of Pandora's finest art during that first series of quakes in '73. She had been a volunteer at the museum desk down under when the collapse came and commandeered an old delivery sub. Instead of saving herself, she loaded artwork into the sub even as the seams of the museum dome split, sending streams of waterspray powerful enough to slice a human in half.

"Yes, Mrs. Wittle. Do you like them?"

The elderly woman glanced down at the walk and her eyebrows raised ever so slightly.

"Lovely," she said, and sighed. "They were right about you, my dear. But now I have a problem and perhaps you can help me."

"What is it?"

"Some of the help that we were counting on haven't shown up today . . . the troubles, you know. Could you stay awhile longer and greet our guests at the door? I have the guest list here, and name tags are on the table just inside the hatch. Of course, you are welcome to stay as my guest and enjoy the reception. Would you do that for me?"

Stella had strong feelings about rich people, and they were strong negative feelings. A hundred meters away the starving poor lined up for hours to buy limited rations with their hard-earned pay. Servants of the rich handed over cards stamped "Exception" at the high-security back door loading dock and filled their vans with an abundance of food. Stella had worked parties like this before to be able to take home leftovers. The pay meant nothing, she had always earned more than her ration card allowed her to buy. She had never been able to figure out the red tape process for getting a ration card stamped "Exception."

But today her Cushette was not running and she had no safe way home.

"Yes," she said, "I can stay. But I'm not dressed . . . and I'll need a ride home."

Mrs. Wittle brightened and took her by the elbow.

"You don't know what a worry you've lifted, dear. Of course we can arrange a ride for you, you just leave that to me. Now, let's have a look at my daughter's wardrobe. She had some wonderful things that should fit you nicely. There's an elegant black dress that will look splendid on you, though I'm sure that anything would look splendid on you."

Stella blushed at the compliment.

"Thank you," she said. "She won't mind?"

Mrs. Wittle's face darkened for an unguarded moment, then she set her chin forward.

"No, my dear, I'm afraid not," she said. "She was killed in that terrible scene at the college last season. Terrible."

"I'm . . . I'm sorry to hear that."

"Well, she had her own mind," Mrs. Wittle said, "and she insisted on using it." Then, in a whisper, she added, "I was *so* proud of her. I'll tell you the story someday, this is not the time."

The dress was slinky and black. The fit in the bust was uncomfortably tight, though it seemed that any pressure at all hurt her breasts lately. The neckline plunged a bit, too, showing her off as she hadn't been shown off before.

"I wish Doob could see me in this," she said, turning in front of a pair of mirrors. "He'd love it."

"Then you'll just have to keep it, my dear," Mrs. Wittle said. Tears welled in her eyes but nothing spilled. "In fact, I wish you'd look through these clothes and take anything you can use. It's not right that they just hang here, they're not paintings, after all."

Stella protested but Mrs. Wittle prepared a carton full of her daughter's clothes, then escorted Stella to her position at the small table beside the entryway.

The guest of honor, Alek Dexter, arrived tugging his shirt-sleeves flush with the jacket cuffs and cursing the muggy afternoon. Stella pinned his name tag to his left breast and smoothed the fabric out of habit. Instead of joining the rest of the guests, he lingered beside her and unabashedly appraised her cleavage. She caught his gaze and held it until he looked away.

"Been in meetings all day," he mumbled. "After this shindig that the distributors put together I have to speak at a Progress Club dinner in two hours and then meet with the Director at a cocktail party at eight. No wonder I'm always out of breath and can't lose weight. You look beautiful, my dear—" he squinted at her name tag and moved closer to her chest, "—Stella. Stella Bliss."

They shook hands and she found his palm very sweaty.

*I didn't think these bigshots sweat in public.*

A sheen gathered at his forehead and upper lip and he dabbed at it with a handkerchief.

The Honorable Alek Dexter motioned to his driver, who lounged nearby in the cool breeze of the entryway.

"I'll need another shirt," he said, his voice lowered. "Powder blue will do for tonight."

"Streets are blocked," his driver said. "Couldn't make it back in time to fetch you for dinner."

His voice sounded sullen to Stella and she suspected from the tightening of his jaw that if there was one thing Alek Dexter did not allow in his presence it was sullenness.

"Then *buy* one," he snapped. "Shops are open until curfew, and the market's only a few blocks away." He waved his hand in dismissal. "Take it out of petty cash. Change your attitude or change jobs."

The hatchway behind the driver framed a small street scene capped with a tumultuous sky. Two guards faced the street with their backs to him. A third tilted his head at the sound of three tones that came from the messenger on his belt. He picked it up, spoke into it, then hurried inside. His face seemed to pale more with each of the five steps that brought him to His Honor's side. Their conversation was brief and whispered, but Stella heard every word.

"Code Brutus standby warning, sir. Do you want to secure here or at the compound?"

"Shit!" Alek Dexter said, and he turned his face away as though he'd been slapped. He, like Mr. Wittle, was a possible successor to the Director. He rubbed his forehead while a trackful of security emptied itself out front. His face was as pale as his guard's. He watched the security squad fan out from the track and take up positions outside. A half-dozen armed men covered with grime and streaming sweat shouldered by him and stationed themselves about the reception.

"These ours?" he asked his guard.

The guard shrugged, his lasgun gripped white-knuckle tight in his shaking hands. "Don't know, sir."

"Humph," he grunted. "Guess it's hard to know what side they're on if we don't know what side *we're* on. Just a warning, you say? Flattery's not . . ."

"Yes, sir, a warning. Flattery issued it."

"We'll wait here," Dexter said. "If we're going to find ourselves stuck somewhere, I'd prefer it to be with this lovely young woman."

He bowed, took Stella's hand and kissed it. Then he strolled inside to the hostess and her guests, passing the long table set with an array of the most beautiful fruits and seafoods that Stella had ever seen. The centerpiece was a meter-high chunk of ice carved to represent a leaping porpoise.

The fighting sounded closer, and the security quietly closed the double hatch. Stella was more than a little afraid.

Not once had Dexter glanced at her orchids.

*To be conscious, you must surmount illusion.*

—Prudence Lon Weygand, M.D., number five,
original crew member, Voidship *Earthling*

The series of explosions dropped by Flattery's Skyhawks from the surface wounded the green kelp in sector eight, killed tens of thousands of fishes and a pod of bottlenose porpoises and roiled up enough sediment to clog submersible filters for a fifty-click radius. A huge stand of blue kelp neighboring sector eight retracted all of its fronds instinctively and clamped itself as tight around its central lagoon as possible. In this configuration, its leaves were packed so tight that it could barely breathe. Feeding was out of the question.

The blue kelp, when fully deployed, reached a diameter of nearly one hundred kilometers. Its outer fringes bordered domestic kelp projects for nearly 280 degrees of its circumference; the rest faced open ocean and some of it was growing daily at a visible rate. For its own safety, it kept out of contact with the domestic kelps. These were slaves to the humans, bound to the electric whip, this much the blue gathered from the dying shards that drifted its way. There would be many such shards soon. Kelp death always followed these explosions. Other deaths followed, too, at times feeding the blue kelp into an incredible spurt of growth.

This day something else drifted in on the currents. Something like an aura, a fragrance, something that kept the kelp from hugging itself too tight, too long. Something stirred this blue kelp deep within itself, setting its genetic memories tingling. Nothing would quite come to the fore. Soon, the blue could no longer help itself and it opened its fronds wide in hopes of a good strong whiff.

*Feed men, then ask of them virtue.*

—Dostoevsky, *The Brothers Karamazov*

Turbulence from the blasts hadn't settled yet when the *Flying Fish* pitched, helpless, to the surface. Rico's eyes teared instantly in the sudden glare of afternoon sun that jammed the cockpit. He groped for his sunglasses and tried to blink away the afterglow. To starboard, he saw a long gray line that must be the coast. To port, two or three kilometers away, the surface seethed with a mean white froth as far as he could see.

A puddle of seawater widened into a pool beneath Elvira's command couch. Her nosebleed was slowing and she shook her head, trying to clear the concussion that had hit her with the first of the depth-charges.

*Anybody but Elvira would've been scrat bait out there,* Rico thought.

Somehow she'd made it back into the engine-room airlock by herself, though stunned and quivering from the blast. There were many other blasts, too many to count.

249

"That goddamn Flattery's answer to everything is to blow it up," he grumbled.

Kelp lights winked out all around them as the sea was glutted with shredded fronds and torn vines.

"Sister Kelp," Elvira said, following his gaze across the tumultuous surface, "she retracts, saves herself."

"Elvira, I don't want to hear that 'Sister Kelp' crap. I want to get us out of here."

"Overflights!" she warned, and pointed to two specks at ten o'clock off the port cabin. Her hands automatically worked the dive sequence, but the engines remained still.

"Jammed," she said, her face impassive and dazed. "Silt and . . . kelp in the filters."

"Don't sweat it, Elvira," Rico said. He patted her arm. "They're the ones who dropped the charges. If they carried all that payload, they're short on fuel. At least we're not dealing with a bunch of mines out here."

Rico unharnessed himself and got Elvira a towel out of one of the lockers.

"Here," he said. "Dry yourself off, change into a new dive suit. We might be here awhile and there's no sense you getting sick."

She took the towel, and it seemed to Rico that her senses were coming back.

"Flattery can track a one-seater coracle from port to port with the Orbiter, anyway," he said. "These guys can't set down out here, and with Crista Galli aboard they don't dare blow us up. Meanwhile, we've got to get her and Ben to some big medicine, and fast."

Two sonic booms rocked them further as the overflights dove in on them and pulled out. Rico could make out the pilots' faces as the tiny aircraft flashed past.

"They're young, Elvira, did you see that? With their whole lives ahead of them they chain themselves to Flattery." He fisted the arm of his couch and grumbled, "Why do they do that? They should be out cuddling some young thing in a hatchway somewhere. Didn't their mothers teach them any better?"

"Their mothers are hungry, Rico, and they're hungry *now*."

Rico glanced at Elvira with surprise. He was accustomed to speaking to her but getting nothing but grunts for reply. She was already out of her restraints and fighting the toss of the foil, making her way to the aft lockers.

"You're not going out there again," he said. "The seas are a mess, nothing can get through here."

"You will calm down," she said, and it sounded like an order.

Elvira peeled off her dive suit and toweled off her finely toned musculature with the candor typical of Mermen. "Care for the others. I will clean out the filters."

As she slipped into a fresh suit, Rico realized he'd been aroused at the sight of Elvira's pale body. Even her thumb-sized nipples seemed muscular in the chill. He would never approach Elvira, both of them knew that, but the surprise of his arousal reminded Rico of Snej, and how much he'd missed her.

Elvira's plan was the logical thing, he knew. He ticked off a list of priorities.

*Ben and Crista,* he thought. *Keep them breathing. Monitor the radio, prepare for surprises by Vashon security.*

Elvira swept past him to the hatch without so much as a glance. Rico fought the pitch and roll of the foil to the lockers and pulled out three more dive suits. He worked himself along by handholds in the bulkhead back to the galley. On his way, he listened to the crackle of the radio and the report from the overflights.

"Skywatch leader to base. Charges away. We have your fish, over."

"Roger, Skywatch. We mark your position. Our bird is launched. ETA thirty minutes. Status report."

*Thirty minutes!* Rico thought.

Their bird must be a foil, and a fast one.

*Not room for a lot of hardware or a lot of bodies—good. We might have a few surprises for them.*

The radio continued to chatter about the condition of the *Flying Fish* and speculation on the occupants, but they were quickly out of range.

Rico bent over Ben and saw that he was immobile, his chest was not rising and falling, but his color wasn't bad. He put his cheek to Ben's mouth and detected the slightest breath. Checking the pulse at Ben's neck, he noted that his partner's heart was beating, but only a few beats per minute. His eyes were open, but still. They looked dry, so Rico opened and closed the lids a few times to lubricate them, then left them closed.

He unhooked the restraints and struggled to get Ben into one of the dive suits.

"We're topside," he said, hoping Ben could hear. "They threw some charges at the kelp, but I think it's just surface damage. Elvira's out there unclogging the intakes. Flattery's people have a foil on our tail, they'll be here in no time. We may have to go over the rail.''

He heard a groan from Crista Galli, and saw that she was trying to sit up against her restraints.

"Your girlfriend's coming around," he said. "I'll get her into a suit, then get into the code book and let Operations know what's going on. Everybody else seems to know where we are."

He sealed Ben's suit and inflated the collar, just in case. When Rico turned to Crista Galli, he saw that she was crying. Her red-rimmed, swollen eyes stared at Ben's deathlike form on the galley deck. She seemed to be conscious and aware.

"Can you understand me?" Rico asked. In spite of her restraints, he remained well out of reach.

She nodded.

"Yes."

"Have you ever had this reaction before?"

"Yes." Her voice was slurred. "Once. Before he gave me shots. I pretended to take pills, spit them out later."

"What will happen next?"

She tried a shrug. "More of the same. Maybe seizures. It takes . . . a while." She added, in a slurred whisper, "Nobody's ever made me feel like a human being except Ben."

Rico noticed that the pupils of her eyes dilated and constricted wildly.

*Must be some potent drugs,* he mused. *Damn that Flattery.*

"We are in the open," he explained, "and helpless. You need to have a dive suit on in case we go into the water."

It flashed on him then what Flattery must've realized all along, what Operations warned in their instructions: "Do not let her into the water. Do not let her contact the kelp." This was speculation, precaution. There would be no other choice if Vashon security showed up, there was no point worrying about it.

"I can help you with it if you can't do it yourself. I'm sorry to say this, but I'd rather not touch you."

He held the suit out to her at arm's length.

"I can't get out of this harness," she said.

Rico tapped the quick-release mechanism and she was free. He recoiled from her, partly as a reflex, partly because the foil pitched his way.

At this, she cringed away from him, her face even more pale and her jaw set.

"And what do *you* think I am?" she asked.

"I don't know," he said. "Do you?"

"I know that I don't think . . . I *can't* think that I do this . . ." She gestured limply at Ben. "It *can't* be me!"

"It's the drugs," Rico said.

He tried to keep the anger out of his voice. She needed reassurance, not another enemy. "Remember, the drugs are Flattery's doing, not yours."

Her tears, the way she looked at Ben *seemed* like the genuine article.

*But look at what happened to Ben,* he cautioned himself.

"Get your suit on," Rico said. "We don't have much time."

Crista had to slip out of her dress to don the dive suit. Rico knelt beside Ben, a hand on his forehead. He moved a little, and Rico took it for a good sign. His breathing was much stronger.

Crista did not seem modest at all, nor did she look like a monster.

*Probably spent so much time as a lab animal she didn't have a chance to get shy.*

Rico, like Ben, had been raised among Islanders, a generally shy lot. Rico admitted to himself that Crista had the best-looking legs he'd ever seen. Again, he thought of Snej back at Operations, and sighed. He planned to send a message to her, too, along with whatever he'd think of to say to Operations. He turned back to Crista Galli.

*A little pale,* he thought.

She seemed very weak, and struggled just to pull her suit on and fasten the seals. Her breathing was rapid and shallow. Her forehead beaded sweat and she was still more pale than when Rico had first seen her in the village. Her eyes were doing their dilation trick and he noticed an uncontrollable tremor in her legs.

"Can you get back into your harness?" he asked.

She shook her head.

"No," she said, her voice weaker now. "It's starting . . ."

She was drifting out again. She lay down on her couch, eyes still open.

"Are you still with us?" he asked. "Can you hear me?"

"Yes," she said. "Yes."

Rico still didn't want to touch her. Whatever it was, it had nearly killed Ben and he wasn't about to let the same thing happen to himself. He reached around her carefully and snicked the harness into place, then snugged it up with a jerk. He pushed the head of the couch back so that she lay flat. By then Crista was unconscious again.

Rico hurried into his own suit and noted that the seas had calmed somewhat. He could hear the thump and scrape of Elvira at the hull ports, and hoped that the kelp wouldn't set her hallucinating as it did some people. She seemed to have been all right before.

"It'd be just our luck," he muttered to himself. "Best damned pilot in the whole damned world thinking her gauges are grapefruits."

There was a very loud scrape, more of a long, slithering rasp across the top of the foil. Then another. It was the same serpentine sound that the kelp had made when it grabbed them. Rico jumped for the cabin, but it was too late.

The whole foil tipped on its side and he was thrown against the port bulkhead so hard it knocked the wind out of him. He saw, through the swarm of black amoebas across his vision, that they were airborne. He was jostled again, not so much this time, and as the bow of the foil tilted upward he saw them being pulled up into a mass of hylighter tentacles.

"Shit!"

He struggled to his knees and crawled the upended bulkhead to the command couch under the plaz. He could flip open a port and get a shot at it with his lasgun . . .

That was when he saw how big this hylighter really was. He guessed it at a hundred meters across, with its two lead tentacles, which gripped the foil, at nearly that length. Even the smallest tentacle was thicker than Rico.

They were already a hundred meters or so in the air, and rising. *That pitch back there,* he thought, *it must've dumped a helluva ballast to be able to pick us up.*

It was then that he thought of Elvira, and scrambled for a view of the seas below. She was there, dive suit inflated, floating on her back. She must have seen him, but she didn't wave.

"Damn!"

He couldn't drop her a flare, he couldn't try the engines. Either of these might touch off the hundreds of cubic meters of hydrogen in the monster hylighter. It tucked the *Flying Fish* upside-down against its great orange belly. Rico had never been this close to a hylighter before, but he'd seen them explode. A hylighter considerably smaller than this one had flattened the first tiny settlement at Kalaloch. Six hundred people cooked alive in that firestorm. He and Ben had covered that one, too.

The living were the worst. He remembered that Ben wouldn't settle for the easy story, the inevitable films of cooked flesh on living bone, shaking chills, vomit and screams.

"Just shoot their eyes," Ben had told him. "Leave the rest to me."

Ben asked them about their lives, not about the blast. The dying and near-dying filled eighteen hours of tape before the dashers hit. It was Rico's footage of the team fighting for their own lives against a dozen hunts of dashers in a feeding frenzy that chilled the holo audience worldwide.

Rico saw that the coast was coming up fast and black weather pushed behind them. He hoped that the weight of the foil wouldn't pull the hylighter too low to clear the gray bluffs ahead. He worked his way back to the cabin along the ceiling and sat below the command couches. This coliseum of a hylighter had a destination in mind, and that destination was land. If it didn't bash them to bits against this cliff face it would blow them up inland.

Rico reviewed their odds and didn't like what he came up with, though he was sure he'd rather clear the cliff than not. He wondered whether Operations had a code provision for this one. He hoped that Operations could beat Flattery's people to Elvira. Rico refused to mull over the consequences if they didn't.

Just off the cliff face the daily afternoon squall whipped up. The sky fisted down on them without warning, clouds churning in their typical black and lasgun gray.

*No lightning,* Rico prayed to himself. *We don't need lightning.*

They did need the cloud cover, this he knew. With good cover more overflights and Flattery's spies in the Orbiter would be worthless. The ride got bumpier as the squall moved inland with them. Rico was close enough to the face of the bluff to see the markings on the back of a flatwing when an updraft sank his belly. They almost cleared the top, he saw that clearly, but the stern of the foil caught the lip of the bluff, cartwheeling the bow of their craft deep into the leathery belly of the hylighter.

Unrestrained, Rico was flung like a toy about the cabin. The foil tumbled down the cliff face as the hylighter deflated and collapsed on top of it. When the foil came to rest Rico lay dazed across the plazglas windshield of the cabin. All he could see under the shadow of the hylighter's canopy was an immense cloud of blue dust. He flexed his arms and legs, coughed to test his ribs. Bruised, but nothing broken.

"Great!" Rico told himself. "'Keep her away from the kelp,' they said. Here we are, smothering in the stuff."

He tried calming himself, but a few deep breaths did not still the shaking in his hands. He hoped the foil had slid all the way to the beach. He didn't relish being perched halfway up a cliff.

The afternoon downpour washed over the canopy and their foil. Rico thought of Elvira, caught in open water in the squall, and assessed her chances. They summed up close to zero. She might now be one with her sister kelp.

"At least there's not much hydrogen left in that monster," he muttered.

He switched on the cabin lights and radio. A couple of the lights worked, but the radio was gone. He took a deep breath of the kelp-laced air before heading aft to check on Ben and Crista.

*If you think that vision is greater than action, why do you enjoin upon me the terrible action of war?*

—from *Zavatan Conversations with the Avata,*
Queets Twisp, elder

Mack was awaiting a call-back from security when suddenly his instruments showed random explosive damage to the kelp in sector eight.

*He didn't wait,* Mack thought. *Flattery wants whatever's in there in a bad way.*

Mack was sure that the "something" included Crista Galli. Instrumentation showed merging patterns between the wounded domestic kelp and the massive neighboring stand of wild blue. Mack and Alyssa Marsh had done peripheral studies of that particular stand of blue, the largest wild kelp bed in the world.

*It learned to hide from us, to convolute itself so it could grow inside a ring of domestic kelps and outmass them without detection.*

Now that it had broken through, he suspected that it could wreak havoc with Current Control. If it was as big as the Gridmaster said it was, then the blue kelp could possibly *be* Current Control.

*If this kelp's on our side, then Flattery's surrounded,* he thought. *But what if it's not on our side?*

Beatriz was his big worry now. She always checked in from the docking bay, but this time he had heard nothing. When she was incommunicado inside her studio he suspected trouble. It wasn't like her at all. Just a blink after Spud left, a spinjet jockey reported seeing a body expelled from the shuttle airlock. Nobody was answering his calls in security or inside the studio.

"Dammit!"

Now the Gridmaster was getting a response from the kelp, an incredibly healthy and powerful response. This stand that the depth charges had stunned back into mere reflex reawakened immediately—with a corresponding shift in frequency.

*This is the new kelp,* he thought. *It's absorbed the memories of our domestics and taken them over.*

All of the hardware from the domestic kelp was intact, but instead of dozens of frequencies dancing the screens, there was now only one kelp frequency on the Gridmaster.

Mack's screen showed the grid reforming, except for an unresponsive area in the northwestern corner. He hoped that wasn't pruned back too far.

"Well," he muttered, "so far it seems to like us."

He had planned to use Current Control to turn the kelps against Flattery. He'd groomed as many sentient stands as he could muster for one last try, for the time that Flattery went too far. MacIntosh saw war as a drug, an extremely addicting drug, and he didn't want Pandorans to start using it.

"I want that sector on visual," he told the sector monitor. "We should be able to spot them."

All he got on visual was the gray-black whirl of afternoon squall that obliterated his view of the entire sector. Ozette, LaPush and Galli were under there somewhere. He hoped against hope that the depth charges didn't turn them all into soup.

*Com-line's still down to the studio,* he thought. *If Spud doesn't get in there, we'll have to get their attention somehow.*

A feeling stranger than his weightlessness flipped through his stomach. He shook it off, as he had shaken off the chill that slipped into the air after her shuttle docked. He wondered how many had come up on that flight. The shuttle could carry thirty to forty, depending on equipment. Then there was OMC life-support, and the techs. Everyone aboard would have to know what happened.

He didn't like thinking about the OMC, where it came from, what Flattery had done to it. She had been *Alyssa,* not "it," but he found "it" a lot easier to handle at the moment. Life-support was Mack's responsibility, as it had been aboard the *Earthling.* He did not relish the notion of that job.

"Well," he muttered to himself, "before we get that far I might have a few surprises for Flattery."

A soft tone went off near the turret, alerting him that something was forming up on the kelp's private holo stage. MacIntosh had built the thing after consulting Beatriz on holography. He had routed it through the Gridmaster in hopes of getting images from the kelp. In the two months that it had been experimental it had far exceeded his dreams.

The kelp had been frustrated for a long time, and it had a lot to say. So far it was all images, flashing lights and odd sounds. The images were clear—usually solid information about real things in real time. The sounds and lights seemed to be "talk," or inflection, or philosophizing. MacIntosh had not yet been able to interpret anything but the more obvious images.

He launched himself across the small office toward his new setup at the base of the turret. He didn't care much for the near-zero-gee environment this close to the axis, but it was the most practical location for an observation station. At first, he had liked the immediate access to the shuttle port.

To get the near-normal gravity rimside he would have to put up with the annoying two-minute spin of the Orbiter that made visualization of anything nearly impossible. His body was lanky enough that it got in the way more often than not. Since he'd become acquainted with Beatriz Tatoosh, he had come to like the immediate access to the Holovision studio, too.

His experimental holo stage lit up with the image of a giant hylighter dragging its ballast across the wavetops. This projection was the best quality he'd ever seen. It was a perfect miniaturization and the collating data identified this as the source of the disruption within the kelp. A metallic glint off the ballast drew his attention closer to the tiny three-D scene in front of him.

"That's not ballast!"

The miniature holo played out the incident with the *Flying Fish* and the hylighter. He watched from the hylighter's view as they bore down on the cliff. They came in fast, and when MacIntosh realized that they wouldn't clear the top he caught himself pulling his feet up. Then the hylighter burst, and the screen went blank.

"There's an Oracle somewhere near there," he muttered. "Maybe we can muster up a rescue team."

He handed himself back to his command console and paged Spud on the intercom. That was when all hell broke loose from the klaxons.

The four-klaxon alarm meant a fully involved fire somewhere in the forward axis section, *his* section. His greatest fear was for the shuttle docking station and its spare fuel stores.

With a four-klaxon alarm the fire could be in Current Control, the studio area or the shuttle docking bay. All areas sealed off automatically. Warning lights winked on in all axis quarters and the Orbiter intercom repeated calmly, "Vacuum suits mandatory in all sealed areas. In case of fire, vacuum will be installed. Vacuum will be installed. Vacuum suits mandatory in all sealed areas . . ."

MacIntosh typed out the "area clear, visual" code for Current Control on his console. If the area sensors detected no fire danger, then Current Control would not be sealed off. He snapped open the hatchside locker and followed the prescribed drill. He sealed himself into his pressure suit and activated the communication unit beside the faceplate. He sprung the hatch to the passageway in time to see a groundpounder security slap Spud across the face with a lasgun butt. Spud spun against the studio hatch, and the security grabbed a closer handhold for the leverage to try again.

MacIntosh hollered, "Hold it!" but the man hit Spud again. Spud floated, unconscious, in midpassageway.

MacIntosh turned his set on "full."

"Hold it!" he yelled. "Stand down, mister."

The security was obviously direct from groundside and lacked the skills for maneuvering in the axis area of the Orbiter. He spun around at the voice and let go his handhold. The momentum in near-zero-gee sent him spinning up the passageway toward MacIntosh. The man let go of his lasgun as he flailed for balance and Mack scooped it up as he sailed by.

Mack reached Spud as he started coming around.

"I heard them say they'd kill her," Spud said, through a mouthful of blood. "I pulled the alarm because I didn't know what else to do."

"Good thinking, Spud," he said. "Get a suit on in case we break vacuum."

The arriving volunteer fire squad crowded the passageway as Spud suited up, and close behind them the usual throng was forming. In spite of their bulky suits the squad moved with a grace that MacIntosh envied. He looked around for the owner of the lasgun, but the man had disappeared. The hatch to the studio remained sealed.

MacIntosh plugged his communicator directly into Spud's headset.

"Beatriz knows the drill," he said. "She'll suit up."

"Does she know the visual 'all clear' code?"

MacIntosh nodded.

"She knows it, but I'll bet she knows better than to use it."

It took two things to prevent a sealed-off fire area from being committed to vacuum: an automatic sensor signal "all clear" to the Orbiter computer, and a coded visual "all clear" signal to the computer. Since the sensors in the studio undoubtedly reported no sign of fire, the computer awaited the visual code indicating that a human had inspected the scene and declared it clear. Meanwhile, the suspect area remained sealed off, accessible only by fire personnel.

The intercom warned: "Attention axis deck, yellow sectors eight through sixteen. Vacuum instillation in three minutes. Vacuum in three minutes. Full pressure suit mandatory in these areas . . ."

The electronic device that the fire squad used to enter sealed hatches didn't work on the first try, or the second. MacIntosh plugged his set into the bulkhead receptacle and tried direct contact with the studio.

Spud plugged into MacIntosh.

"Anything?" he asked.

MacIntosh shook his head. "Static. They're just not . . ."

On the third try the hatch sprang aside. The fire squad rushed in and MacIntosh shouldered himself behind them, hiding the lasgun as best he could. He was glad he did.

Beatriz was the only one who had managed to don a suit. She stood to the side of the hatch and grabbed MacIntosh as he raced through. The momentum spun him into the bulkhead beside her, but she had a good grip on a handhold so they both stayed put.

The others fumbled with the seals of their suits, surprised at the suddenness of the fire squad's entry. One of the newcomers made a clumsy dive for the back of the studio, but he was grabbed in flight by a firefighter and his partner who wrestled him to a handhold and restrained him. MacIntosh made sure the rest of them saw his lasgun and they stayed put.

Mack's squad finished their sweep of the room in less than a minute and one of them sent the "all clear, visual" signal back to the computer. The intercom announced "all clear," and MacIntosh unfastened his headgear. Beatriz beat him to it.

"They killed my crew," she shouted. "They killed your security squad and they have weapons back there in the lockers."

One of the firefighters sailed to the back of the studio to search out the weapons cache.

"Hold these men," MacIntosh ordered, "and hand out whatever weapons they have, we're likely to need them."

The firefighters used various lines and straps from their pockets to truss up Leon and his two men. All three were confounded and helpless in zero-gee. The fire squad lived and worked in it every day, but MacIntosh still had to admire their ease of movement, even with three struggling captives in tow.

Beatriz hugged him tight and kissed him. Even through the added bulk of the vacuum suit, she felt good to him.

"I was hoping we could do that under other circumstances," he said. He felt her trembling and held her close.

"There are more of them," she said, "I counted thirty-two altogether. My guess is that their leader, Captain Brood, is with the OMC."

"Spud, you heard?"

"Yes, Dr. Mack."

"All this action's going to bring somebody down here. Seal off axis sector yellow, code admission only. We might seal a few of them in here with us, but it'll give us time to deal with the rest of them."

Spud activated the nearest console and completed the order in a blink.

MacIntosh motioned to the firefighter with the white headgear.

"There's a big storage locker across the passageway that's empty. Seal these men in there and then meet me in the teaching lab next to Current Control. If you can find any weapons from our own security, bring them. I want your best tunnel rats, as many as you can muster."

"Aye, Commander," he said, then added, "these men are groundsiders, sir. You saw how clumsy they are. Our best weapons here are zero-gee and vacuum."

"You're right," MacIntosh said, taking Beatriz's hand, "and strategy. Let's move."

*While the fat and flesh cleaving to the flame are devoured by it, you who cleave to it are yet alive.*

*—Zohar: The Book of Splendor*

Spider Nevi hoped that Flattery was getting a humbling at the hands of the rabble, because Nevi was certainly getting a humbling out here at the hands of the kelp. He'd spotted Zentz floating on his back, only the whites of his eyes visible, the mouthpiece to his breathing apparatus discarded. A long strand of kelp wrapped his middle, and it reeled him steadily toward the side of the lagoon.

Lucky for Zentz that he'd had the presence of mind to inflate the collar of the suit. It kept his head and shoulders on the surface, though fat as he was his body floated nicely enough without it. Lucky, too, that Nevi had hit the vine quickly and on the first shot. He had Zentz all the way back to the foil before he felt the seethe of kelp anger on his heels. Zentz appeared to be breathing.

*It would've been so much easier if he had drowned,* Nevi thought. *But I still might need him. A live body is a lot more useful than a dead one.*

Nevi knew one thing for sure, he was getting out of reach of the kelp. One zombie on the crew was enough. The foil started a slow spin, and Nevi swore under his breath.

*It's channeling us into its reach.*

He managed to secure Zentz's collar with a line from the aft hatchway and pulled him aboard the foil. He used a boathook to brush off pieces of kelp frond that clung to the unconscious Zentz.

The whole situation had passed beyond the ridiculous for Nevi, now it was simply comic. It didn't matter to him whether Flattery stayed in power or not. Whoever was up there would need Spider Nevi and his services, and Nevi enjoyed that position. It was like having three or four good chess moves already set while the opponent was in check. Well, it was time Flattery learned his worth.

*Send me out here, will he?*

Zentz had been kelped, and the automatics in his dive suit kept him from swimming off to who-knows-where. They didn't keep him from struggling blindly against rescue. At sixty-five kilos, it took Nevi a while to wrestle the nearly one hundred kilos of Zentz inside the foil and harness him into his couch. He didn't know why he bothered, except that it would give Flattery something to play with if they didn't come back with Crista Galli and Ozette.

Nevi quickly maneuvered the foil to the center of the lagoon and prepared for vertical takeoff. It would eat up more fuel than he liked, but it would cut his odds of getting grabbed by that kelp stand.

He punched in the automatic VTO sequence and all of the power of the foil kicked him right in the seat of the pants. It swayed like a bug on a blade of grass until they were a safe hundred meters above the lagoon. He set the controls for straight-and-level and turned the foil loose. A routine ten-minute refueling had turned into nearly an hour's delay, and Nevi couldn't afford to waste another blink.

He listened to the radio and couldn't make heads or tails of the situation back at the Preserve. He'd tried to raise Flattery on their dedicated channel, but no one keyed him in at the other end. One fragment of transmission from an overflight came through and he shook his head in wonder.

*What idiot talked Flattery into depth-charging the foil we're hunting?*

He snapped off the radio and relaxed his grip on the controls. The afternoon turbulence didn't sit well on his stomach, so he flipped off the autopilot. He needed something to do besides listen to Zentz breathe through his drool. He kept the yellow arrow on his viewscreen pointed toward the green coordinates set down by the overflights.

He could tell, by the way Zentz squirmed in the copilot's couch, that the Chief of Security might be coming around.

Nevi had trouble suppressing a sneer at the mere thought of Zentz as chief of anything.

*Chief* Breach *of Security,* he thought. *Chief of* In*security.*

Nevi had to admit that Zentz had held a difficult line against the increasing hostility of the villagers for nearly a year. A mob of villagers was one thing—this Crista Galli and her Shadow playmates were quite another.

"A hundred meters across!" Zentz gurgled.

Zentz's eyes were wild, the pupils dilating and constricting on both sides, dancing to some strange rhythm.

Nevi didn't answer. Zentz had started this raving about some giant hylighter as soon as Nevi had gotten the foil back in the air.

"Crista Galli, kelp gone crazy," Zentz went on, "giant hylighter grab whole foil . . ."

"That's hocus-pocus, and it's in your head," Nevi said.

He knew Zentz couldn't hear him, but it made Nevi feel better. His voice was calm and flat, a practiced calm that paid off whenever he had to work with Zentz. He knew it gave Zentz the creeps, and that always gave Nevi the edge. He wondered whether it would give Zentz the creeps in his dreams. He hoped so. It was this flying that made Nevi nervous.

The storm buffeted Nevi against the restraints in his command couch. Some of the updrafts along the coastline nearly emptied his stomach. Like most Pandorans, he preferred traveling the kelp's subways, particularly during afternoon storms, but today speed was critical. The cat had played the mouse too loose. Maybe Zentz was right about their foil. Who knew what the kelp had shown him?

If Ozette and Crista Galli got loose afoot in this country they might just wind up being dasher bait. Ozette didn't strike him as the survival type. Nevi knew that Flattery needed both of them alive—for now. For now, what Flattery needed Nevi needed, and he didn't want to get so comfortable out here that he forgot it.

*Zentz needs them alive more than anyone,* he thought.

The big question mark for Nevi was the hylighter—what would contact with that thing do to Crista Galli?

*Or what might it do* for *her?*

And something about those damned Zavatan squatters upcoast gave even Nevi the creeps. Nobody could farm the open country like that without some kind of protection. He wanted to know what that protection was. Or who. They kept one jump ahead of Flattery and the dashers—accomplishments that captured Nevi's personal respect.

The squall cleared occasionally, allowing Nevi glimpses of the coastline. Cloudfront pushed across both suns and confounded his perspective. He knew that thousands of square kilometers lay under Zavatan camouflage. It didn't take much imagination to appreciate the value of the new fertile land below.

In a matter of weeks the Zavatans turned bare rock into garden, pumped water and started up their smelly labs. The entire upcoast region was laced with streams and pockmarked with hundreds of small lakes. They'd already turned many of the lakes into fish farms. Their pitiful farms grew more than enough to sustain them, this Nevi knew. His information was better than Flattery's, but Flattery didn't pay him for information.

*Where does their surplus go?* he wondered.

He knew that when he discovered the answer to that one he would answer the Shadow question as well.

*No food, no Shadows,* he thought.

It would be a pity if Flattery managed to wipe out the farms to stop the supplies that he was sure were channeled to the underground. There must be a more profitable way . . .

It occurred to him that the Shadows might win. He shrugged.

Nevi admitted an admiration for these Zavatans, for their independence that Flattery couldn't yet control. He didn't intend to muddy his own hands, though this trip had already proved messy enough.

Nevi smiled, a rare break in the steel of his countenance. He had plans for his retirement, and this upcoast region with its farmland and its new, burgeoning forests appealed to him. The people up here just might want some professional protection soon. Protection from the likes of Flattery and his bungling Chief of Security.

*Lot of new squatters this year,* he thought.

Since the earthquakes started a few years ago people had turned to the surface for safety. Even with burmhouses it was easier to spot a dwelling than a tunnel, it wouldn't take that much effort to map these people. Nevi flew into a sudden wall of weather and there wasn't much possibility of spotting anything.

Nevi kept his attention on the screen. The slash of rain against the metal skin and plaz of the cabin nearly deafened him. He switched on the landing lights to clarify the terrain. Still, visibility was a few hundred meters, tops. A buzzer reminded him that he was flying at the stall point.

They were only a couple of kilometers downcoast from the overflight coordinates. Zentz came around enough to set his couch up and hold his head.

"So, how was it?" Nevi asked.

"I don't ever want to go back."

"Where'd you go?"

"Everywhere." Zentz wiped his drool with his sleeve. "I went everywhere . . . at once. I saw them picked up."

"They're around here somewhere."

"Beached," Zentz said. "Down the cliff. Beached."

Nevi grunted his amusement. He imagined this gray land on a sunny day, blooming.

*Flattery couldn't possibly send troops,* he thought, *they'd never come home at all.*

"Approaching set-down," he said, and throttled back. "See them yet?"

"No . . . yes!" He pointed a shaking finger starboard. "There, look at the size of that . . . thing! I knew it was more than a dream."

Nevi was disgusted at the spit-spray of Zentz's excitement. The squall was moving on already as quickly as it had come, and visibility over the downed hylighter was good. The terrain, however, looked deadly. The crumple of downed foil was plainly visible amid the orange shards of the deflated hylighter.

It was a monster, all right, and deflated it covered far more than the hundred-meter diameter it had occupied in the air. Almost half of it trailed the fifty meters down to the sea, and the rest lay crumpled in the narrow stretch of beach between the sea and the precipitous rocks. The foil appeared to be nearly intact right at the foot of the cliff.

Nevi did not want to set down inside the perimeter of that thing—he'd seen what that blue dust did to some of those burned-out Zavatans who wandered dazed around the village. The strip of tideline was too narrow and the tides less predictable than he liked. The beach itself, from tideline to cliff, was a jumble of boulders. That meant a water landing or a set-down at the top of the cliff. He didn't like the look of all that kelp in the water, or the positioning of the dead hylighter.

"Electronic and infrared scan," Nevi ordered. "I'm making a couple of passes so that we don't get surprised down there. Then we'll worry about how to get them out from under that thing."

Their situation suddenly struck Nevi as absurd. Flattery had positioned his precious Orbiter and had the Voidship nearly ready to go; he had plans to establish a steppingstone colony in a debris belt over a million kilometers away. Pandora's moons were even more unstable than the planet. Even Nevi agreed that fleeing was the ultimate answer. But he doubted that it would be worth it in his own lifetime.

Especially if he insisted on risking his life in a wrestling match with a hydrogen gasbag of hallucinatory dust and tentacles. He chose a set-down atop the cliff, near a trail that didn't look too difficult. Zentz should be clear of his kelping by the time they reached bottom.

*If the girl's as holy as they say, let's see her get herself out of this one.*

*That's all Ship ever asked of us, that's all WorShip was meant to be: find our own humanity and live up to it.*

—Kerro Panille, from *The Clone Wars.*

Rico sprung the galley hatch with a crowbar from the tool locker and saw Ben sitting up, fumbling with the catch of his harness.

"Ben, buddy . . ."

He stumbled over the crumbled deck to Ben's couch, but was careful not to touch him. Ben's Merman-green eyes seemed clear when they looked at him, but they weren't tracking all that well. Both Ben and Crista were half-buried in debris from what was left of the galley.

"Can you talk?"

Ben's voice caught in his throat. "I . . . I think so," he said.

"Sit back," Rico said.

His own head started a strange buzz, so he took a deep breath, let it out slow. "We're not going anywhere for now, so relax."

He hesitated short of unclipping the last two restraints.

"Crista . . ." Ben's voice sounded foreign, distant. "Is she all right?"

Rico felt his lips tingling, and his fingertips, too. It was just like

269

Ben to think of someone else first. He glanced over at the other couch. There was no movement. All the lights in the galley were out, but from where Rico knelt in the rubble it looked as if she wasn't breathing.

*Shit!*

"Sit back," Rico repeated, pushing Ben back. "I'll check."

His muscles didn't work quite as they should, and he felt as if he was moving in slow motion. The heavy rain that pelted their foil dimmed what little light seeped through the single uncovered port. Rico noticed that the shadows weren't just shades of gray, but dancing hues of blue and green, backed up by flickering tongues of a cold yellow flame.

A halo of yellow flame surrounded the prone form of Crista Galli. Rico couldn't see any movement, but her lips were pink and that gave him hope. He moved to check for a pulse at her neck, then backed off. He couldn't bring himself to touch her.

She lay still, absolutely sagged, her mouth a little open. The inflated dive collar kept her head back and her airway clear. Even this way, Rico had to admit she was beautiful. For Ben's sake, for the sake of the hungry people of Pandora, he hoped she stayed alive. As he watched, a green glow smoldered over her body. A fainter glow, also green but lighter-hued, came from himself. Pockets of green oozed out of him and, amoebalike, they crept the air. One of these joined with a similar pocket oozing away from Crista Galli. She was alive, no question about it. Now all he had to do was keep her that way.

"Rico?"

"Yeah, Ben," he said.

His voice sounded a long way away to himself.

*But it's right here my voice is right here.*

"Is she all right?"

Rico breathed in a deep breath, and some of the lime-green glow sped into his lungs like fog or dust.

"She's OK," he said, fighting for control of his tongue. "Flattery gave her drugs a while back."

Rico turned slowly and saw his partner backlighted by the one piece of uncovered plaz. The rain that spatted against it struck sparks that shot out from Ben and ricocheted around the galley. Ben sat up rubbing his eyes, and a roil of fire moved with him. It was not the blue-green glow that captured Crista and Rico, but a sensuous warm glow like the throb of some membrane from the inside.

*The spore dust . . .*

"I think I'm dusted," he told Ben in his new, slow way. "How do you feel?"

"Headache," he heard Ben say. "Helluva headache."

Ben's speech was thick and slurred.

"And my muscles don't all want to go right, but they work. That shot did it."

Rico helped him sit up. Their two haloes arced and whirled around them. Ben held his head between his hands, doubled over nearly to his knees.

"I see what you mean . . . I'm starting to feel a little dusted, myself. Long time."

"Yeah," Rico said, letting out another slow breath, "long time. With Crista it's drugs. Flattery's drugs."

"Drugs, yeah," Ben said. "She's been laced up with something, something that Flattery wants people to think is kelp juice. Figures."

Ben stood on wobbly legs, holding Rico and the bulkhead, and made his way to Crista Galli. Rico watched as Ben checked her pulse, bent to her breathing.

"She's in there," Ben said. "If she's like I was, she can hear us, too."

He leaned down to her ear.

"You'll be all right," he said, and patted her arm.

Rico hoped it wasn't a lie. Some panicky feeling in his gut told him that none of them would ever be all right. The green of his aura sucked itself tight against his body. When he stuffed his unease away, it crept out from him again and mixed with the others.

*The drugs are the danger, not her touch,* he reminded himself. *How long before they wear off?*

Rico knew that a single-dose dusting didn't last that long in real time. He would have to remind himself that it was the dust that warped time. He knew they didn't have much of it to spare. They could count on help from the kelp. This was something he felt, intuited.

*It's the dust,* he thought.

"We'd better see what we have left," Ben said.

Rico forced himself to focus. He knew Ben was right, and if they were both dusted then they both had to pay attention.

"If we don't pay attention, we're dead," Rico heard himself say.

Ben just grunted.

Rico pulled the lasgun from his belt, checked the charges.

"They'll know we're down," he said. "We have to get out from under this mess, we're too easy to spot."

He braced himself against the upside-down bulkhead.

"Things were tough enough without all of us going to dreamland."

Rico started out the buckled-in hatch.

"Bring me some dust," Ben said. "That's what we need to get her out of this."

"No way," Rico said. "She's had enough, right here. We don't know what Flattery's been doing to her. A heavy dose might kill her, you don't know . . ."

He heard his voice going on without him. Ben was insisting that he was right, that she'd already been dusted and it was bringing her around, that what she needed was more . . .

"I'm serious, Rico. She needs it, and the antidote—you saw what it did to her. Think about it."

Rico didn't understand, and he knew they didn't have time to think about it.

He didn't say anything more, just turned on his heel and picked up Crista's legs under the knees. Ben reached under her arms and they stumbled with her through the hatchway into what was left of the cabin.

A few of the lights still worked, illuminating the burst-in walls and ceiling. The galley and aft portion of the foil remained upright, but the boat was twisted nearly in half at the cabin hatchway. The entire bow lay on its side. One of the wings had sprung from its retraction bay and sliced into the fuselage, peeling a section of hull away like a rind.

Ben brushed away debris with his feet and they set Crista down. She called his name and gripped his arm. Rico went immediately to work trying to free them from the deflated hylighter and the wreckage. Some pockets of undissipated hydrogen worried him. The rain helped, but he worried about sparks—not the spiritual kind he'd seen in the galley, but the metal-to-rock kind that might flash the hydrogen.

"There's still some gas around here," Rico warned them. "It shouldn't be a problem but we should be careful. Our judgment's been dusted, too, so we have to be extra careful. Don't move around much until we get free."

Rico's legs stood in the fuselage rip while the rest of him

worked at using the wing section as a shield to push the dead hylighter away from the foil. With his head and shoulders in the open he could see that the foil lay next to the cliff, with the hylighter spread out between the foil and the sea. A small flap of the bag and two tentacles covered the foil. The whole scene whirled in a lightshow of spore-dust.

*No gas out here,* he thought. *A good offshore breeze.*

Rico smelled a greasy char, sickly sweet, as he burned through the hylighter flap with his lasgun. Peeling it back from the fuse-lage made him even more lightheaded and wobbly-kneed. A thick, steamy smoke filled the cabin and Crista coughed behind him.

"Crista!"

Ben's voice sounded happier than Rico had heard it in a long time. Releasing the flap of hylighter let in some air and some light. The rain had muddied most of the dust, but they'd still had a pretty stiff dose. Rico's head felt as if it was ready to take a big plunge, as if he was clinging to some giant fluke just before it sounded for the deeps. He kept reminding himself aloud, "We've been dusted, it will pass soon."

He ducked back inside and Crista leaned on one elbow, cough-ing and gasping, and shook her head.

"Ben," her voice was gravelly and deep, "we are saved. Avata will see to it."

Just then a tentacle slithered through the hole above them. In less than a blink it snaked around Rico's waist and in another it snatched him through the hole. Its grip on his waist was stronger than anything he'd felt in his lifetime, but it didn't hurt. He heard a shout and felt a grab from Ben, then the hole and the foil disappeared from sight and Rico couldn't see anything but water.

> *Therefore, if it was more necessary in those days to satisfy the soldiers than the people, this was because the soldiers had more power than the people. Today . . . all rulers find it more necessary to satisfy the people than the soldiers, because the former now have more power than the latter.*
>
> —Machiavelli, *The Prince*

Holomaster Rico LaPush was a fine prize indeed. The Immensity respected this human LaPush as a sculptor of images, the best that the humans had ever mustered. For nearly a decade the Immensity had monitored human transmissions in all spectra. Through these transmissions it witnessed the inevitable unraveling of human politics. When it had its own data to compare, it compared, and it found significant facts wanting. From humans it learned to lie. Then it learned the subtle differences between lie and illusion, truth and illumination.

The Immensity intended to learn holography. On its own it had mustered transient illusion at times—ghost ships at sea, phantom radio transmissions—the parlor tricks of broadcast. Holography was more precious than that. The Immensity knew humans, now, and human history. It knew that holography, the pure language of imagery and symbol, would become the interspecies tongue.

There were the other forms, of course—electrical voice-talk of the humans. They spoke to each other of fish concentrations, weather, delivered the mysterious modulations that humans called "music." Except for the music this had been easily understood, but not very interesting. Then the human they dared call "Kelpmaster" began using the kelp itself as a medium of conduction. This private communications channel linked the Orbiter with the Zavatan world, and the kelp heard everything. The Immensity spoke in pictures, and these words over the kelp channel helped weave a picture of the world as it was, and as it could be. Though the Kelpmaster listened, he lacked the subtleties of holography that the Immensity required.

The Immensity could think of no better place to start than with LaPush, the Holomaster. The Immensity knew good holos from bad. In this matter it would apprentice itself to Rico LaPush.

The hylighter tentacle that gripped LaPush was, in turn, gripped by a huge frond of blue kelp. It transmitted every move directly to the kelp. Rico's automatic lapel camera unreeled a ten-second broadcast every hour, beamed back to its recorder in the foil. The Immensity received all broadcasts, including these.

Flattery was the dominant human, but the Immensity saw no future in him. He enslaved the kelp, but worse, he enslaved his own kind. Flattery didn't trust any creature that might know what he was thinking, including humans. He had plans to hide the future of a world from its people, and the kelp noted a heavy stink of greed about him. Except for the kelp channels, Flattery controlled communication among humans. He discouraged it, as he discouraged their education. The kelp often marveled that humans survived themselves. They appeared to be their own fiercest predator.

*Flattery would sacrifice many to save himself*, it realized one day, *perhaps even to the last human*.

The Immensity harbored no illusions about its position in Flattery's hierarchy.

The kelp knew that as long as humans accepted Flattery as the Director they would never realize their potential as One. If they did not do this, then neither would they recognize the need for Oneness among the kelp. Flattery saw this need as a threat, in humans and kelp alike. There would be no true Avata again as long as Flattery ruled. Whenever the brain grew, Flattery dealt it a stroke.

Since the day of insight, the Immensity had set about the downfall of Raja Flattery and the unity of pruned-down stands of kelp throughout the seas. The answer, it knew, was in holo. If it could project holo images, it could communicate in a way that humans would understand. It could speak to distant humans and to kelp alike.

*A language between sentients,* the Immensity thought, *this is the Pandoran revolution.*

Rico LaPush had been difficult to follow. He moved quickly and under cover, and spent most of his time landside these days. He'd been exposed to the kelp from organic islands that were the old cities and on assignment with Ben down under among the Mermen—still, he had chosen not to communicate directly with the kelp throughout most of his adult life.

*It is simply a matter of privacy.*

Unlike Flattery's political fear of betrayal and death, Rico's was simply a reluctance to let the kelp eavesdrop through his psyche. It did not make him feel "at one with Oneness" as it did many of the Zavatans, this the Immensity knew. What the kelp knew of Rico it had gotten from other sources, and from the airwaves of Holovision.

Perhaps the Holomaster Rico LaPush would become the kelp's Battlemaster if the image alone was not enough. Timing and presentation of images were essential. As a kelp channel, a simple conductor, the Immensity allowed itself to be used by the faithful in their struggle with the Director. Now it was time to use them in that same struggle.

The Immensity would win over other stands and reestablish Avata as the true governor of Pandora. It planned to help humans win over Flattery and to come to some symbiosis with these fearful humans. Oracles and kelpways were not enough. Images were tools beyond value, and the kelp would learn to use them.

"Seeking visions in the kelp violates civil rights," Flattery had proclaimed. "If your son uses the kelp, then he and all who use it, including the kelp, know the most private thoughts and dreams of your youth, of your entire life before his conception. That constitutes mind-rape, the ultimate violation."

He passed his law making contact "for the purposes of communication" an offense punishable in varying degrees, all of them unpleasant. The Zavatans universally ignored this law, much to the benefit of the kelp.

The Immensity had to snatch Rico quickly, before he alarmed the others. The enemy Nevi approached, and there was no time for petty confrontations. The Immensity had appropriate reverence for the kelpling Crista Galli. She would be the instrument that would complete the symphony of the kelp. But without Rico's genius the kelp saw hopelessness, death and despair in Crista's future, and in all of their futures.

The hylighter had turned in a superb performance. The *Flying Fish* now rested atop an Oracle, an old one secured by a small but hardy Zavatan band. Its cavern, much larger than Flattery's, was occupied equally by the live kelp root and the Zavatans. Passage from the water side was too dangerous for a foil The humans had burrowed a passageway down from the top of the bluff to meet the kelp's burrow in the rugged rock near shore. It was identical to the Oracle that lay at the foot of Twisp's command center beneath the high reaches.

Flattery had scoured the kelp clean from his cavern, to make it suitable to his tastes. He had destroyed one of the kelp's nests, a socket where the kelp rooted into the continent itself. Zavatans protected hundreds of these stations along the coastline, careful to keep Flattery's people at bay. Each Oracle was a strategic kelp-work of communication, a link with the entire world and with the Orbiter above it.

The Immensity had learned from certain Zavatans how images are formed on the matrix of the human brain, and how its own flesh correspondingly formed the images that it saw against the dreamscape of the sea. When it had learned to project its thoughts, its images, as Rico LaPush projected his holos to fill empty space, then it would commence the salvation of Avata and of humans.

*Woe to Flattery,* it thought. *Woe to selfishness and greed!* It dragged Rico inside the Oracle and among his own kind as quickly as it could so that he would not be unnecessarily fearful of his new pupil, Avata.

*What happiness could we ever enjoy if we killed our own kinsmen in battle?*

*—Bhagavad-Gita*

When he announced after their midday ration that he would run the P, the Deathman's squad beat him up. They thought that would bring him to his senses, or at the very least make running around the demon-infested Dash Point physically impossible. It didn't work.

"I know why you're doing this," his squad leader told him. He was called "Hot Rocks," and his sister was married to the Deathman's brother back in Lilliwaup. They talked in private behind some boulders bordering Kalaloch's refugee camp.

"Just like everybody else who does this, you're fed up with killing. You want to do something for somebody, leave your insurance to your family, right?"

The Deathman just leaned back against the boulder and stared at a clear patch of blue sky scudding with the clouds.

"Who gets your back pay? Your mom? Your brother? That little piece of blonde action you've been plugging in the camp?"

The Deathman's hand snapped toward Hot Rocks but stopped

still at his throat. Hot Rocks didn't flinch. Hot Rocks never flinched.

"My brother."

Hot Rocks cursed under his breath, then whispered, "Wouldn't it be better to go back there? Tour's almost over, the worst is over. We're all going home in a month. One month. If you still feel this way . . ." he looked both ways, ". . . then fight this thing at home. Work it out at home."

"I'm no good for home," the Deathman said. "The things I've done . . . I'm not normal, you're not normal. We can't go back there. We *can't!*"

"So, instead of going home you run the P, you make the dash out Dash Point and back. You know the odds. Lichter made it a month ago. Spit made it and collected a year's worth of food chits. Two out of twenty-eight—it's suicide and you know it."

"Either way, my family's better off," the Deathman said.

His voice was a monotone, and Hot Rocks could barely hear him above the light breeze.

"They get my insurance and back pay if I don't make it, and the winnings if I do."

"Yeah," Hot Rocks said, "but they don't get what they want—which is you. If I come back without you my sister will have my ass."

"I can't go back. You know that. You of all people should know that. They should make a place for us, or let us go after these Shadows and take over wherever they are and stay there and then we won't have to hurt anybody anymore . . ."

The Deathman choked up, and Hot Rocks looked away. He peeked around the boulders and saw the rest of the squad near the beach, backs together, watching for demons or a Shadow attack.

"You're my brother-in-law, but let's forget that," Hot Rocks said. "You're the best man I've got. These guys are alive today because of you—doesn't that count for something?"

"It don't mean shit," the Deathman said. "It means I've got more ears in my pouch than anybody else. They throw rocks and garbage at us and we hit them with lasguns and gushguns—shit, man, if they were animals we wouldn't even say it was good sportsmanship."

"I think—"

"I think you better stop thinking for me, and start thinking for yourself," the Deathman said. "I've learned how to kill here, but I haven't learned how to like it and I sure as hell haven't learned how to sleep nights. Last I heard, there were no openings for assassins in Lilliwaup.''

He stood up, brushed off his fatigues and hefted his lasgun.

"Now this is how it's gonna be," he said. "I'm doing the running whether you let me take the bets or not. You gotta admit, a sizeable winnings is good incentive, and I intend to add an attractive twist.''

Hot Rocks flicked his gaze around the beach, the cliffside, the tumble of boulders around them. This was hooded dasher country, and his caution was automatic. Besides, they'd burned out two boils of nerve runners here in the past week and nothing gave Hot Rocks the creeps more than nerve runners.

"Let's do it," he sighed, and they joined the rest of the squad at the tideline.

The bright afternoon suns ate away the tail of the daily squall and glistened off the wet black rocks of Dash Point. The narrow point jutted three kilometers into the ocean, and was named for its popularity as a place to run the P.

"Running the P" was a game as old as Pandoran humans. The first settlers took bets, then ran unarmed and naked around the perimeter of their settlement, hoping to beat the demons for a thrill and a few food chits. Though technically illegal, it was a game resurrected by the Vashon Security Force. In the old days, survivors of the run tattooed a single chevron over an eyebrow to mark their success. Though this tradition, too, had been resurrected, the runs were set in places like Dash Point that were famous for high demon populations. The two in twenty-eight that Hot Rocks had seen survive were exactly twice the actual average.

"Bets are always two to one," the Deathman said. "The six of you match my month's pay, then that means I get a year's pay when I get back.''

"*When* he gets back," McLinn muttered. "Listen to him.''

"Well, I want *five* to one," he said.

"Five to *what?*''

"You been hit too hard in the head.''

"No way.''

"Shit," McLinn said, "for five to one he just might make it. I'm out.''

"Hear me out, gents," the Deathman said. "See that big rock yonder off the point? Not only will I run the P, but I'll swim out to that rock and back. For five to one.''

"Stay awake, men," Hot Rocks warned, and everyone swept

the area quickly. "Standing here this long we make excellent bait, remember that. OK, let's get it on. Bets or not? Run or not?"

"I'm in."

"Me, too."

"In."

"Here's mine."

Each of the men handed five of their food coupons to Hot Rocks to hold. Each coupon represented a month's rations in the civilian sector. The Deathman handed over five of his own against their twenty-five. Hot Rocks stayed out of it, and the Deathman didn't press him.

"Do me one favor," the Deathman asked.

"Name it," Hot Rocks said.

"Name that rock after me," he said. "I want something around for people to remember me by. Rocks, they're a lot more permanent than people."

"'Deathman Rock,'" McLinn chimed up. "I like the sound of it."

Hot Rocks gave McLinn one of his paralyzing stares and McLinn busied himself with sentry duty.

' If you're going to do it, do it," Hot Rocks said. "Myself, I'd just as soon shoot you here as see you go out there. Stick around much longer and I just might."

"Here's the paperwork," the Deathman said, handing Hot Rocks a small packet. "Back pay, retirement, insurance all go to my brother."

"Who gets the ears?"

"Fuck you."

The Deathman reached into the neck of his fatigues and showed Hot Rocks the necklace he'd made out of the brown little dried-out ears Though human ears, they looked like seashells now, or twists of leather. He unfastened his fatigues and stepped out of them without a word. He handed Hot Rocks his lasgun and started running toward the point dressed only in his boots. The heavy necklace spun around his neck like a wot's game hoop as he ran.

They took turns at sentry, keeping him in sight with the glasses.

"He's almost at the point," McLinn reported. "What do you bet he leaves his boots on for the swim?"

The quiet one they all called "Rainbow" took him on for a month's worth. Everyone else was quiet, scanning the point with their high-powered glasses for signs of dashers or, worse, nerve runners. Rainbow lost. They were all surprised when he made the rock.

*Nobody more surprised than the Deathman,* Hot Rocks thought.

"Well, he's earned his place in history," McLinn said, and laughed.

The Deathman stood atop the offshore rock, yelling something they couldn't hear and shaking his necklace of ears at the sky like a curse.

The dasher must've been lazing in the sun on the oceanside of the rock. The impact from its leap carried the Deathman and the dasher a good ten meters into the narrow stretch of sea off the point. Some of the froth boiling up with the waves was green, so Hot Rocks knew that somehow, before he died, the Deathman had drawn dasher blood. Neither the Deathman nor the dasher ever came up.

Hot Rocks paid off the debts and pocketed the Deathman's packet of paperwork. While he packed up the fatigues, the lasgun and the rest of his brother-in-law's gear, none of his men's eyes met his own. He barked a few orders and walked flank while they finished their long sweep back to camp.

*Reveries, mad reveries, lead life.*

—Gaston Bachelard

This was the dream Crista had endured for years, the one of her return to the arms of kelp, cradled again in a warm sea. She rubbed her eyes and images flickered across the lids like bright fishes in a lagoon: Ben, beautiful Ben beside her; Rico in a cavern beneath them. There were others, fading in and out . . .

"Crista!"

Ben's voice.

"Crista, wake up. The kelp's got Rico."

She blinked, and the images didn't go away, they were just overlain with more images like a stack of wot's drawings on sheets of cellophane. Ben knelt at the center of these images, holding her shoulders tight and looking into her eyes. He looked tired, worried . . . scenes from his life dripped from the aura around him and spread out on the deck beside her.

"I saw something around his waist, a tentacle," he said. "I think it pulled him into the water."

"It's all right," she whispered. "It's all right."

He held her as she got her wobbly legs under her. She breathed deep the thick scent of hylighter on the air and felt strength pulse out from the center of herself to each of her weary muscles. Everything seemed to work.

"I see Rico," she said. "The kelp has saved him. He is well."

"It's the dust," Ben muttered, and shook his head. "If the kelp has him, he's probably drowned. We need to get out of here. There are demons, Flattery's people . . ."

*He doesn't believe me,* she thought. *He thinks I'm . . . I'm . . .*

A vision gelled in front of her out of thin air, one of Rico wet and gasping in the cavern. Rico tipped back his head and laughed, surrounded by . . . friendly feelings. It was a side of him she hadn't seen. Someone approached him, a friendly someone.

"Zavatans," she said, cocking an ear, "they will be coming up from the caverns."

"It's the dust, Crista," Ben insisted, "it'll wear off. These are hallucinations. We've got to find Rico and get out of sight. Flattery's people . . ."

". . . are here," she said. "They're already here. It's not hallucination . . ." she giggled, ". . . it's cellophane."

She had unraveled some cellophane in her mind and she saw the sinister figures looking down from the clifftop. Two of them. She reeled her vision closer and saw that she knew them both from Flattery's compound: Nevi and Zentz. Zentz's face and body were grossly misshapen. With Nevi, it was his soul. This she could see in the boiling black aura that seethed from him and sought her out. It sniffed the wind with its black snout like a dasher on the hunt.

She felt Ben pull her backward through the rip in the *Flying Fish.* The bright sky trailing the storm forced her to squint and focus on a double rainbow that lazed in the sky above them. She wondered whether Ben might be right about the dust. The pink of the rainbow's arch blazed brightest of all the colors and it pulsed in time with her own pulse.

"Do you see it?" she asked.

"The rainbows?" Ben said. "Yes, I do. Give me your hand, I'll help you down here."

"Don't rainbows mean something?" she asked. "A promise of some kind?"

"Supposedly God placed a rainbow in the sky as a promise that he would never destroy the world by flood again," he said. "But that was Earth, and this is Pandora. I don't know whether God's promises are transferable. Here, give me your hand."

The impatience in his voice just made her move slower.

*Rico's safe,* she thought. *He doesn't believe me, so he's worried.*

She shielded her eyes from the glare and scanned the cliff. The clifftop was identical to the one in her vision, except for a void, a nothingness where she'd seen the images of Zentz and Nevi.

Another image of Rico, in the cavern. He reached out for the kelp frond that had brought him there and she felt him transported to the dead hylighter at their feet. He stood there, facing them, head cocked and hands on his hips. It was as if he were impatient, waiting for them to make up their minds.

"Look there," she said to Ben, "can't you see Rico?"

She pointed to his image, seating itself at the point where the hylighter touched the sea. He was smiling at her for the first time and beckoned her with a finger.

"I see the sun shining off the water," Ben said. "It's too bright to look at. You'd better be careful of your eyes."

"It's *Rico* . . ."

"We're dusted enough," Ben said.

He stepped down from the foil to the ground and reached up for her.

"Try not to touch the hylighter. We're probably safest scaling the cliff."

"No!"

The word was torn from her throat before she could think about it.

"Not the cliff," she said. "I feel something there. I saw them up there, Nevi and Zentz. They're after us."

Ben pulled her free of the wreckage and they stood on the unsteady footing of the slickrock beach.

"OK," he said, and sighed, "I believe you. If not the cliff, then where?"

She couldn't help looking at the sea.

"We can't go there," he said. "Please don't ask me to take you there. Maybe you can live in there, but I can't."

He glanced quickly around them, biting his lip.

"If you *can* see Rico, how do we get to him?"

She couldn't resist caressing the remnant of hylighter draped over the foil. Though a plant, and clearly dead, it emanated a warmth that pleased her. It tickled something in her memory, something distant about her childhood. The kelp had protected her, nurtured her, educated her chemically in the customs of her fellow humans. She knew at a touch that this hylighter was from the same stand.

She turned in a slow circle, scanning the beach. She knew Ben was wise in some things, that she had to have faith in him. Without the kelp's cilia, she, too would have died in the sea. Much was rushing back to her, in fragments and colors. What she wanted more than anything was to run to it, to bury herself in the kelp's great body, death or not.

*That is selfish,* some voice warned her. *Selfish is no longer acceptable.*

She had heard about the barrenness of the upcoast regions, and at first glance black rock was all she saw: sheer black cliff, then black rubble, then a foaming churn of green sea. But there was life among the rubble. Little bits of green squatted among rocks, clinging to crevices in the cliffside. Something, maybe the something that spoke inside her head, pointed her upcoast.

"There."

She took Ben's hand and pointed out a huge black boulder with a single silver wihi clinging to its top. It was about thirty meters upcoast, halfway between cliff and tideline.

"That's where we want to be."

That was when Nevi and Zentz stepped out from behind the boulder, lasguns drawn, picking their way across the rocks toward them. Crista wasn't surprised, nor frightened. She heard Ben mutter "Shit!" under his breath and saw his head twitch quickly left to right, looking for a dodge. But she knew it wasn't necessary. She *knew.*

The moment came together for her like a great conception. All the world silenced itself—the waves, the breeze, the cautious footsteps of two murderers clattering across wet stones.

"Hands on top of your heads, step away from the foil." Zentz delivered his orders with a shaky voice tinged with slobber.

"Yes," Crista told Ben, "that's where we want to be."

They clung to each other's hands in the stone-still afternoon and watched the huge boulder lift itself back from the ground behind Nevi and Zentz. It came up smoothly, quietly, as though on hinges. Neither man heard a thing.

"Hands on your heads!"

The boulder laid itself carefully down behind them and out of the shadow beneath it climbed a half-dozen men armed only with ropes and throwing nets.

"Tell me you see it, too," Ben whispered. "Tell me I'm not still dusted."

"It is as it should be," she whispered back, her voice a sing-song. "There is a great moment at our feet, and it will not be stayed."

Something about the way Nevi's gaze met her own must have given it away. Without a backward glance he sprang sideways, beachward, and whirled. The first net was already settling over the surprised Zentz and another, poorly thrown, grazed Nevi's arms. Two flashes from his lasgun brought down both netmen, but Zentz flailed in a hopeless tangle. When Nevi whirled back, Crista Galli stared down the business end of his lasgun. Even at thirty paces it looked huge.

"I'll kill her," he announced, just loud enough for all to hear. "Trust me. I am very quick."

Everyone froze, and in the silence that went with this stillness Crista felt that they were all graceful subjects inside some great painting. She knew who the painter must be.

Nevi half-crouched in careful aim, his colorful face unreadable, his eyes fixed only on Crista Galli. She felt her head clearing, the return of wave-slaps against rock.

*But there's something . . .*

It was something she hadn't felt since she'd been dredged up from the sea, something familiar . . .

"Connection," she whispered.

Ben breathed beside her and she felt it as her own breath. They were one person, pulses synchronized with rainbows, waves and the great heartbeat of the void. She knew the choices in his mind and marveled at the sacrifice he was prepared to make. She saw the play in his mind: spin her by the hand, get between her and Nevi, take the hit while the netmen brought him down. At the moment he elected to move, she touched his shoulder.

"No," she said, "it's not necessary. Can you feel it?"

"I feel those sights on my chest," he said. "He's the only thing standing between us and—"

"Destiny?" she asked. "There is nothing between us and destiny."

The image of Rico stood behind Nevi, gesturing wildly to her, still smiling.

Nevi came out of his crouch, moved carefully across the rain-wet rocks toward them. She liked the smell of the rain, a different wetness than the smell of the sea, easier on the lungs but not as rich. The scent of the sea, of the dead hylighter. lay heavily beside her like a sleeping lover.

"Do you see?" she asked Ben, and smiled.

"I think I do," he said.

Nevi barked a few orders and two of the surviving netmen slowly began to disentangle Zentz. Crista Galli had that feeling again, the feeling of being a subject in a painting.

"Be still," she whispered.

Ben didn't move.

Nevi stopped walking, a look of surprise washed over his face.

"Where are they?" he shouted, and he shaded his eyes even though the sun was to his back. "Where did they go?"

Crista suppressed a giggle, and the figure of Rico applauded silently from behind Spider Nevi.

"I don't understand," Ben said. "Are we invisible?"

"We're not invisible," she said, "we're simply not visible. He can't pick us out of this landscape. I think it's a trick that Rico has taught the kelp."

Ben squeezed her hand and started to speak, but that was when the shooting started.

*I will this morning climb up in spirit to the high places, bearing with me the hopes and the miseries of my mother; and there . . . upon all that in the world of human flesh is now about to be born or to die beneath the rising sun I will call down the Fire.*

—Pierre Teilhard de Chardin, *Hymn of the Universe*

Twisp walked Kaleb to the flickering lights at the Oracle's edge. This was a small cavern, a subset of the great root that Flattery had burned out a few thousand meters downcoast. This was a hushed place, a place to breathe iodine on the salt air and feel the cool pulse of the sea.

Kaleb trod the well-worn path with his father's bearing—tall, shoulders back, large eyes alert to every nuance of light and motion. While his parents lived no one had consulted the Oracle as often as he. In the dim light by the poolside Twisp saw that Kaleb's adolescent gangliness had transmuted into the epitome of athletic grace.

"You are the man your father would most like to know," Twisp said.

"And you are the man my father most liked."

The two of them stood together at the poolside, watching the flickerings of kelp just beneath the surface. Both men kept their voices low, though the kelp chamber carried every whisper to its farthest crannies. Behind them, at a discreet distance, stood the complement of Zavatans who tended the pool. They busied themselves cleaning and reassembling one of the great borers that helped them tunnel out their habitations in the rock.

"When your parents met they were younger than you are now," Twisp said. "Is there someone in your life?"

The perceptible blush that rose from Kaleb's collar reminded Twisp even more of the young man's father. Kaleb's skin was darker, like his mother's, but his naturally kinked, reddish hair was a gift from Brett Norton.

"Yes? So there *is* someone?"

"Victoria is a big place," he said, "I've seen a lot of women." His voice bordered on sullen, bitter.

"'A lot,'" Twisp mused, "and which one broke your heart?"

Kaleb snorted, half-turned away, then turned back to face Twisp. He was smiling.

"Elder," he said, "you are truly a force to be reckoned with. Am I *that* transparent?"

Twisp shrugged.

"It is a recognizable affliction," he said. "I endured it myself one day. Thirty years, and I still daydream."

He didn't go on. It was more important that Kaleb do some talking.

Kaleb sat at the poolside, dangling his feet in the water, caressing the kelp with his bare soles.

"When I travel the kelpway, and take my father's branch, I see you as he saw you himself. You were good to him—firm, kind, you let him talk too much." Kaleb laughed. "He was a good man, I know. And you, you were a good man, too." He bowed his head and shook it slowly. "I would like to be a good man, but I think I'm different. My life is different."

Then he lowered himself into the pool and lay on his back on the kelp as though reclining on a great couch. His head and chest rested above water. Even in the colorful blue and red flickerings of the kelp-lights about the cavern Twisp could see a new life come into Kaleb's large eyes.

"How are you different, Kaleb?" he asked. "You breathe, you eat, you bleed . . ."

"You know why we're here," Kaleb interrupted.

His voice was firm now, none of the hesitation of youth deferring to age.

"How many people died out there today because they wanted to tear Flattery apart but settled for tearing *anything* apart?"

Twisp remained silent, and Kaleb went on.

"I'll be truthful, I respect you, I want your respect for myself, I want your approval that what I'm doing is right. If this doesn't work, we will probably have to attack him, you know."

His voice was becoming dreamy, and Twisp knew that the kelp was gathering him in, guiding him down the eddies of the past. Twisp steered him past thoughts of failure, past the matter that gave him the sense of failure.

"There is a woman who won't let you sleep," Twisp said. "Tell me about her."

"Yes," Kaleb said, closing his gray eyes.

Kaleb's eyes, like his father's, emanated a maturity beyond his years.

"Yes, she's here. She had two wots before we met. Qita, she knew the kelp as you and I have known it. As an ally. She had other lovers, but I was her last. As she will be the last for me."

This wrenched out of him with such an agonized moan that Twisp's hair raised up on his neck. Kaleb splashed the pool with both fists, but stayed immersed in the kelp, quieting with the caress of the waves.

"Elder," Mose whispered, tugging at Twisp's sleeve, "did you see his eyes?"

Twisp nodded, and before he could respond the kelp's display of flickering lights took on an intensity he'd never seen before. It was like one of the winter magnetic disturbances in the night sky, with great leaping rainbows of color that seemed to transcend water, rock and air. Mose stepped back from the pool in fear, but Twisp reached a hand to stop him.

"Old friends," Twisp whispered. "They are glad to see each other."

Perhaps Kaleb's bloodlines led to this moment. His mother, Scudi Wang, and her mother before her had been the first two to communicate with the waking being that humans called "kelp" and the kelp called "Avata."

When Twisp met Scudi Wang she was a dark young woman passionately working in her mother's wake to reestablish the kelp worldwide. In her own words, she "mathematicked the waves," and in doing so made Current Control possible, a system that saved thousands of Islander lives and revolutionized travel in Pandora's seas.

Scudi Wang was beloved by the kelp—this Twisp had heard from the kelp itself long before Kaleb was born. When Flattery attacked the kelp, lobotomized it, Scudi ordered her inheritance, Merman Mercantile, to stop trading with him. She and Kaleb's father were assassinated three days later.

It seemed to Twisp that Kaleb took on his mother's features as he lay there in the pool. His hair appeared darker, and so did his skin. The kelp enveloped him as though he were in the palm of a giant hand. The lights around them leaped and danced to some silent music. Twisp recalled that day when Scudi placed her hands into the sea and pleaded with the kelp, "Help us," and it did. It saved their lives, and that moment had changed his life forever. It had changed all of their lives.

In the years since Scudi's death she had become something of a Pandoran historical monument, with many plaques and statues erected in her honor. When a massive earthquake ravaged the old Current Control site undersea, the carved glass statue of Scudi Wang was found intact, clutched in the fronds of a nearby stand of kelp. That sign of love from the kelp, that recognition of a symbol enraged Flattery and he entered into a vendetta against the kelp that continued to this day.

Twisp watched Kaleb recline on the back of the kelp root and it seemed as though the root surged up to cradle the young man closer.

"Twisp," he called from the pool, "that was what my mother wanted to do, isn't it? Shut off all supplies to Flattery, starve him out. All these years I have hunted in vain for the day she died, and now I have it . . ."

Kaleb started to weep, and Twisp had a difficult time making out his words.

"It would have worked then, it would have worked. But now he owns everything, *everything* . . . and now there is no way. No way short of a miracle to reach all of the people at once . . . to get them all to shut him out would take . . . would take a sign from God . . ."

His voice faded into a hum that seemed to keep time with the red and blue lights.

*Increase the number of variables, but the axioms
themselves never change.*

—Algebra II

Beatriz liked the feel of the free-fall spin. She kept her eyes closed
and imagined herself sprawled across one of those warm organic
beds the islanders grew. She wanted to be in a bed like that now
with Dwarf MacIntosh, on some other world, under some other
star. But of course a bed like that made no sense in near-zero-gee.

MacIntosh gave her one more gentle shove and drifted them
both into "the webworks." This was a cavernous room at the
Orbiter's tubular axis, sometimes called the "privacy park,"
often used for naps or meditation between duties, or for an occasional tryst by a desperate pair of lovers. A fine white netting
crisscrossed the area, segmenting the huge space into a blur of
booths and bins. Holo scenes turned some sections of webwork
into fantasy worlds, further removing the occupants from the worries of life aboard the Orbiter. All this Beatriz knew from her last
tour, so today she kept her eyes shut tight.

"The disorientation is lasting longer this time," she told Mac-
Intosh. "I really don't want to open my eyes."

"After what you went through today, I'm not surprised," he said. "I wouldn't want to open them, either."

She heard his fingers clicking at the keys on his belt messenger, and felt the sudden play of a warm light across her exposed hands and face.

"Well, we're now at Port of Angels, that lush Islander resort you've heard so much about. It's warm, feel it?"

Yes, the movement of air across her cheeks was warm, caressing. She could imagine herself on the beach at Port of Angels, letting her hair dry in the suns and stirring a cold drink. A plate of mango and papaya slices waited at her elbow. There was no wavesound here in the Orbiter, no pulse of the surf against her back that sometimes took her breath away . . .

She opened her eyes. A sandy beach stretched away from her in both directions. Greenery poured over the clifftops down to the beach, and several little huts waited under their thatched hats to cool her sun-drenched skin. As the two of them turned, the holo turned, responding to a reference point in the messenger.

The holo came complete with their footprints in the sand, following them up from the edge of a blue-green sea. The fictional ferry that had transported them to this illusion had already settled under the waves, leaving only a swirl of current and a trail of bubbles toward the horizon. Sea-pups yapped and dove from the rocks that lined the harbor, hunting fish startled out of hiding by the ferry.

"We needed a few minutes alone," MacIntosh said. "It will take more than a few minutes to clean up the mess up here, track them all down. We've got an exceptional crew, that's why they're up here. Warning's out, so this Brood doesn't stand a chance."

He held one of the overlarge loops at her belt to steer them lazily around inside the holo.

"No one knows who the Shadows are," he said. "Do you?"

"I . . . no, I don't."

"That's because the Shadows don't exist. Ask any of them. They don't have meetings, pass messages or recruit. Things simply get done—a power blackout, kelpway shift—and something of Flattery's is lost. Supplies circle him, but don't land. Replacements don't show . . ."

"That's what I mean," Beatriz said. "I want to know *who* does it, how do they know *when* to do it, and what happens."

MacIntosh held her tether and they spun in a lazy spiral through the webworks. The illusion that played across the nets, the beach resort, was tailored for her, designed to help reduce her orientation stress.

*He's at home up here,* she thought.

She was aware then that *up* didn't make the same sense now that it had a few hours ago.

"They call it 'tossing the bottle.' You throw something out to the waves, and it's chance. But if you *control* the waves, or a little part of them, then it's not chance anymore, it's a sure thing. The Shadows' nonsystem encourages every citizen to frustrate Flattery when they see the chance. Divert something *this* way—say, a subload of hydrogen generators—and go about your business and never do anything like that again. Someone out in the waves sees this diverted load of generators coming along, diverts it *that* way . . . and in blinks it's headed upcoast to a settlement of Pioneers."

He spiraled a finger across the space they shared and bull's-eyed the palm of his other hand.

"Delivery." He winked. "Flattery's project loses and the people gain. No Shadows." He smiled. "It's brilliant. And everyone can play."

"Yes . . ."

Again, her thoughts were with Ben.

*I wonder how long Ben's been playing . . .*

"The Zavatans, Rico and Ben . . ." MacIntosh hesitated, choosing his words, "they don't want Flattery killed. They just want him removed. After all he's done to them, they still don't want to kill him, simply because he's a human being. Do you know how incredible that is? Do you know how far you Pandorans have come from us?"

"Our enemies on Pandora have always been more vicious than ourselves," she said. "Except for the kelp. The kelp has killed its share of humans over the years."

"But who rattled its leash?" MacIntosh asked. "Who threw fire into its cage?"

She closed her eyes again and breathed in slow, deep breaths.

"Are you OK?"

She breathed in and out again, slowly.

"I don't know," she said. "I look around this scene, and I know it's manufactured, fiction, not real . . . but people are following us. There are lasgun barrels behind the rocks and plants. Out of the corner of my eye I keep seeing people scurrying for cover."

He hugged her, and they finally kissed that kiss she'd been waiting for. This was no chap-lipped peck on the cheek, and it was just what she needed to bring her back to the world.

"I've wanted to do that," she said. "But it seemed . . . out of place with all this death."

"Yes," he said, "I've wanted it, too."

He brushed her lips with his fingertips.

"You know, you're going to be jumpy for a while, maybe a long while. We're going to go back out there in a few minutes and finish this matter with Captain Brood. He might think otherwise, but his men have already discovered how little they know about getting around up here. Then we'll see what we can do about your friends groundside."

"You don't think they're . . . dead?"

"No," he said. "I don't."

"How do you know?"

"The kelp."

Her face must have registered surprise, because he chuckled.

"You know how much the kelp interests me," he said. "Since Flattery gave me Current Control, I've been able to experiment a little. It paid off."

He kissed her again, then told her about the kelp communications system he'd devised, and his attempts to unify the kelp.

"Which kind of god would the kelp be?" he asked. "Merciful? Vengeful?"

"That's not important now, is it?" she asked. "Brood's a smart one. I won't be able to think of anything else until he's . . . neutralized."

MacIntosh steered them into a holo of sky that unfolded throughout their webwork—360 degrees of sky and high clouds covered the latticework that cradled them in free-fall.

"I worry more about Flattery," he said. "Brood's small-time. Flattery's got big things afoot, things big enough to crush anything in his path."

"But he was a Chaplain/Psychiatrist," Beatriz insisted. "He's trained to be better than that."

"He's trained to cope with the necessary thing and to see to it that we all adjust," he reminded her. "No romantic bullshit, just the straight facts. He's programed to see to it that we don't unleash a monster intelligence upon the universe."

"If he hasn't adjusted and he hasn't coped, why assume that he'll take us all with him?"

"Simple," MacIntosh said. When he smiled his face wrinkled all the way up his shaved head. "The number five Flattery hit the 'destruct' switch, you've read *The Histories*. That Flattery was a lot more likable than *this* one. It's just that the program had already come alive, had already anticipated his move and headed it off."

"Maybe we can do it!" Beatriz tried to shake his shoulders but all she did was set them both gyrating through air. "You're right, use the kelp to head him off!"

"Well, now that it knows Flattery's out to get it, the program's already inserted, wouldn't you think?"

"Well . . ."

"I have another possibility, and it's regarding Crista Galli."

She felt a curiosity about Crista Galli that went beyond her newsworthiness. Ben saw something in Crista, something in her eyes that swept him up and further away from Beatriz. Even though things were finished between Ben and Beatriz, a woman who could do that—a *younger* woman who could do that interested her mightily.

"What's that?"

She heard the rusty bitterness at the edge of her voice, the unnecessary *snap* of the words past her lips.

"I think the kelp's beat us to it," he said.

She looked up from her nestling spot at his neck to see his wide grin. "I think that Crista Galli is the kelp's experiment in artificial intelligence. I think she's manufactured, incomplete, and alive. It would be nice if we could keep her that way."

A musical tone sounded from the messenger at his belt. He did not take his arms from around her shoulders, but voice-activated the device with a simple command.

"Speak."

"Brood and two of his men sealed themselves off with the OMC. He says if you're not there in five minutes he's going to start scrambling some brains."

*And we are here as on a darkling plain*
*Swept with confused alarms of struggle and flight . . .*

—Matthew Arnold, "Dover Beach"

The Orbiter collared the Voidship's nose in a flat wide ring of plasteel. The two cylindrical bodies spun in concert on their long axes. Soon the ring would slip away to remain in orbit around Pandora while its Voidship plied the dark folds of the universe. At the helm would be an OMC, a stripped-down human brain.

The Organic Mental Cores had a definite edge over the mechanical navigators, and this had been determined clearly long ago by experimenters at Moonbase. Navigation in all planes required subtleties of discrimination and symbol-generation that hardware never achieved. The disembodied, unencumbered brain took pleasure, or so they said, in plotting the impossible course. One goad worked on OMCs that had no effect on mechanical navigators—the OMC needed this job to stay alive.

The particular OMC that the techs were preparing for installation, the Alyssa Marsh number six, felt no pain or bodily pleasure as the microlaser welded in the necessary hookups. She had been trained in astronavigation at Moonbase and had borne a child in

298

the year after splashdown on Pandora. The story that she filtered back to Flattery had the child die in an earthquake, and Alyssa Marsh had launched herself into her kelp study project with a passion. Her body had been crushed in a kelp station accident, but Flattery saw to it that her silent brain lived on.

Soon she would be silent no more. Soon her brain would have a body that it could move—the Voidship *Nietzsche*. She would navigate knowing the differences between ability and desire, knowing the need for dreams. Right now she lay genderless behind a pair of locked hatches dreaming of a banquet where Flattery was the host and she was both the honored guest and the main dish.

Dwarf MacIntosh gathered his forces outside both hatches and tried once more to contact Captain Brood. There was no reply from the OMC chamber. Three of the four monitors inside were blacked out, but the one remaining showed an overhead view of the long, specialized fingers of a nerve tech probing the webwork that encased what remained of Alyssa Marsh.

"Hookup's not scheduled until next week," someone said. "What's going on in there?"

A lasgun barrel appeared on the screen, pointed at the tech. The long, spidery fingers froze, then ascended from the surface of the brain toward the screen, then backed out of view.

"That fool better not touch off his lasgun in there," somebody else drawled, "or we be stardust."

"Hold your fire, Captain," MacIntosh ordered. "This is MacIntosh. You're in a high-explosive area—"

"Brood's dead," a voice interrupted, a voice that cracked with youth and fear. "May Ship accept him. May Ship forgive and accept us all."

The lasgun barrel tilted up toward the viewscreen and in a flash the last monitor went blank.

Beatriz tugged at Mack's sleeve.

"He's an Islander," she said. "The old religion, like my family. Some believe this project, to build an image and likeness of Ship, to be blasphemy. Some believe that the OMC should be allowed to die, that it—*she*—is a human being held here against their will and enslaved."

MacIntosh covered the intercom receiver with his hand.

"I don't necessarily believe that Brood's dead," he told her. "That would be too easy. And why shoot out the monitor instead of the OMC? You're an Islander, you talk to him. Play the religion angle, set up to get him on the air if that's what he wants. My men here will help you out."

"Where are you going?"

He saw the unbridled fear in her eyes at the prospect that he would leave her.

*What have they done to her?* he wondered.

He gripped her shoulders while his men floated the passageway feigning inattention to their covert affections.

"Spud and I know a few ins and outs of this Orbiter that don't show up on schematic."

She held him as close as their vacuum suits would allow.

"I could take anything but losing you," she said. "I know I'm making a spectacle of myself in front of your men, but I couldn't let it go unsaid."

"I'm glad you didn't," he said, and smiled. He kissed her in spite of the throat-clearings, harrumphs and chuckles of his crew.

"Chief Hubbard will stay here with you while his men secure this area. By your estimate, we're still missing a few of Brood's men. He's up to something, I have that feeling."

With a half-salute to the chief, MacIntosh propelled himself toward Current Control with his compressed-air backpack.

*Dark, unfeeling and unloving powers determine human destiny.*

—John Wisdom

Rico couldn't see through the illusion and he knew that Ben could not see him, either. Nor could Ben see Nevi and Zentz. Rico whistled the "get down" signal, hoping that the couple wouldn't run out of the boundaries of the image. They would be visible then, and in the open against an incoming tide. Rico dropped when Nevi started shooting.

*Time to send him a more suitable surprise,* Rico thought.

He wriggled into a position of better cover.

Nevi laid a pattern of fire into the rocks that hid Ben and Crista. Zentz covered Nevi's rear, keeping the dozen local Zavatans pinned down. Nevi stopped firing, but kept his wary crouch.

"Save charges," he warned Zentz. "We might be here awhile."

All was quiet except for their harsh breathing, the seething of the incoming tide and the high-pitched *ping* of weapon barrels cooling.

Rico was held firmly around the waist by a budding tip of kelp vine. It reminded him of his father's arm, and the way it used to pick him off the deck in one swoop. The feathery bud of kelp felt like the palm of a small woman's hand on his belly, covering his navel, hugging him from behind.

An image of Snej flashed through his mind and just as suddenly Snej's face appeared in thin air about ten meters in front of Nevi. The rising tide licked at the hylighter skin beneath her and hissed over Nevi's boot.

"What the hell . . . ?"

Nevi advanced a step, two steps. Zentz moved with him, backward, step for step. He glanced over his shoulder and paled when he saw Snej. He snapped his attention back to their rear defense.

"The redhead," he gurgled, "where's the rest of her?"

Rico found he could reinforce the intensity of the image by looking at it, concentrating on it. It was like a huge coil of energy feeding on itself, refining itself, awakening. After a couple of slow, calming breaths he was able to materialize the rest of her. She stood there in her green singlesuit, hands on her hips, staring at Nevi. She was a bit larger than life size. He wondered if he could make her speak.

"Well," Nevi said, "she's here, now."

Another glance over his shoulder and Zentz began a wet, ragged breathing that Rico could hear a dozen meters away over the surf. He placed his back tight against Nevi's.

"Shit, Nevi, a head that grows a body," he whined. "Let's get back to the foil."

"Shut up."

Nevi stopped and looked over the scene behind Snej. It was nearly the same view that Rico had: black rocky stretch of beach between the tide and the cliff, a cluster of large basalt boulders and a foil draped with the wet shards of an unexploded hylighter. In the downcoast distance the great expanse of sea glowed like green lava against the black cliffs.

"Where are they?" Nevi asked her. "I want them."

A two-toned whistle told Rico that the Zavatans were in position to rush the two men. He noticed that his illusion of Snej didn't cast a shadow.

*Don't think I can manage that, too,* he thought. *Talking will be enough of a challenge.*

Her shadow melted from her feet on the hylighter skin to where it met the beach, no more. It lay parallel with the other lengthening shadows of the day, but amputated at the rim of the skin. The tide already rushed the edges of the image, breaking up the light. With luck, Nevi wouldn't notice.

Rico smiled, concentrating on Snej, and quickly thanked Avata in the back of his mind.

"Put your weapons down," Snej said. "It is finished."

But no sound came from her lips.

"Shit!" Rico muttered.

Zentz responded with a burst from his lasgun. It came so fast that it startled Rico out of the illusion and it pulverized a rock just a meter in front of him. Avata brought the lost image back. Nevi fired, too, advancing them another step.

"It's not real," he told Zentz. "Watch yourself."

"Maybe we're dusted," Zentz said. "All this hylighter crap . . ."

"Ever know two dusters to share the same hallucination?" Nevi asked. He stopped a pace from Snej, squinting.

"Something's not right . . ."

Rico held his breath. If Nevi stepped across the plane of the image, he'd see Ben and Crista, and Rico wouldn't be able to see Nevi. The entire area over the downed hylighter became a dome of imagination, a hypnotism of light, a life sculpture.

> There must be a threshold of consciousness beyond
> which a conscious being takes on the attributes of
> God.
>
> —Umbilicus crew member, Voidship *Earthling*,
> from *The Histories*

Mose's eyes were open so wide that he looked even smaller to
Twisp than he had when a refugee band had carried him in half-
starved ten years ago. Memories—they kept him from the kelp as
they drew Kaleb. Twisp had watched the struggle for nearly a
quarter-century. The kelp must be like a drug to Kaleb.

*Not the kelp,* Twisp thought. *The past.*

Twisp knew, too, how the kelp always drew him to a particular
part of the past, a particular year, a particular woman. Twisp had
thought her the most beautiful woman on Pandora. Later, after
Flattery and the others had been removed from the hyb tanks,
Pandorans got a look at unmutated humans for the first time in
over two hundred years.

*They were all so testy about being clones,* Twisp recalled, *when
"clone" wasn't even something you could see.*

He remembered the bitter ceremony, with Raja *Lon* Flattery
presiding, in which the hyb tank survivors purged the telltale
"Lon" from their names forever. It was done with a ridiculous

solemnity, and did not bestow on Flattery's people any of the attributes that Pandora demanded of them: better reflexes, more intelligence, teamwork.

"What they didn't tell you in school," Twisp told Mose, "was that Flattery couldn't control Kareen Ale. She was killed, like Kaleb's parents, by Flattery's death squad. She was the first victim. There are those who believe it was Nevi himself who did it. Shadow Panille was head of Current Control in those days. He was in love with Kareen Ale. The combination killed him, too. He was my friend."

Twisp's voice barely rose above a whisper.

"I quit searching the kelpways, finally. I prefer my memories the way they deal themselves out. The kelp keeps them too true. Memories are not the drug for me that they are for some. I prefer to go to the kelp for the *now,* not the *then.*"

"The kelpways would pink my wattles mightily, Elder," Mose said. "The blue dust takes me to my heart and leaves me there sometimes. I don't know where it would leave me in the kelp."

"With the dust, you face your own conscience," Twisp said. "In the kelp you face the conscience of us all. That does pink your wattles, all right. It demands truth, and singularity of attention. One is easily lost in the cruel maze of someone else's life. Kaleb has learned to filter the kelp as we learn to filter our senses."

"What will he find in there, Elder?"

Twisp shook his head.

The red, green and blue lights intensified and their flicker quickened until the cavern was awash with light. The borer workers left their machine to stand at poolside with the others who gathered in wonder.

"I have heard of this," said one, "but never have I seen the like "

"Not even his mother, the great Scudi Wang, was such a one," said another.

Twisp found it difficult to hold back the torrent of words that memory triggered at his tongue. Memories—they kept Twisp out of the kelp, just as they drew Kaleb inward. The kelp was like a lifeboat to Kaleb, an anchor to Twisp.

A strange mist coalesced above the top of the pool. Every atom in the cavern became charged with a visible hum, and everything above the waterline glowed in a cool green haze. Half-formed images—fragments of someone's past—flickered in and out of the haze. Twisp saw fire and a baby at the breast, a memo to

Captain Yuri Brood, the brown, sensual curve of a wet breast in candlelight. It was a tumble down a soundless tunnel, just the *slosh* and *thlip* of the sea accentuating the drift.

Twisp had the sense of reliving something, of déjà vu without the vu. He heard a voice out of the mist, a woman's voice.

"He will contact one of the upcoast Oracles," it announced, "there is news of Crista Galli and the others. Through me Kaleb will meet my son, and through him, Raja Flattery. He will explore Flattery's inner being. Without secrets he cannot rule, and with the kelp there are no secrets. Kaleb will pick up the DNA path that leads to Flattery's hatch. Avata will transmit what he sees there throughout Pandora."

The whole cavern had become the stage for a giant holo projection. Soon, the babble and squall of life that went with the images swelled in the background. The mist had become a whirling ball of color and sound, its movements jerky and confused.

"Kaleb must focus his attention," Twisp said. "It is easy to get lost following the maze of someone else's life. He must filter Avata as we filter our senses. Then we will have a plan."

*One who withdraws oneself from actions, but pon-
ders on their pleasures in the heart, such a one is
under a delusion and is a false swimmer of the Way.*

—Zavatan Conversations with the Avata,
Queets Twisp, elder

Flattery took his afternoon coffee in the Greens, enjoying an
impromptu stroll among the orange-throated orchids. They clung
to the rock clefts deep in the cavern, their blossoms a pastel
cascade. Condensation drip-dripped its paltry rain on leaves and
wet rock, on the great flat surface of the pool.

Kelp lights surged bright in the pool, reflected in from the
nearby bed. He paused a moment. This was something different,
and the kelp, like Flattery, seldom did anything different.

Flattery turned on his heel and dog-trotted back to his command
bunker.

"I ordered this stand of kelp pruned," he snapped, and jabbed a
finger seaward for emphasis. "I want it pruned *now*."

Marta snapped something into her messenger.

"Not good enough," Flattery said. He signaled his personal
squad.

"Franklin, see that it's done. Use the mortar unit down on the
beach."

"Aye, aye."

Franklin carried a pouch at his waist. Inside were the sandals, papers and diary of the first man he'd ever killed. He said he was saving them for the man's family, they would want them. Franklin slipped with a warrior's shadowy ease out the hatch.

"We can't loosen up, now," Flattery told Marta. "Everything will go perfectly if we don't get careless. That kelp bed is our only back door. We need it secure *now*. Do you understand my concern?"

Marta nodded, then sighed.

"Well," she said, "I have some concerns of my own. Strange things are happening to communications."

"What kinds of 'strange things'?"

"Random transmission sources of high-speed images, hundreds of sources, strong ones, and they seem to be all around us."

"They are all around us," he hissed. "That kelp. Well, we've taken care of that. Damage news, Orbiter news, Crista Galli news?"

"Nevi and Zentz have landed. They spotted the Galli girl and Ozette and anticipate no problem bringing them in."

"LaPush?"

"Snatched by the kelp. The pilot was caught in our charges, condition unknown."

*Snatched by the kelp!*

All this kelp talk was making Flattery nervous. He caught himself running his sweaty hand through his hair. Aumock's gaze caught his own, and he knew that his guard had seen that moment of fear.

"Kelpways secure?"

"We think so," she said. "We—"

"You *think* so?"

"Brood's squad is aboard the Orbiter. No further reports. The Holovision Newsbreak that was scheduled from the Orbiter did not air."

"We're on auxiliary power," the colonel interrupted. "Failure at main plant . . . shit, it's no wonder that these troops got through our security. They *are* our security. 'The Reptile Brigade,' we called them. Shit."

"Does that mean a 'Code Brutus'?" Flattery asked.

The colonel shook his head.

"No, Director. This is an isolated unit of troops, here. Their objective was the power station and now that they've taken it we expect them to defend it.''

"*Defend* it?" Flattery raged. "They don't have to defend it, they blew it up! What would you do if you were them?"

"I'd—I'd know that I'd crossed the Rubicon,'' the colonel said. "Since there's no turning back, I'd head right for the top.''

"Well, goddammit, take appropriate measures. Your ass is on the line here, too, mister.''

Marta flagged his attention.

"I ordered sub coverage of the seaside entry doubled," she said. "I received no confirmation and don't know whether they heard me. Also negative messenger contact with the beachside mortar. The response we get is gibberish.''

An icy panic tightened his stomach.

*Not the kelp,* he thought. *It can't be that. It has to be somebody controlling the kelp. But who?*

The likely possibilities came to two: Dwarf MacIntosh or the ambitious and resourceful Captain Brood. Crista Galli was an unlikely possibility. Suddenly Flattery felt the full impact of this interference.

*We're cut off,* he thought. *Our whole strength was in coordination, and now we're cut off.*

A rally was clearly in order.

"We got a little flabby, people," he said, "a little careless. This harmless little exercise could have cost us our butts, let's tighten up our action.''

He'd caught them with their pants down, whipped them a bit, now he'd have to coddle them, comfort them.

"Reports on the bomb in the upper office just in.''

He picked up Marta's messenger and held it over his head.

"Dick and Matt are alive, the rest didn't make it. May the perpetual light shine upon them.''

They all responded, "May the perpetual light shine upon them," and drew a little closer out of reflex.

"It could have been us, folks. It could *still be* us if we don't tighten up. Consider direct orders the only secure communication. Information in, nothing out.''

"Aye, aye.''

Viewscreens and holo stages in his bunker began to flicker, barely perceptibly, then splashed high-speed displays of color throughout the room. Occasionally he glimpsed a face he recognized in the blur. It was his own face.

"What do we know about Current Control?" he asked.

His staff and guards stood transfixed in the surreal wash of color that visually drenched them all. They stagger-stepped to their posts, displaying the same disorientation that Flattery himself felt.

"Current Control turned the kelp in sector eight loose," Marta reported, "then it turned loose all the kelp worldwide. Sensors now indicate that everything's intact. The kelp appears to be on-line again. High suspicion for Gridmaster failure."

"Brood's mission?"

"No news. Holovision covered the launch site incident with a Newsbreak report on the deaths of the Tatoosh field crew 'at the hands of Shadow extremists.'"

The colors that dazzled the room remained as bright but their swirl slowed to a less dizzying rate. Flattery thought he detected a woman's voice, faint in the distance, somehow familiar. Almost as though she called his name.

"Continued fighting in food distribution centers," Marta said. "Too many looters to shoot. The usual 'we're hungry now!' crowd. Some of our people opened warehouses. All stores outside our perimeter have been breached."

*That's thousands of shuttleloads of food,* he bristled. *That's my contingency, my lifetime Voidship supply.*

"Dried grains to feed three thousand for ten years," he said. "Dried fish enough to feed *fifty* thousand. Add water, pat together and cook. Instant wine—add a package to a liter of plain water and stir. Bread and fish for the multitudes, water into wine . . . if this Voidship could time-travel I could be Jesus Christ himself. Shit."

*Consciousness, the gift of the serpent.*

—Raja Lon Flattery, number five model,
*Shiprecords*

A lean-faced security, armed with both stunstick and lasgun, blocked MacIntosh at the hatchway to Current Control.

"Halt!"

He motioned Mack and his men to stop, and gripped a handhold to keep his bearing.

"Orbiter Command," Mack said, "who the hell are you?"

"Security," the man said, and emphasized his point with his lasgun. "Captain Brood has the details. We are under the Director's orders to secure Current Control."

MacIntosh pushed off from the bulkhead behind him and sprang the gap. A push to the shoulder and a spin to the wrist later, MacIntosh had both the stunstick and lasgun. The sputtering security was pinned head down against the passageway bulkhead by two of Mack's firefighters.

"You'll get the hang of it in a day or two," MacIntosh said, and smiled, "if you live that long. Whether you live that long depends on how much you tell me, right now."

311

"That's all I know," he said, his voice edging a whine.

"Airlock time," Mack said. His men tumbled the security down the passageway to the freight airlock adjacent to Current Control.

"No, no, don't do this," the security pleaded. "That's all I know, that's really all I know."

"How many in your squad?"

"Sixteen."

Mack opened the inner hatchway to the airlock.

"My information says different—how many came up on this load, and are there more already aboard?"

"It's just us, Commander. Sixteen troops and sixteen techs."

"Where are they?"

Silence.

"Airlock time, gentlemen," Mack said. "Let's decompress slow. Anything you might think of to tell us, you can tell us from inside the lock. We'll stop decompressing when we've heard the whole song."

As Mack spun the hatchdog closed behind the security, he saw a half-dozen more of his men step off the elevator in full gear. Mack twisted the dial that sent air hissing audibly from the lock. His prisoner immediately became hysterical.

"Shuttle crew is ours," he said. "Two troops, three crew stayed aboard. Holo crew was two troops, three techs. OMC crew was three troops, two techs. Current Control, four troops, four techs, counting myself and Captain Brood. The rest secured the Voidship. Please, don't let the air out. Don't put me out."

"Keep him inside in case I change my mind," Mack ordered. "We can add to our collection here as things develop. We need Brood so we can find out what Flattery's up to. Hooking up the OMC, taking over Current Control and the Voidship . . . sounds like things are going worse for the Director than he lets on. Maybe he's getting ready to take the Voidship for a little spin around the system."

The intruder code, a tone-and-light warning, flashed at all corridor intersections. It was a drill that Mack had never taken seriously, now he wished he had.

"Rat, you and your people take the shuttle. Barb, you work the Voidship and know it better than anybody here. Take Willis and his engineers. Remember, no lasguns. You have your vacuum suits on, use them. The rest of us will handle this little nest here. If Flattery doesn't trust us anymore, let's make it worth his while."

Mack knew that he had the edge over Brood as long as they met in the near-zero gravity in Current Control. Brood's techs might figure out the old hardware that ran Current Control, but the new organic hookups throughout the Orbiter and ship, grown by Islanders specifically for MacIntosh, might be a surprise. These kelp fibers bent light and encoded messages chemoelectrically within cell nuclei. This enabled kelp to bring light to the ocean depths and messages to the Orbiter. The switching speed and capacity of kelp hookups far outstripped any hardware that Pandorans had developed.

*Too late, Raj,* Mack thought. *Current Control will never be the same.*

Brood could only fail. In the time it would take his techs to figure out Mack's secret system they would all be grandparents.

The is *is holy and the void is home.*

—Huston Smith

Hot suns melted through the thick, post-squall mist to scorch the albino nose and exposed arms of Crista Galli. When an offshore gust caught the mist in a whirl it freshened her hot skin like silk. She had felt the *whump* of breakers in the surf beyond the fog and now she could see just how close the waves really came.

"Tide's shifted again," Ben told her.

He held her right hand but his voice sounded empty with distance, thick-tongued. He blinked a lot, and his motions were slow, exaggerated.

*Dusted,* she thought. *I wonder how it feels.*

She was convinced now that the dust had returned her to reality, rather than removed her from it. It was her personal antidote, an antiamnesiac that spun valves and opened the stream of memory.

She remembered Zentz, too. He had been a mere captain when he came into the lab at the Preserve that made up her home. He took away the researcher who was talking with her at the time, a young Islander woman who taught social psychiatry at TaoLini

314

College. Once a week Addie came to question Crista about her dreams and always spent the afternoon with her in the solarium over tea. Crista had awakened in that lab a twenty-year-old female human without a single memory.

The psychiatrist, Addie Cloudshadow, tried to get those memories back. In the process she became Crista's first friend. Because of Zentz, Crista hadn't dared another friend until Ben. Zentz had walked into the lab that day with his weapon drawn, said simply, "Come with me," and shot Addie just outside Crista's hatch. Crista was sedated through her hysteria, and Flattery promised to take care of Zentz. Four years later Zentz surfaced as Flattery's Chief of Security and Crista vowed to escape the Preserve.

Today the mist kept her from seeing either up or down the beach. That glimpse of Zentz would have terrified her a day ago, but today she was not afraid. Something in the flash of kelp-memory warned her of Nevi, the other shadow in the mist, but it also illuminated a tension between the two that she knew would work to their favor.

The kelp had replayed for her Nevi's refueling incident, and she'd even forayed briefly into Zentz's mind. She had never seen anything so filled with horror and fear. She felt hate there, too, but it had long ago given way to a fear of Flattery that, itself, became an intense personal fear of Spider Nevi.

*Divided they fall,* she thought.

Flattery's world was coming apart, fighting itself, dying a thrashing death faster than it could inflict death on others. This was what Zentz had seen when the kelp grabbed him, and only Crista knew the strength of his resolve not to die at Flattery's feet or at Nevi's hand.

Crista had one open view from where she stood in the rocks, over the boil of breakers and out to sea. Though the tidelands wallowed in their salty fog, the sea itself glistened out to meet the sky somewhere in the distance. As far as the eye could sea, huge fronds of kelp rose lazily from the sea and splashed lazily back. Crista found comfort in the play of the kelp and the infinity of the horizon.

"What a time to be dusted," Ben mumbled, and shook his head.

"Rico has a plan," Crista whispered, "and he's ready to start it right . . . *now.*"

Crista Galli felt her hair prickle when Rico's electric dance of light crackled up like a shield around her. The high suns roiled fog off the wet beach and coated her skin with a fine grit of salt. The mist enhanced the surreal quality of Rico's lifesize hologram. From the back side it was like looking through a fogged mirror that refused her reflection. Crista watched the barest shadows of Nevi and the others as they ghosted the boundaries of the holo image that erased herself and Ben from the visible landscape.

Nevi and Zentz positioned themselves behind the light curtain, calling out strategy codes to each other.

"Flank sweep, left," Nevi said. His voice was unhurried, precise. "Cover high. I'll take point and ground."

"But they . . . they *disappeared!*"

"It's a trick," Nevi said, "a camera trick. They're in there and can't get out. Position?"

"Secure. Ten meters, left flank. I can't see shit in this soup." Zentz spoke more with a gargle than with real words.

"Ozette!" Nevi called, "she's sick. She goes back or she dies, you know that. It's not a choice. Send her out."

Ben's finger went to his lips.

"He can't see us," Ben whispered. "Don't move."

She couldn't tell one person from the other. The gigantic holo danced on its curtain of mist. Surreal figures outside the holo field became a futile blur. Three lasgun flashes burst the curtain of rippling light and a cascade of prisms lighted up all around her. Ben pulled her to the ground and in a blink the image reformed.

"Stay low and don't move," he whispered. "This is the perfect holo. *Perfect!*"

She wriggled with him into a fold of hylighter against a black lava boulder. Though faint, a wisp of images rose out of the hylighter skin and filled her mind in a steady unraveling of Pandora's tangled politics. The thick skin of the hylighter held the warmth of afternoon sunlight. With Ben tucked close against her she felt safe. Flashes of sunlight sparkled intermittently throughout the hologram that surrounded them. Crista drew a new strength with the hylighter's touch, and a confidence that insisted Nevi would fail.

"They can't see us as long as we stay inside the image," Ben whispered. His voice strained with the effort of focusing through the dust coursing his veins. He kept low, but his quick eyes took in all of the scene that they could.

"This is incredible!" he marveled. "We're *inside* a holo . . . where the hell did he get the triangulators to bring this off? And the *resolution* . . . ?"

"From the kelp," Crista said. "He got everything he needed from Avata."

"I wish we could see what the hell's happening," Ben whispered. "Right now we're inside a hole in the light show. See this edge here? Rico's holo follows the outline of our hylighter. He's made a stage out of a hylighter skin."

His finger reached out to the edge of the hylighter skin and appeared to disappear as he pushed it through the hologram. A momentary flutter of light and shadow around his finger was the only sign of disturbance of the image.

"The mist makes the illusion especially colorful," he said. "All the tiny flashes that you see are the lasers catching a water droplet spinning in the mist—kind of pretty."

"I can take her back dead or alive, Ozette," Nevi's voice insisted. It was closer now, only a few steps away. "If she's dead, the world will think you killed her. If she's alive . . . well, then everyone gets another chance."

"Going back there," she whispered, "that is not living."

"Don't worry, he knows how it's got to be."

Three more flashes burst through the light screen and pitted the boulder above them in a dazzle of red and violet. Ben wrapped his arms around Crista to sandwich her between himself and the rock. It seemed that the dust was bringing her out of a dream instead of into it. She felt her head and senses clear beyond anything she'd experienced in Flattery's custody.

"I think the dust . . . you were right about it," she told Ben. "It's offset whatever it was that Flattery gave me."

She pulled Ben's arms tighter around her and felt as though she were melting into him, her busy atoms scooting between the oscillations of his own. She felt herself disassemble into her qualities of light and shade. She was no longer so much a substance as an idea, an image, a dream. She felt no pain or pleasure, just a sense of transmission, of movement with purpose over which she had no control.

"Ben," she asked, over a stab of fear, "Ben, are you here?"

"Yes," his breath puffed her ear, "I'm here."

"I'm sorry," she said. She knew something was coming, some feral intensity crested her awareness and would not be cowed. "I'm sorry."

A sensation like the one she had felt at the dockside in Kalaloch welled up inside her, then burst with a loud *crack* that rolled outward from her heart like angry thunder. Everything around her stilled except the wet rush of the incoming tide.

*Welcome home, Crista Galli.*

The voice spoke through her mind, without the impediment of sound. It came at a rush from the dying hylighter, from Avata itself.

A refreshing sense of detachment, then a familiar disembodiment overcame her. The distinction between hylighter skin and her own blurred. She was encompassed within a familiar tingle. It was a muted, struggling tingle that she knew to be a kind of death in body that hatched the great hylighter of her mind. Her mind flexed its great sail in the sun and caught its first breath.

*We hatched of the same vine, Crista Galli.*

She remembered, now. Before the bombing that cut her free she had been rooted for safety in a pod of kelp. The memories filled her head so fast they stunned her. Ben's groan in her ear reeled her attention back to their huddle on the beach. The holo was gone, and enough of the mist lifted to reveal a scattering of bodies in the rocks.

"I thought I was dead," Ben said, rubbing his temples. "How . . . what have you done?"

Crista couldn't answer. She felt as though she straddled two worlds—one on the beach, with Ben, and one in the sea with her great guardian, Avata. The holo had switched off with the thunderclap, and Nevi lay on the beach, nearly within her reach, his eyes bli. king stupidly and blood oozing from his red-veined nose. She got up slowly and retrieved his lasgun. Rico, though wobbly, was the first to recover and he did likewise with Zentz.

"My apologies, sister," Rico said, with a slight bow and a quizzical smile. "There is much this ignorant brother did not understand."

He reeled and nearly fell, but caught the side of a great rock and steadied himself.

Others around them, the stunned ones, began stirring and shaking their heads. A few, victims of the lasguns, would never stir again. She felt bigger now, taller, and it seemed that even Rico looked up to her. A deep breath of the mist-laden air cleared her mind and helped pulse a new strength to her young legs. The tide hissed up to her feet, and a few meters away it licked Nevi's outstretched form in the sand.

"So, Rico, do you still want to keep me from the kelp?"

He managed a laugh and shook his head.

"Two rules," he said. "The first: never argue with an armed woman."

She hefted Nevi's lasgun as though seeing it for the first time, then inquired, "And the second?"

"Never argue with an armed man."

She returned the laugh, and Ben joined them.

"You argued with Nevi," Ben said, "and look what it got *him*."

"I didn't argue with him," Rico said, "I tricked him—that is, Avata tricked him. Now we've got more work to do. Believe it or not, we have to save Flattery. If we don't—"

"*Save* Flattery?" Ben's bitterness dripped from his voice. "He started all this, he should suffer the consequences."

"Not if we all suffer," Crista said. "Not if human life on Pandora is extinguished. He can do that, I feel it. Rico is right. Flattery must be stopped, but he must stay alive."

The dozen stunned Zavatans struggled to regain their feet and their senses. Ben picked up Nevi under the arms and dragged him out of reach of the water. A Zavatan scout took over and trussed Nevi's thumbs together behind his back with a stout length of maki leader.

"That holo," Ben said, "I've never seen anything like it. How did you do that?"

"Thought you'd never ask," Rico said.

He picked up a length of kelp vine from the water's edge, caressed it momentarily and then dropped it back into the sea.

"That was the trick. I think our Zavatan friends here have these two zeroes under control. Follow me, I'd like you to meet my friend, Avata, the greatest holo studio in the world."

A warning shout went up from a scout at the clifftop, and simultaneously a hunt of dashers splashed out of the upcoast mist in a sinister blur. Ben snatched the heavy lasgun from Crista's hand and pushed her toward Rico. He fired a quick burst and the barest scent of ozone accompanied the snapping of the weapon. Two dashers crumpled in a flurry of screams and sand only a dozen meters away. The others began to feed on their dead, as was their instinct. A Zavatan scout emptied his charges into the rest of the hunt.

"They're so . . . so *fast*," she gasped, and discovered herself clinging to Rico's arm.

He did not cringe or push her away, but put his arm around her shoulders and gave her a squeeze.

"Not much time to think topside," Rico said. Then, to Ben, "I see you're still quick in your old age."

"Some of us stay young forever," he laughed. "Must be the company I keep."

Ben's hand took her own and the three of them caught their collective breath.

"If they're not too chewed up, we'll get you one of those hides for a souvenir," Rico told her.

"What would I do with a dead thing?" she asked. A huge cold finger ran a shudder down her spine. "I'm a lot more interested in life."

"Touché," Ben said. "Let's get going. I want a look at Rico's mystery studio."

A gust of breeze puffed the last of the mist off the tidelands and both afternoon suns caressed Crista's pale skin. The fabric of her dive suit rippled in sunlight as the tide reclaimed, amoebalike, the tumble of rocks that marked its upper reaches. With her hand clasped in Ben's she followed Rico as he scrambled away from the sea up to the cliff. Two Zavatan scouts in green singlesuits flanked a great entryway between boulders.

"In here," Rico said. "It's not nearly as scary as the way I came in. Watch your step, the wet rock is mighty slick."

Crista stood at the dark entry, feeling a pulse of damp air rush out at her. A series of carvings decorated the wall inside, carvings of intertwined kelp vines, fishes and suns. She turned her face upward for one more dose of light before facing the darkness.

"Look there," Ben said, pointing skyward, "hylighters. And they have the foil that these two came in on."

A half-dozen of them appeared from somewhere landward, two of them cradling the shiny foil in a snarl of tentacles. They all dropped in lazy circles to within a hundred meters of the beach. They valved off their hydrogen, fluting their peculiar songs that included one long shrill "all clear" whistle. Their great sails fluttered and snapped, tacking the coastal breeze. Sunlight through their sail membranes made them glow a dusky orange, and even this far away she could make out the delicate webwork of their veins.

"Guardians of the Oracle," one of the Zavatans said. "They, like you, are sent by Avata to help us. There is nothing to fear."

It seemed to her that their flutings called "Avaaaata, Avaaaata," on the wind.

"Come," Rico said, "let these guys mop up. There isn't much time."

They passed through the high portal of carved rock and, though she had expected darkness, they entered a chamber of magnificent light. The light came out of the pool itself, fanning out from the kelp and, like the warm breeze on her cheeks, it pulsed ever so slightly as though it, too, were alive.

"Avata brought me in through the sea," Rico told them. "There's an entry through the kelp itself into the pool. The entry closes off as the tide rises, then opens again at ebb. I just squeaked through. As you can see, it's well-occupied."

The strong sea-smell of the beach had been replaced with the scent of thousands of blossoms, but there were no blossoms in sight. A kelp root rose out of the pool at the center of the cavern, crowding all the way to the high domed ceiling.

"The root comes out of the ceiling," Ben said. "This rock was folded upside-down during the quake of '82. Look at that monster!"

She saw that it was true. It did not rise out of the pool but dropped into it. The top portion of root, thirty meters or more above their heads, was indistinguishable from the rock it clung to. Around it sparkled the thousands of reflections from its mineralization.

"This is an old one," she said, craning for a good look. "A very old one."

The cavern walls were terraced up to where the root joined the ceiling. The terraces were cultivated, and thick fruit vines carpeted the walls. A welcoming committee in brightly embroidered costumes smiled down at her from among the greenery. As the three of them stepped from the passageway to the edge of the pool applause broke out and the chant of "Cris-ta, Cris-ta, Cris-ta" pulsed with the brightening light.

"Look at yourself," Ben said, over the din, "you're *glowing*."

It was true. Except for where his hand held hers a light surrounded her body. It was not a reflection of the glow of the kelp on her white skin and white dive suit, because the pulse of this light matched the throb of her own heart. She felt stronger with every beat.

"Thank you," she said, bowing to the crowd. "Thank you all. Your hopes for a new Pandora will soon be fulfilled."

She stepped to the edge of the pool and became one with its

emanation of white light and felt herself enter again the great heart of Avata. It was as though she opened a thousand eyes throughout the world and looked everywhere at once, and with some of these eyes she watched herself watching Avata at the pool.

She heard her voice rise to fill the cavern with a richness it had never held before.

"Fear is the coin of Flattery's realm," she announced. "We shall buy out his interest in kind."

Images leaped from the pool's surface at the sweep of her outstretched arms and filled the cavern like quick bright ghosts. Her body swelled to its limit in the seas, and she reached her thousands of arms skyward in joy.

A gasp escaped one of the sentries, then a shout.

"The kelp! Look at the kelp!"

But no one had to go outside for a look, it was all played before them inside the cavern. Throughout the seas of Pandora the kelp reached its great vines high above the surface. Colorful arcs of light bridged the gulfs between stands. Even hylighters trailed great streamers of light from their ballast, providing a link between isolated patches of wild and domestic kelp alike.

Rico smiled through the dazzle of light and Crista realized the difference between the Rico she had first met and the Rico who had saved them on the beach: This Rico was *happy.*

"You're looking at Avata," he shouted. "The kelp has risen. Long live Avata."

Applause and exclamations of joy gave way to the heavy background rhythms of water-drum and flute.

"But how . . . ?"

Ben swallowed his question back, his eyes desperately trying to follow the display that surrounded him. A parade of ghosts from all over Pandora washed among the people in the cavern like a hologrammatic tide.

"Like the kelpways of the mind," Rico explained, "only it's no longer just a function of touch."

Rico turned to Crista and took both her hands into his own. The light around them leaped even higher.

"Though it seemed like moments, I was gone from you for years," he said. "I witnessed your life, my life, Flattery's life. He buried a secret in his own body that would kill the kelp should he die. If his heart stops a trigger releases his stockpile of toxin worldwide. It would paralyze the kelp in moments and kill it all off in hours. You see now we must isolate him, stop him, save him from his own ignorance. Enter the kelp. Tell the world what you know.''

Crista felt herself pulled to the edge of the pool, and a murmur swept the chamber when she stepped onto the thick root of kelp. What she felt in that instant was joy. She became the very force of life in all of those present, and she entered the being of a young Kaleb Norton-Wang.

In blinks the webwork grew. In Oracles throughout the world people consulted the kelp and she entered the minds of them all as they entered her own. It was more a giving up of mind, a joining of the piece to the whole. She felt as though she spun like a mote on a current of air, and filaments of light snaked out from each of her cells into the world. One of them, from the center of her forehead, reached beyond the world to touch the faithful above it. From her perch aboard the Orbiter, she watched Pandora's seas become ashimmer with light.

*So you see, Crista Galli,* the voice inside her said, *the severed vine regrafts itself. In you the parts are joined, and Avata is much more than the sum of its parts.*

*If you take any activity, any art, any discipline, any skill, take it and push it as far as it will go, push it beyond where it has ever been before, push it to the wildest edge of edges, then you force it into the realm of magic.*

—T. Robbins

Dwarf MacIntosh had the axis areas of the Orbiter evacuated and sealed off, with the exception of a handful of volunteers from the fire crew who remained as his security force. Mack was sure that Brood, when cornered, would resort to sabotage, so he instructed Spud to prepare separation charges that would blow the Orbiter free of the Voidship, if necessary. He was sure that Brood's focus would be Current Control, easily the most important and most sensitive installation in space.

*With luck, he won't get both the ship and the Orbiter*, Mack thought. *With luck, he won't get anything at all*.

Mack had always hated the feel of a weapon in his hand. Moonbase had taught all of them well, and his recent life in free-fall gave him the advantage over Brood, but he didn't rise to the killing challenge as eagerly as some of his fellows. Mack was older than the rest of his *Earthling* shipmates. He had trained a lot of Voidship crews, finally gotten a flight of his own, at Flattery's request.

324

He didn't rise to the dying challenge anymore, either. Since Beatriz had come into his life he had found he wanted to live it more than ever. The prospect of facing Brood at the end of a lasgun struck a cold blow in his belly and set his hands to trembling. He gripped a handhold outside the main hatch to Current Control and tested the latch.

*Unlocked.*

He and three of his men sealed themselves in full vacuum suits and tested the squad frequency in their headsets.

"Ready one," he said.

"Ready two."

"Three."

"Yo, four."

"Foam only, if possible," he reminded them. "We didn't build all this to blow it up. Remember, the kelp hookups in there won't survive a vacuum, so we don't want a breach if we can help it. Blow vacuum as a last resort. Two and three, you're right and left. Four, I follow you. Check?"

Three fists clenched aloft, though "aloft" to Two was upside-down.

"Now!"

Mack pulled the hatch free and they spilled into the room that had been home for him for the past two years. Two was hit before he cleared the hatch but Three, using him as a shield, foamed both of Brood's henchmen and they hardened to immobility in blinks. Four tumbled to a ceiling position above Brood.

Brood himself sat calmly strapped into the control couch, his lasgun aimed idly at the Gridmaster. He had not even donned a vacuum suit over his fatigues.

Mack hesitated, his complete attention caught in the sighting dot of Brood's lasgun, which rested on the brain that controlled all the domestic kelp in the world.

"Dr. MacIntosh, shoot your two men or this thing is history."

In the immediate few blinks that followed, Mack's mind unreeled some light-speed logic.

*He's got to be bluffing. If he wipes out the Gridmaster, there's no way he or anybody else could live on Pandora a year from now.* That was when Mack realized that Brood didn't *have* to live on Pandora—not if he had the Voidship *Nietzsche.*

*But he doesn't have the Nietzsche. Not yet.*

"I might add," Brood said, "that if I'm killed, your OMC is also history. We can accommodate everyone, you see."

Mack saw the four techs reflected in a console panel. They ducked behind the next row of machines and were tracked by the muzzle of Four's lasgun. Mack hoped it wouldn't come to that. The men inside the foam cocoons might survive if they were cut free soon, but a lasgun firefight—messy, depressing.

Brood tapped the intercom on Mack's console.

"I left my man Ears back there to look after the OMC. You might've noticed how young he is. Nervous, too. That's been a problem in the past. You can ask your holo star what happens when Ears gets nervous. You OK back there, Ears?"

The voice on the intercom cleared its throat a couple of times before answering.

"Y-y-yeah, Boss, they're talking to me out there. But I ain't listening."

"Making progress on the hookup?"

"Yeah." The voice was young and reedy. "Tech says two more hours, tops."

"You're hooking up the OMC?" Mack's voice sounded as incredulous to him as he felt. "What the hell for?"

"We might want to take this thing out for a little spin, Doctor," Brood said. "Now, about those two lumps of shit, here. I told you to get rid of them."

"I won't do that, Captain," Mack said.

He unsealed his headpiece and set it aside. He sat in Spud's control couch and affected the same casual sprawl as Brood's.

"If you think I'm bluffing . . ."

"No, you're not bluffing. You'll do *something*. But the Gridmaster is one of your aces. You're not going to throw it away on something as trivial as my two men."

"They can leave."

Mack nodded to his men, and spoke into his headset.

"It's OK," he said. "Secure the hatch. Take these two and those four with you."

"They stay!"

"Everybody goes but you and me," Mack said. "You knew it would be that way, anyway. Your two guards may have a chance, this way. And the others, they wouldn't get anything done here until this is . . . settled. Am I right?"

Brood snorted his annoyance and waved them away. They backed out, pulling the wounded behind them, and Brood never wasted a glance. His attention remained on the Gridmaster's many screens that charted the world. A faint glow leaked out from behind the viewscreens, and Mack noticed a fine mist spreading from his holo stage near the turret.

The mysterious spill of a distinct white glow leaked under the console and licked at the heels of Brood's canvas boots. A similar glow lighted the base of their holo stage like a small moon on the deck. A reflection of light on the plasteel bulkhead meant that the turret, too, was suffused with this glow.

*The kelp*, he thought. *What could it be up to?*

Brood's lasgun still pointed at the Gridmaster, and by its displays Mack saw that the grids had reformed, but into neat rows of convoluted waves. Either Brood didn't notice the glow, or he didn't know it was unusual.

*Something's overriding the whole system!*

That, whatever it was, meant that the Gridmaster didn't matter. It was merely a recording instrument, no longer a tool of manipulation.

"Did Flattery send you?" Mack asked.

Brood's face, not an unhandsome one, turned up a lopsided smirk.

"Yes," he said, "he sent me."

"And are you following his orders, blasting in like this?"

"I am following the . . . the *intent* of his orders."

"Why wasn't I . . . ?"

"Because you're part of the problem, Doctor."

Brood swung around to face him fully and Mack saw an age in his eyes that was much older than the boyish face that held them. Now Brood's lasgun pointed at his chest. The light continued its ooze from all of the kelp linkups. A similar glow shimmered on each viewscreen behind the pale-faced captain.

*The whole planet's lighting up*, Mack thought. *It must be the kelp, but what could it be up to?*

"My orders were to secure Current Control and keep the lid on the Tatoosh woman," Brood told him.

The man's voice was quiet, almost wistful. "We were to keep Ozette out of the news, replace any of her crew as needed, accompany her up here. The Director thought she might try to—influence you, thereby endangering the security of Current Control as well as the Voidship project."

"So, you terrorized her, executed her crew, murdered my security squad and are now prepared to destroy Current Control and steal the Voidship—even Flattery won't buy this one, Captain."

Brood smiled, showing his fine, sharpened teeth, but his eyes remained hard as plasteel.

"Perhaps it is a family trait, this madness," he said, his voice rising with an edge to it. "You haven't heard the scuttlebutt, then. They say Flattery's my father . . . whoever my mother was, she was one of his diversions back at the beginning. I was the 'poor fruit' of that diversion, as some might say."

Mack was not as surprised at Brood's ancestry as he was by the cold anger with which Brood related it.

*Hot anger stings,* he thought, *but it's cold anger that kills.*

Mack started to speak but Brood's upturned hand stopped him.

"Spare me your sympathies, Doctor. It's not sympathy that I require. I am not the only one so privileged, there are others. If he knows, he finds favor in me because I do not challenge him. If he doesn't . . ."

A shrug, a pull at the lip. The ghost-light pooled his ankles.

"Others have not been so fortunate. My mother, whoever she was, for example. The Director requires power and I require power, that is clear. One way or another, I will have it."

"They've called a 'Code Brutus' down there. Are you a part of that?"

Brood snapped out a laugh. Those sharpened teeth sent a shudder down Mack's spine.

"I'm a winner, Doctor," he said. "I side with winners. I can't lose. If Flattery wins, then I've saved his Voidship for him, saved his precious kelpways, and I win. If Flattery loses, then I've captured the Voidship and the precious kelpways to hold for the winner."

"What happens if one of the others asks your help?"

"Then we'll suffer a communication breakdown," Brood said. "That's nothing new up here, is it, Doctor?"

Mack smiled.

"No, no it's not. We've been having that problem all day."

"So I noticed. My men, they are new to these airwaves, but thorough. We have monitored you here for quite some time—for practice, you understand. I know you quite well, Dr. MacIntosh. How well do you know me?"

"I don't know you at all."

"I wouldn't say that," Brood said. "You knew that I wouldn't blow the Gridmaster—not yet. You knew if I *really* wanted your men dead they'd be dead, and yourself along with them. Tell me what else you know about me, Doctor."

Mack stroked his chin. Leakage from the body of the number-two man drifted close, globs of blood floating with it like party decorations. Mack kept trying to remember which of his men it was, but it wouldn't come to him. But Brood was in a talkative mood, and Mack tried to keep him at it.

"You've covered all bases," Mack said. "If you take the wrong side, you can always run off with the Voidship—provided you can muster a crew."

"I have you, Doctor," Brood smiled. "An original crew member. I have the OMC, too. And I'll bet that you, a smart man and commander, would have a backup system—probably something handy, like the Gridmaster? Yes, a backup for a backup . . ."

Brood laughed again, more to himself this time. He reached out his lasgun barrel and nudged the blood globules enough to clump them together and push the glob out of reach toward the turret. A smear of dark blood glistened on the muzzle.

From somewhere deep inside his training-memory, Mack recalled one of his instructors telling him how clean a lasgun kill was, how the charge neatly sealed off blood vessels in its quick cone of burn through the body. In practice, as usual, this wasn't always the case.

Suddenly, the entire Current Control suite filled with overwhelming, blinding light. A stab of pain punched at both of Mack's eyes and he covered them reflexively. He heard Brood struggling nearby, bumping a bank of consoles toward the hatch.

"What the hell . . . ?"

Mack tried his eyes and found that he could see if he squinted tight enough, but tears poured down his cheeks anyway. What he saw made his already racing heart race faster.

*If light were a solid, this is what it would look like,* he thought.

It wasn't bright now as much as it was all-encompassing. He could actually *feel* the light around him. It wasn't heat, such as sunlight would deliver, but the pressurelike sensation of an activated vacuum suit.

Mack kicked off and made a grab for Brood's lasgun as he fumbled upside-down with the hatch mechanism. He missed the lasgun. Brood happened to open his eyes at that moment and the barrel snapped up to take aim between Mack's eyes.

"Doctor, you just don't get the picture, do you? I ought to cook you on the spot, but I'll wait a bit. I'd rather have you and your girlfriend together for that. Now you tell me what the hell is happening here."

A frightened voice came over the intercom:

"Captain Brood, we can't *see* in here. There's a light filling the OMC chamber, and it's coming from this *brain* . . ."

This was cut short by sounds of a struggle, and Mack assumed that his crew had penetrated the OMC chamber. For the first time, Brood looked worried, perhaps even a little afraid.

"I don't know what's going on here . . ."

"Don't give me that *crap*, Doctor," Brood yelled.

A fine spray of saliva skidded into the air around his head.

"It must be the kelp," Mack explained.

He used the calmest possible voice he could muster.

"There are kelp hookups in here and in the OMC chamber."

An eerie, strangled cry came from Brood's throat, and the man's eyes widened at something behind Mack's back. Mack grabbed a handhold and spun around, shading his eyes with his left hand. The bank of viewscreens that faced him seemed to be unreeling wild, random scenes from Pandora, some of them from the early settlement days.

"That's . . . those are my *memories*," Brood gasped. "All of the places we lived . . . my family . . . except, who is she?"

One face faded in and out, turned and returned and gathered substance from the light. Mack recognized her right away. It was Alyssa Marsh, more than twenty years ago.

A soft voice, Alyssa's voice, came from all around them and said, "If you will join us, now, we are ready to begin."

A great hatch appeared in the light, and a thick stillness took over the room. Nothing else was visible. The hatch hung in mid-air, looking as solid as Mack's own hand, but the pocket of light that contained them had solidified to exclude Current Control completely—there were no deck, ceiling or bulkheads; no consoles, no sound, nothing but the hatch. Even Brood's heavy breathing got swallowed up in the light. Mack felt as though he were alone, though Brood was near enough to touch. He was tempted to reach out, just to make sure he was real.

*Shadowbox,* Mack thought. *Maybe they've figured out how . . .*

"What is this shit?" Brood asked. "If this is some kind of kelp trick, I'm not falling for it. And if it's *your* doing, you're a dead man."

Before Mack could stop him Brood fired a lasgun burst into the hatch. But the burst wouldn't stop, and Brood couldn't let go of the weapon. The detail of the hatch intensified, and the hatch went through dozens of changes at blink-speed, becoming hundreds of doors and hatches that peeled off one another.

The weapon became too hot for Brood to hold and he tried to let it go, but it stuck to his hands, glowing red-hot, until the charges in it were depleted. Though he struggled to scream, with his veins bulging at his neck and his face bright red, Brood did not issue a sound. When it was over, his eyes merely glazed and he floated there, helpless, holding his charred hands away from his body.

Mack heard nothing during this time, and smelled nothing, though he saw the flesh bubble from the man's fingers. Still, the hatch waited in front of him. It had first appeared as one of the large airlock hatches that separated the Orbiter from the Voidship. Now it looked like the great meeting-room door that he remembered from Moonbase. Every time Mack had entered that door it was to be briefed on some new aspect of the Moonbase experiment on artificial consciousness. Some of those briefings had raised his hair and bathed his palms in cold sweat. The door did not frighten him this time.

He did not doubt that this was an illusion, a holo of near perfection. He had been accustomed to working with fourth- or fifth-generation holograms, but this one *felt* real. The light had been given substance.

"What did it take to do this?" he wondered aloud. "A *thousandth*-generation holo?"

It was as though every atom in the room, in the air, on his breath had become a part of the screen. He reached out his hand, expecting to pass through the illusion. He did not. It was solid, a real hatch. Brood was no longer nearby. Like the rest of the room, he had simply ceased to be. All that existed were Mack and the great, heavy doors dredged out of his Moonbase memories. He thought he heard voices behind the door. He thought he heard Beatriz there, and she was laughing.

"Please join us, Doctor," the soft voice urged. "Without you, none of this would be possible."

As he reached for the handle, the door changed once again. It became the hatch between Moonbase proper and the arboretum that he visited so often throughout his life there. A safe, plasma-glass dome protected a sylvan setting that he loved to walk through. Here at the edge of the penumbra of Earth's moon he had strolled grassy hillsides and sniffed the cool dampness of ferns under cover of real trees. His mind, or whatever was manipulating it, must want him to open this hatch pretty bad.

The latch-and-release mechanism felt real against his palms. He activated the latch and the hatch swung inward to a room even brighter than the one he stood in. This time, the light did not hurt his eyes, and as he stepped forward a few familiar figures materialized from it to greet him.

*I've died!* Mack thought. *Brood must've shot me and I've died!*

*To confront a person with his shadow is to show him his own light.*

—Carl Jung

The Orbiter's fire-suppression crew floated in their odd vacuum suits up and down the passageway outside of the OMC chamber. Most of them were women, as was the majority of the Voidship crew. Each was equipped with a beltful of tools for bypass or forced entry, and several pushed smothercans of inert gas ahead of them as they patrolled behind Beatriz. All of them had left their job stations to rally against the threat of fire. Only uncontrolled vacuum was more feared than fire aboard the space station. The pithy jokes that they tossed among themselves through their headsets offset the nervousness that their eyes betrayed.

Beatriz had suspected from the start that the young security who had sealed himself inside the OMC chamber was trying to get the OMC on-line. The firefighting captain who stayed with Beatriz was a structural engineer named Hubbard. Like all of the firefighters aboard, Hubbard was a volunteer and accustomed to getting twice as much work done in half the time. He deployed his crew according to their real-job skills. In a matter of moments all circuit boxes were opened, their entrails spilling into the passageway.

Four women positioned two plasteel welders, one at the hatchway, one at the bulkhead seam to the OMC chamber. The operating arm of the welder alone weighed nearly five hundred kilos, but here near the axis the only maneuvering problem was its bulk.

*These women must've been up here from the start of the project,* Beatriz thought. They used their feet as she might use her hands, and their vacuum suits had been adapted to accommodate their more dextrous toes. When she first visited the Orbiter she had thought that this skill came from a particular breed of Islander, but later visits proved otherwise. MacIntosh himself exhibited great facility with his feet and toes, and his vacuum suit reflected these changes, too.

"Buy us fifteen minutes," Hubbard was telling her, "and we'll be all over that guy."

"These guys killed my whole crew," she said. "They *joked* about eliminating your whole security squad and then they did it. Being all over that guy in fifteen minutes won't be enough to save that . . . the OMC."

"How would *you* do it?"

Beatriz detected no challenge in his tone, just urgency.

"I helped Mack install some hookups to the OMC chamber. There's a crawlway that starts in the circuit panel in the next compartment and leads into the control consoles inside the chamber. I know the way and I can . . ."

"Shorty, here, can squeeze through some mighty tight spaces," Hubbard said. "She can bypass their air supply and divert in CO-two . . ."

"No," she said, "that's too risky. It won't hurt the OMC but I've seen people panic when their oxygen gets low. We want to keep these guys calm, they might just start shooting up everything in sight."

"You're right," Hubbard said. "Shorty, tell Cronin to whip up some of his chemical magic. We want this guy down and out in a blink, and anybody else that's with him. We want that OMC and the tech in operating condition when this is over, got it?"

"Check, Boss."

"Listen up, everybody," Hubbard said. "Set all your headsets to voice-activated fireground frequency three-three-one." He made the proper settings in her equipment, then explained to

Beatriz, "That way we talk and he can't listen, and we don't have to go through the intercom."

Beatriz noted the tools in Hubbard's jumpkit.

"Let me see what you've got there," she said. "I may be able to activate some of the sensors in the chamber through the intercom box. It would help to have eyes and ears."

She slid back the cover and a faint glow pulsed from inside the box. It was not an electrical glow, the cherry-red simmer of bare wires or the blue-white *snap* of a short-circuit. This glow was pale, cool, with a slight pulse that seemed to intensify as she watched.

Hubbard's hand moved reflexively to a small canister at his belt, but Beatriz stopped him.

"It must be luciferase," she said, "from the kelp leads that we fed in here last year." She selected a current detector from Hubbard's kit and applied it to one of the fistful of unconventional kelp leads.

"Kelp leads?" Hubbard asked. "What the hell was he stringing . . . ?"

"Circuits made with kelp don't overload, and they have a built-in memory, among other features. We've done some experimentation with it at Holovision . . . OK, there's something here," she said, watching the instrument's flutter in her hand. "I wouldn't call it a current, exactly. More of an excitation."

When the bare back of her hand brushed the bundle of kelp fibers, Beatriz had a sudden unexpected look at the inside of the OMC chamber. The young guard stood across the lab from her, lasgun at the ready, his eyes wide and clearly frightened. Beatriz watched the scene from two vantage points. One was halfway up the bulkhead behind the OMC, probably the outlet connecting with the hookups she held. The other was from about waist-height, facing the security, and she realized she was watching this scene from inside Alyssa Marsh's brain. The kid kept flicking the arm-disarm switch on his lasgun.

"Get inside," she whispered to Hubbard. "Get someone inside. He's going to panic and kill them all."

She gripped the bundle of kelp fibers tight in her fist and dimly heard Hubbard snap out orders to his crew. She felt herself drawn both ways through the fibers, as though she were seeing with several pairs of eyes at once. The sense of herself diminished as she flowed out the fibers, so she gripped a handhold on the bulkhead and forced the flow to come to her.

*I can't let this go on,* she thought. *It has to stop. Oh, Ben, you were so right!*

It was nearly more than she could bear, but magnetizing as well. She knew she could let go the fibers, stop the headlong tumble down a tunnel of light, but her reporter instinct told her to hang on for the duration of the ride. She raced through the hookups aboard the Orbiter and the Voidship, then felt herself launched toward the surface of Pandora. She tightened her grip and wondered who was moaning in the background, then realized that the moans were her own.

She was a convection center for the kelp. The pale-faced young security with the huge ears and filed teeth stood barely a meter from her eyes.

*Alyssa's eyes,* she thought, and repressed a shudder. *I've become Alyssa's eyes.*

The tech's hands trembled as they worked, and with each new fiber glued in place the eerie glow increased.

"Brood didn't say this was supposed to happen," the kid said, more nervous than ever. "Is this *normal?*"

"I don't know," the tech said. Beatriz heard the fear in her near-whisper. "You want me to stop?"

The kid rubbed his forehead, keeping his gaze on the OMC. Beatriz knew that he saw Alyssa Marsh's brain being wired to some tangle of kelp-grown neurons, but it was Beatriz who looked back at him. Perspiration dampened his hair and spread dark circles from his underarms.

*Fear of the situation?* she wondered. *Or is he afraid of the OMC?*

He was Islander extraction, there might be some superstition but physical abnormality itself would not scare him. A Merman would have a harder time facing a living brain, something an Islander would shrug off.

"No," he said. "No, he said to hook this one up no matter what. I wish he'd answer us."

The kid flicked a switch on his portable messenger and tried again.

"Captain, this is Leadbelly, over."

The only answer was a faint hum across the airways.

"Captain, can you read?"

Still no answer. Leadbelly sidestepped to the intercom beside the hatch. The near-weightlessness made it difficult for him to keep his back in contact with the bulkhead as he went.

"What's the code for Current Control?"

"Two-two-four," the tech said, never looking up from her work. "It's voice-activated from there."

He fingered the three numbers and instantly the glow in the chamber intensified to a near-glare. He armed his lasgun with a metallic *sklick-click* and Beatriz heard herself shout, "No! No!" just as Shorty propelled herself like a hot charge out of the service vent and onto Leadbelly's shoulders. The tech shrieked and jumped aside, and Leadbelly shouted a garbled message into the intercom.

His lasgun discharged and for Beatriz the world slipped into slow-motion. She saw the muzzle-flash coming directly at her, homing in on her as though pulled by a thread.

*This can't be,* she thought, *a lasgun fires at light-speed.*

It was such a short distance to the muzzle that the charge hadn't fully left the barrel yet when it hit the glow around Alyssa Marsh's brain. Beatriz watched the lasgun sucked dry of power in less than a blink. Leadbelly screamed and struggled to fling the hot weapon from himself, but it had melted to the flesh of his hands. Shorty clung tight to Leadbelly with both hands and feet, spinning them across the center of the chamber. The charge triggered some reaction in the glow, and Beatriz found herself surrounded by it, curiously unafraid.

All was quiet inside this bright sphere. Beatriz hung at the nucleus of something translucent, warm, suspended in yellow light.

*This is the sensation that the webworks mimicked,* she thought.

Beatriz found comfort in the familiar rush of some great tide in her ears and she felt, more than saw, the presence of light all around her.

*The center,* she thought. *This is the center of . . . of me!*

A hatchway appeared and though she did not have hands or feet she flung it open. There stood her brother when he was eleven, his chest bare and brown and his belt heavy with four big lizards.

"Traded three in the market for coffee," he said, and thumped a bag down on the table in front of her. "You won your scholarship to the college, but I'll bet it don't cover this. Let me know when you need some more."

She had been sixteen that day, and unable to know how to thank him. He hurried past her out the hatch, the dead lizards making wet sounds behind him.

A flicker of hatches raced past, each connected to the artery of years. Some dead-ended at years-that-might-have-been. She opened another, this time an Islander hatch of heavy weatherseal, and found herself inside her family's first temporary shelter on real land. It was an organic structure, like the islands, but darker and more brittle than those that ran the seas.

Her grandfather was there, hoisting a glass of blossom wine, and all of her family joined him in a toast.

"To our busy Bea, graduate of the Holographic Academy and new floor director for Holovision Nightly News."

She remembered that toast. It came on the 475th anniversary of the departure of Ship from Pandora. It had become an occasion for somber celebration over the years, with a place left empty at table. Originally this was intended to represent the absence of Ship, but in more recent times the gesture had become a memorial to a family's dead.

"Ship did us a great favor by leaving," her grandfather said.

There was much protestation at this remark. She hadn't remembered hearing this conversation years ago, but it pricked her curiosity now.

"Ship left us the hyb tanks, that's true," her grandfather said. "But *we* went up there and got them down. And we got them down without any help from anyone or anything inside of them. *That's* what will raise us up out of our misery—our genius, our tenacity, ourselves. Flattery's just another spoiled brat looking for a handout. You talk about ascension, Momma. *We* are the ascension factor and, thanks to Ship, we will rise up one day to greet the dawn and we will keep on rising . . . that right, little girl?"

The party laughter faded and a single hatch floated like a blue jewel ahead of her, waiting. It was like many of the Orbiter's hatches, fitted into the deck instead of the bulkhead. Across the shimmering blue of its lightlike surface the hatch cover read: "Present." She reached for the double-action handle and felt the cool satin of the well-polished steel in her palm. She pulled the hatch wide and dove inside.

She had the same sense of a headlong tumble, like her early clumsy progress in the near-zero-gravity of the Orbiter's axis. She sensed everything about her as though she had a body, and that body was hyper-alert, but she still saw no evidence of one. She sensed others, too, not far away, and part of this sense told her she had nothing to fear. The translucence of the glow about her folded and thickened, forming a shadow at her left shoulder. In a blink it precipitated into Dwarf MacIntosh.

"Beatriz!" He wrapped his arms around her and kissed her. "Now I know I've died," he laughed, "I must be in heaven."

"We haven't died," she said. "But we may have gone to heaven. Something's happened with the kelp hookups. I know that I'm still holding onto them outside the OMC chamber, but I also know that I'm here with you . . ."

"Yeah, the kelp hookups and holo stage in Current Control got a glow to them, then the viewscreens . . . the whole world seemed to be shining down there. At first I thought it had something to do with those goons that Flattery sent up here. Now I think it has more to do with the kelp disturbances, the grid collapse. I think that your friend Mr. Ozette and Crista Galli are at the bottom of this."

"But how? We're in orbit. The kelp we touch here touches nothing else. It could just be a psychic disturbance, but then you wouldn't be here with me."

"It's the light," Mack said. "The kelp uses chemicals to communicate, this we've known for some time. Now we've taught it to use light. That holo stage I built for experimentation—it works perfectly, and all components came from the kelp, only the kelp has gone a few steps further. The kelp takes pieces of light, breaks them into components, encodes them chemically or electrically, then reproduces them at will. It's something I refined from what cryptographers used to call the 'Digital Encoding System.' You know more about holography than I do, you tell me what's going on."

"If you're right," she said, "if this is the kelp's holography, then it's learned to use light as both a wave and a particle. We can hug each other, yet we're just holo projections of some kind, right? Maybe the kelp has found another dimension."

"Yes," a woman's voice said, "we are the reorganization of light and shade. Where light goes, we go."

"Are you . . . Avata?" Beatriz asked.

A gentle laugh replied, a laugh like moonlight across flat water. A third figure began its mysterious materialization out of the glow. It was a woman, as radiant as the light around them, and because of that she was barely visible. Beatriz recognized her immediately.

"Crista Galli," she gasped. She looked around for sign of

another figure, for Ben, but all she saw was the translucent sphere that held them.

"Don't worry, Beatriz, Ben and Rico are with me. As you and Dr. MacIntosh are with the Orbiter crew. What they see now are the shells of our beings, the husks of ourselves. What we meet here is the being itself."

"But I can *see* you, hear you," Mack said. "Beatriz and I actually touched."

Crista laughed again, and Beatriz felt a giggle coming that she couldn't suppress.

*I am safe here*, she thought. *Brood, Flattery, they can't get me here*.

"That's right, we're safe," Crista said.

Beatriz realized then that thought was as good as speech in this strange place.

*Or is it a place?*

"Yes, this is a place. It is a *who* as well as a *what* and a *where*. Dr. MacIntosh, we have substance because our minds have made a perceptual jump along with the light. Things change to accommodate our differing subconscious. Did you see a lot of hatches?"

Beatriz watched him hold out his hands, look down at his feet, puzzled.

"Yes, I did, but . . ."

"And one reminded you of something pleasant, so you opened it?"

"Yes, and I wound up here."

"So did I," Beatriz said. "But an earlier one led me . . . back. Back to my family years ago."

"It was Avata's way of reassuring you," Crista said. "It took you to a familiar, comfortable place. You have been terrified lately. Avata does not want your terror. She wants your expertise."

"Expertise?" Beatriz swept a hand out to indicate their surround. "After *this*, what could I possibly offer?"

"You'll see. Think of this as Shadowbox, as the biggest holo studio in the world, with nearly the whole world as its stage. We will put Flattery at its center, show him off to the world. What then?"

"Stop people from destroying each other," Mack said. "They have not been able to get at him, so they will destroy his engines of power. If they do that, they endanger all of us, Avata included. Exposing Flattery might be more dangerous than you think."

"But look at our *method*," Beatriz said. "It's incredibly powerful. It will appear as a message from the gods, a vision, a miracle."

"I saw light shimmering above all kelp stands from Current Control," Mack said. "Is that really happening?"

"Yes," Crista nodded, "it is."

"Then we already have the world's attention, right? Everybody must've stopped in their tracks to take a look."

"My people stopped long enough to enjoy the light show," someone said. "They're heading for Kalaloch with everything they have."

Another figure precipitated out of light, a muscular male figure with red hair. Though Beatriz had never met Kaleb Norton-Wang before, she realized that she knew his past nearly as well as her own. At the same moment, she realized this was true of Crista Galli and Mack, as well.

*Then they know me, too,* Beatriz thought, and saw Mack's responding grin.

"We are part of Avata, now," Crista said. "Others float this drift, too, but we are Avata's ambassadors to our own kind. You, Dr. MacIntosh, believed me to be a manufacture of the kelp. Until this day I, myself, did not know my origins. I owe my life to Avata, my birth to humankind, and my allegiance to both. Are we all not of the same mind?"

Beatriz agreed. "We are. Flattery must be stopped, the killing must stop. Can we do it without becoming just another death squad?"

Beatriz paused, felt a surge of light within her and watched a replay of the encounter with Nevi on the beach. Then she discovered something interesting about being one with Avata—all of them could talk at once and she could follow everything perfectly.

Kaleb said, "I can speak to all of my people, using the kelp . . . I mean, Avata, as you used it to beat Nevi. Who could ignore a giant holo in the sky?"

"*I* didn't use it to defeat Nevi," Crista said. "I was merely a witness. Avata and Rico worked out a magic between them, but neither *used* the other."

"I stand corrected," Kaleb said, and bowed slightly. "How are we to cooperate with Avata?"

"We initiated it by seeking contact with Avata in the first place. Each of us has done that, for our own reasons, which we all now know," Crista explained. "Where there is kelp, Avata can project holos. As you can see, these are being refined even at this moment. Our holo selves, here, can hug each other *and we can feel it!*''

"Our problem is Flattery," Mack said. "He has never been easily persuaded, and now that he's made an emperor of himself he believes only himself capable of rational decisions. Anything else is a threat. He is paranoid, therefore it's a given that he's set traps of one kind or another to protect himself from attack. Remember, he's a psychiatrist, too. He can defend himself from both emotional and physical attack. The ultimate threat, of course, is that if he dies, Avata and, eventually, all humans die as well. We can't have him panic and start lighting fuses."

"Why can't Avata just . . . *capture* him, as it has taken us?" Kaleb asked. "He's not the type to kill himself, and it would buy us some time."

"Flattery takes excruciating pains to stay away from the kelp," Crista said. "He won't even have kelp-paper products in his compound. He must be drawn out to the kelp."

"Or driven out," Kaleb said.

"Or the kelp has to come to him," Beatriz said. "Maybe that's possible. There are the Zavatans . . ."

*Yes,* a voice that surrounded them said, *Yes, the Zavatans.*

Suddenly the light cleared around them and Beatriz saw what was left of Kalaloch sprawled out, wounded, beneath her. She floated above the settlement at a great height, with a comfortable sense of well-being that could only be wind buoying her.

"Ah, Beatriz, you have found the hylighter," Crista's voice said. "Let us all join hands in Avata and be with her, now."

Beatriz was vaguely aware of her existence in the light. She felt Mack's hand on her right and Kaleb's to her left, but the sensations she received were from her hylighter perceptions, and these steered her in a tightening circle high above Flattery's Preserve.

Three more hylighters tacked her way, and each one snapped its full sail in their traditional greeting.

She hovered directly above the blackened remains of the earlier hylighter explosion. Hundreds of people scrambled in and out of the cover of rubble, pressing in on Flattery's compound. Many of them wore the drab fatigues of his own security forces.

"We must get to Flattery before they do," Crista said. "If he's killed, there may be no hope for Avata, no hope for any of us."

Beatriz valved off some hydrogen and dropped closer, tightening her gyre. Though certain of the combatants below pointed upward to her presence, none raised a weapon or fired on her.

*Everyone topside is on one side now,* she thought. *Exploding a hylighter would be suicide.*

She wondered whether Flattery had any faithful snipers in the nearby hills.

Now that she was only a few hundred meters above the compound she noticed dozens of people in orange singlesuits popping out of underground cover throughout the area. The dozens became fifty, a hundred, more . . . all Zavatans of the Hylighter Clan. Swiftgrazers had fled the fire zone and scrambled into their burrows about the compound, and now the Zavatans were placing small orange flags at the entrances to these burrows.

*They're showing the villagers the way into Flattery's bunkers,* she thought. *If we can get inside first, we might be able to trap him.*

"Excellent!" Mack's voice said. "And even if we don't, he has his seaward escape and we drive him straight into Avata."

The other three hylighters were immense, their supple tendrils dragging ballast nearly fifty meters below their gasbag bodies.

From this vantage point she had the opportunity to see the wildlife from Flattery's Preserve scattered at the periphery of the scene. They had been a luxury, these mysterious Earthside animals. They got food and health care when people starved, but she did not regret their survival.

*The people will care for them at least as well as Flattery did,* she thought. *Ben was right, there isn't a shortage of food, just a very selective distribution.*

She drifted low enough to the ground to make out individual Zavatans waving at her and shouting their greetings. The tips of her two longest tentacles stung when they touched the wihi tops. This close to the ground she found maneuvering nearly impossible, but felt no fear-sense from her hylighter host.

*Fear not, human,* the Avata voice said. *Let the ending for this spore-bag mark our birth together on Pandora.*

"What do you mean, 'ending'?"

*Unlike humans, we crush ourselves under our own weight when grounded. Without the ultimate fire our spore-dusts are trapped forever inside their shells.*

"You mean, unless you explode your spores are sterile?"

*Yes. Now, you see, we are already too low to recover. I will live in you, now. Hurry. The others, too, must hurry. Find each tentacle a hole, chase Flattery out. Avata will . . . Avata . . .*

Beatriz felt as though a ballast rock lay on her chest, she could barely breathe. One by one her ten tentacles found burrows marked by the Zavatans and began their twining into the depths of Pandoran stone. She heard the other three hylighters valving off their hydrogen nearby.

"What is this like for them?" she wondered to her friends. "Like a mother smothering a crying child to save the village?"

Then she was alive in the tentacles. It was like having ten sets of eyes, and the light that grew from the dying hylighter turned a groping mystery into a warren of horrors. Eyes looked back at her—eyes and tiny, needlelike teeth pulled back in a hissing snarl. She pushed forward and they attacked, biting off chunks of tentacle as she backed them further into the maze.

"I can't stand it!" she screamed. "They're biting my face! They're horrible little . . ."

"Beatriz, listen to me."

It was Mack's voice. Mack was nearby, but he didn't know what was down here, he hadn't seen these little . . . *things* biting and biting, and down here she couldn't close her eyes because it seemed that the whole hylighter became eyes to her.

"Beatriz, talk to me," Mack said. "Don't pull back, now. I'm here, we're all here, holding hands in Avata. We're holding hands in Avata and you're in the Orbiter, holding a kelp hookup. Do you feel me beside you? I'm setting down beside you now."

The Avata voice spoke to her. It sounded like Alyssa Marsh.

*Remember it as holding hands, even if you know it wasn't so. When you tell the story, say that you all held hands. It is a symbol, these clasped hands, as the clenched fist is a symbol. Choose which of these you would pass down. Avata taught through the chemistry of touch, the "learning-by-injection" method, as some called it. Humans keep their kind alive by symbols and legends, by myths.*

She felt him. She felt a bulk press against her own and the weight on her chest eased off. She could breathe, and wondered whether hylighters breathed, too.

*We are . . . more similar to you . . . than different,* the presence said. *I will enjoy a deep breath . . . when you are free . . . to take one.*

The swiftgrazers kept at her, their little mouths biting, snatching off bits of flesh from her face . . .

*From this hylighter's tentacles*, the voice reminded her.

"I'm down."

This was Crista Galli's voice.

"Me, too," Kaleb said. "Let's kick some ass!"

The burrows were too narrow for the swiftgrazers to launch their typical swarming type of attack. Tentacles pressed them further into their burrows and all they could do was turn for a savage little nip every meter or so. Beatriz felt that she had snaked about half of the length of her tentacles into the ten burrows when they broke into the open. What she saw there with her battered stubs of hylighter flesh was a sight to make her gasp.

A blur of fast little animals streaked into a magnificent garden, a place so beautiful that Beatriz thought she must be in the throes of some hylighter death-vision. She heard cries and groans from the others as they encountered the vicious swiftgrazers and she tried to comfort them by concentrating on the scene before her.

"You're close," she said, "don't give up, you're so close."

Her wounded stubs sniffed the blossoms thick in the green foliage. Mosses and ferns hung down the black-glazed ceiling and carpeted most of the walls. She could not stop the light from spilling out of her into the chamber, but she wouldn't have chosen to even if it had been possible.

She heard other screams, then. Screams of a man being shredded to bone. She saw him, an older man, flailing at the panicked swiftgrazers with a pruning rod. He seemed to melt at first, then he toppled and his screams were muffled by hundreds of little bodies upon him.

A couple of big cats came to the fray. They were bigger than dashers, stronger, but they were no match for the tide of swiftgrazers that continued to pour from the thirty other tunnels nearby. Troops raced inside from an opening across the lagoon, firing their lasguns and smoking up the place. They, too, were no match for the fury of the swarm.

A foil that must've been Flattery's fled beneath the surface of the pool, the splash of its crash-dive drenched the walls. There was nothing more she could do here. Rather than watch the horror, she withdrew to Avata and to the comfort of the light.

Flattery heard trouble before he saw it. He had secured the upper bunker system and moved his most trusted personnel to the smaller office complex adjacent to the Greens. It was cramped, but it met his needs and could not be penetrated from above. Here he would have the luxury of waiting out the results of the fighting topside.

"If we sit tight here we can watch everything resolve around us," he told Marta. "Fires burn themselves out, people get too tired or hungry to lift a weapon—then we'll sort out who's who. It will be dark soon. No one will want to be out there in the dark with a breached perimeter. Demons."

He couldn't suppress a shudder and he supposed, under the circumstances, that it didn't matter. Marta and the others were here because they knew him best and they shared his passion for leaving Pandora. They were all a little giddy after the quick move to his private bunker. It helped that there were few claustrophobics on Pandora.

Flattery was pleased to see that, even though they were under fire, his people rallied even more strongly to his cause. Still, he double-latched the security hatch behind him when he returned to the Greens.

*If we're required to stay down here for any length of time, I'll have to bring them in here,* he thought. *I'll put that off as long as possible.*

Throughout his life on Moonbase, from his implantation in a surrogate womb to liftoff aboard the *Earthling,* Flattery remembered no place that was private, unguarded. Part of his training as a psychiatrist had taken this into account. The ultimate privacy was death, he knew this lesson well, and it was because he knew this that he was designed to be the executioner of his species. Who was better trained than a Chaplain/Psychiatrist to recognize the Other—artificial intelligence, *alien* intelligence? And who could be prepared better to deal with such a threat properly? Moonbase had made the right decision, of this he was certain. Of this he was truly proud.

*Pride comes before a fall,* a voice said from the back of his head. He shrugged it off with the shudder.

It was possible that he had erred slightly in this matter of the kelp. He needed the kelp—Pandora needed the kelp—therefore keeping it alive was not so much a matter of prudence as necessity. The first C/P on Pandora had ordered the kelp destroyed and that act had very nearly destroyed what remained of humanity and the planet itself. Pruning was risky, Current Control was risky, because there was always more kelp than people to control it. Ten years ago it had already gotten out of hand and he had been forced to concentrate solely on stands that marked important trade routes around Pandora's new coastlines.

Then, five years ago, Crista Galli came into his life. He had suspected at the start that she was an agent of the kelp. He should've known better, but this kind of wariness had kept him ahead of the kelp all along. A chromosome scan of the Galli girl proved she was human. He'd had the tech who did the scan killed with the kelp toxin, and so began the rumors about the death-touch of Crista Galli. Subsequent adjustments to her blood chemistry provided opportunity for other evidence against her. These rumors had suited his purposes better than entire legions of security.

*A well-placed rumor along with some sleight-of-hand has immeasurable value in political and religious arenas,* he thought.

Flattery was comfortable in spite of the conflict raging around him. In fact, he had to control his glee at the prospect of the aftermath.

*This will adjust the population problem,* he mused. *Old Thomas Malthus comes through again.*

The survivors who opposed him would starve, it was that simple. He had all the time in the world, all the world's resources at his fingertips. From his bunker he had access to three of the largest food bins in the world—enough grain and preserved foods to keep five thousand people healthy for at least ten years. The Greens would not provide enough fresh fruit for everyone, but he and a select cadre could be quite happy there indefinitely. All he had to do was wait it out.

His first warning of trouble inside his personal perimeter was a faint hissing that he heard above the wave-slaps in his pool. At the same time he heard high-pitched squeaking above him, then intruder alarms went off. Most of his sensors topside were gone, destroyed or covered by rubble. These, placed in the dozens of swiftgrazer burrows, were not true visual sensors but presence-activated alarms. Flattery summoned his caretaker and the squeaking intensified all around them.

"What is it?" Flattery asked. "It says 'level A activity.'"

"Swiftgrazers," the caretaker said. "Level A is set for them, since they're the most common intruder into the fissures. This shows a lot of them, and deeper than they're usually found."

"This squeaking—it's getting louder."

"There's a lot of them, all right," the caretaker said. He studied the sensor scan and bit his prominent lower lip. "And they're still coming this way."

"Trigger your trapsets."

The caretaker pressed a red spot on the scanner. The hissing that had become squeaks now rose to high-pitched shrieks of anger and terror.

At that moment a few dozen brown swiftgrazers tumbled from a fissure above Flattery and to his right. They were uncomfortably close, spilling from above the hatchway to Flattery's bunker.

"You'd better clean these up here. We don't want them established—"

"They're still coming," the caretaker said. He pointed further back to where there was obvious movement in the foilage against the wall. "I'll need some help here."

"We're not bringing any more people into the Greens than

necessary. *You* told me it was safe to keep these rodents around, *you* take care of them. *Now!*"

"Yes, sir." The older man sagged, sighed and armed his lasgun. "There's a lot of them," he said, "I'll need more charges."

A flurry of little bodies and shrieks caught their attention to the left of the pool, near the loading dock and Flattery's foil. Behind them a bright, white light broke through the cover of ferns. Now Flattery could see a similar light approaching through the fissure above his hatch.

"I don't like this," Flattery said. "What do your precious sensors say now?"

The caretaker flurried his nervous fingers across the face of his portable control unit.

"Dead," he said. "Something's shorted out the power to all of the sensors."

Flattery heard the low-throated purr of Archangel behind him, and for the first time realized that it wasn't merely a handful of swiftgrazers invading his garden. In blinks there were hundreds of them. Something had whipped them to a fever pitch, and they displayed none of their usual wariness of humans.

"Start shooting," he said, his voice low. "I'll get some fire-power in here."

By the time he had undogged his hatch and signaled for help, the light inside the Greens was too great a glare to let him pick out anything but little blurs of movement across his path. He hurried to dockside and secured himself inside the foil.

Flattery had started the foil's engines and begun his predive checkout when he realized he'd left the mooring lines secured. He glanced up at the caretaker, who was firing wildly at shadows in the greenery, and saw him suddenly disappear under a thick wad of fur. It was as though he'd slipped on a giant coat of swiftgrazers and then disappeared. The coat melted to the deck and disappeared, leaving only the man's weapon, bloody tatters of clothing and a scatter of fleshy bones. Archangel, too, was no match for them, and Flattery had his doubts about the five-man security squad beginning their sweep.

"Not even smart enough to shut the hatch behind them," he mumbled through gritted teeth. "If they don't stop them . . ."

Flattery didn't have to dwell on the unpleasantness, he had plenty of evidence of swiftgrazer vengeance all around him. The

squad had pushed them back far enough that Flattery could make a
dash for the mooring lines and free himself from the pier. His only
escape now would be to dive out of the Greens and wait. The light
in the Greens was so bright that he could barely read his instruments. It nearly surrounded the pool now and he was sure it was
some kind of weapon that the Shadows were using against him.

"Rag-tag bunch of bums," he hissed. "Why don't they leave
well enough alone? Even *they* must be smart enough to know I'll
be off this planet soon."

As he flooded the dive compartments he thought he saw faces
swirling in the light of the Greens—Crista Galli's face, Beatriz
Tatoosh, Dwarf MacIntosh and some young fuzzhead that he
didn't recognize. He shook his head and attended to his instruments. As he settled beneath the surface of the pool he breathed
easier. The foil's atmosphere was contrived, it was not the cool
freshness of the Greens, but it was heaven now to Flattery.

His intent was to wait out the incident safely suspended in the
waters of his personal lagoon. The foil had full rations for six,
enough to last him months, and it could continue to manufacture
its own fuel and air supply as long as the membranes held out.
They were Islander-grown from kelp tissue in a method perfected
several hundred years ago, and had been known to last up to fifty
years.

The light above him continued to intensify and the water began
a rhythmic chop that alarmed him. He had been reluctant to ven-
ture into open water now that the kelpways were down. The idea
of picking his way through a tangle of kelp by instruments alone
dried his mouth and he forced himself to slow his breathing.

"I'll head for the launch site," he told himself. "The nightside
supply shuttle should be ready for launch in three hours."

He marked the time on his log and swung the bow of the foil
seaward. Ahead of him lay the vast coastal kelp bed and its
infernal lights, blinking at him.

*The beachside mortar . . . they didn't stump this stand as I
ordered.*

Somehow, the sight of blue and red flickerings across the
depths ahead of him filled him with as much fear as the mysterious
glare that backed him out of the Greens. Flattery didn't like the
feeling of fear.

*What if they lob their charges in now? I'd be a dead squawk.*

Out of habit, Flattery turned his fear to aggression and throttled
himself into the kelp.

The going was much easier than he'd anticipated. Waters off Kalaloch were quiet in spite of the loss of Current Control. That is, they were quiet except for a strange tidal pulse that pursued him from the Greens into open water. The uncontrolled kelp kept the major kelpway to the launch site open. Flattery attributed this to habit, or to perseverance of the last signal sent from Current Control. He was well into the thick of the stand before he realized his mistake.

Several things happened at once, any one of them enough to shake Flattery's resolve to regroup at the launch site. He ran out of fuel less than a kilometer from the perimeter of the site. Instruments showed all fuel-filter membranes functioning normally. Before the foil stalled out and left him adrift in the kelp, Flattery noticed that the $CO_2$ in his cabin was higher than usual. The gas diffusion membranes were functioning, but seemingly in reverse.

*I'm out of fuel, in the kelp, and my foil is filtering $CO_2$ instead of $O_2$ to the cabin.*

He looked at these facts logically, hoping that logic would stave off the hysteria that bubbled at the back of his throat. He could shuttle ballast as long as his power supply lasted, but if he had to maneuver by battery he wouldn't last long. No one responded to any of the undersea burst frequencies, and his Navcom sent back no signal. It was as though he floated in the center of a black hole. Everything that went out from his foil was swallowed up.

*It must be the kelp,* he reasoned. *It's fouled up our communications before, even the histories tell us that.*

He regretted his leniency with the kelp. It was something that made his life easier, so he had let the explosive growth of this reportedly dangerous species continue beyond his ability to control it.

*Couldn't herd people and kelp at the same time,* he thought, and yawned.

*$CO_2$'s getting me already.*

The yawn frightened him into a flurry of activity, but the oxygen level in his cabin was already low enough to slow his thinking and his hands. He found that, even under electrical power, he couldn't nose any further through the kelp. Blowing ballast did no good, either. It simply depleted his already feeble batteries.

*This damned kelp is sucking the life out of me!*

He stabilized the foil at fewer than twenty meters below the surface. His instruments refused to function, and visibility faded quickly as sunset tipped the scales toward night. Around him, the kelp pulled back from his foil and certain of the kelp fronds began to glow. It was the same kind of cold white glow that had filled the Greens just before he dove.

"This is some kind of Shadow sabotage," he growled. "You'll all regret this!"

Within moments he was wrapped inside a sphere of light so bright that details inside the foil became invisible to him. The glare continued to be bright even though he shut his eyes and covered them with his hands. Voices babbled like red music at the back of his mind.

A warning buzzer droned from the overhead panel and the automatic repeated: "Cabin air unsafe, don airpacks."

How long had it been warning him? He remembered, he remembered . . .

*Light.*

This was a woman's voice, someone he knew well. But it wasn't the Galli woman . . . The buzzer exhausted itself to an electric rattle and Flattery shook his head.

"I need air!" he gasped.

The sound of his own voice broke him free of the suffocation trance of the carbon dioxide.

Flattery clawed through a crew locker for his dive suit. He didn't bother with all of the fastenings, but tightened down the faceplate and activated the air supply. The Director's white hands trembled beyond his control, but at last he could breathe.

*I've got to show them who's in charge!* he thought.

His training always lurked inside, but something about adrenaline slung it free. An old Islander proverb echoed in his mind: "Stir a dasher, feed a dasher."

*I am the dasher and I will strike.*

Flattery repeated this to himself a few times while carefully slowing his breathing.

"What do you want?" he shouted into the faceplate. "If you kill me, you'll die. You'll all die!"

His breath fogged the plaz in front of him but it didn't diminish the cold white glare at all. In fact, as he looked closer at the beads of condensation on his faceplate he saw faces inside, hundreds of tiny faces suspended in translucence, one or more glittering inside each droplet.

*Killing is your way, not ours.*

That voice, inside his own head, chilled something deep in his belly. He could not mistake the familiar Moonbase accent of his shipmate Alyssa Marsh. She had been more than shipmate for a while, but hers had always been a cool intimacy. But it couldn't be Alyssa Marsh because she was . . . well, not dead exactly . . .

"What . . . what is going on here?"

The rasping that he heard across the cabin ceiling and around the foil could only be kelp vines. They snaked across the cabin plaz without diminishing the white radiance that pierced his eyelids, his retinas, his very being. The foil lurched, then its metallic skin shrieked as the kelp began to tear it apart. Flattery hurried to seal his dive suit. He had already armed two lasguns, but he grabbed a couple of spare air packs instead.

*You may fight if you wish,* Alyssa's voice told him, *you will not be killed. You will not be harmed in any way.*

"She had a terrible accident in the kelp" had been Flattery's official version of her body's demise. Now scenes from her life danced in the light around him. And he saw her great secret. Cool as Flattery was, it chilled him just the same.

Alyssa had slipped away on a long-term job in the kelp, knowing she could stretch six months of research in wild kelp beds to nine or ten months without any trouble. He'd wanted to be rid of her, she'd sensed that. If he knew she were pregnant he would destroy the child, of this she was sure. He would probably destroy her, too. Not one in ten thousand clones ever got the chance for a baby. Flattery, Alyssa and Mack were very possibly the last living members of their original crew of 3,006, each one the clone of some long-lost donor.

The Broods took him, and Yuri he was called. There were no other children at this kelp outpost, so Yuri spent his first two years undersea with fourteen adults.

Flattery closed his eyes, retreated into himself.

*It was just the once,* his mind pleaded. *Just the time . . .*

"Do you think it's what I expected my body to do?" she asked.

The images stayed on the other side of his eyelids, but her voice came right into his mind.

*How would I suspect, you didn't stick around . . . your work in the kelp . . .*

Now the scenes came inside his head. Flattery watched as he personally "dismantled" Alyssa and he himself performed the transplant to the life support surrogate and severed her brain forever from its body.

"All you have to do is consult the kelp," he heard Mack telling

Brood. "You'll have your answer for sure, then. You can follow your genetic line back as far as you have the patience to follow."

"I know who my father is," Brood said. "It's him, Raja Flattery."

In one gigantic twist the foil ripped apart at the cabin seam and the sea burst in on Flattery. When the pieces fell away from him the sphere of light remained, and more images danced across the surface of the sphere. He saw Nevi and Zentz captured at the beach, and Brood's attack on the Orbiter. A panorama of disaster played out for him and he watched his precious Preserve go down in plunder.

All along the coastline huge whips of kelp flung themselves skyward and lit up the sea with their pale green glow.

*You have much to learn, Raja Flattery,* Alyssa said. *You are an intelligent man, perhaps even the genius that you believe yourself to be. Ultimately, that is what will save you.*

Something grabbed at his right ankle and he spun away. It grabbed again and held, then pinned his arms when he tried to batter at it with a spare air pack. He was already exhausted, and found himself in a dreamlike state that made resistance more work than it was worth.

*As I told you the night you killed me, I don't think you understand the immensity of this being.*

Beatriz watched Flattery's memory take over, and he broadcast the entire scene of Alyssa Marsh's separation from her body. Holo screens, viewscreens, kelp beds, the air and sky themselves lit up with Alyssa Marsh's memories of her final encounter with Flattery.

*You owe me a body,* she said, and she said it in that same flat, emotionless tone that had made her his first pick for this crew a lifetime ago.

The kelp began to enciliate Flattery, to encapsulize him inside a life-support pod. It had been the same with Crista Galli, as it had been with Vata and Duque before her. Beatriz felt the cilia seeking out his blood vessels to adjust his oxygen level and pH. Others would feed him, recycle his wastes and protect him from flesh-eaters. She felt this as she sensed the world through the hylighter's skin.

Flattery had the show, and the whole world was watching.

> *So many things fail to interest us, simply because they
> don't find in us enough surfaces on which to live, and
> what we have to do then is to increase the number of
> planes in our mind, so that a much larger number of
> themes can find a place in it at the same time.*

> —José Ortega y Gasset

Twisp felt a moment of hysteria play flip-flop with his stomach as
a sphere of cool light encompassed the young Kaleb. Twisp had
sent a boy upcoast and now a man came back. He had known the
boy's father the day he changed from child to man. Suddenly that
old sense of loss iced his spine, and he stood a little straighter at
the poolside.

*Kaleb's a lot like his father,* he thought. *Obstinate, sure, outraged . . .*

Kaleb's father, Brett, had been outraged at the sight of thousands of fellow Islanders stacked dead in a Merman plaza, outraged that humans would murder children in their beds and parents
at their prayers.

*An entire Island, sunk!*

Twisp had heard about the sinking of Guemes Island, he'd seen
holos of the grim rescue scene, but Brett had seen the sledges of
limp bodies, heard the rattle in dying throats.

As though picking up his thoughts, the bright surface of the sphere played back some of those moments, far clearer here than in his memory.

Other images played there, too—nebulized, indistinct, as though making up their minds about being. He saw in them replays of the scenes Kaleb fought with his people. He had resisted the majority of his forces who wanted Flattery's blood. They chose to move without him, and Kaleb stood up to them.

"You're willing to die in battle anyway," he told them. "Why not die feeding the poor?"

He was sending an army against Flattery, all right—an army of angels laden with food.

"Everything stops until everyone eats," was written on each pilgrim's shirt as they set out by the hundreds for the camps.

Twisp had renewed confidence that Kaleb's hatred of the Director would not turn the boy into another Flattery.

*He's not a boy,* he reminded himself, *and he's safe in Avata. His mother saw to that.*

Twisp remembered the time when he had needed convincing himself, when it was Kaleb's mother, Scudi Wang, who first thrust him into the kelpways of the mind. Her face came up in the sphere and it was the smiling face of the precocious teenager that Twisp remembered so well.

*How could Brett not have loved her?*

Twisp tugged his gray braid that tickled his neck. In the halo around Kaleb more images precipitated out of the light. They all seemed to be people he knew, and they all had one other thing in common.

*They're all dead!*

He heard a whimper behind him that must be Mose.

In that moment Kaleb became a bright shadow inside a brighter sphere, and he seemed to hover above the pool rather than float upon it. The manifestations, the flickering images around him, recited a few scenes from their pasts. Twisp was awed, but not afraid.

Everything swam in a pale radiance that pulsated slightly, like a child's fontanel. A similar pulse began to beat in the wave-slaps around the rim of the pool. The onlookers had ceased their chatter and begun their chant of renewal. It was a call-and-response chant, typical at blossom-time, an improvisation on an old theme that Twisp had heard his grandparents sing.

"Open the leaves . . ."

". . . and the blossoms, open . . ."

Kaleb was no longer visible inside the light. The light now was brighter than anything Twisp had experienced, but this cool brightness did not hurt his eyes. Indeed, he could not take his gaze from its hypnotic spell.

"It's everywhere," a tremulous voice shouted from the cavemtop. "There's light on the waves, in the sky . . . everywhere."

Twisp recognized this breathless voice as Snej, the young assistant at Operations.

"And there are pictures in the light," another gasped, "just like this, only it covers the whole sky!"

When a great light took over the whole cavern, it became impossible for Twisp to make out the faces of his fellow Zavatans. Even Mose, as close as he was, became just another light inside the light.

Snej's voice came to him again, bell-like in its joy.

"Crista Galli is safe," she announced. "They are all safe. The fighting is at a standstill."

The bright sphere in front of Twisp unreeled the tideline drama of Ben and Crista Galli and their near-fatal encounter with Zentz and Spider Nevi. It seemed to Twisp that the event was more than visual. Though it must've taken up nearly an hour of real time, the scene was communicated to him in a matter of blinks. A cheer filled the cavern when Spider Nevi fell, and the images on the sphere shifted to another cavern, and to the terrified face of the Director.

All fell silent at the sight of Flattery, except for a few angry mutterings across the pool.

"Is this a miracle, Elder?"

"Flattery's being driven out," Twisp said. "I'd say that was more inevitability than miracle. Avata has decided that it's time to meet the Director."

The brightness inside the Oracle spread out from the sphere to bathe each observer. The darkest of them was a dazzle of light against light.

"Look, Elder!"

Twisp watched Mose lift his arms as though flying, and streams of thick white light pulsed from his fingertips to join with other light nearby. Though it was impossible for him to see detail, Twisp watched these same streams of light merge with others in midair. He was reminded of the time as a child when a cell bioarchitect visited his crèche to show his classmates many wonders. One of these was a blowup holo of cytoplasmic streaming, of an amoeba pumping parts of itself into other parts of itself in order to move, to capture and digest prey.

"What are we, here?" he wondered aloud. "Predator or prey?"

The answer came in a rush that rocked Twisp back on his heels. *You are brother to me, as I am sibling to you.*

His long arms shot out over the pool for balance. A hand reached out of the light and gripped his own. The grip felt real, the hand, wet. Kaleb stepped from the kelp root to the rim of the pool and kept a hold on Twisp's hand. The cavern around them was a din of babble as the Zavatans consulted Avata and each other. They encountered spirits of their ancestors that Avata released from the prisons of their genetic code.

"Let us join hands and thank Avata," Kaleb announced. His voice took on a new projection that stilled the babble but did not shock the ears.

"Avata has dismembered the monster that Flattery built out of our people and has taken him prisoner. He will be reeducated, as we have been, in the inviolable rights that the living have to life. Tonight, everyone will eat. Humans are through suffering at the hands of fellow humans."

Everyone in the cavern linked hands, and the light flowed through them from the pool and then flowed back. Figures and faces, bits of imagery tumbled along the brightening stream. Gasps of wonder and cries of delight filled the chamber.

Then the cavern itself dissolved from view. Ceiling, walls, the rock beneath their feet were no longer visible. All Twisp could see was a serpentine of people holding hands surrounded by something he could only describe as a light-mist. All Pandorans were linked with this group and they all stood together on an immense plain of light. It was warm there, and for once there was no fear of demons, or security, or hunger.

Twisp withdrew quietly from the poolside celebration, found his robe in his quarters and sought out his favorite rock overlook above Kalaloch.

Below Twisp's rock outcrop the night air clarified against a glisten of sea. An old tracked vehicle clanked its stubborn way up the trail and at first Twisp's reflexes tightened. A Cushette followed the track, both vehicles piled high with belongings and wallowing with the effort. These people were already leaving Kalaloch, bound for something better with their bedding and their hope.

"Welcome," Twisp whispered. His attitude was exuberant, but his body exhausted.

*They will be all right,* he marveled.

He thought first of Kaleb, who had left his bitterness behind him in the kelp, who would soon enough bring the grandchildren of Brett and Scudi to hear stories at their uncle Twisp's knee.

He could guess how it would be for the rest from what he'd seen in the kelp.

Ben and Crista were a match made on Pandora, but sealed in Avata, and they would help develop opportunities to improve the lives of Pandorans for many decades to come. Twisp had a feeling, when the light penetrated him, that Rico and Snej would take up housekeeping somewhere nearby.

The Voidship *Nietzsche*, with Alyssa Marsh at the helm, would speed Mack and Beatriz beyond the limits of light-contact with Pandora. It would take the humans and their new-found symbiote, Avata, to another world, which, if not perfect when they discovered it, would make humans happy with the work toward perfection.

Some new insight told Twisp that Yuri Brood would receive a reprieve aboard the *Nietzsche* and would acquire the necessary spirituality by tending his mother, the OMC Alyssa Marsh. Through the kelp hookups, Alyssa Marsh had found her new body and her son. Her son would write out the musings of this OMC, which would become the manual for human behavior for generations—*A Sociology of Ascension*. Their shipload of pilgrims would people a new star, and the sea of a planet of that star.

Raja Flattery would live on in the kelp, his needs met, a prisoner of his own selfishness and greed. People would meet him there from time to time, and legends of him would prevail throughout the generations.

Though Pandora's days were numbered, Twisp would live his days out roaming Pandora, working hard to improve the lot of everyone. He knew now that he would not be the one to see the end, and was happy for that.

*I'll be known as "the old man of the high reaches," I suppose,* Twisp mused.

All was quiet in the settlement below. The glow that had swelled out of the sea and encompassed Kalaloch now sank back to the sea. A cool shimmer remained, ghostlike, at the surface. Two moons and a skyful of stars beamed down on Twisp's gray head. An occasional cheer broke the silence, and Twisp listened as the tinkling sounds of nighttime laughter rent the ancient cloak of death and fear.